W9-BQU-800

DISCARDED

bump

Diana Wagman

CARROLL & GRAF PUBLISHERS
NEW YORK

BUMP

Carroll & Graf Publishers
An Imprint of Avalon Publishing Group Inc.
161 William St., 16th Floor
New York, NY 10038

First Carroll & Graf edition 2003

Library of Congress Cataloging-in-Publication Data is available.

ISBN: 0-7867-1106-X

Interior design by Paul Paddock

Printed in the United States of America
Distributed by Publishers Group West

acknowledgments

I would like to thank Officer Elizabeth Albanese of the Beverly Hills Police Department and Officer William Crook and his Web site, www.lifeonthe beat.com, for helping me understand what it takes to be a police officer. The entire Beverly Hills P.D. has my deepest gratitude and respect.

I would also like to thank Kay Redfield Jamison for her extraordinary volume, *Night Falls Fast: Understanding Suicide,* and A. Alvarez for his wonderful book, *The Savage God: A Study of Suicide.* I was helped immeasurably by the members of the Los Angeles Suicide Prevention Center, as well as the brave folks at the Los Angeles Suicide Prevention Hot Line (800-784-2433).

Very special thanks, in alphabetical order, to Sally Harrison-Pepper, Dorian Karchmar at Lowenstein & Associates, Claudia Kunin, Dinah Lenney, Kerry Madden-Lunsford, Diane Mesirow, Tina Pohlman, and Ellen Slezak.

Finally, this book never would have been written without the patience of my children, Benjamin and Thea, and the support of my husband, Tod Mesirow. They have kept me from becoming one of my own statistics.

For my father

S omething fell in the living room and woke me up. My wife's side of the bed was empty.

"Honey?" I called. "Linda?"

I looked at the clock. 4:43. It was my least favorite time of day, just before dawn. Bleak, as if the sun will never rise. The light in the bedroom was dark gray and hazy. The dresser loomed too large. The closet door was open a crack even though I knew I'd closed it the night before. I could see inside to the black cave of all my childhood monsters.

"Honey?" I called again.

I heard a scraping sound from the living room. I was awake then. I sat up and pulled on my boxers. I reached under the bed to my secret shelf and got my gun. I walked quietly to the bedroom door and opened it without making a sound. I stepped through the tiny hall and into the living room with my gun ready.

"Goddamn it, Ray. Put that thing away."

Linda, my wife, stood at the card table we used for a dining-room table. She was dressed in weekend clothes even though it was Friday. Her hair was combed. She had her lipstick on. I could smell the perfume she usually wore to go out at night. There was an open cardboard box on the table. I saw our candlesticks inside.

"Linda?"

"I'm leaving."

"What?"

I had expected something else. A hundred pictures had gone through my mind: rape, robbery, hostage, but not this.

"Where are you going?"

"I'm driving to Phoenix."

Phoenix wasn't right. Linda hated the sun. She hated it here in Los Angeles. She said the California sunshine made her sick. She wanted winter, snow, clouds, and rain. Not Phoenix. I shook my head. Linda tapped her foot on the floor.

"Put that gun down. You're making me nervous."

"Phoenix?"

"Ray. Come on," Linda said. Her voice softened but her eyes were hard as ice. "This has been over for a long time."

"Why Phoenix?

"Look at you." Linda shook her head. "Gun in your hand."

"It's perfectly safe," I said. "I'm a cop."

"That's right. You're a cop. I'm tired of it. You're always late coming home, and when you finally get here you're distracted, you're in some other world. Even when we go out you can't relax. You always expect the worst."

"I know what can happen."

"It's depressing."

I saw her eyes flicker toward the bookshelves. I collect people's last written words. I had two rows of albums all filled with them. But I knew she didn't like it.

"I'll get rid of them," I said.

"Forget it. Keep your stupid notes. I just don't care anymore."

I looked at her pretty face. She was twenty-seven years old. We'd been married three years. I thought we were happy. Actually, I guess I hadn't thought about it at all. She had lost some weight. She'd started having her nails done. She'd been to Arizona three or four times on business trips and once with her sister. Phoenix was beginning to make sense.

"What does he do?" I asked. "Work in a bank?"

"Something like that."

She didn't deny it. She didn't even try. I sat down on our couch. I saw her two suitcases by the front door. She packed a few more things into the box and then taped it up.

"Aren't you going to help me out?" she asked.

"I don't think so."

It took her two trips. When she came back for the box, she put her key to the apartment on the card table. She looked at me.

"Well," she said.

I had nothing more to say. I couldn't speak anyway. My throat was too dry. My tongue felt so swollen, it was a wool blanket in my mouth.

She took off her wedding ring and set it down next to the key. I wanted her to leave then. I wanted her to leave right away. She walked to the door and I turned my face away from her. I pretended to look out the window even though the venetian blinds were closed. The first rays of the sun lit up the bottom two strips. In the crack, the light was blinding. It was going to be another beautiful southern California day. I heard the front door close and her footsteps walking away.

I sat on the couch in my underwear for a long time. The thing about an apartment is, no matter how well it's made and this one wasn't well made, you can hear your neighbors. I sat on that couch and I heard everybody wake up. I heard their feet hit the floor, their toilets flush, the gurgle of their coffeemakers. All around me, below me, above me, my fellow renters were having their normal mornings; they were listening to the radio, eating breakfast, deciding what to wear. My wife was in her two-door red Toyota on her way to Arizona. I sat on the couch in my plaid boxers with the cold weight of my service revolver pressed against my thigh.

A single shot would stop everything. Not just for me, but others in the building. I imagined the guy in the suit two doors down pausing with his coffee cup almost to his lips. What was that, he'd think. Sounded like a gunshot.

"Shit," I said out loud.

Suddenly I had to take a piss. I had to pee so badly, I thought I wouldn't get to the bathroom in time. The relief I felt standing over the bowl made me laugh. Then I started crying. The bathroom looked weird. She had taken everything—even the stupid knit cover that went over the extra roll of toilet paper. That naked roll on the back of the john made my stomach hurt. I got in the shower, still crying, and made the water really hot like I like it. One of her long strawberry-blond hairs was stuck to the tile. I had always loved her long, long hair. I turned my back to it. I washed myself sideways avoiding her only remaining body part. I sobbed like a kid. My shift started at noon. I had to be at the station by 11:30. I had plenty of time to be sad.

I tried to avoid my reflection in the mirror as I shaved. The skin around my nose was red and flaky. My skin is sensitive, I'm always breaking out in rashes. Irish skin, Linda called it. She told me over and over to see a doctor, but I never did. I cut myself twice trying not to look at my own face.

My eyes hurt as I got dressed. I keep my uniform at the station—they have them cleaned for us—so I wear regular clothes there and back. I just put on the jeans and T-shirt I'd worn the day before. I picked them up off the floor. It didn't matter. No one would care what I wore home.

The building was quiet. Everyone who had work to go to had gone and the writers, musicians, artist-types were all still sleeping. I went into the kitchen. She had left a piece of paper on the counter. It had her address in Phoenix and a single word, "Good-bye." She'd been planning to leave without even waking me up. I put the note in my pocket. I couldn't look at it, but I wanted it with me.

I made a pot of coffee. She'd taken the nice coffee mugs, left me the beige plastic cup with the police academy logo half worn away. I looked at her ring sitting on the black vinyl top of the card table. She hated that table. She thought after three years of marriage we should have a real dining-room table and chairs. But we were saving for a house. We'd gone to look at a lot of houses. We'd even made an offer on one. We thought we had it. When someone else outbid us, she was really disappointed. She hated this apartment. I guess she hated me.

I picked up her ring and threw it in the garbage. I went into the bathroom and combed my hair. I told myself I was glad her stuff was gone. There was more room in the medicine chest for my shaving cream, my razor, my box of Band-Aids. There was lots of room. There was room in the bathroom and in the bedroom. The top of the dresser was all mine. I didn't look in the closet. I just shut the door.

I decided to go to the station a little early. There was always something to do. First I went back to the trash can and fished out her little ring. I had to dig for it. It had fallen to the bottom underneath the old coffee grounds and pizza crusts. The night before she had ordered pizza. She didn't even cook me one last dinner. I washed her ring off and dried it and put it in the silverware drawer, way in the back in the plastic dish where she kept the rubber bands.

At the door to my apartment I stopped. I had my keys in my hand, my gun in my shoulder holster under my denim jacket. I leaned my forehead against the door. I thumped it against the cheap wood. I thumped it hard. It hurt, but it matched how my chest was feeling. I thought about her hand on my thigh and the way her feet were always cold. My legs gave out and I just sat down right there, right on the dirty carpet in front of the door. I was so tired. So damn tired. I didn't know when I'd be able to get up again.

Note #4 05/02/99

Dear Tom,

I'm sorry you had to see me like this. Don't worry, I did my research. I think I fell asleep and died without any pain.

It's not that I'm leaving you. I'm just going ahead. I can't do this anymore. I will be happier in the next world.

I'll be waiting for you.

Love,

Donna

chapter two

Come on, come on, come on. Dorothy banged her hand on the steering wheel. She rocked in the seat of her car. Come on. The truck in front of her was stopped. She was late. As always. It was rush hour in Los Angeles and she was late. She had the radio on. She was singing along, practicing the breathing she had just learned in her voice class. Which had run long, of course, fifteen minutes over the regular hour. She should never have gone to her voice class. Not today of all days. She had the directions in her hand. She had to pick up her wedding dress and the shop closed at five-thirty and it was twenty minutes after and she was lost. She had to be at the rehearsal dinner back on the other side of town by six. Her eye makeup itched. She had put it on in the car. She hated her shoes. This was the day before the happiest day of her life, and what she really wanted was to go to the movies.

She turned right and immediately realized she was wrong. She did an abrupt, illegal U-turn. A young construction worker in a pickup truck honked at her. She smiled, mouthed "sorry." He gave her the finger.

She had been to this stupid, idiotic, sentimental bridal salon three times for fittings. Tighter here, looser there, raise the neckline, no, too much. She still couldn't find it. Rosemary's Bridal Fantasies.

Dorothy had no memory for directions. Places she had been turned into sounds and smells in her head; they lost their addresses, their walls and foundations. She knew there were flowers planted outside. She knew there were plump white cushions on the love seat and conflicting odors of potpourri and fabric starch. She tried to read a passing street sign. She was driving too fast. The green rectangle blurred and stretched in the corner of her eye, the white letters sliding away from her. Rosemary's Bridal Fantasies could just as easily be in Iowa as Beverly Hills, California.

Lewis, her boyfriend, soon to be her husband, would be really annoyed if she was late to the rehearsal dinner. They weren't rehearsing anything, but there were people coming from out of town. Twenty-four minutes after five. She had no idea how far she still had to go. She could give up, turn around, be on time to the restaurant. But she wouldn't have her wedding dress, and she didn't have time tomorrow before the wedding to pick it up. She couldn't come all the way across town, all the way to the west side of town tomorrow. She should have done this yesterday, as she had planned, as Lewis had told her to, but she had been too busy giggling with her friend Lani, too happy to be drinking blender drinks on her front porch with a girlfriend, not thinking, not talking, not caring about getting married. Stupid, stupid, stupid.

The radio was scratchy and annoying. The truck in front of her began to move. She stepped on the gas. Was that the street where she was supposed to turn? She fiddled with the radio. Her fingers let go. The directions floated to the floor of her car. She thought about physics, the idea, property, law, whatever it was called, that the car could be moving, but inside the car the air was still. A piece of paper could fall so slowly through the air, so much slower than her measured miles per hour. There was so much she didn't know.

Come on! She looked in her rearview mirror. Maybe that had been her street. The truck went through the intersection. She followed close behind. She looked to her right.

A car headed toward her. She saw the young man's unhappy Latino face clearly through his windshield. She saw his hand on the horn, heard the blast. Don't do that, she thought. Don't honk at me. She put up her hand to stop him. He closed his eyes. There was a jolt and a terrible loud crunch and her head hit the window and then her car was spinning. She saw another face, a woman's frightened face surrounded by swinging blond hair, as she spun toward her. She heard the thud, felt the hard thump of impact, scraped and slid toward the curb and then she went over. And over. And over again.

She woke up in the emergency room. Her head hurt.

A man was standing by the side of her bed. A skinny young man, sort of handsome, with a good haircut, but so worried. Her first clear thought was to wish she could smooth the worry from his forehead with her hand, brush it away.

Her second thought was that this was Lewis, her almost husband. For one moment, she'd had absolutely no idea who he was. She had opened her eyes, known immediately that she was in the emergency room, remembered the accident, recognized a passing nurse's dry, brisk efficiency. But the man standing by her bed had been a complete stranger. The downward turn of his mouth, the way his hair curled over his forehead, the stubble of beard on his chin and cheeks were unfamiliar. Alien.

A mild concussion, the doctor said, some bumps and bruises. Thank God she was wearing her seat belt.

The young man kissed her hand. Lewis. His name was Lewis.

"How are you feeling?" he asked.

"Weird," she said. "Dreamy."

"They gave you something."

"Let's get some more to take home."

He laughed and let go of her hand. Lewis.

A policeman appeared by her bed. She saw him and started cry.

"It was all my fault," she said.

"Shhhh." Lewis turned to the cop. "She's been sedated."

"Is everybody okay?" she asked.

"You got it the worst of anybody."

The worst.

"Good," she said. "No one else was hurt?"

"Nope."

The officer took out a pad. She looked at his strawberry blond hair. It needed conditioner. It was dry and badly cut. There was a nick, a scabbed indentation on his cheek from shaving. His skin was red and irritated. He needed a different kind of shaving cream and a good lotion.

"What happened?" he asked her.

She liked looking at him. His lips were thin, barely visible in his rosy face. His jaw was firm now, but he had jowls that one day would wiggle when he talked. She liked the way his neck swelled over his collar. He was a big guy. She wanted him to smile at her.

Lewis was frowning. "Does she have to talk about this now?"

"Yup."

"It's all right," she said to Lewis. "I remember. I was behind a truck. I couldn't see the light. The truck went through the yellow I guess and I went right after it."

"And you struck the Pontiac?"

"The red car? It hit *me*. Then I went into that other car, the woman's car."

"The Mercedes."

Lewis groaned.

"I think it was black," she said. "You're sure she's all right?"

"Yup. Fine. Those are good cars in an accident."

"I'm sorry," she said. "I'm so sorry. I wasn't paying attention."

"Dorothy," Lewis said. "Shut up."

"I'm getting married tomorrow," Dorothy said. She had suddenly remembered that she was.

"Congratulations."

"This is my—" But the word for Lewis escaped her. It was gone.

There was a word for what he was to her, but she had no idea what it was. Carpenter, she thought. No. Teacher. Definitely not.

"This is Lewis," she said. Her mind continued its explorations. "My golfer," she said out loud.

"Excuse me?" The officer looked up from his pad.

She had said something wrong. He and Lewis had the same puzzled, disapproving looks on their scratchy male faces.

"I'm sorry." She almost whispered it. She reached one hand over the metal bed rail and put it on the officer's arm. She wanted to stop him from thinking badly of her. She smiled at him and expected him to give her the finger.

Instead, he put his porterhouse palm over her hand. He leaned down, brought his face close to hers. She could see the flakes of skin on the sides of his nose, the white-capped lumps and pustules of his rash.

"You've suffered enough, don't you think?" he asked.

She thought of all her past boyfriends and how she had cried. Every one of them had broken up with her. She was always getting dumped.

"Yes," she said.

"You don't need this," he said.

"No." She looked at Lewis. "I guess not."

"Will you promise me you'll be more careful next time?"

One thing she knew for certain. "There won't be a next time," she said.

The officer patted her hand, gave it a squeeze. His irises were the palest blue, the surrounding white pure and bright. He was handsome, the policeman, but he needed better care. She had just the right product at the shop. Dorothy was a hairdresser at a neighborhood salon in Silver Lake. She specialized in teenage girls and older men. She would choose a good skin cream, mail it to him with a thank-you note and a coupon for a free haircut. Thank you for everything.

"That's what I wanted to hear," he said.

He stood up and tore the top page off his pad. He crumpled it and tossed it in the wastebasket across the room.

He nodded at Lewis. "Two points."

"Well done," Lewis replied. "Well done."

The two men stood at the foot of her bed and looked smug and proud of themselves. A perfect shot in the hospital trash can.

"Can I go home now?" Dorothy asked.

"What about the rehearsal dinner?" Lewis said. "Everyone is waiting for us." He turned to the officer. "We're getting married tomorrow."

"I know," the policeman said softly, "And tomorrow is the first day of spring."

"March twentieth," Lewis said proudly.

"A perfect day." The policeman sighed.

"I want to go home." Dorothy said to the policeman. She implored him. "My head hurts."

He looked into her eyes. She stretched her fingers toward him. She waited for him to touch her hand again. But he stepped back from her bed.

"She should probably rest tonight," the policeman said to Lewis.

Lewis began to object, but was stopped by the blue uniform with silver buttons, the handcuffs hanging from the leather belt, the visible authority of the other man.

"I don't have my wedding dress." Dorothy suddenly remembered. "I was on my way to get it."

"You'll make a beautiful bride," the officer whispered. His nose went red, even redder than it was before. He shook his head so sadly. "Lovely. Really." He reached out to touch her, but his hand stopped in midair. "Have a good life."

He started out of the room, then stopped and gave a backward glance at her, a sad smile, before trudging away.

"He liked you." Lewis sounded surprised.

"He did." Dorothy was just as puzzled.

"He didn't give you a ticket."

"Why not?"

"I have no idea. You were wrong. So wrong."

Dorothy looked at his face. Her failure behind the wheel seemed to satisfy him. He stood taller.

"I didn't get my dress," she said.

"We'll pick it up tomorrow."

The doctor came in and told her she could go home. Then he looked at her seriously. "You're lucky to be alive. Very lucky."

How do you know? Dorothy wanted to ask. Maybe death is wonderful. Maybe the light at the end of the tunnel is the dawn of overwhelming joy. She got out of bed. Her bare feet were sticky on the beige linoleum tiles. She teetered, grabbed the back of a chair.

"You okay?" Lewis had picked up an old newspaper. He held it in both hands. He looked down, reading, before she answered.

"I'm fine." She slid her dress on over her head. She ran her fingers through her hair. She'd had one of the other girls at the shop cut it boy-short and streak it white-blond for the wedding. It had probably been a mistake. Lewis just shook his head when he saw her.

She picked up her high heels, but didn't put them on. "I bet I had the accident because of these shoes."

"I thought you loved them."

"Your mother loved them."

"Then why did you get them?"

The answer to that was obvious. It didn't even need a reply.

Outside the hospital, the night had come. It was dark and cool, and the lights in the shops across the street were friendly. The people in those stores were not getting married tomorrow. They had Saturday to look forward to; sleeping late, going out to breakfast, eating popcorn at an afternoon movie. It wouldn't be a day they had to remember for the rest of their lives.

Dorothy buckled her seat belt carefully. Lewis started his car. She turned off the radio.

"Petey's in town. And Brian." He chatted on, naming their friends, mostly his friends, from out of town who had arrived for the wedding. "We'll run by the restaurant, just for a moment. Just to say hi. Then everyone can come to our house."

She looked at Lewis's face flushed green from the dashboard lights. She watched his hands on the steering wheel. His thumbs bent so far back, the wrong way. Willpower, she had read in a palm-reading guidebook. His thumbs had fascinated her on her breasts, between her legs. Now on the black plastic wheel they stuck out, repulsive and demanding.

He swerved around a car, leaned on his horn. She put her hand up.

"Sorry," he said. "Got you right back on the horse, didn't I?"

She couldn't help but watch the houses go by, stare at the yellow lights in the windows, wish that she was there, or there, or there, behind those curtains, eating that dinner, still waiting for the boy to call.

chapter three

t was 7:18 P.M. I left the hospital feeling lower than I had all day. I had finally gotten up off my floor that morning and gone to work. At the station, I had felt a little better. I put on my uniform. I had coffee. Everything was just like always. The sergeant frowned once at my face, but he didn't say anything. I worked my first seven hours and I was okay.

But when I left the E.R., I could barely put one foot in front of the other. The sun had just gone down and the sky was a deep blue. I trudged out the double glass doors. A nurse was coming in. I held the door for her, but when she said thanks, I forgot to reply. That girl in the E.R. bed, Dorothy P. Fairweather, the one I should have given the ticket, I couldn't get her face out of my mind. She had these little squished-up features. Small blue eyes, a pointy nose and a tiny mouth with full curvy lips like a cartoon character. Her hair was really short and bleached white. I don't like short hair on women. I don't know why I kept thinking about her, but I did. And it made me so goddamn sad.

I hadn't told anyone about Linda. I got back in the squad car and turned to my partner for the shift, Ronald Jackson. He's a good guy. He has a great marriage. I was about to say something to him when the radio crackled. The police-car radio still makes that crackly sound, even though now they're all digital and computerized. I guess it's just something a police radio must do. And we still call them police cars, even though we drive tricked-out Chevy Tahoes.

The call came in. A 6-4-7, disorderly conduct, just up the street at a jewelry store on Bedford. A young male, and they said he was non-white which means fair-skinned black or Indian or Hispanic, was talking crazy, shouting how they were all out to get him, standing in the middle of the fancy jewelry store and screaming how life sucks.

"Idiot," said Ronnie. He was driving. "What is he thinking?"

I like Ronnie. A lot. I like his wife, Jet, and his two girls, Izzy and Francine. He has a marriage you can actually admire. He's African-American and magazine-model handsome and he graduated from Cal State Northridge in criminology before going to the police academy. I'm big and white and five years younger and I never graduated. I did two years as an English major at L.A. City College until I dropped out and enrolled in the police academy. I thought I wanted to be an English teacher like my dad, but things change. Ronnie's the smartest officer I know and I always feel lucky when riding with him. We've both been on the force for six years. We've been through some stuff together.

We are Beverly Hills' finest. I know the jokes about being the best-dressed and the movie-star police force, but we're not just cute. We're good cops. Really good. We have to be because we do it all. Beverly Hills is a little city surrounded by the gargantuan city of L.A. We have our own mayor. There are only 33,000 residents, but the population swells during business hours to almost 200,000 with the shoppers and the tourists and the people who work here. Our small police force of 60 officers has to deal with everything from jaywalking to homicide. We work hard. We take really good care of Beverly Hills.

Ronnie and I pulled up in front of that high-end jewelry store just as the suspect ran out the door and down the alley that led to the parking garage. I jumped out of the car. Ronnie was right behind me. We had our guns drawn.

The guy—high on something, hop, rippers, crack, or just flying on the back of his own despair—turned to face us. He pressed his back against the wall.

"You haven't done anything," I said. Sometimes my size can persuade them. I'm 6'5" and the extra eighteen pounds of bulletproof vest makes me huge. "Just give up. Put your hands over your head."

"Come on, buddy," said Ronnie, calling the suspect his friend, reminding him there are friends, somewhere.

"Don't do this," I said. I knew he could hear the disappointment in my voice. I wanted him to hear me praying. "Don't do anything stupid."

The suspect shook his head. He looked up at the little strip of sky above him, and I saw tears coming from his eyes. Tears like rain falling on his smooth, caramel-colored cheeks. The evening sky was barely dark. The Beverly Hills alleyway was impossibly clean.

The boy, because he was a boy, curled his back to us and his hand went inside his jacket. He whirled around with the gun, with his finger on the trigger. He pointed it at us.

"Drop it," Ronnie commanded.

The kid didn't move.

"Drop your weapon!"

"Shoot me," the kid said quietly. "Aren't you going to shoot me?"

"Don't," I said.

And then he pointed it at himself. He pushed the muzzle up against his temple.

"Don't," I said again. I was feeling sick to my stomach. "Please," I whispered. He looked at me. For a moment I had him. His eyes were looking into mine. My eyes told him it would be okay. I reached my empty hand out to him.

"Yes," I said. I nodded at him. "That's right."

But he closed his eyes and fired. Once. It wasn't a very big gun, but it was enough. The suspect was down. The suspect shuddered, twitched, and died.

I had to turn away.

Ronnie went up, did what he's supposed to do.

"Isn't it the first day of spring?" Ronnie asked.

"Tomorrow. That's tomorrow. Officially."

"Whatever. I hate the goddamn spring. Brings out all the nutcases."

He was right. The kid fired a gun, but it was springtime that killed him. It's a little-known fact. Most suicides happen in the spring. Not the winter, like everybody thinks, not Christmastime or New Year's Eve, but when the air turns sweet and the fruit trees blossom. All that fresh new life makes people crazy.

We made the calls. We waited with the body. A crowd of well-heeled shoppers gathered at the street end of the alley. Some guy in a suit came out of the parking garage.

"Go around," I said.

He didn't want to. He stood at the end of the alley. He tapped his stupid feet. He was annoyed. Somebody died right where he wanted to walk.

"Go on," I said. I didn't want him standing there. Not another minute. It was all I could do for the kid who was dead. It was all I could do.

Traffic was heavy. I could hear rush hour going by.

Ronnie put his hand over his heart. He wasn't saying a prayer, he was checking for something. He collects vintage baseball cards. He's got some that are worth thousands of dollars. We had stopped that day so he could buy a new one, a 1959 Roberto Clemente for over a hundred dollars. He was bending over the body and checking to make sure the card was still in his pocket.

I collect suicide notes, even though Linda thought it was depressing. She wasn't interested. Never wanted to look at any of them or have me read them to her. I have to steal some of them from the evidence room, but I wait until any investigation is over, until no one wants them anymore. I read them. And I keep them preserved in albums with acid-free paper between each one. They'll last longer than I will. I like to look at them. Some of them are bloodstained. Some of them are sad. Some are funny. And sometimes I write them. Not for myself, but I imagine what they would say—the ones who don't leave a note. Like this kid. As I stood there, I knew I'd write him something, what I think he wanted to say. This kid on the sidewalk. Otherwise only his blood would leave a mark.

It was an unusual event for us. Ronnie's face was flushed and he kept blinking, squeezing his eyes shut. It's hard to watch someone die. I looked at the body of the boy. His pants leg was pushed up. His calf was pale and hairless. Like a child's leg. I was mostly numb. I just thought about how he didn't have to worry anymore. I have to say, at that moment, I envied him his relief. The girl, Dorothy P. Fairweather, flashed through my mind. Her face, her mascara smeared under one eye, her perfect white skin on the less-white hospital pillow. Her fiancé standing there tapping his feet. No. Maybe he wasn't. Maybe I imagined that.

I heard the siren. It was Friday evening, the nineteenth of March. It was rush hour in Los Angeles.

Rush hour. Seen from space, the people would be like ants scurrying, hurrying away from one place to another. What are they running from? What terrible calamity is behind them? And what safe haven awaits?

But it is only the end of the day. They dash out of their offices, get in their cars and drive, angry, frenzied, desperate to arrive home and sit in front of the television or eat or sleep or get in their cars and drive somewhere else. From a point of view way up in the sky, we would wonder what the rush is all about. Where are any of them really going?

It is my personal and professional opinion that they run from death. Their only true motivation is their frantic fear of what happens next. They work, eat, make love, and go to the movies to escape it. And they don't even know what it is. It just isn't this. It's the great beyond or the hereafter or the cosmic oneness.

Or, hardest to stomach, Heaven just might be that wise old face waiting for us, waiting to judge our lives, waiting to tell us where we will spend eternity.

It seems most religions think of our time on earth as a little blip, a nanosecond in the context of forever. Then why bother? What makes life worth living? That is the most important question we can ask. It's the only question. When I first got interested in suicide, the guy at the bookstore told me to read an essay by Albert Camus called "The Myth of Sisyphus." Camus said, "What is called a reason for living is also an excellent reason for dying." That thought goes around and around in my head. If we live frantically only to cheat death, then suicide seems like another method to deceive it. It's our way of saying, "You can't fire me. I quit." We are so helpless most of the time. So much is out of our control. We have only one permanent solution to all of life's accidents.

chapter four

Madelyn Morrison waited in the front hall with her head bent and her smooth blond hair hiding her face. The front door was wide open and she could hear her husband, Mitch Morrison, out in the driveway.

"Jesus fucking Christ!"

The car looked bad, she had to admit. The driver's side was scraped and badly dented. She couldn't open her door or the passenger door behind her. When she got home she had to climb over the gearshift and skootch across the other seat.

Mitch came in and slammed the front door shut. Madelyn was expecting it, but she jumped.

"Sorry," she said.

"It wasn't your fault," he replied. "Fucking bitch, was she on a cell phone? On drugs? Out of her mind?"

"No. I don't know. I didn't see her."

Madelyn had not noticed a cell phone, but she had seen her; the small face looking worried, concentrating, eyes squinting, teeth clenched together. Madelyn had seen that she was young, and unhappy, and not particularly pretty.

"Are you okay?" Mitch asked.

"Sure."

"Really?" he said. "A lot of damage to the car. She's gonna have to pay."

Lawyers and insurance agents, rental cars and the Mercedes dealer. It sounded time consuming, and exhausting. But what else did she have to do? She was going to paint that little bookshelf. Plant a row of daylilies along the back fence. She had her photography class every Friday. She had been driving home from class. Her latest interest. If she had continued with Intro to Watercolor on Tuesdays or Personal Poetry on Thursday mornings, the accident would never have happened.

She saw dust under the front hall table. And the corner of the stairway runner was coming up. She loved this house, Victorian, enormous, out of place in Beverly Hills; but it overwhelmed her, even with help twice a week. She needed to vacuum.

"Did she?"

Madelyn hadn't been listening. "What?"

"Did she give you her information?"

"The ambulance took her. The police came. She was knocked out, out cold. She could have been hurt, I mean, really hurt."

"What happened?"

"She ran the light. That's what it looked like to me. Poor thing."

"Fuck her. Now we have to deal with this."

Mitch stamped out of the room, the tassels on his Italian loafers bouncing. Madelyn watched his back heading for the kitchen, blue dress shirt, khaki pants, brown leather belt. When had he started wearing a belt? He hadn't worn a belt to their wedding. He hadn't worn underwear to their wedding. Their first legally sanctioned sex was standing up in the ladies' room at the reception. He had pulled her expensive lace panties to one side, just enough to make room for him.

"No underwear," he whispered in her neck. "The only way to go."

She had been worried about her hair.

"Mom? What happened?" Mason, her twelve-year-old son, hung over the upstairs railing.

"Where've you been?" Her ten-year-old daughter, Morgan, sounded just like Mitch; mistrustful, accusatory.

"Somebody hit me," Madelyn said, "I'm fine."

And she started to cry. Morgan galloped down the stairs, wrapped her skinny little-girl arms around her mother's waist. Mason started, then stopped, looked at her sideways.

"Where's Dad?"

"In the kitchen."

"He's really mad, isn't he?" Mason asked.

Madelyn nodded, rolled her eyes. "The poor girl," she said.

"Did she die?" Morgan's eyes went wide and interested.

"No. Maybe. Her car flipped over and over. I should call the hospital and find out."

"What's for dinner?" Mitch called from the kitchen.

"Pizza?" Madelyn said.

"Hooray!" Her accident, the smashed car, her sore shoulder took on a celebratory air. A special day. Something new had occurred.

"First the candles," she said. "Friday night."

"I have to make a call."

Mitch practically ran to the phone. Madelyn took the sabbath candles from the cupboard in the breakfast room. She moved the newspaper and Morgan's homework so she could put them on the kitchen table. She looked at Mitch and raised her eyebrows, are you coming?

Perhaps he had the security of birth, of being Jewish in his blood. Madelyn had converted, broken her Episcopalian mother's heart, gone through lessons and meetings with the rabbi. It had not been enough to give her heart and her body to Mitch. She had wanted to give him her spirit as well.

Now she was Jewish and Mitch ate bagels and lox. She observed the Friday-night shabbat ritual. She cooked special foods and cleaned out the kitchen during Passover. She went with the kids to temple on the High Holy Days while Mitch went to work. She took them to

Hebrew school, which they hated. And hated her for making them go. She wanted them to have a sense of belonging to something larger, greater than their school or Los Angeles or even America. She wanted the whole family to be one thing. Before her parents died, they kept sending Christmas presents in bright religious paper; red and green Virgin Marys and shiny Hark, the Herald Angels Sing. Madelyn missed the angels, the stained glass, and the music. At first, she had tried to sing the Jewish prayers, but they never sounded right. She found herself humming Christmas carols in the car sometimes at night. Even when it wasn't near the holidays. It wasn't religious. Judaism made so much more logical sense. They were just old, familiar tunes.

Mitch would not get off the phone. She called the children. They lit the candles. She recited the prayers. Her head was pounding. Her neck and back growing stiff. She used her cell phone to order the pizza. Mitch was still talking.

chapter five

Leo Martinez couldn't drive his car away from the accident. The front axle was bent, the radiator was crunched and leaking fluid fast. He didn't want the police to come, but she was hurt. He didn't think it was his fault, but he wasn't sure. He had hit her and her car was nice and his was old and she was white and especially in Los Angeles he was not. She had gone through the red light and he had not seen her behind the minivan beside him. The minivan stopped and he didn't. He hit her.

His car ended up sideways in the intersection. A man came and helped him push it to the side of the road. Someone called 9-1-1. Leo thought he should run over to the girl's car, upside down in the flowers on the side of the road, see if she was okay. But other people were going and he didn't want to. He kept one hand on his car, holding on to the half-raised window. He wouldn't let go.

The ambulance came and the police. Even a fire truck. Everyone was quick and did their jobs so well. One of the paramedics looked in his eyes with a little light, put a comforting hand on his shoulder. Leo was fine. His hands hurt from gripping the steering wheel so tightly.

The police were nice, too. They asked for his driver's license and registration, but they didn't accuse him of anything. They sympathized and explained that her insurance would pay for his car. Then they called the tow truck.

But they didn't understand about his car. They didn't know how much it meant to him. They didn't know he had been sleeping in it for the last six weeks. The tow truck would come and take away his clothes, his shoes, his toothbrush, his apartment.

"Where will my car go?" Leo asked the policeman.

"Wherever you say. Got a mechanic you like?"

"No."

The policeman looked at the Maryland license plate crunched on the front of Leo's car.

"New here?"

"Six weeks," Leo said.

"From where?"

"Maryland. Not Mexico. Everybody here thinks I'm Mexican. I mean, I am, but four generations ago or something. Ancestrally. I can't even speak Spanish." It was the most he had said to another human being since he had arrived in Los Angeles.

"The tow-truck guy can recommend a mechanic. Where do you live?"

Leo knew not to answer with the truth. He wasn't ashamed of living in his car. It was cheap, enterprising in this expensive city. And he wasn't staying long. He had driven across the country six weeks earlier to find his girlfriend Tess. She had come to Los Angeles to be a star more than a year ago. She had stopped calling him about a month after that. He hadn't seen her picture on any movie posters, but he was still looking, hanging out at the small theaters, the ones that showed the indies.

"Hollywood," he said. It was the first place that came to mind.

"Okay. He'll tow it somewhere over there."

Leo rode in the tow truck. It smelled of peppermint and pine-scented air freshener. The tow-truck driver was big and African-American with his dark curls slicked against his head. As he drove, he drummed the dashboard with his fingers, the pink palms in sharp contrast to the black skin. Black and pink, like the wallpaper in Leo's mother's bathroom. Big and callused, strong like Leo's dad's hands. Taped across the dashboard were little school photos of eight different kids, boys and girls, looking clean and brushed and smiling for the camera. Leo could tell their ages by their teeth: the youngest ones missing a couple, the middle ones smiling crooked with front teeth too big for their mouths, the oldest two in braces.

"All yours?" Leo asked.

The driver nodded. "I'll be driving this truck 'til the day I die." He laughed. "I'd have eight more, but the old lady says she's done."

"I come from a big family, too."

"How many?"

"Eleven," Leo said.

"You got me beat." The driver slapped the dashboard. "Eleven. Where are you in the lineup?"

"Number seven," Leo said, "I'm the seventh child of a seventh child, born in the seventh month."

Leo always said that, even if it wasn't quite true. His mom was really number six in her family and Leo's birthday was actually the first of August, but it was close to true. The girls liked it.

The driver looked at Leo sideways. "You don't look like a devil."

Leo shrugged.

The driver looked at him again. Leo smiled at him.

"You got some yellow eyes." The tow-truck driver didn't smile back.

"That's how I got my name," Leo said, "Leo, like a lion. 'Cause of my yellow eyes. My mother thought I had jaundice, but that's just the color they are."

The driver resumed drumming his fingers on the dash.

"Where am I taking you?"

"I don't know."

"Tell me something, Leo," the driver said, "I saw your clothes and stuff, that string across the back with that little flashlight hanging from it. You living in that car?"

"Well. . . yes, sir."

"I see."

"I'm not staying in L.A. long."

"If it don't run, they won't let you park that car on the street. They'll tow you. And I don't know a mechanic gonna let you sleep in it on their lot."

Leo had assumed he could stay with his car. It was his car. His mouth was dry, but he knew his forehead was shiny with sweat.

"How long will it take to get my car back?"

"A while, what with insurance having to come through and all and your car looking pretty smashed up."

Leo's stomach hurt. He had four hundred dollars in his wallet. He had started out with almost eight hundred. When he first arrived in L.A., he thought he would find Tess pretty quick. He imagined her standing on a street corner, under a palm tree in those tiny white shorts he liked. He'd pull up beside her and she'd be so happy to see him. That first week he had spent money foolishly, drinking beers, going to a movie in which she might be appearing. Now he had it down to under five dollars a day. Living in the car, going to the grocery store and eating green apples and saltine crackers for meals, drinking from the park water fountain, that four hundred dollars would last a long time. But not if he had to get a motel room. A bed sounded good, a hot shower and a night behind a locked door where he could really sleep and not worry sounded like the sultan's Taj Mahal, but he had better find Tess first.

"Insurance oughta pay for you to rent a car."

"Would I have to give them any money up front?"

"You got a credit card?"

"No."

"They won't rent you a car without a credit card."

"Oh."

That was that, then. Leo felt his throat begin to close. His heart was beating hard against his skin, he could look down and see the front of his T-shirt thumping.

The tow-truck driver looked at him. "Why don't you get a job?"

"Why don't you?" It was a reflex, a reaction to what people had been saying to him for so long. Even Tess had said it to him, more than once.

The tow-truck driver was looking at him with dark, angry eyes. "You can get out right here, sonny boy."

"Sorry," Leo said to the father of eight happy kids. "Sorry. I was thinking about something else."

Leo could tell by the photos on the dash that none of those kids would commit suicide, or end up in jail, or make their little sister give them a blow job, or draw pictures on their arms with battery acid.

"Call your mom," the truck driver was saying. "Or one of your brothers. They can rent you a car over the phone maybe."

Leo nodded. It wasn't worth going into.

chapter six

stood at the counter and held the paper cup of coffee gingerly between my thumb and middle finger. It was hot, too hot even through the cardboard sleeve; it'd be half an hour before I could drink it. I don't like hot things.

Bridget, the counter girl, smiled at me and handed me another cardboard sleeve.

"Hey, Officer Cork, your rash is looking better."

"Thanks," I said.

I fought the impulse to cover my nose with my free hand. I sighed. Bridget smiled at me as she turned away, but I felt deformed and disgusting. I wondered how my wife managed to sleep next to me as long as she did. Ronnie was already sitting at a table with his coffee. He stared out the window into the dark parking lot. I waited for my change.

Bridget was pretty. She was always happy. She had this curly hair that bounced all over her head. Her coworker said something to her and her laugh was like a roller coaster, I held my breath on her way up and exhaled with her on the way down. I was a free man. I could ask Bridget out. I could ask anyone I wanted. If I wanted to. Suddenly I was thinking about Dorothy P. Fairweather again. I shook my head. I hoped she was home in bed with her feet elevated.

Behind me, at the table to my left, I knew there was a couple in

T-shirts and tattoos. On the couch to my right was a guy in a suit reading a newspaper. What makes me a cop? It's not my dark blue uniform. It's not the weight of my bulletproof vest. It's not the way the gun sits in the holster against my hip, the creak of the leather as I move. It's the watching. I'm watching, always watching. I was the only one who noticed that the guy in the suit wasn't a businessman. That the shopping bag at his side wasn't new. He hadn't been shopping. A woman with a little girl came in for two hot chocolates with whipped cream. A couple of college girls entered, laughing about trying to stay up to study. I watched the guy in the suit. There were five other adult customers in the coffee bar, but he was the one I watched. I watched the way his hand wouldn't stay still on the newspaper. I watched the way his other hand fluttered to his nose, his hair, the front of his white shirt. I watched the way nothing about that man was still. His shoes were too big; his ankles swam in them. He eyed every woman as she went by, but not her ass; he was checking her purse, her jewelry, her leather jacket. If I had watched him long enough, if I had followed him out of there, across the street, down the next street, maybe the next, I'm sure he would eventually have done something I could have picked him up for. Instead, I got my change and I sat down with Ronnie.

Ronnie looked at me. His brown eyes had a cloud over them.

"I don't know why that kid did it," I said.

"You're the expert." Ronnie wasn't accusing me. He was really asking for an answer.

"There's a predisposition," I explained. "Some people, no matter what happens to them, will never commit suicide. Some people it only takes a little thing. They've done studies on the size of the hypothalamus gland and the levels of serotonin in the victim's brain. Some people are predisposed."

"Did you know he was going to do it?"

"How could we know? He pulled a gun. First thing he did, he pointed it right at you."

"And you."

"And me."

"He wanted us to shoot him." Ronnie shook his head. He couldn't understand it.

"Suicide By Cop." It happens often enough that there's actually a term for it.

"But we didn't shoot him," Ronnie said.

"He shot himself."

"Good Lord."

We both stared out the window at the parking lot. We watched the college girls get in their car. We watched them back up and run over the curb. They were laughing. Then they saw us watching and the girl driving got serious and frightened. I wanted to tell her, go ahead, run over every curb in the parking lot. I don't care.

"Did I tell you that the girl in the accident, the one who was knocked out, did I tell you she's getting married tomorrow?"

"Poor thing."

"Why do you say that?" I was confused. Ronnie hadn't met her fiancé. Ronnie hadn't gone into the hospital to give her the traffic ticket. We had flipped for it and I had lost.

"Because she's all scraped up for her wedding. What do you think?"

"Oh. Right. Of course. I just keep thinking about her," I said.

"Why?"

"I don't know. I just do."

"Look at that guy."

We both turned to look at the man in the suit. He was over at the rack with the free newspapers. He was putting every one of them into his shopping bag. Then he started loading up on the sugar packets and the little plastic creamers. He even took the stirrers. I looked at Ronnie. He shrugged. I shrugged back. Bridget and the other counter girl were watching him, too; then they turned away. A good cop can watch and figure out what will happen next. A great cop stops it before it happens. I'm learning. But it's tough. I can't arrest some guy just because of the way he wears his shoes. He'd bought a cup of coffee; he was entitled to as much cream and sugar as he wanted. And the newspapers were free. Maybe he was a foreigner. Maybe he had a medical problem. Or he was just a nervous guy. And that I understand. My job has made me nervous.

Note #87 06/07/00

Dear Mom,
    Life has been hell.
    Death will be a cool glass of water.
        Jamie

This was written by a thirty-four-year-old schizophrenic who had a long history of suicide attempts. I didn't feel bad about Jamie when he finally died. In his first try, he took a step off a bridge. He lived, but he ended up with one leg shorter than the other and a terrible limp. The third or fourth time, he went to some flophouse and injected rat poison in his arm. He screamed so horribly that a junkie saved him to shut him up. He lost his arm, but not his life. So then he was a limping, one-armed paranoid. The voices in his head were louder, if anything. Finally, time number six, he used a gun. Guns are the method of choice for men. And they work. Ninety-six percent of the time, they work.

A lot of cops are collectors. I don't know why that is, but a lot of us keep things. Hats. Rocks. Model trains. Ronnie's baseball cards are worth a fortune. It's something we can control, line up, leave, and return to find it just the same. At least my collection doesn't cost much. Suicide is just something of interest to me. It's not morbid or prurient. I mean, Ronnie thinks I'm nuts. And I've never told the sergeant because it's illegal for me to have them. They belong to evidence. But if I ever got caught, I'd tell him it's better than the notes being lost in some police file in the basement. These are the last words, the last wishes of people desperate enough to die. It's their very last chance to be heard, to be understood. They deserve preservation. Respect.

And it's not that I'm depressed. I was. I admit it. But the department shrink gave me a booster pack of Prozac and some good therapy. I'm not embarrassed. It's an occupational hazard. And it was before I married Linda. She helped a lot in the beginning. Anyway, what's the Beverly Hills breakfast? A nonfat latte and a Prozac. The choice between life and death is the most important choice we have and most of us never make it. We just go on living until we don't anymore. I've read. I've studied. I've talked to lots of people, both survivors and the friends and families of victims. I'm trying to understand making the choice, making the decision to die.

Ronnie wanted more from me, an explanation, but I didn't know what to tell him. Some people just can't think of any other alternative.

chapter seven

The Electric Shiva Indian restaurant in their neighborhood was Dorothy's favorite place. She had originally wanted to get married there, but Lewis said it wasn't big enough and there wasn't any air conditioning and there was no place for him and the band to perform. So she had settled for the rehearsal dinner. She loved Indian food. It wasn't necessarily the taste, it was the soft, slippery textures, the muddy colors, the heat in her nose, the foreignness.

Her head began to throb as they pulled up in front of the restaurant. There were sudden tiny, sharp flashes of light in her peripheral vision, but when she turned her head to look left and then right, nothing was there. She blinked, looked at Lewis in the driver's seat.

"I'll wait for you," she said.

"Don't you want to come in?"

"I need to go home."

"These are your friends," he said. "Everybody in there is worried to death about you. We'll just say hello, show them you're all right."

"You could have called them. I'll see everyone tomorrow. At the wedding."

"Your mom is here."

"Send her out."

"Everybody wants to see you."

"The policeman said I should rest."

"Dorothy." He was exasperated with her.

She crossed her arms. She was not going in. Her right eye sparked lime green, her left eye pale pink, but each intermittently, and only in the corners. Sometimes her left eye, sometimes her right, sometimes both together. She might learn to enjoy it.

Lewis left the car running. He slammed the door. She winced. She watched him disappear inside the restaurant. She looked up at the blue neon Shiva above the double doors. He had six arms that lit up in sequence like a fan, back and forth. His bare legs were bent as if he were dancing. Bracelets of red light blinked on his ankles. His eye was a single dot of bright orange. Shiva the destroyer. One of the Hindu holy trinity. He was the most interesting of the three. He was the violent, the sexual, God of both reproduction and disaster. He was the conflicted.

She reached her hand out the window toward him. Her palm turned blue. The inside of her wrist was iridescent with reflected color, blue and bright spills of red. What would it be like to have six arms? She could scratch her nose, read a book, eat an apple, comb her hair all at the same time. She wanted to go to India. She wanted to study Hinduism, but she didn't have the patience to read the books. She was lazy. She was without conviction. She was a hairdresser for old men and Hispanic girls. She was still taking her voice lessons, but only once a week. She hadn't been to an audition or to sing at a club in months.

Well, she thought, soon she would be married. Soon she would be a wife. They were going to Hawaii two days after the wedding. Lewis's band had a gig in Honolulu, then she and Lewis would go by themselves to the Waka Maka resort. Waka Maka. She frowned. That couldn't be right. Wiki Miki. Wucka Mucka. She had no idea.

The door to the restaurant opened and Lewis's Great-Uncle Bob emerged. He had his cell phone in his hand. He waved it at her.

"Damn!" he cried as he walked over to the car. "Goddamn it!"

"Hi, Uncle Bob."

"I was just gonna call that fellow of yours."

"What for?"

"Find out where the hell you all were."

"Right here. Here we are. Well. He's inside."

"Who?"

Dorothy had to concentrate for a moment. "Lewis!" she announced. "He's just telling everyone I'm going home."

"Your young man."

"Right. My young man. I'm sorry, Uncle Bob. I need to rest."

"Of course you do."

He opened her car door. She shook her head, but then it just seemed easier to get out of the car. She held on to Uncle Bob as she put her shoes on. They were sleekly black and spike-heeled. Grown-up shoes, Lewis's mother had called them. Dorothy felt like an impostor.

"I have to go home," she said again.

"I told everyone I'd see what was goin' on-and then here you were." Great-Uncle Bob looked at his cell phone proudly, as if his technology were responsible for her timely arrival.

Lewis's mother, Elaine, burst from within the restaurant, knocking Great-Uncle Bob off balance so that he stumbled and grabbed onto Dorothy for support.

"My baby!" Elaine threw her arms around Dorothy's neck.

Dorothy stood like a coat tree, draped with Lewis's family members. The sparkles in her eyes continued. She looked down on Elaine's head, the hair thinning, the scalp mottled gray under the frosted blond. A coconut-oil conditioner would help her dandruff.

"Bob! Get off of her. Can't you see she's hurt?"

How could Elaine tell? Was she bruised? Were the spasmodic flashes visible in her eyes?

"My baby. My poor baby. I was so worried. I thought I was going to be sick. I thought I might actually throw up, and you know I haven't been eating. I haven't eaten anything all day and only a slice of toast and a hard-boiled egg, a little tomato yesterday. I thought if I lose that little bit, well, I might just pass right out. I was so worried."

Dorothy liked Uncle Bob. His white dress shirt accentuated the white hairs sprouting from his ears. She had met him yesterday for the first time. He was in from New Jersey. He wanted her to come sing at his retirement home. An important contact from New York might come, he had told her; someone's niece's brother-in-law was a record producer. She smiled at him. His eyes grew warm and moist and he suddenly pulled her to his chest. He hugged her hard.

"Thank God you're all right," he whispered, his voice thick with teary gratitude.

Elaine looked at him in surprise. "Jesus, Bob," she said, "it was just a fender bender."

"More than that, Mom, it was more than that."

Lewis, her young man, her fellow, had come out of the restaurant. Dorothy looked at him and felt something. Relief, she thought, a settling back into herself, into a quiet alone space deep inside. A child's space. Now that he was here she didn't have to talk or even think; he would take care of everything.

"The doctor said she was lucky to be alive," Lewis continued.

Dorothy looked at Elaine's face. It needed powder. It was shiny and the blue and red neon light of Shiva glittered off her forehead. There was a tiny speck of something—lettuce, spinach—in the corner of her mouth, stuck in the thick red lipstick.

"Her car rolled over and over and over. They said she ended up upside down."

An actual tear rolled down Great-Uncle Bob's face. He put his hand on Elaine's shoulder. "My God," he said. "Oh my God."

Lewis put his arm around Dorothy. She felt him thin and sharp against her. She stepped away from him. His face had a lavender tinge in Shiva's light. She wished she could remember what that other word was for him, her young man, her fellow, her—but it was gone.

"My head hurts," she said. She didn't mean to say it out loud. It was just a thought that turned into words before she could stop it.

"Let's get you home, little girl." Great-Uncle Bob took one arm.

"You have such a big day tomorrow," Elaine said, slipping her small manicured hand through Dorothy's other elbow.

Dorothy turned to Lewis. "Where's my mother?"

"Michael's bringing her to the house."

"Is she here?"

"She's inside talking to your cousin."

"She knows I'm out here?"

"Yes."

"Where is she?" Dorothy heard her voice get high. She didn't mean to sound desperate.

Elaine—Lewis's mother, such a good mother-pursed her lips and shook her head. She patted Dorothy's arm.

"She'll see you at home," Lewis said. "Let's go."

Bob and Elaine ushered her into the car. Dorothy looked back over her shoulder at Shiva. His orange eye winked. Her eyes twinkled back.

chapter eight

Leo stood beside his car in the mechanic's garage. He was sweating and he couldn't swallow. The mechanic, thick black curly hair, olive skin, Greek or Armenian or something, wiped his hands on a greasy blue rag and took a clipboard from the tow-truck driver. He made a couple of check marks on the form, then signed at the bottom.

"What's that?" Leo had to ask.

The two men turned their dark faces to him.

"That paper? That thing you signed? What is that?" Leo heard his voice get high and dry, cracking in his throat.

"It just says your car got here," the mechanic explained.

The tow-truck driver shook his head. He didn't like Leo anymore. He didn't care about him. He went around to the back of the truck, turned on the automatic winch, and put Leo's car back on the ground. He slid under the front and unhooked the big chain. He didn't speak. He didn't look at Leo or at the car.

"See you, Gus," he said. He got in his truck and drove away.

"Okey-dokey." Gus, the mechanic, turned to Leo. "Someone gonna pick you up here?"

"Why would they do that?"

"Because you don't have a ride no more."

"No," Leo said. "No one's coming."

He stood by his car. Gus waited. When Leo didn't move or speak, Gus said, "I'm closin' up."

"Okay."

"No. I mean, you gotta go. Your car'll be fine. No one's gonna steal it looking like that." Gus laughed. Leo felt sick.

Leo sat right across the street from the garage in a 24-hour doughnut shop. He sat in the window. He could see his car, abandoned, on the lot in front of the garage. He ordered a cup of coffee which he didn't need because he was shaking already and a plain glazed doughnut, the cheapest thing they had. He hadn't had a sweet of any kind, a treat, in five and a half weeks. The sugary glaze stuck to his teeth and the back of his tongue. His head began to hurt. The smell of cooked sugar was strong. He took a gulp of the hot black coffee, swishing it around inside his mouth. It burned but he wouldn't swallow. He was trying to melt the sugar off his tongue.

A homeless guy shuffled past the window. His hair was matted against his head, the patterns of stains on his ancient pants like rings of a tree, evidence of the life he had led, the accidents he had had. Leo pulled his backpack closer to him on the sticky plastic bench. He had retrieved the most important things from his car. His toothbrush. His flashlight. His only photo of Tess. Clean underwear, T-shirt and socks. His book. He was reading the Bible. The Old Testament. Not because he was religious, but it was thick and he had pulled it off his mother's shelf of bestsellers and romance novels because he thought it would last the longest. He had driven across the country with the Bible, reading the creation of the world in Ohio, Adam and Eve and Cain and Abel in Illinois, Noah and the flood in Nebraska. The Bible was pretty interesting reading. Wait until he told Tess how little God thought of women. God put them just above a snake; one small transgression, and He gave them terrible pain in childbirth for eternity. But Eve didn't complain. Everyone in the Bible was so passive. Now Leo was reading about Abraham and Isaac. Why didn't Isaac run away? Leo wanted to know. Why was

Isaac such a wuss? Sure, Dad, tie me up and kill me. No problem. Here, Dad, let me carry the rope.

Leo did not know his dad very well. He was big and dark, and he didn't live with them most of the time. He showed up every few months to collect some money and fight with Leo's mom or whoever else was around. Leo remembered his dad's fist going through the wall and the frying pan filled with hamburger meat crashing through the closed window. He remembered the grease stain on the curtains that was there forever after. Leo had seen his mom's face bleeding, his older sisters' eyes black and blue. Even when he was little, Leo had known enough to keep out of his dad's path. He had sneaked around, behind the couch, out the back door without letting the screen slam. He hid, lied when he had to, tried to say as little as possible. His dad had given him the creeps, or the back of his hand. Every once in a while, Leo's big brother would go someplace with Dad. His mother would hold her bruised face and watch her skinny oldest boy walk out through the front door with his father, leaving his high girlish laugh in the hot air outside as they drove away.

And then when Leo was older, his dad still didn't take him. Leo always had to stay home with the girls. And the two of them, his father and his brother, then three of them with the next brother, and four of them, and five of them, and finally six with the wildest of his younger sisters, would come back when it was almost the next morning and slam the doors and tip over the iced tea pitcher in the kitchen, waking up the babies. Leo's mother would call out from her room and Leo's father would go in, and nine months later there'd be another mouth to feed and another reason not to come home.

He and Tess would never have children. They would make love until they were fifty years old, eighty years old, one hundred years old, but she would never swell up, leak milk, get tired of it like that. He shivered. It was cool, too cold in stupid sunny southern California. His hands hurt and now his head was throbbing. He looked out at the Hollywood night glittering with neon and electricity. Somewhere Tess was waiting for him.

chapter nine

Madelyn had to hold on to the kitchen counter, her head hurt so much. She took a deep breath. There wasn't much to wash. She put the forks and knives in the dishwasher. She tried to fold the pizza box so it would fit in the recycling bin, but she couldn't. She didn't have the strength.

"Let me do that." Mitch took the box from her. His big brown eyes were soft and worried. Sweet.

"I'm exhausted."

"You sure you feel okay?"

"The paramedics looked at me. I'm fine. Just tired. Headache."

"Go to bed," he said.

His eyes lit with that look, the one she called to herself the Sex Look. He wanted to do it. Tonight. His response to any problem, injury, concern, even food poisoning, was sex. It'll take your mind off it, was always his excuse, even if you throw up later.

At forty-two years old, Madelyn had finally admitted to herself, if not her husband, that she just didn't like sex. She never had. She had used it when it got her what she wanted. She had gritted her teeth and endured when it was necessary. In high school and college, she was blond and pretty and popular with the boys. She liked to party. She drank plenty and did whatever drug came around. Her lack of sexual appetite was an asset. It made her seem pure, unattainable. No boy had ever made her crazy. She enjoyed her power over their blue balls, but sometimes she wondered what she was missing. Maybe she wasn't able to relax. Maybe her body just didn't work right. She had very rarely felt anything at all. There were a couple of episodes with Mitch, before the kids were born, with the additions of alcohol and oral sex, when she had actually enjoyed herself. Now, after fourteen years of marriage, she spent the time making to-do lists in her head.

"I'm going," she said and sighed.

She said good night to her children. They were watching television, their eyes glazed, their perfect faces glowing blue in the reflected light of canned comedy.

"Feel better, Mom," Morgan said without looking away from the show.

"Thanks, Monkey. I will."

No word to her from her son, Mason. He was oblivious to pain. Other people's pain. She had ruined him. Done too much for him early on, never wanted him to be hungry or tired or anxious or bored. Now he was never much of anything. She watched his long boy fingers folding and unfolding the hem of his T-shirt, rubbing one knuckle against the seam. It was his habit. His fingernails needed cutting.

She closed their bedroom door with relief. The walls were pale aqua and the carpet thick and blue. It was an ocean of comfort; she was underwater in another world. She put on her favorite flannel nightgown and crawled into bed without washing her face or brushing her teeth. She didn't need to wash, in here she was a mermaid, a mythical creature of the deep who didn't have a sore shoulder, a throbbing head, those same ten pounds to lose.

At the accident, that handsome African-American policeman wanted to call her husband. He looked at her and knew she had a husband, assumed she had kids. He asked her about a car pool, or if she had anyone to pick up from dance class or soccer practice. He reminded her it wasn't her fault in case her husband was angry. She had "wife and mother" tattooed on her forehead. Yes, she drove a

Mercedes station wagon, but it could have been for dogs, or plants. Maybe she was a gardener, an artist, a photographer who needed room for all that interesting gear. She might be a photographer in another year or two. He nodded at her sympathetically when she said she had already called her husband, but he was in a meeting and couldn't come. The policeman knew who she was by the extra flesh on her thighs. He knew because of her clean creased khaki pants and her pink man-tailored shirt hanging over her waistband, her blond hair curled under. She looked like all the others.

She pulled the blanket up higher and rolled over on her side. Her hip was sore, too. What about that girl, Madelyn wondered, the one whose car had flipped over. She could be dead, lying in the morgue. Her family could be just now finding out. She could be gone, done, finished with all of it.

Madelyn looked at the small black phone by the bed. She wanted to call her friend Steve. He could make her feel better, but Mitch was home. She didn't talk to Steve when Mitch was around.

He was her phone friend. She had met him on the telephone at her volunteer job. One night a week, she answered phones at the Suicide Prevention Hot Line. She had been trained. And she seemed to have a knack for getting people to talk to her, unload, explain, reveal themselves. Steve had been one of her first calls.

"I'm going to kill myself," he said.

Yes. She knew that. "Why?" she asked.

He explained that he was a double amputee, legless from just below the hip. His girlfriend left him when he woke up from surgery, right after losing both his legs.

"What happened?" she asked.

"She stopped the car," he said. He had a beautiful deep voice. He spoke softly, intimately. "She wanted ice cream. I ran across the street and got hit by a truck. I was looking at her. I was smiling back at her. She asked for Rocky Road."

Madelyn's eyes filled with tears.

"It's fine about my legs," Steve said.

"How can you say that?"

"I don't need legs. It's not my legs. It's her. It's my life without her."

Madelyn leaned her head on the wood-grain Formica desktop. It felt cool against her forehead. Her eyelashes brushed the surface when she closed her eyes.

"You're very brave," she said.

"I'm not. I can't live without her."

"Yes you can."

"But why should I?"

She said what she was supposed to say. "You'll meet someone else."

"It's too late for that."

"No. No. You sound so young."

"I don't want anyone else," he reminded her. "Only her."

"You have a beautiful voice." She wasn't supposed to get personal that way. It just came out.

"So do you," he whispered. "You sound like my girlfriend. May I call you again?"

"Oh, yes."

"Tomorrow?"

"I won't be here. Only Monday nights. I only work on Mondays."

"I'll call you then."

"Good."

"'Til Monday."

"I look forward to it."

She did.

And he called the next Monday, and the next and the next. He kept her going to the hot line. Usually she gave up on her hobbies, her enthusiasms, after a few weeks. She had quit the watercolor class and the poetry, as well as furniture refinishing, cake decorating, power yoga, and hat design. She had been taking photography for only a couple of weeks. But she returned to the hot line every Monday. Every Monday for more than six months, and it was all because of Steve. Eventually she gave him her home number, just in case of emergency. Now he called her at home, too. In the mornings, when Mitch had gone to work. Steve gave her his number. She had never called him, but she wanted to. She wanted to tonight.

The longer she worked at the suicide hot line, the more suicide seemed a viable alternative. The people she talked with had terrible lives. They lived with abusive parents or spouses, or on the street or in the backs of cars. They heard voices. They saw monsters no one else could see. They were unskilled, unwashed, and unemployable. And they were all in such pain, a pain she would not be able to stand. Even Steve. He had no girlfriend, no legs, and a cosmic hospital bill. He convinced her that he was right. Yes, she finally said, yes. Suicide is a choice you can make. It's not certain what happens after death, but it must be better than this. At the least it is oblivion. At best there is the possibility of heaven or maybe you come back as a dog, or a bird or a lizard in the desert, and you can sleep and eat in the hot sun without sunscreen all day.

Perhaps the best service the hot line could provide was a booklet of various methods, along with ways to protect against the messiness of death: plastic drop cloths, diapers, recommended final meals that coat the stomach. There would be a chapter for things to take care of beforehand like emptying the fridge and returning videos, and another chapter with sample notes to loved ones with suggested guidelines. Don't blame your children. Don't use four-letter words.

She turned over on her back and stared at the ceiling. There were cobwebs in the corners that her housekeeper never saw. She closed her eyes, but the headache was worse without anything to see.

Her husband loved her. Her children were wonderful. She began to cry.

chapter ten

Ronnie and I sat in the alley off Bedford above Wilshire behind a whole building that sold just perfume. We were watching the stop sign at the intersection below us. A pedestrian had been hit a couple of days previous and the residents wanted the stop sign watched. We'd already nailed two drivers. One in a BMW, one in a Rolls Royce. They had each driven right through the intersection.

I looked at my watch. 9:22 P.M. Linda would already be in Phoenix. She had probably arrived around dinnertime, maybe earlier. I imagined her pulling into her boyfriend's driveway. He was standing out front. He was waiting for her. It was a flat suburban neighborhood. He had a big ranch house with a circular drive. His arms opened for her. She cried a little.

"Was it hard?" her boyfriend asked.

"No." Linda shook her head against his chest. "He didn't say a thing."

I had the address. Sunday was my day off. I could just show up. I could say a couple of things.

I cleared my throat. I sniffed.

"You okay?" Ronnie asked.

"Fine."

I could have told him then. I sat in the passenger seat and said nothing. I twisted my wedding ring around and around on my finger. What if I did show up in Arizona?

What if I didn't? It hit me. I'd have all day Sunday by myself in the apartment. All day and all night. The loneliness fell over me like a heavy shroud. It bent my shoulders, turned my legs to sand. I peered out from under it, and everything I saw was suddenly sharp and magnified. I saw the pebble pattern in the plastic of the dashboard and the chipped paint on the radio and the screw and worn nut in the shotgun mount. Everything was clear to me. I saw the pores in Ronnie's skin and the way his hair sprouted from his scalp. I saw the fingerprints someone had left on the windshield. The rest of my life was absolutely clear to me.

Note #91 08/15/00

Honey,

I'm staying with Mr. Harrison. The weather's bad. The rescue team won't get to us in time. He's not going to make it through the night. I know I won't make it if I stay. But I got him into this mess. I don't want him to be alone. I have to stay.

I love you,

Scott

I bought this note off the Internet. It's from a guide who made some stupid decisions up on Everest. What really got me was that it was being sold by his wife. What kind of wife would sell her husband's final note? For fifty bucks?

Linda would. My wife. I loved the way she smelled. I liked the way she slid her hand under my thigh while I was driving. I liked it that her feet were always cold. But the rest of her was pretty damn cold, too. She had been a news dispatcher; she listened to the police frequency and sent reporters to cover the worst disasters. If it bleeds, it leads.

She had heard me crying on the radio. It was the woman who dropped her three little kids off the balcony before jumping herself. I'm not ashamed that I cried. She heard me. She knew how easy it would be. She dated me. She married me. And then she left me.

chapter eleven

Leo had a new plan. He could meet a girl. Three dollars for a beer and an evening spent lying to some not-very-pretty thing at a bar would get him a free night in her apartment.

He asked the small Asian woman behind the glass doughnut case if he could use the bathroom. She nodded to him, quickly, many times, shaking more dandruff onto her black sweater.

He followed her finger through the kitchen and past the old, fat Asian doughnut cook reading a newspaper in his own language. The man didn't even look up. Leo slid down a hall stacked high with paper supplies, boxes, and bags. He opened the dirty pink door.

The bathroom was not clean. Leo didn't want to think about the doughnut he had eaten. His head was killing him. He brushed his teeth and ran his wet fingers through his thick hair. He gave himself a boardinghouse shower: face and armpits washed, lots of deodorant. He put on his mostly clean amber T-shirt. It made his eyes brighter, yellower, even more unusual. He knew what he had.

He left the doughnut shop and walked across the street, just to say goodbye to his car. He had to figure it was safe behind the chain-link and barbed wire. A mangy pit bull growled at him from a dark spot under a truck.

If Tess walked by, she would recognize his car. She knew the dark red color, fading on the top. She had given him the Grateful Dead sticker for the back, not because she liked the Grateful Dead or even knew who they were really, but because she thought the different-colored bears were so cute. She would see the front end smashed in and know he had been in an accident. She'd be worried. She'd call the hospitals and the police; then she'd probably figure out to come by the garage and ask someone about him.

Tomorrow he would spend the day with Gus the mechanic and his car.

He chose a bar on La Brea. It had a small happy-hour sign out front and no name over the door. The Latino valet sat on a folding chair beside a brushy palm tree. He spun a set of keys in his hands. His black wing-tips looked cheap and uncomfortable, but required. He leaned forward around the palm and nodded at Leo, smiled a little, man to man, Mexican to Mexican. Leo nodded back, but hoped the guy didn't speak to him.

There were two girls standing outside the door, trying to decide whether to go in. One wore pants. The other, the larger one, wore a stretchy skirt that was too tight; she kept pulling it down with one hand. She'd pull and Leo could see it creep back up her thighs.

"Goin' in?" he asked.

Two pairs of over-made-up eyes turned to him. The girl in pants looked him up and down and dismissed him. The big girl just smiled.

"We're tryin' to decide," Pants said.

"Been here before?" Skirt asked.

"Just checkin' it out myself," Leo replied.

Skirt wore a little top with skinny straps. She had beautiful skin and no obvious bones. He couldn't see her collarbones or any definition in her shoulders, just the pure expanse of her smooth white hide.

He smiled at her, but she wasn't the one. She lived at home, or with Pants as a roommate. She would want to see him tomorrow, and the day after that.

"See you inside," he said. "Or not."

He went in. It was nicer inside than he expected. It was soothing, with cream-colored walls and a dark wooden bar. The bar stools were upholstered in navy blue and turquoise. He chose a stool in the back where he could watch the door.

It was quiet. A little early for a Friday night. The bartender was bored. Leo ordered a beer. Pants and Skirt never came in. That's good, Leo thought, that's a good sign. He didn't like them. He didn't want to see them again. He sipped his beer. His foot tapped against the bar rail. He pushed his hands flat against the smooth wood and waited.

chapter twelve

Dorothy should have said she wanted to go home alone. Instead, everyone came home with her. They moved the rehearsal dinner to her house. She sat on the sofa with her legs up on the coffee table and a blanket around her even though she wasn't cold, just to remind them she was not herself. They all arrived, laughing, looking for alcohol, carrying bags of cold Indian food that had already been bought and paid for. Dorothy's mother sat next to her and held her hand. Lewis's family and their friends came over one by one and asked if she was all right, what the doctor had said, what happened. She repeated the story until she couldn't anymore, and then her mother started telling it. Embellished, of course; her mother believed that the truth could always be improved. The truck was bigger; the signal impossible to see; the red car that hit her was moving too fast, over the legal limit, beyond the speed of light.

Dorothy's mother, Jane, held her daughter's hand possessively, but for her own protection. She had her back against the couch facing the enemy: Lewis's mother, his father, his great-uncle, and the rest of them. She held Dorothy's hand and her mouth was grim. No one had better forget that she was the mother of the bride, the only one who had claim to the space beside the wounded girl. Jane was tall and bony, with a beautiful New England face. Her blue eyes were large, her nose patrician. She wore a blood red dress, rich and dangerous; never mind that it was a wedding sort of thing. Her free hand fingered her single strand of pearls. She wore plain black pumps and no stockings. She had wonderful blond hair, still thick and glossy with hardly a gray hair, and pulled back on one side with a yellow plastic child's barrette shaped like a bow. Dorothy admired her mother's hair. Her own hair was wispy, thin, of indistinct color and texture. It was unfinished looking, haphazard, no matter what hairstyle she chose, what product she used, what color she made it. She ran her hand through the short bleached spikes.

Jane turned to her. "You're getting married tomorrow," she said.

Dorothy's right eye was still sparkling. It flashed neon green and obscured her mother's face. Dorothy shifted so she faced her mother head-on. Jane hadn't asked once about the accident or how she was feeling. Of course, everybody else had asked and kept asking, so maybe Jane didn't think it was necessary. More likely, when Jane had first heard about the accident, she had assumed the worst: her daughter dead with her body mangled beyond recognition the night before her wedding. Dorothy's ordinary survival had disappointed her.

Dorothy heard a woman's high peal of laughter and turned to look. In the kitchen, her older brother, Michael, was pouring drinks for the members of Lewis's band and their chic girlfriends. It was a black hole in there, everybody dressed for espionage. Michael was drunk. She could tell by the way he leaned as if on the deck of a listing ocean liner. His short hair was pushed back and up from his forehead, gelled to stand straighter than he in that same ship's breeze. He glanced over, through the doorway at her and Jane, lifted his glass to them both. Tomorrow, after the ceremony, he would drive Mom back to Walnut Hill. The funny farm.

"It's not an institution," he always said. "It's a place for her to live without worries."

Without them worrying about her, Dorothy knew. They had

spent so many years worrying. And Jane wasn't miserable there, not most of the time. Anyway, everybody hated their life occasionally.

Dorothy had inherited her mother's long legs. She wanted her mother's hair. She wanted her straight nose and large eyes, the wide mouth that wore lipstick well. But that was all she wanted from her mother.

"We're so much alike," Jane would tell her. "You think just the way I do."

It was a liturgy that Dorothy didn't repeat, could not believe. Her mother was crazy. All through her childhood, there were clothes Dorothy was not allowed to wear—not because they were inappropriate, but because they had evil in them. A white peasant blouse with red embroidery sent Jane into conniptions. There were words Dorothy and her brother needed permission to say—"butter" for instance, because these ordinary declarations opened doorways to bad places. Only Jane knew what these places were. When Dorothy asked, Jane shuddered and told her she was too young to know.

Her mother saw things that no one else could see. Dorothy came home from a high-school party, unhappy, rejected by the boy she liked. She wanted to go right upstairs to her room and listen to some sad music. But she found her mother hiding behind the sofa.

"Make it go away, Dorothy. Please." Her mother whispered. Terrified, sweating.

Dorothy saw nothing. She waved her arms at the air, shouted "shoo!"

Jane shook her head."No." Her voice was hoarse from crying. "Over the fireplace."

Something in the way her mother spoke scared Dorothy. She knew there was nothing there, but the hair stood up on her neck when she turned to look. Nothing, but what was that? Nothing. Come on, Dorothy told herself, don't be ridiculous. She got the broom from the kitchen. She swept the wall above the fireplace. Still her mother cowered. Dorothy sighed. Now she knew what it was. There were evil rays emanating from the clock on the mantel. It had been Jane's mother's clock. Anything old, anything from Jane's childhood, was dangerous. Dorothy took the clock from the mantelpiece and put it in the front hall closet, behind the outgrown snow boots.

Dorothy understood her mother. Michael frowned, shook his head, moved out at seventeen, coming home for all the holidays and few of the emergencies. Dorothy stayed.

Her mother walked away from dinner one night, angry at something Dorothy had said, and marched out the back door, letting the screen slam behind her. She didn't come back for three days. Dorothy didn't go to school. She waited at home for her mother. She stopped eating, did not watch television. She sat at the kitchen table her mother had left, the same dishes in front of her, the same food, rotting, spoiled.

"You're just like me," Jane would say.

Dorothy cringed. Anything but that. I am not like my mother, Dorothy chanted, prayed, hoped.

"Dorothy." Jane sounded annoyed.

"Sorry," Dorothy replied. She pulled her hand from her mother's large grasp. "Sorry," Dorothy said again. For whatever, for everything.

"Do you love him?"

"Who?"

"Lewis," her mother said.

"Of course."

"Bullshit."

Dorothy gasped. "Mother!"

But Jane laughed, a peculiar sound in a woman who was chronically and helplessly depressed. "You should have seen the look on your face." Then her mother's face grew serious. "I want to talk to you."

"Not now."

"After the party."

Dorothy was exhausted. She wanted them all to go away. The smell of congealing curry, the laughter and music conspired against her, kept reminding her of how badly she felt and what would happen to her tomorrow. She should have gone to India that summer after she and Seth broke up. India. Enlightenment. She might never have come back.

She managed to avoid the conversation with her mother. Michael was impatient to leave; he had his eye on a guy, the only gay band member. They were meeting at a bar after Michael dropped Jane at the hotel. He didn't want to wait for his mother and sister to have a heart-to-heart.

"In the morning, Mom," Dorothy said.

After everyone was finally gone, Lewis sat down next to her and stroked her cheek.

"Our last night," he said, "living in sin."

"I've enjoyed sin," she said.

"Me, too." His fingers took a lascivious turn down her neck and under her dress.

She leaned into his arm, took his hand, and kissed the palm. "I'll help you put the food away."

He laughed. "First things first."

Dorothy stood up. Her eyes flashed. Her head was aching. Her neck and back were stiff. She was suddenly dizzy, and her stomach was unhappy. She stumbled into the kitchen. Dirty glasses and half-eaten plates of food covered the counters. A bag from the Indian restaurant lay on its side on the floor. Shiva looked up at her. Her glittering eyes made him sparkle and shine. Fine Indian Cuisine. She didn't want to cry, but it seemed suddenly she was crying.

They didn't have sex, after all, their last night unmarried. Lewis was a little disappointed, but he understood. Dorothy couldn't stop crying. She wasn't sobbing, but the tears kept dripping from her eyes no matter what she did as if the faucet was broken.

Lewis went to bed. She could hear him snoring, the sputtering of too much alcohol. She sat in the living room on the couch with ice cubes on her eyes. Here it was. The night before. This was it.

Lewis loved her more than anyone ever had. She couldn't wait to get married.

She picked up the phone. Two years later, she still knew Seth's number by heart. It was midnight. He might not be alone. She let it ring. Twice. Three times.

"Hello?" His voice was the same. "Hello? Hello? Anybody there?"

He didn't sound like he had been sleeping. He sounded just the same. He sounded like he had been waiting for her call.

"Hello?" he said.

She hung up. She felt it begin, just like two years ago, the weight in her chest, the thickening in the back of her throat.

Hello? It was him. His voice.

Dorothy went to the bathroom and threw up. She never wanted to feel that much pain again. She had thought, she had prayed, that she would die.

She sat on the bathroom floor, the tiles cold on her legs through her dress. She remembered the day in March, almost exactly two years ago, when he left her. They had plans for St. Patrick's Day, but he left two days before. March fifteenth. Beware the "ides." She showed up at his house, as always. She checked her lipstick in the rearview mirror, jumped out of the car, hurried to his door. He wasn't home. The door was unlocked and there was a note on the kitchen table.

"Dot—" it began. His name for her. Sometimes Dottie. She loved that he called her Dot. No one else ever had. And never once had he made a comment about her name and the Wizard of Oz. Her first baby shoes had been tiny ruby slippers. Since then, she avoided any kind of red footwear. And she refused to ever, ever sing "Over the Rainbow."

Dot—

I have to go. You do too. This isn't working. You want more than I can give. You want everything. Sorry. Sorry. Sorry.

She waited for him. Slept on his couch waiting. When he finally returned, she saw the look on his face. He was standing there, but he was gone. He shook his head, started backing out the door. She fell off his couch. She crawled toward him.

"Don't," he said. And "I can't do it anymore. You love me too much. You're destroying me. I'm suffocating. Get up. Get out."

For the next two weeks, Dorothy stayed in her studio apartment. She stayed in bed. She didn't shower. She didn't read a book. She brought the box of cereal under the covers and ate it dry, spilled it in the sheets they had shared. The clock radio played pop music beside her head, and she cried at every song. The phone rang but she didn't answer. She listened only for his voice on the answering machine. He didn't call.

A friend from work came by and rang the doorbell. She yelled at him to go away.

"Are you sick?" he called.

"Yes."

"Are you coming back to work?"

"I don't know."

"You're gonna get fired if you don't call them."

"Go away."

He went. She got fired. She heard her boss on her answering machine. Older, exasperated and, worse, disappointed.

"We can assume you have quit. If you haven't quit, don't bother coming back. We'll be mailing you your final paycheck."

It was the thought of her mother that finally got her out of bed. Her mother and a future at Walnut Hill. She was turning into Jane. Dorothy got out of bed because she couldn't stand herself anymore. The smell. The bits of honey-coated oat and wheat flakes against her bare skin. The ache in her hips from not moving. And the complete absorption in her own misery. Just like Mom. She forced herself to leave her apartment, to get a newspaper, to read the classifieds.

But the agony continued for a long long time. It was a lengthy convalescence. One errant thought of Seth and she might collapse wherever she was, even in the grocery store by the ice cream. She swayed. She thought of him and her legs would not hold her. She grabbed at the chrome handle of the freezer case. She sank to the dirty linoleum. Her heart had split again. Her suffering blossomed there, in the left side of her chest, and made it impossible to walk, to speak, to breathe. The store manager should have been able to tell. The woman pushing the cart who muttered "drugs" under her housewife breath, should have known by looking at her that she was mostly dead from love.

Eventually she decided to take a beautician course at City College. It was time to learn how to do something. And she found a night job waitressing at a popular bar. She needed to be out and busy at night. She wanted too many people around her. That was where she met Lewis, playing at the bar with his band. One Saturday she drank too much and got up onstage. She sang a sad and silly song with them, low and breathy, with her mouth pressed against the rough microphone. People applauded. She held onto the sides of her waitress apron and curtsied. Lewis laughed. She told him she wanted to be a singer. She had always wanted to be a singer.

Lewis took her home to his house and made love to her and she let him and the rest, as they say, was history. And in that history, she stopped driving by Seth's house. She stopped looking for him in every restaurant, art opening, crowded concert. She stopped waiting for him.

Like a prisoner of war with Lewis as her only ally, Dorothy began to hate Seth. He was her torturer. Her memories of him, his arms around her, his tongue, his taste, his skin, were smothered by the twisted acts he had performed on her. His face appeared in her mind and she recoiled. She scrambled backwards on her hands and butt. She felt desperate to get away from her recollection of him. But time passed, and like the captive who eventually knows nothing else, she sat on the cement floor in her mind's cold cell and relished the ache. It was all she had left of him. Then, she welcomed those memories of him, the worst thoughts, the most hurtful moments. She focused on the terrible things he had done to her. She concentrated on when he said good-bye, when he said "Get up. Get out," when his face told her he hated her. The ache was him. The agony was all that remained. She could not let it go. And she could not die, because if she died, she would have nothing of him, not even the pain.

chapter thirteen

I decided to drive by her house. Dorothy P. Fairweather. It was 1:13 A.M., early morning on the official first day of spring. My shift was over. I'd done all my paperwork. I had her address from her driver's license. It was clear across town, but it was impossible for me to go home. I couldn't go home. I'd had a moment, back at the station, when I wondered if Linda had changed her mind; maybe she turned around. Maybe I'd get home and she'd be there, sleeping, waiting for me. Then I thought, what if she wasn't?

I drove east on Beverly Boulevard. In Larchmont, I stopped at a light. The sidewalks were empty. Even the chicken place on the corner was dark. I was in the left-hand lane and I looked out my passenger window at the car next to me. It was a late-model four-door Buick sedan, two-toned, brown and beige. The driver was Caucasian, middle-aged, fat and bald, and he was screaming at the top of his lungs. I saw him shouting, yelling and gesturing with one hand. Then he banged the steering wheel. He had his windows rolled up. I couldn't understand his words; I heard only a distorted whine as if he were underwater. I leaned forward to look past him, to see who had made him so angry, but there was no one in the passenger seat. I looked in back, afraid I might find a small child, a woman lying on the seat with her arms over her head, but there wasn't anybody there. He was just angry. He was screaming at the world.

The first suicide note I ever kept was from The Angry Guy. We found him naked with his head blown off in his girlfriend's bed. He had the name "Amanda" scratched in his chest with a razor blade. His name was Sam, but we called him The Angry Guy. His girlfriend/mistress found him, just like he wanted, but it didn't seem to have the desired effect. She didn't even dial 9-1-1. She called the regular number for the station and said a man had killed himself in her bedroom.

"Can someone please come quickly?" she asked. "Blood is dripping on the carpet."

I was dispatched to the scene. She answered the door eating a piece of toast. She was very pretty, but her face was a veneer. There was nothing behind her eyes.

"Do you know this man?" I asked.

"Well," she said, "it's a little hard to tell, but I think so."

"Do you know why he killed himself?"

"He was an angry guy," she replied.

Note #1 03/18/99

Dear Amanda:

Fuck you. Fuck you. Fuck you. They say suicide is one big fuck you. So fuck you.

I don't fucking care if you never get over it. I arranged it so you would find my disgusting bloody faceless body and I hope you have a fucking heart attack. But if you die don't come to my heaven. My heaven won't have you in it. You can go straight to your own private hell.

So fuck you. And your stupid fucking dickhead husband.

I hope that guy you're married to fucks you good and hard. I hope he gets all his friends to come over and fuck you too. I wish they would fuck you in the ass and in the ear and in the nose and in your eyes.

You don't know what love is. You don't know how much I

love you. I am writing your name over my heart with a razor blade right now. When the police come they will see your name in blood on my chest. They will read this note and they will know YOU DID THIS TO ME. YOU DID IT. YOU. YOU.

I don't know why you couldn't love me. You stupid cock-tease bitch. FUCK YOU.

Sam

Dorothy P. Fairweather's neighborhood was on the east side of L.A. I turned down her street. It was dark. One of the streetlights was out. The wind was rattling in the loquat trees. I could smell a skunk somewhere in the distance. I pulled up across the street from her house. It was a nice-looking California bungalow, clapboard with a couple of big trees out front. I could imagine the hardwood floors, the built-in china cupboard in the dining room, the brick fireplace with bookcases on either side. It was exactly the kind of house young couples buy. I knew it had a small bedroom in the back and that when they first looked at it, they were too shy to talk about it, but they both knew it would be perfect for a baby. I've seen this house and the roof that needs fixing and the real estate agent who smiled at them when they signed the papers. Dorothy and what's-his-name planned to paint the kitchen themselves, they found just the right chair to go next to the fireplace, over dinner they talk about knocking out that back wall and making a real family room.

There was a lamp on in the living room and no curtains, just some oleandar bushes in front. I sat across the street and watched. And I saw her. I didn't know she was there, but then she stood up from the sofa and I realized the lump in the window I had thought was a pillow was her head. She bent down and got a tissue and I watched her blow her nose. She looked so slight, a shadow of a girl. She wiped her eyes with the same tissue. I knew she was crying. I hoped it was just her head that was hurting.

A broken heart should be visible. Something that hurts that much should not be hidden. The pain, worse than broken bones, knife wounds, gunshots, chemotherapy, tumors or boils, should be swathed in long white bandages. The wounded should appear on crutches or in a wheelchair for their heart. Then people would know. They would recognize the injured, they would see the damage and understand, care, offer a kind word. Love is so much like war and a relationship only one long siege, the defenses going up and down as the fortunes change and alliances transfer. Couples should wear combat uniforms. They would be bright and freshly ironed in the first days of romance. Then the material would become stained, begin to fray. We would lose a button or two. Anyone looking at us would know where we were, how far we had come. Only one shiny epaulet still attached, but somehow a symbol of hope. We will emerge victorious.

chapter fourteen

Leo spotted his victim the moment she walked in. She was long-haired and slim-hipped. Too skinny for his taste. But she had a bad eye. Her left eyelid drooped. She couldn't quite open it. It gave her face a sad look, the eyes of Quasimodo, or Dr. Frankenstein's pathetic assistant. There was something wrong with her left hand as well. It was subtle, but two fingers curled together in an abnormal way. She came in and sat at the bar with her good side toward him. Leo watched the other guys look at her and dismiss her. She didn't seem to mind. She was used to it.

She ordered a vodka martini and that impressed him. She paid with a twenty and that was good, too. She was a little older than him, but not much. She was definitely still in her twenties. Maybe it was her deformity. Maybe living with being ugly had given her wisdom, a maturity beyond her years. She sipped her drink and looked around the bar slowly, taking it in. She came to Leo and paused for a moment as he looked back, right into her one good eye. He smiled a little. She flushed and looked away, then glanced back at him from behind her hair. He grinned. This was a piece of cake.

He slid over to the bar stool next to her. She kept her face hidden by her hair. She smelled like perfume, too strong and chemical, but clean anyway. He spoke softly, making her listen.

"Hey," he said. "That drink looks so pretty in your hand."

He didn't know why, but she laughed. "What's your name?" she asked.

"Leo."

She turned to face him. Both eyes, bad and good, went wide and surprised. She grinned. Happy. Really happy.

"Leo?"

"My mom named me Leo. 'Cause of my eyes. See? Like a lion."

He leaned in close. She smiled and it was a smile that was sure to last all night long.

chapter fifteen

Madelyn made silent, parental love with her husband. She kept her eyes closed and her mind on tomorrow's schedule of birthday parties and soccer games. She put her hands there and moved her hips like that and it was over quickly. Of course it didn't help her headache, but Mitch was happy. It was actually masturbation—she was just another form of his hand—but it kept the peace. He rolled over and slept right away, like a cliché, with his familiar pattern of snoring in and huffing out.

Madelyn got up and went downstairs to the kitchen. The last thing she should do was eat, but there was one piece of pizza left. She took it out of the fridge, unwrapped the aluminum foil, and ate it cold while standing at the counter.

She picked up the phone and dialed information.

"Beverly Hills," she said to the operator. "I need the number for the Beverly Hills Police Department. No. It's not an emergency."

She let the operator connect her. She thought to hell with the ninety-cent charge. She felt extravagant. Usually she was thrifty, even frugal, although Mitch the movie producer was doing very, very well.

"Hello?" she said. "Police?"

"Yes. This is the sergeant on duty. How may I help you?"

The voice was businesslike, but comforting. The Beverly Hills

Police Department had won an award for being the best- dressed police force in the country. It wasn't that their uniforms were so well appointed, it was that the men wearing them were all movie-star material. She was probably old enough to be this man's mother, certainly his aunt.

"I was in a car accident today," Madelyn said.

"Did you file a report? You have to call back during regular business hours to request a form."

"I did. I mean, the police were there. It was a bad accident."

"I'm sorry."

"Not for me," Madelyn assured the handsome voice. "I'm fine. But the young woman who hit me, her car flipped over and over. She was upside down. I just wanted to know if she's all right."

Madelyn assumed the officer would know exactly the accident she was talking about. She knew they were Beverly Hills cops on the scene. She couldn't imagine they had more than one terrible accident a day. Beverly Hills was so pleasant.

She heard the sound of computer keys. The sergeant on duty typed very well.

"She was treated at Cedars and released."

"She's okay?"

"Guess so. It doesn't say more than that."

"Thank you," Madelyn said. "Thank you so much."

She hung up. She had to admit she was disappointed. She had decided if the girl was dead, then she wouldn't ask for any money, even from the insurance company or whatever. It didn't seem right. She had imagined showing her friends her damaged car, telling the story at her book club, at the health club, at the tennis club.

She stood in the dark kitchen and was embarrassed by her disappointment. Thank God she's alive, she wanted to think, but it sounded false, even when she said it out loud. She rubbed at a spot of tomato sauce on her counter. Her kitchen was so nice. She had fought for the glass tile countertops, begged that funky glass artist who never left his studio to do them for her. Between her begging and the amount of money Mitch offered, how could he refuse? He complained the whole time, but finally he did a beautiful job. At dinner parties she told the story of when she caught him smoking a joint in her downstairs bathroom. She said how shocked she had been, but he offered it to her and she took a toke and then giggled all through Morgan's piano lesson. It always got a laugh.

Pathetic, she thought now. I used to do a bong hit every morning before I got on the bus for high school. I went to Freshman Orientation at Stanford tripping on mescaline. I sold enough cocaine to pay for my three weeks in Paris. There wasn't a drug she hadn't tried, enjoyed, used. No one knew that now. Even Mitch had come later, after she was working seriously at the documentary film company and only a weekend party-girl.

She stared at the phone. She took a deep breath and decided to do it. She dialed Steve. She looked at the digital clock glowing green on the back of the stove. It was almost midnight. She had never called him before, but she knew his number by heart. The phone rang. And rang.

Just lately, maybe because she worked at the Suicide Prevention Hot line, she had begun to think seriously about how she would take her own life.

In the mornings, after Mitch had gone to work and the kids were off to school, after she had walked the dog and done the breakfast dishes, planned what to have for dinner that night and spent her twenty minutes on the exercise bike, she worked on a list.

Shotgun.
Handgun.
Rope.
Knife.
Razor blade.
Poison.

There were obvious drawbacks to these methods. She preferred

>Sleeping pills.
>Head in the oven.
>Head in a plastic bag
>>plus pills.
>>plus alcohol.
>>plus alcohol and pills.

And what about freezing to death? It was supposed to be a pleasant way to go, once you got over the initial cold. But it was a problem since she lived in southern California.

>Meat locker.
>Oversized upright freezer.

Her sister in Ohio had one of those. She had a big carnivorous family. She kept a side of beef in it, white paper packages of hamburger and rib roast. Madelyn was not a small woman, but she was certainly smaller than half a cow, even half a cow in pieces. If she removed the shelves and put the meat packages in the camping cooler with some dry ice, there would be plenty of room for her.

She crossed that out. She didn't want her sister to find her. Or her brother-in-law. His heart was bad. He might have a heart attack. He might die. She wanted to go alone.

She wondered if it would be best to just disappear first—not necessarily be dead, but gone. It might be easier on her family if she just evaporated, lost, possibly kidnapped. The authorities could find her body after she had been missing for a while, after time had passed. When her body, or what was left of it, was found, Mitch and the kids would already be accustomed to her absence. Tragic, but that way the blow would come slowly, in stages. Her children would have a new housekeeper and a new routine. Her husband would already be taking his shirts to the cleaners, not depending on her to make sure there was milk, and bread, and dog food. Of course they would still be hoping she'd turn up. But when the news of her death came, Mitch would say, "At least we know. At least we're not wondering anymore." They could get on with their lives, grieve and move on.

And then the day would come when there were no more of her dirty clothes in the laundry. Nothing she had wrapped and labeled left in the freezer. There wouldn't be any more of her notes on the calendar. Her handwriting would be gone, buried with her. There would be no smell of her left in the towels or the bedsheets. Even the dust bunnies under the bed would not contain flakes of her skin and hair and dirt.

How long would that take? When would she really be gone? She flipped forward in the calendar hanging by the refrigerator. There were things written in her slanty, proper hand for months to come, until after school began again in the fall. October. By Halloween, she'd be a ghost.

Flight.

She wrote it down that way. Not "Jumping" or "Falling," but "Flight."

But she wasn't sure that jumping off a bridge or roof was really doable. Not for her, not since she had mentioned it to Steve. He said the pain was bad when he was hit by the truck on Glendale Boulevard running across the street to buy his whiny girlfriend ice cream. He said it hurt. Like hell. Forget them saying you're in shock, he told her; forget them saying he never felt a thing. You would feel it when you hit the ground. You do, he said. You feel everything.

"But before the pain, flying would be grand."

"No," Steve said. "I'd be too afraid to enjoy it."

Drowning was Steve's favorite option. His legs obviously couldn't help him and his arms wouldn't be strong enough by themselves. If he could get his wheelchair into the ocean, he'd never get out.

Take a deep breath and surrender.

"I don't like cold water," she told him. "Anyway, I'm a good swimmer. I think I'd fight back, just by instinct."

Steve called her during the day. She might be in the laundry room, or in the yard picking up the dog shit and she would hear the phone ring and know it was him. She would run to the kitchen.

"Yes," she always answered the phone breathless with anticipation. "Yes. What else?"

"Car accident," he whispered.

"Can you drive?" she asked.

"Yes," he said, "But not me. You. Think of the lesson you could give your children. Don't take a ride on the freeway for granted."

"But it would hurt."

"If you figured it out," he said, "scientifically, the kind of car you drive, the kind of wall you hit, so you could go fast enough and hit something at exactly the right angle, it'd be over instantly. Not like hitting the ground."

"What about you?" she asked. "What about you?"

"I'm doing it slowly. Very slowly."

"I don't want you to suffer," she said.

She imagined his blood dripping by single red drops onto a white tile floor. His wheelchair on its side, the wheel in the air turning and turning. He was in the tub, one arm hanging over the edge, the other arm across his pale naked chest. The blood, his blood, sliding from his wrist, across his abdomen, down between his legs, and finally mixing with the bathwater. The human body contains less than two gallons of blood, barely enough to cover the bottom of the tub. She heard the gurgle in the back of his throat and saw his sad eyes—eyes she had never seen, but thought were blue—staring, watching, seeing everything but all of it blurred by pain, until the last breath, the last moment.

She didn't want that.

"I've quit taking my medication," he said.

"Oh."

"Other things were damaged in the accident. I could have a stroke at any moment."

At least he had medication to quit taking. If she knocked her head against the closet door enough times, could she produce a brain tumor? If she didn't have her mammogram or her Pap smear or a regular checkup, could she will herself to have cancer? But that wasn't suicide. That was giving them the power, the same power as if you grew old and died.

She took up cigarette smoking. It wasn't much, but it was something. She had to hide her smokes from Mitch, from her kids, from her friends. Only on Monday nights—sitting at the beige folding table, her skin blotchy green from the fluorescent lights, her alien hand on the phone in the basement of the Boys' Club, fielding calls from troubled teens and desperate housewives, men who had lost money and women who had lost men—only then could she smoke.

"Yeah?" Finally Steve answered the phone, not sleepy but belligerently awake. "Who is this?"

"Steve?" she asked stupidly.

"Madelyn." he said. "Madelyn." The change in his voice was palpable. It deepened, softened. She smiled.

"Yes," she said. "I was in an accident."

"Where are you?" he asked. "I'll be right there."

"Really?"

"Don't worry. I'm on my way." Then he laughed. "You don't care what I'm wearing, do you?"

"It's after midnight."

"Just tell me where you are. I'm coming."

And that was it. The thought of him getting in his wheelchair and leaving his house and driving his specially made van through dark streets to save her was all she needed. She had been leaning in that direction; now she tumbled, she fell and she landed at his feet.

"No, no, no," she said.

"Your husband is coming?"

"No. It happened earlier. I'm home now. I just—" She paused, then she said it anyway, "I just wanted to hear your voice."

"Are you all right?"

"My head really hurts."

"Tell me you're all right."

"I'm fine."

"Good."

She laughed, nervously, unhappily. "What are you wearing?" she asked.

"Why?"

"You asked if I would care. Of course I wouldn't, but now I am curious."

There was a long silence.

"Steve?"

"I'm naked," he said.

"Oh."

She had never seen him. They had never met. She didn't know if he had dark hair or blue eyes or ears that stuck out from his head. Now he was naked.

"What are you wearing?"

Should she lie? "My flannel nightgown."

"What color?"

"Pink."

"Are you wearing underpants?"

"Steve."

"Answer me."

"Yes." She had picked her dirty ones up off the floor and put them on when she left the bedroom. She didn't want to leave a spot of her husband's semen on the back of her nightgown if she sat down to read or watch television.

"Do you always sleep with your panties on?"

"No."

"What color are they?"

"Light blue."

"Bikini or brief?"

"Hip huggers." She giggled and was embarrassed that she had.

He was quiet. She sat down on one of the stools in the kitchen. Then she stood up. She carried the phone to the living room and sat down on the cool leather couch.

"Madelyn."

"Yes."

"Take them off?" Steve asked. "For me?"

"I don't know," she said. "I've never done this."

"Hold on to the phone with one hand. Take off your underwear with the other."

Madelyn suddenly felt warm all over. She felt something. Why not? He couldn't see her. She slid her panties off and stuffed them under the couch cushions.

"Okay," she said. "Okay."

She and Steve had discussed his sex life, or lack of it. She knew that his equipment all worked, was still there, it was only his legs that were missing. She also knew he was shy about his stumps.

"I'm so glad you're all right. I'm glad you're not hurt. I'd like to kiss you," he said. "Would you like that? If I kissed you? If I put my tongue in your mouth? Would you like that? Do you kiss with your mouth open?"

"Yes."

"I can feel your breath on my face. I'm kissing your neck now. I'm running my tongue over your soft skin. My hand is on your breast. I'm touching your nipple."

"Maddy?"

It was Mitch. He called from the top of the stairs. She heard him coming down. She hung up. She didn't say anything to Steve, she just hit the "off" button on the phone.

"Oh," Mitch said when he came into the living room, "You're not feeling well, are you? Your face is all flushed."

Madelyn stared at the phone in her hand.

"Did you take some aspirin? Do you want to call the doctor?" Mitch was looking at the phone, too.

"No. I called the police. You know, to find out about the girl who hit me. She's okay. Her car turned over a couple of times, and she went home."

"It's sweet of you to be concerned about her."

"Well."

Mitch sat down beside her. He took her hand. The one that had been on her own breast. "I'm sorry I didn't get there. To the accident, I mean."

"It's okay."

"You sounded pretty shook up, but I was about to go into a meeting. These damn writers. Why we have to talk, talk, talk about everything."

Mitch was a producer, a big executive at a movie studio. The writer was always his nemesis. He hated all of them, any of them, before they even started. Madelyn listened to him complain about those fucking writers all the time, but she never reminded him that he started as a writer himself. That was a long time ago.

"It's okay," she said to him.

"You smell like pizza." He smiled at her. Indulgently, she thought. Condescendingly.

She stood up. "I'm going back to bed," she said.

"I'll come with you."

Of course he was coming with her, Madelyn thought, where else would he ever go?

Madelyn climbed the stairs. Her inner thighs were sticky and rubbed together. She took a deep breath and had to grab the stair railing suddenly.

"Are you okay?" Mitch asked from behind her.

"Yes," she said and thought, Yes. I'm in love.

chapter sixteen

Leo shifted his backpack from one shoulder to the other and waited while Jenny fumbled with the three locks on her apartment door. He leaned against the hall wall and breathed in the smell of human life. Door after door and behind each one was at least one human, farting, burping, eating, defecating, leaving their disgusting refuse behind. Coming from a big family, he was more than aware of a body's waste. He walked down the hall, listened at the next door for someone inside who might be coughing or grunting.

"Are you coming in?" Jenny called to him.

He turned around and smiled. He went into her apartment and shut her door behind him. He turned the three locks and dropped his backpack on the floor. It was nice to be inside. It had been a long time since he'd been in somebody's home. Jenny was okay. They'd had a few laughs at the bar. She touched his arm and his T-shirt and his face. She ran her good hand along the bar and up and down her martini glass. She ate the olive with her eyes closed. She held it in her mouth for a long time before she chewed and swallowed. He watched her. It seemed she was trying to absorb the bar and the bartender and her drink and even him, to pull them inside her with her hands and her mouth and all of her senses. He remembered his mother saying, "I'm going to eat you up" when she tickled him, and he thought, that's what Jenny wanted to do, too. Eat it all up.

Her apartment was so clean and empty. There was a small sofa and a lamp. One little wooden table with two folding chairs. A framed picture on the wall of a fairy or something looking at her own reflection in a pond. There were no books or papers, no shoes left lying on the floor. It didn't look like anybody really lived here.

The kitchen was spotless. He opened the refrigerator. It had been a long time since his doughnut and black coffee.

"There isn't much," she said.

There wasn't anything except a box of baking soda and one can of Coke. He took the soft drink.

"Mind?" he asked.

"No. I want you to have it."

He popped the top and took a long drink. He put the can down on the counter and put his arm around Jenny's neck and pulled her to him. He kissed her. Maybe in the morning she would take him out to breakfast, eggs and sausage and toast and hash browns. He slid his mouth across her cheek and behind her ear. They could go to Denny's and have a Grand Slam.

She was more than willing, but she kept asking him to slow down. She wanted it all, she said, but slowly, a little at a time. It had been so long, she told him. She said she wanted him desperately.

And then she said, "Let's pretend we love each other."

He must have frowned because she continued hurriedly, "I know we don't, I know I'll never see you again after tonight, but just for now let's pretend we're madly in love, that you love me more than anyone in the world. Close your eyes. Let's love each other."

Leo felt bad for her. She was pretty desperate. Her bedroom had a double-bed mattress on the floor and a child's white dresser. On the dresser top was a clock radio and a vial of prescription pills and a blue envelope. No cosmetics, no perfumes, no jewelry.

She pulled him down onto the mattress and it crinkled beneath him. He recognized the sound of a plastic sheet, the protection against bedwetting and sex stains and blood. Maybe her deformity affected other areas of her body. He hoped he wouldn't find out.

She was a lousy kisser. She pecked and nibbled. In the dark he couldn't see her odd eye, her twisted fingers. He was so hungry. He took his time, he performed well, and he kept his mind on breakfast. He deserved it. She owed him a big hot plate of eggs, spaghetti and meatballs, anything he wanted. They could even get up afterwards, after this, and go out right away.

"No," she said a little later when they lay side by side on the mattress. "I don't want to go anywhere."

She got out of bed and, naked, picked up her prescription from the dresser. She took it into the bathroom. He heard the water running.

"I'm hungry," he said. He pulled on his blue jeans. There wasn't a lamp in the room, but he opened the curtains. The streetlight cast a rectangle of ashen luster across the bed.

"I'm hungry," he said again and louder. He sat down on the bed and leaned against the pillow.

"I'm not," she said from the bathroom. The water was still running. "I have to take my pills on an empty stomach."

"You don't have to eat."

She came in without the vial and crawled back onto the bed next to him. She snuggled close.

"Come on," he said. "I'm starving."

"I'm not going."

"Then I will." He started to get up. He knew her purse was in the living room. He could snag a twenty or a couple of them. She wouldn't even miss them from that wad she had waved around at the bar.

"Don't go," she said.

"Hey. Jenny. It's been great. You're a fox. I'll call you."

"Don't leave yet."

"I have to work in the morning."

"Remember. You love me."

She grabbed his arm. Her strength surprised him. She wouldn't let him get up.

"Stop it," he said.

"I love you."

"No, you don't."

"I do. For as long as it lasts." She laughed. "I do."

She wouldn't let go. He tried wiggling his arm out of her grip.

"Stay with me," she said, "for the rest of my life."

"Let go!" He tried to peel her hands from his arm. She held on. Her weird crippled fingers dug into his skin. "Let the fuck go!"

"No! No!" She was screaming. And holding on.

He picked and pulled at her fingers. Her face was getting red; he saw snot in her nose. Disgusting humans made of blood and pus. He wrenched his arm free and stood up. She doubled over, moaning sort of. But then her hands came out, reaching for his leg, her strange fingers clutching at the bottom of his blue jeans.

"Stop it!" he said.

She crawled off the mattress and wrapped her arms around his legs. "Don't go!" she moaned. It was a gurgle filled with spit and mucus.

He struggled to get away, but fell backwards onto his butt. He tried to slide out of her grasp. She kept coming and coming and reaching for him and grabbing and plucking and pulling. He heard her mouth opening and closing, her tongue slurping, her lips smacking. She was going to eat him up. Her head came up, her face terrifying, the drooping eye sliding around in its abnormal socket. He could see that the eyeball wasn't round, but distorted and grotesque.

"Get away from me!" he cried. He kicked at her with his free leg. He was in an awkward position; he could only manage a push, really, but his bare foot caught her nose and knocked her head sideways.

She swayed. Her awful eyes rolled back in her head. Then she smiled.

"What did you do that for?" Her words were slurred. Abruptly, she let go of him and collapsed forward on his legs.

Shit, he thought as he scooted back from her and stood up. He hadn't meant to kick her. It was just a reaction, a reflex he couldn't stop.

"Hey," he said, "Jenny?"

She had made him angry. She had scared him. She was weird and crazy, but he had barely touched her.

He squatted. "Jenny?" he asked again.

She didn't move. He heard her breathing, a low wet sputtering through an open mouth. He was afraid suddenly to touch her. They had been naked and belly to belly forty-five minutes ago; now he was frightened by her flesh, her hair, her naked skin. She gurgled, she slurped. He would get in trouble. He didn't want any trouble.

He took a deep breath and lifted her head. Her eyes opened for a moment and rolled back until only the whites showed. There was drool coming out of the corner of her mouth. This wasn't his doing, not her open wet mouth, the saliva dripping off her chin, not her rolling odd eyes. There was something wrong with her.

Her head slipped out of his hands. Her forehead hit the floor. She lay still and crumpled like a used tissue.

"Jenny. Wake up."

No response. This must be her disease, her deformity. He could appreciate that; he could feel sympathy for her. But it wasn't his fault.

"I'm borrowing some money," he said. "Your money. I'm borrowing it."

He went in the other room and found her purse. He looked in the wallet. She had almost two hundred dollars, minus the cost of two vodka martinis and another beer for him. He took all of it and put it in his pocket with the rest of his cash. Maybe there was more money. She had lots of money if she carried this much in her wallet. She was rich. She should buy some furniture and a lamp or something.

He started in the kitchen and opened a cupboard door. One plate, one bowl, one glass. It was too depressing. Another cupboard. There was a can of soup and an unopened bag of raisins. He pulled apart the cellophane package and ate a handful of raisins. He kept eating as he opened two more cupboards, both empty, and a broom closet with only a mop and a broom. There was no sugar bowl or flour canister, no place to hide any money.

The living room was too bare for hiding places. He put down the bag of raisins and dumped her purse on the couch. A comb, a package of tissues, and her wallet. No more money.

He stepped over her in the bedroom and went to the dresser. He opened the bottom drawer. It was empty. He opened the one above. Also empty. Did she even really live here? What was going on?

The middle drawer was also empty.

In the top drawer there was a pair of socks and a photo. It was Jenny, but she looked younger and fuller and her arms were around two young men who looked like her, but not deformed. They were all smiling at the camera. He shut the drawer.

He put his hand on the blue envelope. It had no name or address. It could be empty, waiting for her to put something in it. But it looked like the kind of envelope that would contain a check. He picked it up, turned it over and opened the flap. There was a small blue piece of stationery folded inside. He put the envelope down. He didn't read other people's mail. He respected people's privacy.

He spoke to Jenny on the floor at his feet. "Hey. Are you okay?"

She didn't move. He sighed, then opened the envelope, took out the piece of paper and read:

Dear Mr. Hopkins:

As it begins, so it ends.

It is March. March comes in like a lion. Then it steps cautiously around those Ides and dances a jig over St. Patrick's Day. Then spring arrives, and March scampers out like a lamb.

I began in March. I was that lion on March 2nd born screaming and kicking. I never wanted to be here. I was never supposed to be here. I was deformed because I was never fully human.

But I will go out the lamb today, March 20th, the first day of spring. Twenty-one years later. I will be quiet. No screams. No fuss. My apartment is clean, nothing to return or throw away. Give my furniture to the next tenant or put it out on the street. I think the plastic sheet will save the mattress.

Away I go, the frolicking spring lamb, following my poor

brothers and no one will even know I've gone until I begin to smell. It should have been me, the freak, who died that day in the car. Not them. Not my beautiful perfect brothers.

Baked ham, asparagus, new potatoes with the red skins shiny with butter. That's what I will eat for my first spring meal. I will sit in the backyard at the picnic table. My father and both of my brothers will be there.

I can't wait to March on.

There will be spring eternal.

As it begins, so it ends.

Jenny

Leo put the note down on the dresser. He walked into the bathroom. He picked the empty vial of prescription drugs out of the otherwise-vacant trash can. He read the label. Nembutal. It wasn't even her name on the prescription. Some other woman, perhaps some previous suicide, had taken what she wanted and willed the rest to Jenny.

Leo sat down on the edge of the bathtub.

They had found his sister Lulu hanging, silhouetted against the ugly green tile of his childhood bathroom. She was a little thing, only fourteen years old, and she hung herself from the fan somehow. It had impressed Leo, even at ten years old; the thought and planning it had taken Lulu, the brains no one knew she had, to unscrew the grating and remove the fan blade and the plastic casing and find the beam running across the ceiling and then attach her yellow jump rope with a good strong knot.

His mother had screamed and screamed. Leo and one of his older sisters had talked later about the way the blood collected in Lulu's hands and feet. The smell of her poop dripping down one leg onto the fuzzy bath mat.

He couldn't blame Lulu. She had never really made any other decision in her life. She had just gone along with what anyone else wanted. And they, especially his older brothers, never wanted good things for

Lulu. Lulu's death was a proud act. She finally took control. She had left a note, too, pinned to her pink nightgown:

Fuck you.
love,
Lulu

He had to make a decision.

He went back in the bedroom. Jenny was still breathing. He could hear it, raspy and unhappy in her throat. He couldn't call 9-1-1, there was no phone in the apartment. He could put her in the car and drive her to the hospital. They would pump her stomach if it wasn't too late. Then they would lock her up somewhere and give her drugs and whatever they called therapy. He looked around. Her apartment was empty. How full was her life if she wanted to spend her last night with a stranger?

He pulled her up onto the bed. Her body was gray in the dim light; only her hips and pubic hair lit by the streetlight outside. The shadow of the window made a cross on her abdomen. She was not unattractive, despite her funny fingers. It turned out her toes were disfigured, too. Leo straightened her out. He pulled her legs down, lifted her head onto the pillow. He crossed her arms over her chest. She looked too dead. He put them down straight at her sides. He put the sheet over her and the blanket and tucked them in, neatly. He tried to make her long hair look okay. He thought about wiping up the blood under her nose, but he couldn't, so he tidied the bedroom, folded her clothes, lined up her shoes against the wall. She wanted to die. Her note was clear. She didn't want to leave a mess.

He sat on the floor against the wall on the other side of the room and waited. It was the least he could do, the only thing left he could do for her. Her breathing got slower and slower and his eyes closed. And when he woke up, the sun was shining and she was quiet.

chapter seventeen

had to go home. Ms. Dorothy P. Fairweather, age 31, female, Caucasian, 5'6", gray eyes, light brown hair dyed blond, 118 pounds, had sat down again on the couch. She hadn't moved for forty minutes. She was probably asleep. My neck was stiff. I had seen what I could see. I wasn't sure why I was there anyway. It was chilly and I shivered. I had rolled up my windows when I first arrived and now the air inside my car smelled used.

I found my way to the Hollywood Freeway. Twenty-six minutes later, I was back in Van Nuys at the Pineapple Grove apartment complex. There aren't any pineapple trees. It's a beige stucco box of sixteen apartments with a tiny swimming pool on one side and a parking lot on the other. I knew Linda didn't like it, but it was cheap. No one on the force actually lives in Beverly Hills except one of the detectives, and she's married to a doctor.

I walked down the hall to our apartment. I stepped over the wrinkled bump in the brown carpeting. I could smell the onions someone had cooked for dinner. I got to the door, our door, and stopped. I put my ear to the peephole. If she, if Linda, was sleeping inside, I would know she was there. The air would be different. I listened. The apartment was silent.

I opened the door. It was an ugly place, but I had never really noticed before. It was only temporary, until we found a house. I always felt we weren't permanent and neither was the apartment. The building itself seemed transient. Nothing was square or fit snugly. The cupboards slanted and the doors waved open if I didn't give them an extra nudge. The overhead light in the living room was never installed. There was a switch on the wall that went up and down, but no fixture. Things rattled inside the plaster when a truck drove by. I would lie in bed at night and look up at the cottage-cheese ceiling. It seemed to cover only air; the sparkles in the paint were just bits of the upstairs apartment showing through. If I sat up in bed to read, I could see the place behind the bedroom door where the wallpaper stopped short. No one had bothered to paste up the last strip. I wonder now what will be left of that building in a hundred years, or even fifty. It was not built to last. It will never be a historic landmark. The corners will go first, crumbling into the jade plants. The whole place will begin to disintegrate and then they'll tear it down. No one will want to save it.

I came into the living room, put my keys on the hook by the door and took off my jacket. I threw it over the back of the one good chair, the one we'd bought for the house we didn't get. Then I saw that Linda had taken the painting that hung over the couch. There was just a gray outline of a rectangle on the wall. It made me feel weird that I hadn't noticed it earlier. I was afraid to look around and see what else was missing. Had she left me anything?

I could feel my neighbors sleeping. I was wide awake. I went into the bedroom. I hadn't made the bed that morning. I could see the indentation from her head in her pillow. I put my face to it. I smelled her sour sleepy smell. I had to get out of there. I had nowhere to go. I put on my bathing suit and my old sweatshirt, grabbed my towel and went out to the pool.

It wasn't much of a pool. The cinder-block wall behind it backed up on the freeway. I could hear the cars, the whine of a semi. I could smell their exhaust mixed in with the chlorine. It was just an aqua-colored hole without a diving board, three and a half feet to six feet deep from one end to the other, surrounded by cement. There was no poolside furniture, but the water was heated and that late at night it was always empty.

I hurried across the cement in my bare feet. I threw off my sweatshirt and dove into the water. I came up in the deep end, beside the sign that says "No Diving." The water was colder than usual. I had to catch my breath. I could feel my testicles shrink into my body, but the water was soothing, the feel of it against my skin, the smell, the sound. I started doing laps. I didn't count, I just did them until I couldn't anymore. It was a long time, forty-five, fifty minutes. When I was done, I turned on my back and floated. I watched the dark windows looking down on me. I thought about the people sleeping inside. A light burned in one apartment on the bottom floor. Someone was up. Maybe Mrs. Curson, the old lady in 1C, couldn't sleep and had turned on her television and found an old movie. Maybe, lying on her couch, she had forgotten that it was no longer 1960. I imagined her laughing with Deborah Kerr and sighing at Cary Grant, who was so much like her husband. "Harry," she called, "come see," before she remembered her husband was dead and had been dead for eight years.

I saw Linda sleeping in a king-sized bed with her new boyfriend. Her cold feet were wiggled in under his calves, just like they used to hide under mine. She snored a little, the ticking sound she always made in the back of her throat. Her boyfriend wasn't sleeping so well. He wasn't used to having her there. In the back of his dreams he was realizing that from now on it would be like this every night, forever, not just when she could make it to Phoenix. Why were her feet so cold, he wondered. Maybe she could wear socks to bed.

And I pictured Dorothy in her little house. She had woken up on the sofa. Her nose was stuffed up from crying. Her face was white in the gloom, whiter than it had been in the hospital when she turned to me, when she had reached her pale, slender hand to me. She was lost. Someone should have been sitting beside her.

I floated on my back and imagined these things. And I knew that even if they were true, I couldn't do anything about them. I couldn't do a thing.

I paddled to the wall and pulled myself out of the pool. I heard a car drive into the parking lot. The door opened and the radio blared. I heard a girl's laughter and then someone turned off the car. The music stopped. The car door slammed shut. I could hear her high heels on the pavement and her date saying something low and urgent. I wrapped myself in my towel and tiptoed back to my apartment.

chapter eighteen

Dorothy spent the entire night before her wedding on the couch. Lewis was asleep in the bedroom. She ate a hunk of cheese and most of a package of oatmeal cookies. She was ravenous. She thought of the Indian food she hadn't eaten with longing, but Lewis had carried what was left out to the trash. She turned on the television and turned it off immediately. The tears finally stopped and she fell asleep.

"Dorothy."

"Dorothy."

In her dreams they called her name. Over and over. Usually a man's voice. Sometimes a woman's. Together. Separately. Quietly. But occasionally loud and insistent.

Whenever she heard them as she slept, she woke up with her eyes turned inward, searching for the bodies to those voices, reaching back into sleep for them. It was the night before her wedding and still they came to visit. She had first dreamed the voices when she was only nine. Once a week or once a month she had heard them ever since. She slept with boys, with Seth; the voices came just the same. She thought a constant male presence would stop them, and for the first month after she moved in with Lewis they were quiet. They seemed to be answered by his presence, the way he said her name. And then, she didn't know why, they started again, less frequently, but always a possibility.

It was 6:30 A.M. when she looked at herself in the bathroom mirror. The ice cubes she had rubbed on her eyes in the middle of the night had not helped. Her eyes would be puffy all day. She looked at herself in the mirror and heard the man say her name, "Dorothy?" She looked over her shoulder but she knew he wasn't there. She was just tired. She should have chosen a veil to cover her face. She wasn't beautiful to begin with. Her features were small and unremarkable. Now her eyes were barely slits in swollen red skin.

The sun was rising. The bedroom glowed in the warm morning light. Lewis slept peacefully in the bed. She smiled at his little toes and his big feet sticking out from under the blankets. The soles were the color of peaches and, like ripe fruit, his feet were so sensitive. He always wore shoes except when he tiptoed out to get the newspaper in the morning, saying ouch, ouch, ouch. Her feet were smaller, but much tougher.

She made a pot of coffee. Her eyes were only occasionally flashing this morning. The sudden burst of green or pink would take her by surprise. Her headache was almost gone, just an echo of the pain she had felt last night. Last night. She had called Seth last night, in the middle of the night. She had heard his voice, his same voice. His voice sounded in her ear and deep in her body like a bass guitar string strummed and reverberating long after the song is over.

The tears threatened again. She pushed Seth away. She thought about the flowers she had chosen and the five-layer cake and how beautiful her mother would look in that blue mother-of-the-bride dress. Jane, her mother, was so lovely—completely nuts, but gorgeous. Michael, her brother, was such a handsome guy. She thought, as she had thought a thousand times, why had the gene pool dried up for her? In her mother's womb, she had done a swan dive and hit the hard cement bottom.

If she had been beautiful, Seth would have loved her. He would never have stopped loving her. The tears spilled over.

"Stop it," she said out loud. It wasn't true. He had loved the way she looked; he told her that. He loved her skinny legs and high, small breasts. He loved who she was, when he loved her at all.

Lewis loved her now. She looked at the clock on the kitchen wall. Five after seven. She would let Lewis sleep. She would take his car and go get her wedding dress. Lewis had telephoned Rosemary's Bridal Fantasies last night. Rosemary, or someone, was expecting both of them at 8:30. She was opening two hours early just for them. Dorothy was supposed to wake Lewis at eight and they would go together. Instead, she would go by herself. She would find it first on the map; then she would drive over there and Lewis could sleep.

She tiptoed into the bedroom and pulled her blue jeans out of the laundry basket. She threw on Lewis's white dress shirt from the night before and rolled up the sleeves several times.

Her ancient sneakers were by the back door. His keys were on the kitchen counter. She started to write him a note, then decided just to surprise him with her abilities. She took her coffee mug with her and closed the front door very quietly.

She was not used to his car, a truck really, an enormous sport utility vehicle which sat up high and had plenty of room in the back for the band and their gear. But she had driven it a few times and it was early on a Saturday, the roads should be empty. She backed out of the driveway, knocked her coffee mug and spilled coffee down the pure white front of Lewis's shirt. The coffee dripped from the bottom of the mug onto her leg and the seat. There were no napkins or tissues in the car.

She stopped the truck, got out, and set the cup on the curb where she could pick it up later, when she got home.

A small yellow light on the dash told her she needed gas. Good. She could do that, too. She drove easily down the hill and pulled into their usual gas station, popped the tank cover, got out with her twenty-dollar bill in her hand, and walked up to the booth.

"Good morning," she said to the sleepy attendant. She could just see the top of his head as he leaned his face on his tattooed arms.

He picked up his head and looked at her through the bulletproof glass. His eyes were heavy, half asleep and beautifully green.

"Long night?" she asked.

"Just a very early morning."

"I know what you mean." She nodded.

She didn't usually talk to people. Not to waiters or salesclerks. Certainly not to a green-eyed, tattooed, and handsome guy under glass.

He grinned.

She smiled back. "Twenty dollars, please."

"Let me pump that for you," he said.

"What?"

He got off his stool and opened the door and came out. He really was cute. There was a red mark on his cheek from pressing against his arms. His hair stuck up funny in the back, the remnants of last night's spiked hairdo. Obviously too much gel. But it wouldn't be bad to wake up with a guy who looked this good in the morning.

She followed him to the pump. He turned his hooded eyes to her.

"What are you doing out so early?"

If she told him she was going to pick up her wedding dress then the flirtation would definitely be over. She could not remember the last time a boy had flirted with her. No one ever flirted with her. She was the one without sex appeal, the only hairdresser who dyed her hair blond, wore see-through tops and leopard-skin capris and no one noticed. Clients came back time after time and introduced themselves as if they'd never met.

She wondered if she and this boy could have quick, meaningless, but incredibly satisfying sex in the back of his little office.

"What are you smiling about?" he asked her. "Looks like you had a good time last night."

If she was brazen, forward, even 15 percent prettier, she could say, I was thinking about you. But she was shy and plain and on her way to get her wedding dress.

"No," she said. "It's just been a crazy couple of days."

And today was going to be even crazier, she thought. Today she was getting married.

Another customer waved from his car.

"Yeah, yeah," the attendant said, "I'll be there."

He finished pumping her gas and twisted the gas cap into place.

"Wash your windows?" he asked.

She had to go. "You have another customer."

"Fuck him," he said. "Cup of coffee? I made a fresh pot inside, in the office."

"Really?"

"Come on."

The other customer honked his horn. He was having some difficulty.

"All right, all right," the attendant said then turned back to Dorothy, "Wait for me. Wait right here."

"No. Thanks." She could see the customer's angry face. "I'm on an errand. I'm late. 'Bye."

She retreated, climbed into Lewis's truck and drove away. The handsome hip boy watched her from beside the pump, watched her until she was out of sight. She didn't trust him. He had something up his sleeve besides his tattoos. He could tell she wasn't wearing any underwear. Or somehow he knew she had spent the night crying and now she was vulnerable. Strange men never asked her for coffee.

She giggled. Then she laughed. She felt like a redhead in a convertible. To be noticed was amazing, powerful. No wonder women wore high heels, dyed their hair, injected cow fat into their lips. She was thirty-one years old. Her mother always told her she would age well. Jane always said that other, prettier girls would lose their looks, that they would get pudgy and their faces would sag.

Dorothy believed in fidelity, but it was easy to be faithful when no one else was asking. She imagined again sex in the back of the gas station, the odor of oil and gas, the feel of new tires against her bare thighs. She would smell sleep on his neck; he would lick the spilled coffee from her wrist.

Thank God the road was empty. She was paying no attention at all. She pulled over and got out the giant map. Los Angeles had a road atlas the size of most telephone books. She looked at the gas gauge. Twenty dollars had only filled half of the truck's enormous tank. She could go back to the gas station again later, or tomorrow. But, she remembered, tomorrow she would be a wife.

chapter nineteen

Before Madelyn opened her eyes, she thought of Steve. She thought of Steve and her stomach flip-flopped, her heart beat faster. Would he call her this morning? Could she call him? He worked at the *L.A. Times,* in the morgue where they filed old stories. He was a victim, he said, of their policy to hire the handicapped. They had sought him out. He had turned down their offers of editorial jobs or "good news" reporting, events easy to cover from a wheelchair. He told them he wanted to be alone in the basement with the dead files. He had been a prizewinning journalist before the accident. He gave it up when he lost his legs.

She wondered how soon he would call her and then she remembered it was Saturday. Her heart sank. Saturday. Morgan's soccer game. Mason's soccer game. The dinner party tonight at the restaurant. Mitch would be home all day. Steve never called on Saturdays.

And anyway, he might be angry with her about hanging up on him. He might not realize that her husband had come into the room. He might think she was shy and scared and not enjoying what he was saying to her, what he was doing to her. She thought about it this morning and wondered if she had dreamed it. Phone sex. Ridiculous.

Her hip and shoulder were still sore. When she sat up in bed, her head reminded her that it hurt. She hobbled down the stairs. Her legs were weak. She loved him. She had fallen in love with a paraplegic she had never met.

The kids were already in front of the television. Mitch sat at the kitchen table with the paper.

"I can't go to the soccer game," Madelyn told Mitch. She whispered so the kids wouldn't hear her, so they wouldn't worry. "I'm so sore."

"What? What time is soccer?"

"Morgan has a nine o'clock game. Mason's game is at eleven." He would never learn to look at the schedule. Why should he? He had her. "I need to take a hot bath. My hip hurts."

"See the doctor."

"I will, if it still hurts on Monday."

"Even if it doesn't," Mitch said, "it's the insurance company that has to pay, pay, pay."

Madelyn leaned on the counter and watched out the window as the dog took a dump under the swing set in the backyard. For once, she didn't care. She looked at the clock. Eight-twenty. Go, go, go, she chanted silently at her family. She wanted to be left alone with this flushed quivery feeling. She wanted to call Steve.

"I'm on my way," he had said, "if you don't mind what I'm wearing."

Her fingers trembled on the coffee pot.

"Four-twenty at the latest," Mitch was saying.

"Okay," she replied without any clue what he was talking about.

He droned on, giving her instructions, writing down a number or something on the pad by the phone.

Morgan, adorable in lime green and orange pajamas, twirled in the kitchen. "How do you feel, Mom?"

"I'm fine."

"You seem a little weird," she said.

Madelyn laughed. She had a secret, all her own, like a hidden treasure in the bottom corner of an old cigar box. Maybe it wasn't much, a bottle cap or a frayed piece of satin ribbon, but it belonged to her.

"Better get into your soccer uniforms," she said.

Finally they were gone. Madelyn cleaned up the breakfast dishes. She put the toast crusts down the garbage disposal; she didn't even feel like nibbling on them. She didn't want to eat at all.

"I'm on my way," Steve had said to her. "I'm coming to save you."

Well. He didn't actually say that last part, but that's what he meant. That's what she wanted. Save me. Save me. Save me. She chanted it as she wiped the counter, folded the newspapers, put pajamas under pillows and made the beds. Save me. As she dialed Steve's number. Save me.

"Hello?"

"I'm sorry," Madelyn said.

"Thank God it's you."

"I'm sorry," she said again.

"Are you all right?"

"Fine. You?"

"I'm okay now. Now that you've called. I'm okay now."

There was a pause. Madelyn had to sit down on her unmade bed. She had to close her eyes. She couldn't talk to him, think what she was thinking, and look at the framed Mother's Day picture from three-year-old Mason or the photo of her with Morgan at her breast or the candle Mitch put by the bed hoping to kindle some of that missing lust.

"Listen," Steve said.

She was listening to him breathe, to him being there.

"I'm sorry about last night," he began.

"Why?" She interrupted him. "What for?"

"I thought—I guess I went too far. You have a husband."

"Don't," she said. She didn't want him to talk about Mitch. "I liked it." She changed the subject. "But one of the kids woke up," she lied. "I had to go."

"Oh. The kids. Are they okay?"

"Fine." She should never have mentioned her children, reminded him how much older she was.

"Listen," he said again, "Maybe I shouldn't, or we shouldn't, you know, I don't know."

He stopped. There was a long silence.

Madelyn waited.

Finally he said, "So. How do you feel? What are you doing today?"

She really should have kept quiet about the kids. He was reconsidering. She was just a problem for him. Married. Older. With kids and a husband and a mortgage and half of her life over.

"Steve," she said.

He didn't reply, but she heard him, heard the squeak of his wheelchair as he shifted in the seat.

"I thought about you all night," she continued. "When I slept, I dreamed of you." She had to tell him. She was too old to wait.

"Me too," he said. "But I didn't sleep at all."

"I want to see you. In person. I want to see your face."

"You'll be disappointed."

"You will."

"I couldn't be." He laughed. "If you were four hundred pounds and covered with green warts, I wouldn't care."

"Worse, it's much worse than that," she said. "I look like a middle-aged mom."

"I don't care." He paused. "Today."

"What?"

"Can I see you today?"

"Yes," she said, already planning the lie in her head. "What time?"

"Now."

"Now?"

"As soon as possible."

"Where do you live?" she asked. "I can be there in an hour."

She was giggling nervously on the phone with a man. They were making a date, a rendezvous, for this morning. They couldn't wait. He was worried about her, he was asking about her hip, her shoulder, her head. He was whispering to her. She was blushing. Suicide never came up in the conversation. She would see him very soon.

"It's the first day of spring," she said to him. "It's spring."

"It's never spring in Los Angeles," he said, "but it is the first day of something. The first lovely, perfect day of something."

When they finally hung up, she hurried to the exercise bike and pushed the pile of mending off the seat. She would be vigilant, she would do this every day. But there was a kind of security in falling in love with Steve. A man with no legs couldn't mind her extra pounds, could he? She cycled hard, letting her breasts bounce and running her hands through her uncombed hair. She was going to have breakfast with him. She was going to meet him, face to face. It was the first day of spring.

chapter twenty

Leo leaned against the bedroom wall. Jenny was not breathing. The room was completely quiet. There was no noise from the street, not even the buzz of distant traffic. This was a silence he had never heard before, as if every sound was captured, held hostage in Jenny's dead body. The whole world could be dead. He was the only one left alive. Out on the street, bodies were lying this way and that, slumped in their cars, fallen at their desks, the checkers at the grocery store collapsed over their cash registers. He would have plenty to eat and drink, but he would die of loneliness. He would search the bodies to find Tess before she decomposed. Eventually he would find her. He would even know her bones.

Leo stood up. He made himself think about the practicalities. He had Jenny's keys. He had her car. He had her money and her apartment. He wished he was sorry that she was dead, but it couldn't have happened at a better time. She said in her note no one would find her until she started to smell. By that time—four or five days, he thought—his car would be repaired.

His stomach growled. His jeans hung on his hips. He knew his face was beginning to look gaunt. But now he had a refrigerator and a bathroom and one hundred and seventy-four dollars that he could just spend.

He ate the rest of the raisins. He took a shower for a long time. He washed his hair twice with Jenny's flowery, girlie shampoo. He got his razor out of his backpack and shaved. He felt like a new man.

He came into the bedroom to get dressed. Jenny's eyes were shut, but she looked creepy on the white pillow. Vampiric, as if she could wake with superhuman strength. He pulled the blanket all the way up and over her face so he wouldn't have to look at her. Too bad about the bed, but he didn't want to move her. He could sleep on the couch. Even the little couch was a big step up from the back seat of his car.

Should he open the window? It was cool in the bedroom. He was afraid the flies would find her. Maggots. Exposed organs. He left the window and the curtains closed and went out to breakfast.

Sure enough, there was a diner a couple of blocks away on Olympic. He could have walked, he realized, as he parked in the lot behind the restaurant, but this way it would look as if Jenny had gone out. It would seem normal for her car to be gone, for her to be up and around on a Saturday morning.

This diner reminded him of something. He sat at a booth against the window. He looked out the glass at the sign, a star rotating in a neon circle. He looked at the long Formica counter and the orange vinyl swivel stools. He saw a sign, "World's Best Pancakes." How could any place have the best pancakes in the world? How would anyone know? He laughed and slapped the table with both hands. Tess had sent him a postcard from this place. Her first week away, she had written to him, "Di-No-Mite Pancakes. Really. LA's Totally Wild. Miss ya', Luv, Tess." She had been here. He slid out of the booth, hurried up to the cashier.

"Excuse me," he said, "Do you know this girl?"

He showed her his only picture of Tess, a snapshot of her with a beer in her hand, laughing, wearing that little T-shirt with "Foxy" on the front in shiny stuff and her long blond hair falling over her shoulders.

"Lemme see," said the cashier.

She took the photo from him and peered at it. She was probably sixty-something, short and stout with hair piled impossibly high and big false eyelashes at eight-thirty on a Saturday morning.

"No," the woman said. "I don't think so."

"Look again," Leo said. "She sent me a postcard from here. I know she's been here."

Leo wanted to scream, take those things off your eyes so you can see something. He wanted to shake her.

"Is there anyone else I can ask?"

"Well. The night hostess comes on at four. Maybe she knows."

There was something in that hair, some kind of plastic something that Leo saw when the woman bent her head to look at the photo. It was a frame, or a basket, some way that she got all that hair to stay up there. It was dirty in there, flakes of dandruff clinging to the whitish plastic.

The woman's long silver-polished fingernails brushed his hand when she handed the photo back to him. He shuddered, tried not to think of what was in her hair, and how long it had been like that.

He would come back tonight and talk to the night hostess. She would know. He would come here every day. Tess liked the food. She would come back.

Meanwhile, a couple had sat down in his booth. Leo hesitated. He had touched that knife and fork. Well, it was their problem. He sat down at the counter. The waitress was older and Hispanic and her hands were clean and her nails short. He ordered scrambled eggs and pancakes and french toast and sausage and bacon and toast and coffee and orange juice. The waitress brought his coffee and smiled at him.

"Here, *niño*," she said. "Happy springtime."

Things were looking up. Turning around. He had money in his pocket and a place to stay and here he was, in this diner. Tess could not be far away.

chapter twenty-one

Dorothy parked Lewis's truck in front of Rosemary's Bridal Fantasies fifteen minutes early. She felt immensely proud of herself; warm satisfaction melted in her veins like butter on toast. She opened the truck door. The sun was bright, and as she got out, she smiled up at the spring sky.

Her head exploded. She lurched, teetered, then collapsed on the patch of grass beside the curb. Her head was gone. Where her forehead and hair should be there was only pain. Her exposed brain radiated agony. Her eyes were burning, flashing electric white and neon yellow. She hid her face from the sun, pressed it down into the sharp green blades. She could feel the hot light beating on her shoulders and neck. She had to get out of the sun. She crawled into the backseat of the truck and cowered against the scratchy upholstery. The truck was spinning. It undulated beneath her. She opened the other side of the car and threw up into the street. She began to cry and her tears splashed into the regurgitated chunks and juice on the asphalt. She sobbed with her head hanging out of the car and her body writhing on the seat. She would die. She could not survive this.

Then the sun went behind a cloud and the pain began to subside. Slowly. Gradually. It slid away like night falling, one shadow at a time, the soothing darkness reassembling her head piece by piece.

She closed the car door and lay, panting and exhausted, on the seat. She could smell her sweat, taste her vomit, feel the trickle of perspiration under her arms. Her legs were trembling as she sat up and got out of the truck.

She hunched her shoulders against the sun's return and put her arms protectively over her head. She hurried to the door of Rose-mary's Bridal Fantasies and rang the bell frantically with her elbow.

She was hiding under her arms when the small Asian man opened the door. His mouth went wide with alarm when he saw her.

"What is it?" he said. "What's happening?"

"Let me in!" Dorothy pushed past him.

Inside it was air conditioned and dark with the curtains still drawn. Dorothy sat down on the white couch and gingerly leaned her head against the artistic scattering of white pillows. The little man hurried to her.

"Are you all right?" His voice went higher with each word. "What is happening? Is someone after you?" He was squeaking.

Her headache was completely gone. Dorothy let herself relax against the matrimonial cushions. She let go. Her limbs melted into the fabric; her hands puddled at the ends of her arms; her fingers dripped onto the floor. If she could just stay here in this cool, dark room. Everyone could come here. They could have the wedding right here. She would get married if she could just stay here.

"What is going on?" He was practically screaming, but softly, somehow managing to yell at her respectfully.

Dorothy remembered him now. Mr. Lee, the tailor, the one who had pulled and folded and pinched her dress and her in it. Now his capable hands were shaking, opening and closing in fear or frustration or reproach.

"It's the sun," she whispered. "It makes my head hurt."

She expected a tirade, a waterfall of furious words, some English, mostly Chinese, to spill from his mouth. When she had told him she wanted the dress taken up another inch because she didn't plan on wearing high heels, he had shouted at her in his own language. His face had turned crimson and dangerously swollen, like a balloon. "You no bride!" he had finally exploded at her. Or at least that's what she thought he said. Maybe it was "turn the tide," or "you're so wide," or "try it fried." Whatever he had said, he really meant it.

Sitting on Rosemary's love seat, she closed her eyes against his wrath. To her surprise, she felt him take one of her hot, moist hands in both of his. His hands were small and dry. He traced a circle in her palm. She felt the callus on his index finger from pushing the needle through miles of tulle and lace and satin. His strong, rough finger was wonderful, an ancient secret from the Orient, the therapeutic mystery of acupressure and massage.

"Thank you," she said without opening her eyes.

"You be okay," he said. "Oh, yes. Yes. Yes. You beautiful girl."

At that, she opened her eyes and looked at him. He had his eyes closed and a half-smile on his lips. His finger kept going round and round in her palm as he leaned toward her.

"Wait a minute." She stood up and pulled her hand from his grasp. "I'm here to pick up my wedding dress."

"I know," he said. "You a fool."

"Why do you say that?" He was the one who worked at a bridal salon.

"I look at you many times," Mr. Lee said.

He took a step toward her. She took a step back. He had barely ever made eye contact with her. Four fittings and each time he turned away when she said "thank you" and "good-bye."

"I listen to you talk," he said, "and I know you not happy."

"The whole wedding thing," Dorothy admitted, "it's such a ridiculous concept. No offense, but I mean wearing white, walking down an aisle, giving the bride away. It's filled with symbols that don't signify anything real. Not anymore."

"You don't like boyfriend."

"Oh, now, come on," she said. "I never said a word about Lewis when I was here. I didn't talk about him at all."

Mr. Lee crossed his arms over his chest with satisfaction. "See?" he said.

"He loves me madly. Lewis. My . . . " That word was still missing this morning. Lewis was not just her boyfriend. He was not yet her husband. What the hell was he? "It's too late for this. I'm getting married today. I want my dress. I have to go."

She took a step toward it. It was hanging on the dressing-room door. She could see the silk roses through the plastic window in the pink garment bag.

Mr. Lee lunged around her and spread his arms in front of the dress.

"You can't wear this dress, this dress is hideous. You picked terrible dress."

"I did not!" Now she was angry. She loved her wedding dress. There were silk roses, big ones, on the shoulder straps and the waistband and in a trail down the back. It was covered in hundreds of roses. She looked like a garden of roses.

"You look like clown!" he said adamantly.

"It's a beautiful dress. Rosemary said it was one of her favorites."

"She desperate to get rid of it. You sample size."

That was true. Dorothy had picked it off the rack and it fit and Rosemary had given her a great deal, almost fifty percent off. There were a lot of roses, but she was skinny. They gave her hips and an ass, only out of flowers. Her mother-in-law loved it.

"What would you suggest?" asked Dorothy.

Mr. Lee beamed. He ran to the rack of dresses and pulled out a simple straight gown in off-white silk. It had a mandarin collar and a white silk frog at the neck. When Dorothy looked closely, she could see a subtle floral pattern in the fabric, white on white. It was too striking, too understated. It needed a movie star to carry it off.

"No," she said. "It's beautiful, but—"

"Try it on," he said. "For me."

His dark, lidless eyes pleaded with her. His black hair had fallen over his forehead. He tossed it back. That beautiful, thick, straight

Asian hair. He was younger than she thought. Not a bad-looking guy, not really. And he did have that magic finger. Her palm was still tingling. Maybe Mr. Lee was really a famous Chinese clothing designer and master tailor to the Emperor who escaped in the hold of some terrible ship and traveled in dirt and darkness to this country, where he was stuck doing hems and alterations for fluffy Beverly Hills brides.

She took the dress from him and went into the enormous dressing room. She looked at herself in the full-length mirror. She looked terrible. Her hair was uncombed and dirty. Her eyes were still puffy. Her forehead was shiny. She knew her breath had to be poisonous. There was coffee and something else on the front of Lewis's shirt, grass stains on the knees of her grubby blue jeans, and her little toe stuck out through a hole in her sneaker. Mr. Lee must somehow, with his Asian powers, be able to see her inner self. The outer self was disgusting.

She turned her back to the mirror and took her clothes off. She wasn't even wearing underpants. She slipped the silk column over her naked body. There was a zipper on the side and she pulled it up without looking at herself.

"Here I come," she said and thought, how embarrassing.

She opened the dressing room door and stepped out. Mr. Lee turned, saw her and fell on his knees. He lowered his head to the salmon-colored carpet and stretched out his arms in supplication.

"Very funny," Dorothy said.

He looked up at her. "You magnificent. A jewel."

Dorothy laughed.

She stepped up on the carpeted platform with her back to the half-circle of mirrors. There was a long slit up one leg that made the dress easy to walk in. She twirled on the dais, but still avoided her own reflection.

"Look. You look," he said.

She sighed and raised her eyes to the mirror. She was shocked. The dress was beautiful. She looked elegant and sophisticated, and the off-white made her skin creamy. The slit accentuated her long legs. It was great. If she could just cut off her head. She had done too much crying.

"Wow," she said.

"Wear it." Mr. Lee's voice trembled. "Wear it, and think of one who made it. It was made for you. You first American bride without all those big buttocks and titties."

"What about my other dress?" she said and stepped down from the platform. "I can't afford two of them."

"My present," he said. "But you take other one, too. Get rid of it."

Mr. Lee bowed again. She slipped past him into the dressing room and locked the door. She carefully removed the virgin geisha girl-dress. It was the stir she would create, the look on Elaine's face and Lani's and Lewis's and her boss from the salon—all those people who expected Dress A—that convinced her to take Dress B. She would wear it. She would walk down that aisle and know that other men saw her finer points. She was choosing Lewis. She had other options, but she chose him.

Mr. Lee carried both dresses out to the truck. The sun was shining and the sour stink of her vomit blew over them in the morning breeze. She looked down at the flattened spot of grass where she had crouched. Now her head didn't hurt at all. She smiled at Mr. Lee apologetically, sorry for everything: the smell, the sun, especially his forlorn face.

She took the dresses from him and hung them carefully in the back seat.

"'Bye," he said and bowed.

"Thank you so much," Dorothy said and meant it.

It was after nine. She hoped Lewis wasn't worried. Now she knew the way. She would be home in no time. They had to be at the place, the rent-a-mansion Lewis called it, by eleven-thirty for pictures. She had to shower and shave her legs. She wanted suddenly to make love to Lewis, one last roll in the premarital hay.

Six months ago, when Lewis asked her to marry him, she said maybe. She couldn't say yes. She couldn't. All the time she and Lewis had been dating and fucking and then living together, some part of her was still waiting for Seth to return. She thought she saw him once coming out of a sandwich shop at the beach as she and Lewis drove by, but she couldn't be sure. She looked for him all that day, by the ocean, at the place where they had lunch, while Lewis shopped for new shorts. She was crabby and distracted waiting for him to appear. Since he had left her, he was always just around the corner, just ahead of her, just out of sight. It was her fault, if she could only move a little faster. Someone at work the next day asked her if Lewis was the love of her life and she answered without thinking, "No."

Seth was an artist, a painter, with some real success. He had a piece in the permanent collection at the Museum of Contemporary Art. She loved the smell of turpentine in his hair and in his house, a bungalow with a view up on Mulholland Drive. His parents had bought it for him years ago. It had a two-car garage he had gutted to make into his studio and as much like a New York loft as possible. He even paid a kid to put graffiti on one wall.

He painted in the middle of the night. He painted after they made love, and before they made love, and sometimes during, he would push off her and run to the canvas. Had a thought, he would say. You inspire me, he would add to make her feel less abandoned. He never painted her. His pictures were always vacant houses or empty streets or barren landscapes, all without any signs of life.

Seth had his chance, Dorothy thought.

She pulled into the driveway. Lewis came out the front door, frowning, coffee cup in his hand.

"Are you okay?" he asked as she came up the walk.

"I just went to get my wedding dress."

"I knew that."

"I wanted you to sleep."

He put his arm around her. "Your mother called and woke me up. She said it was urgent. She has to talk to you. An emergency."

Dorothy turned her face into Lewis's neck and inhaled his sleepy smell. "It's always an emergency with Jane."

He looked down at her. "What did you do to my shirt?"

She felt the vibrations of his chuckle in his throat. She put her hand under his T-shirt.

"We only have a couple of unmarried hours left," she whispered. "I want to make the most of them."

chapter twenty-two

Madelyn was showered and dressed in a light summer dress that she rarely wore. It scooped too low in the front. It was impractical for sporting events and grocery shopping and picking up dog poop. It got in the way in the car and when she walked the flowery fabric gathered between her legs. But it was pretty and the loose, flowing style hid her motherly stomach.

She let her hair dry naturally instead of blowing it straight. With each child it had gotten curlier. She colored it now and the dye changed the texture, but she spritzed it with the plant sprayer and scrunched it to make it curl around her face.

She put on some eye makeup, but no lipstick. She wrote a note to Mitch and the kids saying she was off to the chiropractor. She would be back by four, in time to take Morgan to her slumber party and drop Mason at his friend Montana's house for his.

She was so glad Steve's name did not begin with "M". She was sorry Mitch had talked her into the "M" thing. Every day, a hundred times a day, she was sorry about the "M" thing. Mitch, Madelyn, Mason, and Morgan Morrison. It made her shudder.

The dog, Maisy, wouldn't get a walk. She threw it a rawhide chew and sighed at the crap in the backyard. It didn't matter. Nothing mattered now, except getting there.

She was early. She circled the block in her dented Mercedes. She had never been to this neighborhood, the clapboard boxes small and depressing, no sidewalks, every car ten years old, dark-haired barefoot children playing in the street. Teenage boys with their heads shaved, their baggy pants and tattoos, watched her as she went by. They made her nervous. They made her aware of her breasts and her fair hair. They were so male, like six-foot penises, all muscle and skin. She went around the block another time, passing Steve's house again, giving him, giving herself another two minutes. In the driveway there was a van with handicapped plates and a wheelchair lift on the back. She should have suggested they meet at a restaurant instead of his house. Instead of alone in his house. Maybe, maybe she should have.

She parked in front. It was cooler than she thought it would be and she shivered. She forgot her car was damaged and she kept trying to open her door, feeling frustrated and dreamlike. What's going on, she thought as she watched his neighborhood, his van, his front door. What's going on?

Her door was broken, she remembered and got out the passenger side, pulling her dress behind her, getting it caught on the emergency brake, wishing she had worn something else.

And then he was opening the door and waiting for her. She didn't know whether to use the front steps or the ramp. She used the steps and when she looked up at him, he was watching her and not smiling, and she thought she had known him her entire life. He looked exactly as she imagined he would. His dark hair was too long, his bright blue eyes intense and sad. His mouth and his mustache quivered and then he grinned at her staring at him.

"Hi," she said.

He closed his eyes.

"Hot line," she said. "This is Madelyn. How may I help you?"

He opened his eyes, laughed. "It is you," he said. "I was expecting—"

"What?"

"Come in," he said. "I'll tell you."

He wheeled backwards and spun around and led her into his house. It was warm inside and pretty and more colorful than she would have imagined. There were variegated Mexican blankets on the back of the couch and the chair. One wall was painted red. The hardwood floor was polished until it shone. And everywhere there were books. The bright yellow bookcases were full, and there were stacks of books on the floor against every wall.

"I see you're looking at my furniture," Steve said. "Do paraplegics need chairs and sofas? Well, occasionally I get out of this chair and sit in that chair, just to give my butt a new configuration. And sometimes I have people over who like to sit down."

"I was looking at your books," Madelyn said, mortified. "Of course you have furniture. Why wouldn't you have furniture? I'm sorry. I was looking at the books, and the color. It's so pretty in here. Of course you have people over. All the time."

"Stop," Steve said. "I was joking. Come here. Let me hold your hand."

She walked over to him. He took her hand. She took a deep breath. She felt something enter her from him, travel up her arm, and burst in her chest. She could feel his hand holding hers in the back of her throat and the soles of her feet. She looked out the window and shook her head, trying to clear it.

"I'm glad you're here," he said.

He brought her fingers to his lips and kissed each one, then the palm of her hand and her wrist and her forearm and the inside of her elbow. She had never felt anything like this. Steve's lips on her skin.

How had she gotten here? Madelyn Morrison, born Madelyn Rawlins of Cincinnati. She had been a cheerleader, not slight or small-boned ever, but amazonian, a corn-fed girl with thick blond wavy hair and the skin on her calves tan, tight, and polished. She was born full. She had been the picture of American abundance. Her teeth were white and straightened to perfection. There was a brush of golden down on her cheek and the small of her back. The hair between her legs was as copious and exuberant as the hair bouncing in her ponytail. She was generous and a good student. Now she was married, with two good-looking kids and a successful husband. She refused to cry. She would not think about the tight lines around her mouth, the furrow of worry between her eyebrows. Something had not worked out the way she planned. Something had gone wrong for her. She had been heading in one direction. She had ended up here.

"I'd like to tell you what to do," Steve said.

It was bright in the room, the sunshine strong through the sheer linen curtains. She didn't want to be naked in front of him in this light, but if he asked her, she would do it. I never have to do this again, she told herself, I never have to see him again. She looked into his electric blue eyes. If I do this now, just this once, I'll be over it. It's just this once.

"Lie down on my useless sofa."

He let go of her hand and she felt bereft. She reached for him. He moved away. She stepped out of her shoes and lay down on his old soft couch. He turned his wheelchair to face her, positioned himself at her breasts. She put her hand on his face.

"No," he said and put her hand at her side. "Relax. Close your eyes. I'll tell you exactly what to do."

He ran his fingers across her forehead. He leaned down and brushed her eyelids with his lips. He teased her mouth, wouldn't kiss it, came close, and left again. He traveled down her neck, one hand in her hair. His other hand stroked the skin on her inner arm, up and down, driving her crazy. He caressed her shoulder, her neck and finally her breast. She moaned. She could feel his lips smile against her skin.

His hands continued, and his mouth. She panted. Her inner thighs were sticky, her skin vibrating. She kept her eyes closed. He pushed her dress up, pulled her panties down. She was terrified. She was hypnotized. His hands were so good. She didn't care how many had gone before her, she was just glad he'd had the practice. Finally, finally he kissed her mouth and she squirmed under him. She wasn't sure what to do. She didn't know she knew, but then she did. She pushed against his hand until she exploded, disintegrating into a thousand hot, happy droplets.

She curled on her side. She looked up at his face. He had his eyes closed and his head back. Madelyn started to cry. She had read in a women's magazine that a lot of women cried after orgasms. It was boring and ordinary of her to cry, but she couldn't help it. She sobbed. She crawled halfway off the couch and put her head in his lap.

She had never felt like this. She never wanted to feel any other way. One time and she wanted this forever. More. Now.

"Shhh, shhh," Steve said. "It's okay. It's okay."

Something bulged beneath her cheek. He was hard and she could feel it. She stopped crying. She crept one hand up under her nose and squeezed him there.

"No," he said.

He lifted her head and put her back on the couch. He rolled away from her.

"Why not?"

"I don't want to."

"But you can."

"I can. But I don't want to." His face got softer. "Today is your day."

"It would make me happy."

"Forget it."

He meant it, he wasn't waiting to be convinced or seduced. He wheeled into the kitchen and called to her, "Hungry?"

She stood up and picked up her underpants from the floor. She stepped into them quickly. She wanted to get them up and over her forty-two-year-old thighs before he returned.

"I'm going to the bathroom," she said.

"I'm making brunch."

In the bathroom, she held onto the sink with both hands and

looked at her face in the mirror. She should look changed; her face should be different. She felt the same way after she had lost her virginity, shoplifted for the first time, tried her first drug, gotten married. Her face should look new, the change in her life marked by a straighter nose or an unusual dip in her hairline. But she was only herself, a little flushed, but exactly the same.

Three years ago, Mitch had an affair. She figured it out and he had begged her forgiveness and she gave it. She had no choice but to forgive him. They had kids and a house and their lives were all tied up together. The other woman, she had told herself, only had sex. And sex meant so little to Madelyn, there was no real contest. Now Madelyn could use her husband's midlife crisis to ease her own guilt. Driving over, she had decided she could rationalize Steve as evening the score. But now she knew this was something else. This was not an affair. If her husband had felt like this during his affair, then sex would have won after all.

"Hey." Steve was outside the bathroom door. "Are you all right?"

"Fine." She opened the door and smiled at him. "Great."

"Breakfast is ready."

They sat in his kitchen eating feta cheese omelets and olive bread—adult food, things she would never eat at home. They drank espresso. A platform ran the perimeter of the cabinets with a ramp at one end so Steve could get up to the sink and counters. The bottom cupboard doors were cut to open over the platform. Madelyn was impressed with the ingenuity, the independence it represented. The kitchen tile work was all original and stunning. Green and lavender, popular colors from the twenties, in a complicated pattern over the counters, the back splash, and the entire wall behind the stove.

"The tile is beautiful," she said. "I know tile. And this is remarkable."

"Did it myself."

"You did not."

"No, but I want to take credit for anything you like, everything you like."

He leaned over to give her a kiss on the cheek. She turned her face and kissed him on the mouth. She could taste the cheese and the coffee. They kept kissing. They couldn't stop kissing. His mouth was soft, his tongue active but not insistent, not jamming down her throat half the time like Mitch.

She sat back, looked down at her plate, took a bite of cold eggs.

"I wanted this to happen," Steve said. "But I don't want to complicate your life. I just want you to know, I've thought about it for weeks. I've dreamed about you."

Madelyn smiled. "When I had my accident yesterday, you were the only person I wanted to call."

They sat together at the table without touching, without looking at each other. Madelyn had never felt so happy or so guilty.

chapter twenty-three

I overslept. It had taken me a long time to fall asleep and when I did, I slept too hard. I woke up Saturday at 10:18, groggy and disoriented. I started to call for Linda and then I remembered she was gone. She had ransacked the apartment. She had driven to her new lover in Phoenix. I sat up on the edge of the bed. My head was full of rot and my heart had fallen down into someplace in my stomach.

I forced myself out of bed and into the bathroom. I sat down to urinate, I didn't have the energy to stand up. I told myself to cut it out. I tried to shake it off in the shower. But in the shower, her one hair was still there. I looked away. I saw the bottle of shampoo sitting on the corner of the tub. That bottle of shampoo would last almost a year for just me. I used so little on my buzz cut. It was her shampoo. It was hard to breathe. By the time I bought a new bottle of shampoo, Christmas without her would have come and gone. The steam closed my throat and filled my chest. I turned my face up to the water. That's what I'd write in that kid's suicide note, the kid who had died on the street the day before:

Dear Mom,
   Everything in my life lasts too long. I don't
   have anyone to help me use it up.

And I'd sign it "your son," and whatever his name was. When I got to the station, I'd be sure to find out his name.

The only towel in the bathroom was still wet from swimming the night before. I'd forgotten to get a clean one. I dried myself the best I could with the damp terry cloth. I put on my clothes, shivering. I made the bed and I cracked my shin hard on the metal frame. I looked at my telephone.

It only took a couple of calls. Dorothy Fairweather and Lewis Lapinsky were getting married at the Riverstone Mansion in Elysian Park at 1:00. I had to be at work by 11:45 to put on my uniform and pick up my assignment. I thought of Dorothy in her wedding dress with a big smile on her little face. I knew it was stupid, but I kept thinking about her, walking down the aisle, throwing her bouquet, pushing a piece of wedding cake into his downturned mouth. I kept wiggling the image like that little-kid loose tooth, pushing, twisting until it really hurt.

I sat down at the card table. I was hot suddenly. I could smell the sweat under my arms even though I'd just had a shower. I wiped the perspiration off my upper lip with the back of my hand. I put my gun on the squishy vinyl tabletop. I admired it. It was an attractive piece of functional art. I liked the smoky gray metal on the barrel and the trigger in contrast with the wood-grain butt. I picked it up. It fit my hand perfectly. The metal was cool and I laid the barrel against my cheek. It felt so good. I had a quiet thought, for the first time ever, I might be late to work. I had the thought. I ignored it. I laid the gun down on the table. I touched my forehead to it as if in prayer. I pressed my face into it. If it went off now, by accident, it wouldn't really be my fault. It wouldn't really be suicide.

I closed my eyes. I imagined Dorothy at the mansion, fixing her hair, putting on her eye makeup, giggling with her maid of honor. Linda was at Saturday brunch with that asshole. They were holding hands. He was thinking her cold feet weren't so bad after all. Not after that morning blow job.

I rolled my forehead back and forth over the barrel. I stuck my tongue out and licked the metal trigger. It had no taste, but it made my tongue dry. I sat up straight. I picked up the gun. It was an equation, pure and simple. Logic. I could stand it if I was going to feel this bad only for a month. If I wouldn't miss her after thirty days, I could make it that long. But if I was going to be sad for a year, then I needed another solution. I would never survive a year feeling like this. A month? Or a year? Which was it going to be? Then I imagined her wedding ring lying on the table and I thought I was going to be sad for a very long time.

I was crying again. I wiped my eyes with the back of my hand. The hand holding my service revolver. I looked at it. I didn't have to be miserable. I could take control. I laughed a little. I wouldn't give her the satisfaction of my misery for more than another ten minutes. I was practically an expert on this one act. Maybe I was a lousy lover, maybe I didn't know how to be a husband, but I knew a lot about ending a life. I felt relief knowing that very soon I wouldn't miss her anymore. I was calm. I put my gun down on my right-hand side. I got up and went in the kitchen and got the pad we kept by the phone. It had a drawing of a fat mouse at the top and the words, "From the Big Cheese." I would have liked plain paper, but I didn't think we had any. I found a pen and sat down to write.

Note #327. The last note. 03/20/02

Dear

Then I stopped. I wasn't sure what to say. I wasn't sure even who to address it to. I was supposed to know about this. My note had to be the best suicide note ever. I couldn't just dash something off. I thought about all the notes, the funny ones, the sad ones, and what I had liked about each one. I wanted to do even better. I wanted to write something everyone would remember.

I had never missed a day of work. The next day was Sunday, my day off. I decided to go to work, keep my perfect record, and do it on my day off. That way I would have time to buy some nice paper and an envelope. I could think and plan, even look at some other notes if necessary. And I could make my few farewells.

I put my gun in my shoulder holster. I even smiled a little, thinking about my plan. It seemed so clear. One more day. One last day.

I picked up my jacket and my keys and left. I drove down my street heading for the 405 South. I passed some new graffiti on the backside of my local dry cleaners. "Lexi! I'm sorry for . . . " in dark red spray paint. The three dots interested me. What was he sorry for? Why not say it? Dot dot dot. I looked at my watch. She would be married very soon.

chapter twenty-four

Sex with Lewis was lovely. It wasn't earth-shattering, but it was warm and reliable, and Dorothy liked it, liked doing it, liked having it, liked how much Lewis liked it. They were a good fit and she had his rhythms down exactly. And occasionally they had great sex, wild, a little kinky with the sash from her bathrobe and his fondness for chocolate syrup.

In just three hours from now, he would be the only man she would ever have sex with again. He pulsed above her and she tried not to think of Seth. She had not compared them for a long time. There was no comparison anyway, both because it wasn't right to compare and because sex with Seth was something else entirely.

Why doesn't he love me? She had said it out loud every day, hundreds of times a day, after Seth had left. Why doesn't he love me? Why? What's wrong with me? She was hearing it now in her head. Now, just a few hours before her wedding. She forced herself to remember the way his breath stank in the morning, told herself that the problems he always had with his teeth were only going to get worse. She hated his art, he was second-rate and overblown and quasi-intellectual. Why doesn't he love me? the little voice said and kept saying. I don't want him to love me, she answered. I don't. I'm going to marry Lewis.

Lewis breathed Iloveyou in one slippery word in her ear and rolled off her. She turned over on her stomach. He sat up on the edge of the bed, clasped his penis with both hands and giggled, high-pitched and feminine.

He always grabbed himself and giggled after sex. It was a tic or a habit or a neurosis. She had thought it was sweet and sort of child-like in the beginning; now it was just what he did. She wondered how she would feel in thirty years.

He went into the bathroom. She lay where she was, waiting her turn, waiting to get going, waiting for the roof to fall in. She would be abducted by aliens, fall into the witch's caldron, be spirited away by little blue devils. Lewis would come out of the bathroom and never see her again, only the indentation of her head on the pillow, the scratch marks that her fingernails left on the floor when they dragged her to the underworld.

The phone rang. Perfect. She had to get up. She scrambled across the bed, dashed into the kitchen to get it before the answering machine began.

She was breathless and almost giggling, elated for some reason. She was getting married. "Hello?"

"Dorothy Fairweather?" It was a man's voice, deep and official. Dorothy sat down. This voice had called her before. Called her out of the blue, out of the dark, out of her life. She didn't know this man, but she knew his voice. She wanted aliens or witches, not this.

"Yes," she said, agreeing to everything.

"Are you the daughter of—"

"Yes, yes. Where is she?"

"This is Officer Peters with the L.A.P.D."

"Where is she?"

"She's at St. John's Memorial. I guess your mother has a history of depression?"

"Is she alive?"

"Yes."

"What did she do?"

"We picked her up on Santa Monica Boulevard. She was in the intersection threatening to jump out in front of traffic. In her bathrobe. That kind of thing."

Dorothy knew exactly the kind of thing. She looked down at her naked body, the small blond hairs on her thigh, the blue veins in her breasts. She should have called Jane back. Somebody should have been with her. "Where's my brother?"

"We haven't located him yet. Your mother gave us your number."

Getting hit by a truck. That was new. It was always pills, and once she drove the car into a wall. How resourceful of Jane, visiting Los Angeles without a driver's license or a drug contact, to use the traffic right outside the hotel. Downright creative. Dorothy thought of the hotel, how pretty it was, how hard she had worked to find just the right place for Mom.

"I'll be right there," she said.

She didn't even know she was crying until she opened the bathroom door and saw Lewis's eyes widen with alarm.

"My mother," she said. "She's had an episode."

"What is it this time?"

"They picked her up in her bathrobe, out on the street. I guess she was obstructing traffic."

"Oh, shit." Lewis sat down hard on the toilet seat. His hair stuck up from the shower. He had shaving cream on half of his face. His penis wiggled, small and vulnerable in the nest between his legs as he threw up his hands and shook his head angrily.

"Well, fuck your mother."

"What?"

"What about the wedding?"

"She's in the hospital."

"What else is new?" He wiped his face on a towel, her towel. "Every time we plan anything, Every time it's not all about her, she has an episode."

Dorothy knew what he said was true. It had been true her whole life, long before she had met him.

"I knew she shouldn't come," he muttered into the terry cloth.

"It's my wedding."

"Not anymore. Now it's a goddamn crisis. Forget it. We're getting married anyway."

"I have to go to the hospital."

"Let Michael take care of it."

"They can't find him."

"Of course not. He's probably butt-fucking some thirteen-year-old boy."

"Just because he's gay—"

"Your goddamn family. It's so goddamn awful. Couldn't they leave you alone for one day?"

"I'm sorry. I have to go." She was dressing while he raged, the same old blue jeans over clean underpants, a T-shirt instead of Lewis's white shirt.

"I want to get married," Lewis was saying. "Today. We have the place, the caterer, the flowers, the band—"

"It's your band."

"Your goddamn family."

"You said that."

"When will you be back?"

"As soon as I can. Tell everyone. We'll bring the food here and the flowers and everybody. I don't care about the stupid mansion place. We'll get married tomorrow, or the day after, when Mom's feeling better."

She had to go. Dorothy knew she had to go. She looked at Lewis. He was furious. Her mother needed her, didn't she? Lewis didn't. Not right now. They could get married anytime. They could stay the way they were. She could go back to Rosemary's and marry Mr. Lee.

"No!" Lewis shouted at her as she walked out of the house. "It's one o'clock today at Riverstone Mansion. Do you hear me, Dorothy? Today! Or never."

Better still, she could go see that cute guy at the gas station. She had a feeling he was not the marrying kind.

"Can I take your car?" She had looked at the empty curb and remembered that her car was destroyed. Totaled. A complete loss.

"No, you can't take my truck. My truck is going to the wedding. Not the hospital."

"I have to go. I can't just go get married and forget about her. My mother was wandering down Santa Monica Boulevard in the hotel bathrobe. What kind of wedding memory is that? Maybe the photographer would like to take *that* picture!"

Dorothy started walking to the corner. She would take a bus; she would flag down a cab. There were no cabs in her neighborhood. She would walk to the convenience store, inconveniently far away, and use the goddamn phone to call a cab. She marched down the sidewalk, her old sneakers flapping, waiting for Lewis to pull up behind her, to open the truck door, to take her to the hospital.

He did arrive finally, when she was standing at the pay phone talking to Yellow Cab. He screeched to a stop in front of her and leaned over to open the passenger door. She started to smile. He pushed her wedding dress, Dress A, the ugly one, out onto the dirty blacktop, closed the door and accelerated out of the parking lot, tires squealing.

"It's the wrong dress!" she shouted after him. She didn't want this dress. He hadn't noticed the new one in the backseat. She dropped the phone and ran after him. "Lewis!" she screamed. "Come back here!"

He couldn't hear her. He was gone. She went back to the phone. Yellow Cab had hung up. The pink vinyl garment bag lay crumpled on the asphalt. She picked it up and slung it over her shoulder. It slid off. She tried to hold it under one arm while she fished in her wallet for more change. It was heavy. It felt as if the dress inside was decorated with more than roses; it was covered with two inches of fertilizer, some gardening tools, a deep layer of dirt. Finally, she let it fall. She called Yellow Cab again and got the same dispatcher. She apologized. He said the cab was already on its way. His voice was old and scratchy. She could hear every cigarette he had smoked. Dorothy leaned her head against the graffiti-covered booth and let the tears fall. There was something sticky on the phone's mouthpiece; she could feel it pulling on the skin of her chin as she cried.

"Are you married?" she asked the dispatcher.

"Thirty-two wonderful years," he said.

"What's your secret?"

"It's my two-word method."

"Two words?"

"First I say yes. Then I say dear. Yes, dear. Method works every time."

She could see the guy who worked at the store looking at her through the window, around the magazines and lottery machine. He was overweight and freckled. His brown hair was buzzed, his scalp pink and apparent. He looked like the Midwest, like a football player at a state school. What was he doing here?

He came out the glass doors and walked over to her. He handed her a stack of 7-Eleven napkins even though his store was not a 7-Eleven.

"Can I help you?" he asked. He tugged on the neck of his uniform shirt, ran his hand across his fuzz of hair.

"No thank you," she said and then, "but thank you for the napkins."

She blew her nose noisily. He hovered, looking over his shoulder into the store, worried to be outside and not behind his counter, but not wanting to leave her.

"I'm fine. Really. I just had a fight with my—" the word was still missing. Lewis. That guy.

"That guy," she said finally.

He nodded. "Ass Hole," he said making it two words, serious words. "I'm here, if you need me. What an Ass Hole."

Ass Hole could be her own two-word method.

She could see him watching her through the glass, the worried crease between his little eyes.

The cab pulled into the lot. She waved goodbye to the napkin guy, picked up her wedding dress, and got in the backseat.

The hospital was far away. She had twenty dollars. She hoped that would be enough. The cabdriver was African-American, with short, fat dreadlocks that erupted all over his head. They wiggled and undulated as he drove. Dorothy stared at them, living fingers gesturing to her, pointing this way and that.

The garment bag crackled in her lap. She set the dress on the seat beside her. She wiped her eyes. That counter guy had been so nice. His navy blue uniform was clean and his eyes gentle when he handed her the napkins. He had watched her get in the cab and kept watching until she was out of sight. He would not have let her go to the hospital in a taxi. And Mr. Lee this morning, he would have driven her there himself. And the tattooed and pierced young rocker at the gas station. He let his customers wait. He would have taken care of her. The worse she felt, the more men who had never noticed her before seemed to worry about her. She had always been independent and nondescript enough to be anonymous, sexless. Men didn't notice her. There were no whistles from construction workers or winks from passing drivers. When she was with Seth she had overheard one of his woman friends, a textile artist, say to another woman, "I don't know what he sees in her. She's so ordinary." It had made her feel good, knowing that Seth saw something special in her, something just for him.

And Lewis always said that was exactly what he liked about her, that she was not flashy, just a normal girl. "How the fuck you got that way with your family, I'll never know." He said it over and over, to his friends, to her, to his perfect mother.

The cabbie was watching her in the rearview mirror.

"You like my hair?" He had a thick Jamaican accent.

"Oh, yes," she said. "I'm a hairdresser, but dreadlocks are one style I know nothing about. Could I do it to mine? Would it work?"

She saw him looking at her short hair in the mirror. She still hadn't showered. She had brushed her teeth quickly before hopping into bed with Lewis, but she could smell herself, feel the sweat from earlier dried and tight on her neck.

"It must grow first." He laughed. "But I think so." The driver nodded and the fingers bowed away from her and then at her. "I could show you. You wanna go?"

"I have to get to the hospital," she said. She would much rather have gone with him somewhere, anywhere, a place to make her hair curl.

"Please?" he asked.

"No," she said. "My mother is in the hospital."

"Oh-oh. Then I take you, fast."

He reached over the seat and patted her knee. He left his long brown hand there for a moment, gave her a little squeeze and a stroke. It was a beautiful hand. She slid out of reach.

In one day, more strange men had been nice to her than in her entire adult life combined. Maybe it was the power of getting married, of being unavailable. She looked down at the wedding dress scrunched on the seat next to her.

"You want a wedding dress?" she asked the cabdriver. "Got a sister, someone to give it to?"

"Lemme see it," he said.

She unearthed the dress from the bag. The roses sprang out in all directions. The skirt was enormous, Dorothy could hardly see out from behind it.

The cabdriver started to laugh. He laughed, he hooted, he whooped and banged the steering wheel. Dorothy was crying again. She wiped her nose on the hem of the dress. They were zooming down the freeway in the car-pool lane. There was an exit ahead, for car-pools only, that arced up and over eight other lanes of traffic. She loved this exit. She took it whenever she could, begged Lewis to go this way, even if it was out of the way. To her right, she could see all of L.A. laid out, houses and swimming pools, the mountains in the distance and the Hollywood sign. To her left, along the distant horizon, she saw a thin glittering stripe that was the ocean.

Dorothy opened her window and pushed the wedding dress out of the car. She watched it catch the wind, open, fill and billow like a parachute. It flew, it floated, and finally settled over the cement barrier. It was more beautiful fluttering by the side of the road than it had ever been on her.

The driver kept laughing. He was beginning to seem out of control, but Dorothy felt better than she had all day. Her eyes flashed again, pink on the right and green on the left, but there was no headache—just the bright lights reminding her she was something special after all.

chapter twenty-five

When Leo got back to the apartment building, there was a woman just walking out the front door. An older woman. She frowned at him. He kept his face away from her, looking down into his bag of groceries.

But she stopped on the front stoop and watched him use the key to go inside the lobby. He had Jenny's keys; he knew the teddy-bear key ring was distinctive. He should have changed it, thrown the bear away.

"Are you Jenny's friend?" the woman asked.

He was almost inside; the door had almost closed behind him; he could almost not answer. He turned and smiled, holding the door open with his foot.

"I'm her cousin."

"I didn't think she had any family."

"Distant. We found each other on the Internet."

"Jenny hates computers."

"I found her, sent her a letter."

"Uh-huh."

The woman squinted her watery blue eyes at him, sizing him up. She was probably in her fifties, wearing a beige skirt and a lighter beige raincoat. Raincoat in Los Angeles. The kind with a belt and too many pockets. She had on cheap flat shoes, plastic made to look like leather. This woman should be married, Leo thought. She was too old to be living alone in Hollywood. No wedding ring on her finger.

"How's Jenny?" The woman's voice was flat and suspicious, like her face.

"She's fine. Just bringing home the groceries."

"She hasn't been going out much. She sold a bunch of her furniture. I thought maybe she was moving."

"No, no," Leo said. "She's not moving." That was certainly the truth. "Well." He nodded at his grocery bag. "Gotta go."

He went in and hurried up the stairs. It'd be just like that woman to stop by later, bring them a pie or a casserole or something. He had to go check on his car, push that grease monkey to work fast. He had been excited about having a real place to stay. Until she ruined it. Bitch.

He was going to find Tess soon anyway. He was going back to the diner at four, talk to the night hostess. He could be going home with Tess tonight.

He set the groceries down on the floor beside the apartment door. He started to put the key in the first lock and stopped. There was a noise from inside. A thump. He heard it again. He felt the hair stand up on his arms and down the back of his neck. He saw himself open the door and Jenny's cold, dead face waiting for him, dragging her crippled foot, walking toward him, thump, thump.

He shook his head. Dead people don't walk.

He listened again. The apartment was quiet. His imagination could run away with him, he knew it. His ma always told him he was in the clouds, lost somewhere. Yeah, Ma, anywhere but home with you. He opened the three locks, picked up the groceries, and went inside.

It was quiet. Then he heard it again, the thump, hollow sounding, coming from the bedroom.

He put the groceries down. He held the keys sticking out between his fingers like spiked brass knuckles. He tiptoed toward the sound, through the living room and into the bedroom. She was still in the bed, just the way he had left her, her face covered, her feet making a small uneven hill under the blanket. The sound came again. From the bathroom.

Leo kept one eye on Jenny as he walked quietly to the bathroom door. His feet sank in the carpeting in front of the door. It was wet. Now he could hear another sound, a rushing, a steady whoosh, like water. He opened the door. The floor was flooded. The plastic trash can floated and banged against the toilet making that hollow thumping noise. The faucet was running, slowly but steadily. His plastic razor floated in the full sink. He had left the water on and the stopper in when he finished shaving. He didn't remember. He had been tired, and hungry. He hadn't been thinking.

He turned off the water and pulled the towel off the rack and threw it on the floor. He hoped the water wasn't seeping through to the downstairs apartment. He didn't want the landlord, the plumber, the neighbors coming up. He didn't want to have to hide Jenny's body. He didn't want to know what it felt like when he touched it. He worked frantically, sopping up the water and wringing out the towel into the tub. Before long, the towel was too wet to do any good. The bathroom linen closet was empty. There were no other towels. He went to the kitchen, looked in the one tall cupboard. He thought he had seen a mop and there it was.

He yanked the mop out, scraping the top of the cupboard. Something fell. A manila envelope, wrapped in half around a weight, fell from the underside of the cupboard ceiling and banged the kitchen floor with a heavy metallic thump. The wide packing tape used to hold it up there was yellow and brittle; the envelope had been hidden for a long time.

Leo's heart sank. He didn't want to find something else. Her dead body, one blue suicide note was enough. It was probably a childhood toy, some sexual appliance, a framed photo of the man she loved, something that would make him wish she wasn't dead.

He had to finish in the bathroom. He had to hope he was quick enough to keep water stains off the ceiling in the apartment below him. He hurried to the bathroom and mopped and squeezed into the tub, and mopped and squeezed for thirty minutes before he was done.

He left the mop in the tub, went into the living room, and sat down on the couch. He was depressed suddenly, and he had been feeling so good, so positive about finding Tess. He would find Tess. This girl, Jenny, this body, was not his problem. He had not done anything but obey her wishes. There was nothing wrong in that. Soon he would find Tess and go away with her and leave this mess to be cleaned up by someone else.

He sat on the couch and he could see the envelope lying on the floor in the kitchen. He wanted to ignore it, to tape it back on the cupboard ceiling. He did not want to open it, but he knew he would.

He walked over and picked it up. There were papers inside; he heard them. He put his hand around the bigger object.

"Oh, boy," he said out loud. "Oh, boy."

He went back to the couch. The envelope was addressed to Jenny Dunlop at this apartment. He had not even known her last name. He turned it over. There was a phone number scrawled in pencil across the flap and the words, emphatic in all capitals: "CALL!"

He opened the flap, turned the envelope upside down, and let the contents slide out onto the couch. A yellowed newspaper article, a certificate of some kind, a map of stars, a small pamphlet about astronomy, and some folded papers which looked like stationery, pink with scalloped edges.

And a gun. A revolver small enough to fit in a clear plastic sandwich bag. A gun nonetheless. He took it out of the bag. It was palm-sized, convenient. He checked the cylinder. The gun was loaded. But officer, he knew the punch line if not the joke: I didn't know the gun was loaded. He closed one eye and stared along the barrel, lining things up in his sights. He pointed it around the room and down at the papers on the couch.

On the certificate, partially hidden under the other things, he suddenly saw his name. "Leo" was written there, in fancy Old English script, on a background of dark sky and gold stars. He put the gun down, turned it away from himself. His knees trembled in a sick rush of fear. He had never met her before. None of this was his fault. There was no reason for his name to be anywhere. He pushed the other papers away. His name was in the center of the certificate. He read:

Star Light, Star Bright, Wish Upon a Star Tonight.
Know ye that
Jennifer Anne Dunlop
has her own star hereby named
"Jenny's Light"
in the constellation
Leo Major
and is recorded as star number 239M at 19n x 8'7.
Given to her by her father,
Wayne Cooper Dunlop,
on the occasion of her birth,
March 2, 1979.

Leo had to read it a second time. Her father had named a star after her. Leo didn't know regular people could do that. Maybe they hadn't been regular people, but the certificate looked mass-produced and cheesy in a New Age kind of way. Was a star really named for Jenny? He turned his head toward her prone body. A star with her name.

He picked up the map of the constellations, cream covered in navy blue dots. "Leo" it said again in the center of an area outlined with yellow Magic Marker. In blue marker, dot to dot, someone had outlined the lion constellation, the curving mane, the tail. A tiny dot, down by the lion's foot, was circled in red. A delicate hand, slanted and precise, had written "Jenny's Light."

There was more writing on the back. Leo turned it over.

It was a description of the spring sky, Leo Major was a seasonal constellation, and Jenny's star would return each year for her birthday as the earth rotated and orbited the sun.

Leo had not known there was a constellation with his name. He picked up the fancy printed certificate again to look at it more closely. He turned it over. There was writing on the back of it too, but in pen, handwritten and not neatly. Leo recognized Jenny's round, loopy cursive from her suicide note.

People Who Love Me

Dad..... dead, cancer, 4/26/91
Billy... dead, car accident, 6/10/98
Robby... dead, or might as well be, 3/17/99
Sam..... dead, car accident, 6/10/98
Mom.... nope, never did.

Leo tossed the paper aside. Ridiculous. Who made a list? Who thought that way? People who killed themselves, that's who. She was nuts. There was no point in making lists, but his mind couldn't help it. His dad. His mom. His sisters. His brothers.

He shook his head. Picked up the newspaper clipping. There was a photo of a car, mangled almost beyond belief, and the headline "Two Dead, One Saved in Fwy 29 Wreck." It was an article about the car accident that killed Jenny's twin brothers, Robert James Dunlop and William Brian Dunlop. It talked about the extraordinary and improbable recovery of Jenny, completely unharmed, from the driver's seat. She had not been wearing her seat belt. She was pushed sideways, into the bent door. She missed being crushed with the steering wheel by only inches. She had been driving. Her brothers had died.

Leo unfolded the pink paper. Dear Jenny, it began. A letter from her mother. A letter from her mother hating her, blaming her, calling her a freak, telling her she should have died instead. She should have died with them. She should be dead. Leo couldn't read it all. He couldn't read a hate so cruel, so pure. His face got hot and his throat so full, it was hard to swallow. He gathered all the papers and put them back in the manila envelope. He took the envelope in to Jenny. Her hair was pretty. He was glad he couldn't see her face. He laid the envelope next to her on the bed. Someone should find it. Someone should tell her mother. Poor Jenny. He reached down to touch the lump under the blanket that was her hand, but stopped. She was growing. She was expanding. He looked her up and down. Her belly made a round hill, her legs seemed to be floating. She had become the dog he had seen by the side of the road back home, lying on its side, its stomach huge and bloated, its mouth open, its legs rigid and extended into the air.

He left her and shut the bedroom door behind him. He could pee in the sink. He could skip showers. He looked at the bag of groceries sitting on the floor where he had left it. He should put the milk in the refrigerator.

Milk. . . . dead, spoiled on the floor, 3/20/02.

Bread. . . . dead, molded, 3/20/02.

Who would he put on his list?

Tess . . . Tess . . . might as well be dead, left him to be a star, one year ago . . . 3/16/01.

chapter twenty-six

Steve's dark hair shone in the sun coming through his kitchen window. The skin on his cheek was white and pure like milk in a clean glass. Madelyn reached out and traced the blue vein in his temple.

He turned to look at her. Her finger fluttered down his cheek, onto his shoulder. His eyes were indigo and resolute, prepared for her, for whatever she might offer. He looked down at her hand on his shoulder, his black lashes like paintbrushes in the milk.

He was looking at her wedding ring. She took her hand away.

"Breakfast was delicious," she said. "Where did you ever learn to be such a good cook?"

He didn't answer. He stared at her. He kept looking until she blushed.

"Thank you," he said.

"For what?"

He had done everything. There were eggs on her plate and blueberries in a bowl, and she could still feel the scratchy couch cushions under her bare thighs. She could still feel what she had never felt before, because of him. "Why are you thanking me?"

"For today."

Then this was it. He wanted only the one day. Disappointment settled, hard and cold, in her stomach. She was older. She was married. She had kids, for God's sake. Today should be enough.

"Thank you," she said.

She didn't want to leave. The toast was eaten. He looked tired. His experienced hand lay flat on the varnished wood tabletop. His fingers were long, with each joint pronounced, the knuckles a small bony mountain range. If she had not loved him before, she would have loved his hand. A dancer's hand, skipping, twirling, sliding over her body.

She stood up and took her plate and his to the sink. She would leave him with a clean kitchen, nothing to be sorry for later.

"Don't," he said as she turned on the water.

"Let me." She didn't look at him. "This is something I'm good at."

He wheeled over to her and put his hand on her hip. He was like a toddler at her side; in his chair, he was shorter than either of her children. She was afraid to look at him. She squirted detergent into the sink, watched the bubbles form and expand.

She stepped away from him, picked up the coffee mugs.

"I want more," he said.

"Great." Inane and cheerful mom that she was. She started to pour him more coffee.

"No," he said, "I want more time. I want to talk."

She finished pouring. "We can talk right here." She heard her own voice perky, false.

He spun away. She watched the back of his wheelchair as he went into the other room. There was a sticker on the back that read "Hell on Wheels."

She walked after him.

He was looking out the living-room window through the sheer curtain. She saw children outside, playing in the street, heard the scrape and skirl of their skateboard wheels. She pushed her own children, their soccer games, the other mothers feeding them orange slices and cookies, out of her mind.

"Steve," she said.

"I'm sorry," he replied. "I'm an idiot. If you want to wash dishes, go ahead."

She bent over and lay her head on his shoulder. It was not a comfortable position, but she was glad to be in it. He didn't move, didn't turn away. She knelt, but then she was a little short. She strained to kiss his neck. Her lips collided with his cotton-covered shoulder.

She stood up and took his hand. He lifted his eyes to her. She was terrified, but determined. This was her day. Her day for all the things she had never done before, would never do again, would remember for the rest of her life.

"Where do you sleep?" she asked.

She had goose bumps. She walked backwards down the small hallway. He followed with his eyes on hers. A small smile on his lips. She pushed open the bedroom door with her butt.

The room was small and beautiful, golden walls with big windows on two sides that looked out on a backyard garden full of green and early flowers. There was a double bed under one window. Over the bed hung a metal bar. It looked like a trapeze, but it was obviously something to help him get in and out of bed by himself. Madelyn concentrated on looking out the window and inside at the books, more books. She smiled at Steve. He grinned at her, proudly.

"I'm a gardener," he said.

"And a reader," she said.

She sat down on his bed. He rolled up next to her. Now they were the same height. She kissed him. She kissed him and she felt it in her toes, in her knees, everywhere, all the way to the ends of her hair.

She wanted to do this. She wanted everything. She ached, she wanted so much.

"Move over," he said.

She slid to her left. He reached up for the bar and pulled himself out of the chair and onto the bed. He sat next to her. She smiled. She could put her arms around him. She could feel his chest against hers, her hands on his back. They lay down, sideways on the bed, face to face. She unbuttoned his shirt. She was annoyed with her own fingers for moving so slowly. There was no hair on his chest. A long puckered scar under his ribs. She kissed him there. Her hands went to the buckle on his belt and the button on his jeans. His jeans with the legs sewn together just above where his knees could be.

"Wait," he said.

"Why?"

"Are you sure?"

"I am," she said. "Are you?"

She could see the worry in his face.

"It's not pretty," he said.

Again she kissed the scar on his side. She hid her face against his flesh.

"That scar is the least of it." His hands lifted her head, made her look at him.

"I've never felt like this," she said. "Never."

He groaned and pulled her up to kiss her.

She sat up and took her dress off, and her bra and her panties. She was naked beside him. She was oblivious to the light, to her stretch marks, to the splay of her thighs, to anything but his touch on her skin. He wiggled out of his pants. There were bandages, long and beige, attached here and there with metal clips. He undid the clips. He began to unwrap his stumps. She saw nothing to be ashamed of. She helped him roll the bandages, put them aside. He moved well on the bed. And then he was over her and inside her and she was so surprised she laughed out loud.

chapter twenty-seven

I f you knew you were going to die the next day, what would you want to do? It's a game I played as a child, more often as a teenager. If the bomb was going to be dropped tomorrow, what would I do today?

If I knew I had only twenty-four hours to live, I wouldn't want to sleep, but I would want to wake up. I'd want one last morning when I open my eyes, then close them again and sink down deeper into the soft covers and the warm sheets. I'd want the metallic smell of slumber and the last bit of dream fading in my head. I'd want to stretch and wake up slowly. I drove to work with all the windows down. I listened to the radio, to classical music, composed by people who had died before me. I saw the gravel on the shoulder. I saw the little sparkles of glass imbedded in the cement road. I saw the yellow lines and thought about the crew who had painted them. I wondered where they were. I drove too fast and I looked at the other drivers as I passed them by. They all seemed sad and even absurd to me, the Asian mother and daughter; the Latino man with a tattered straw cowboy hat; the red-haired executive picking his nose. What was the point of going anywhere. They were moving, breathing because they always had. Living is a hard habit to break.

The sun was shining, but I couldn't see it behind the haze. I was sorry my final sky wasn't clear and blue. And I was sorry it wasn't going to rain, just for an hour or so. I love the rain.

I was only a little later than usual to work. I parked in my usual spot, but when I started into the station, I stopped. I had never noticed before how imposing the building is. It is tall and white and manages to be modern and classic at the same time. I thought of all the people inside, not just the officers, but the secretaries and the computer people and the janitors, all working, all doing their usual thing. An old lady with a cane and orthopedic shoes tottered down the sidewalk toward me. She wore those black wraparound sunglasses favored by the geriatric set. Her hair was wispy like a baby's. She wobbled toward me. I could see through her skin to her fragile bones and muscles. I could smell the blood pumping through her veins. She had lived a long time. She could die at any moment. So could I. So would I. My stomach growled. I was hungry. Why do we eat, sleep, breathe? How senseless to perform these rituals for no other reason except we've never thought of doing anything else.

I went inside. Now I was late. I changed quickly and hurried into the big room for my assignment. There weren't any seats left. I had to stand just inside the door.

Ronnie had been given the day off. It was a gift, the sarge said, to help him recover from watching that kid shoot himself.

"What about me?" I said to the sergeant.

"What about you what? You're the suicide man, aren't you?"

That brought my head up. "Why'd you call me that?" I asked. Was my plan for tomorrow written on my face? Would they try to stop me? Lock me in a cell without my belt or my shoelaces? When I first started on the force, a suspect in lockup had hanged himself with the elastic from his underwear.

"I know about your interest in the subject," the sergeant said. "We all do."

I looked around. My fellow officers were all nodding, chuckling. Nothing's really a secret on the force. We work together too closely.

It's our spouses who get left behind. I remembered Linda complaining that I never talked about my work. My throat got tight and thick. I'd been working with these guys for six years. Linda and I had gone to the sergeant's daughter's wedding. I looked at my shoes so they wouldn't see my tears.

"You're with Hayden," the sarge said, "'til lunch."

Hayden was the one officer I didn't like. Perfect, I thought.

I got a cup of coffee and burned my lip on the first sip. The break room hadn't been cleaned properly between shifts. There was sugar on the counter and spilled milk and trash everywhere. On a regular day it would have pissed me off, but instead I stood there and rubbed the sugar crystals between my fingers, breathed in the sour milk smell, saw the half-eaten muffin and thought about the mouth who had taken the first bite. It was too much for me. It was too much life.

I shuffled to the squad car. My eyelids were at half-mast. I could feel my feet sinking into the concrete.

"What's wrong with you?" Hayden asked.

"Nothing," I said.

"Unsettled weather. Low pressure front moving in. Barometer has dropped .42 inches." Hayden was an amateur meteorologist.

"That must be it," I said to him, "why I'm feeling so low. That and driving with you."

Hayden flipped me the finger. His nails needed cutting. I got in the passenger side and leaned my head back against the seat.

Suicide is familial. It has a genetic component. Ernest Hemingway's father committed suicide. His brother and sister did too. Then he did. And thirty-five years later, almost to the day, his granddaughter, Margaux, died of an overdose. They've done studies on identical twins. If one commits suicide, the other is 60 percent more likely to commit suicide as well. Even when they're separated at birth and grow up clear across the country from each other. My dad killed himself when I was sixteen. What was it Hemingway said about death? "Just another whore."

chapter twenty-eight

Dorothy gave the cabdriver her twenty dollars. The fare was nineteen and change. She apologized. He was still chuckling, wiping the tears from his cheeks as Dorothy got out of the cab.

"If you need a haircut," she began, then stopped. "I'm sorry."

"Should I wait?" he asked. "Should I come in? Maybe you need some help? You need me, yes?"

"No. Thank you."

Her stomach hurt. No food, no sleep, the back of her throat raw from vomiting. What would she say to her mother this time? How could she not be angry? It was her wedding day. It had been her wedding day.

Dorothy had had an abortion in her senior year of high school. She figured out what was wrong with her the day she got her acceptance letter to the college of her choice. She wasn't even seeing Tim—Tom—Ted anymore. She never liked him much. She made the appointment, had the abortion, and of course her mother found out. Jane couldn't function well enough to drive a car or make dinner, but she was good at doctors and she knew them all. Dorothy lay on her teenagers' purple bedspread with her knees tucked up against the cramping. Her mother came into the room with a hand at her throat, the other running through her hair again and again.

"How could you do this to me?" her mother asked. "Why didn't you tell me? Why didn't you let me help you? You don't love me enough to confide in me. You don't love me."

Her mother collapsed in tears. Dorothy apologized and cried and told her not to worry, not to feel bad, that she loved her more than anything. Dorothy got up, made her mother tea, filled a special plate with her favorite little crackers. Dorothy tucked the blanket around Jane on the couch, turned on the television for her, sat down and rubbed her mother's feet.

This hospital was like all the others, like every hospital everywhere. The smell of medicine and disinfectant, the waxed linoleum floor, the posters about cholesterol and exercise were familiar, if not comforting. It was bright and sunny outside, but inside any hospital it was always the middle of a fluorescent-lit night.

Dorothy asked for her mother and recognized the receptionist's reproving smile. She knew the way the nurses at the station nodded to each other as she walked past. Mental breakdowns always provoked the same response. The health-care professionals rolled their eyes, sighed deeply, all but snickered. If Jane had actually committed suicide this time, if instead of freaking out she had actually thrown herself under a truck and died, she wouldn't have been on their floor. She would have gone straight to the morgue. A more sympathetic male attendant in white would unlock the drawer, pull her mother out on her metal tray like cookies from the oven. He would lift the sheet and ask for identification.

What if Dorothy said no? What if Dorothy said, "That's not my mother." If that cold, stiff body wasn't hers, then Jane would have to go on living. She was away, on a trip, gone to Bora Bora, but not dead. That'd show her, Dorothy thought. Forget it, Jane, I won't let you die.

It made Dorothy feel better to enter the quiet hospital room equipped with ammunition for a possible future. It armed her against her mother's loveliness, the blond hair and her peaches-and-cream skin. But Dorothy's protection fell away when her mother saw her and immediately closed her eyes against her daughter.

"Mama?" Dorothy whispered. "It's Dorothy."

Her mother's elegant hand waved her away. Dorothy was ten again, she was eight or five years old, her mother's rejection leaving her knees weak, her world and her body without foundation.

"Mama," Dorothy said again, heard herself bleating. "Mama? I'm sorry I didn't call you back this morning. I had to get my dress. I was just going to call."

"Are you getting married?" Jane's voice was rough.

"Not today."

"Good. I want to see your father."

Dorothy's father was miles away, years away. He had left long ago, after the first psychotic episode but before the first hospitalization. Dorothy didn't know him now. She hadn't seen him in seventeen years. She addressed a wedding invitation to him and then threw it away. She wasn't even sure she had the right address.

"Get your dad."

There had been two husbands after him. No more children, but maybe Jane was confused. Maybe the iv dripping into her vein had her drugged and delusional. A different delusion than usual.

"You mean, Sy?" Dorothy said naming her most recent stepfather, gone only two years.

"Fuck Sy. I want your father. Your father. Your brother's father. I want Jim. Idiot. I want him here."

Dorothy wanted to be angry. Her rosy wedding dress was on the side of the freeway, coated with exhaust, peppered with emission particles. She assumed her other wedding dress was still in the backseat of the truck, and she imagined the truck parked in front of Lewis's mother's house. There were flowers she had paid for decorating the rent-a-mansion right now. Wannabe actors in black pants and white jackets were standing around, sitting in the folding chairs, sneaking canapés, wondering if they would still get paid. One hundred and twenty-five people had not done something else so they could come to her wedding. She should be furious with her mother.

"I'll try to find him," Dorothy said. "I'll try."

Dorothy started out of the room.

"Dorothy," Jane croaked.

"What?"

"Tell him I love him. I always have."

Dorothy left the room. Her mother's talk of love surprised her. There had been no mention of her father for the last ten years, at least. Since their divorce, Jane had married, divorced, gone to the state institution, married, gone to the private institution, divorced, gone to live at Walnut Hill. Each marriage after Jim had been played as "it," the one, the love of her life.

Dorothy had almost married Lewis. She had lived with him for longer than her mother's second or third marriages had lasted. She had loved Seth longer than that.

Her knees went out from under her. She sat down on the shiny floor, her back straight but her legs unable to support her. She leaned her head against the wall, reached up a hand to hold on to the safety railing above her. A doctor ran toward her. He was young and Indian or Pakistani. He had beautiful caramel skin and big brown eyes. He was the son of Shiva, appearing in human form, and Dorothy smiled at him as he knelt before her. She scanned his forehead for traces of his third eye. He took a pen-sized light from his breast pocket and shone it in her eyes.

"I have a concussion," Dorothy said. "That happened yesterday."

Was it only yesterday? The car coming toward her. The woman in the black station wagon looking frightened. She had been on a hospital bed just like her mother, but she had not asked for Lewis. She had not even recognized him when she opened her eyes.

"How do you feel now?"

"It's been a hard day," Dorothy said. She struggled to get up, but the doctor put a hand on her shoulder.

"Are you her daughter? Jane Morgenstern is your mother?"

His inflection was lyrical, gently twisting, making every word poetry. She could go to India now. There was nothing stopping her. She could find a school to work in or a hospital where she could hold the sick babies and comfort the mothers. She could put cool compresses on the foreheads dying, but very wise old men. They would have last words of ancient truth to give her. She would find enlightenment. Everyone would be beautiful and helpful like this doctor.

"Today was your wedding?" he asked.

"How do you know?"

"Your mother said she doesn't want you to get married."

Dorothy's mouth opened. The doctor continued.

"I think your wedding prompted today's breakdown."

"Shit!" Dorothy said. She saw the doctor wince. "Sorry, but, honestly, couldn't she have just told me?"

"Would you have stopped the wedding?"

People stepped around them, frowning, curious. Dorothy used the railing and pulled herself to her feet.

"Are you ready to stand?" the doctor asked.

"Yes," Dorothy said. "And no, I would not have stopped the wedding. My mother is certifiable. Actually, she has been certified."

"So I understand. But today she was desperate, not insane."

"You don't think it's nuts to run around half-naked just so your daughter won't get married?"

"If I had a daughter," the doctor said seriously, "and she was about to commit a bad act with a lifetime of consequences, I would do anything to stop her."

Dorothy believed him.

She thought her mother was happy for her. Then she remembered how she had handed her mother off, gratefully, to Michael last night. Jane's eyes looked worried, her mouth opened to say something, but Dorothy hurried her out the door before her mother could speak. And then the urgent phone call this morning. Dorothy had made love to Lewis instead of returning her mother's call.

The doctor was smiling at her. "Did you postpone the wedding ceremony?"

"Well. I guess we kind of canceled it." She hoped Lewis was making those calls.

The doctor beamed. His teeth were startlingly white in his brown face. "Then maybe you would have dinner with me," he said.

"Excuse me?"

"You must feel at loose ends with no plans. We could make a night of it."

Dorothy looked at the small doctor. He was just her height. His hands were delicate, even feminine. He held them clasped in front of him. His eyes were expectant pools of melted chocolate. His lab coat was very clean.

"What time?" she asked.

"Any time you like. We can go anywhere you like. My shift ends at three, but I could probably get away a little earlier."

"For dinner? I have to go home first."

She said "home." She wasn't sure what else to call it. Lewis's house? He had bought it. It was all his. She felt sticky and offensive. The doctor nodded happily. Maybe the smell of vomit and sweat, plus the grass stains and the dirty hair, were all some kind of turn-on. Maybe for her entire thirty-one years she had been wrong to bathe. To meet men, a girl simply had to stink.

Her brother Michael got off the elevator in front of the nurse's station. He saw Dorothy and the doctor and hurried toward them. He stopped and looked Dorothy up and down.

"What the hell happened to you?"

His nose wrinkled. Obviously, her dirt didn't have the same appeal for gay men.

"Where've you been?" she said. "I canceled my wedding."

"Thank God." Michael turned to the doctor. The handsome Indian prince was still grinning. "How's Mom?"

"You must be the brother. I was just telling this very attractive young woman—"

"Dorothy?"

"Dorothy." The doctor sighed with satisfaction. He looked gently at her and then back to Michael, man to man. "I was telling Dorothy that your mother is doing quite well."

"What does that mean?" Dorothy said.

"She is actually very—"

"No." Dorothy looked at her brother. "What does 'thank God' mean?"

"It's just an expression."

"It is not."

Michael looked down the hall. He seemed to be suddenly fascinated by an orderly wheeling a patient into the elevator.

"Michael." Dorothy pinched his arm. Hard.

"Ow! Nothing. It means nothing. I mean, I'm sure that makes Mom happy."

"You knew she didn't want me to get married? You knew that? When did you know?"

Michael looked at the doctor. "So, Mom's doing well?" He changed the subject.

Dorothy spoke before the doctor could answer. "She wants to see Dad."

"Our dad? Really?"

"Maybe it's the medication."

The doctor piped up in his official capacity, "Oh, no. This is not the effect of medication. I do not think so."

"I'll call him," Michael said.

"I have an old address in Reno. Maybe information—"

"I have his number."

For the second time, Dorothy's mouth fell open. Everyone knew something she didn't. Michael knew everything.

And again, Michael looked embarrassed. "I talk to him. You know. From time to time."

"Why didn't you tell me?"

Michael shrugged. Dorothy's knees trembled. She grasped the railing, forced her back to stay straight, her legs to hold her.

Michael turned away from her. He looked up at the ceiling. "Dad's here," he said to the light fixture.

Dorothy's shock turned to pleasure. Michael had told him. He couldn't miss his baby girl getting married. "Really? That's so sweet of him. To come to my wedding."

"Dorothy. He knew Mom would be here. He came to see *her*."

The words crept from Michael's mouth, each one a bigger secret than the last, until Dorothy and the doctor had to lean in and watch his lips move.

"He wasn't coming to your wedding."

Dorothy saw crow's-feet at the corners of Michael's eyes. She saw the large open pores on his nose, the sharp vertical lines beginning around his lips. He would age like a woman, she thought. His neck would sag and the flesh under his arms would go flabby.

"Give me your car keys," she said.

He looked at her blankly, stupidly.

"I want to go home."

"Where's your car?"

"Totaled, remember? Remember? I had a car accident last night. I got a concussion. I ended up in the hospital. I was getting married today. Remember?" She was shouting.

The doctor's eyes were wider than ever. She turned and snarled at him. He backed away.

"Okay, okay." Michael put the keys in her hand. "It's in the garage. The parking garage. Third level by the elevators."

"Ten dollars."

Michael didn't even ask. He opened his wallet, put a twenty-dollar bill in her waiting palm.

"I will see you back here, for dinner?" the doctor squeaked.

Dorothy stamped her feet at him. He nodded as he backed away.

"I see you are upset," he said. "I understand completely."

His lyrical accent was getting annoying. She took the stairs.

chapter twenty-nine

Leo's car sat exactly where the tow truck had left it. A bird had crapped on the back windshield. The three garage doors were wide open, but the place was empty.

Leo went into the office. He smelled the gasoline and grease. He started to lean on the pale blue counter, then thought better of it. There were two chrome and black vinyl chairs with a chipped Formica table between them. The magazines looked too well read. There was a calendar on the back wall. A girl in a leather garter belt straddled a red and black motorcycle. Leo saw today's date. March 20, with small red words printed underneath, "First Day of Spring."

Leo cleared his throat. The mechanic, Gus, the same guy from yesterday, came out of the bathroom, expelling the odor of shit and industrial soap.

"Hey," Leo said. "Gus."

Gus frowned at him. He had no idea who Leo was.

"I'm here about my car," Leo said. He nodded toward it. "I came in yesterday. The tow truck brought me."

"Oh, oh, oh. Sure."

"How come you haven't started working on it?"

"It's Saturday."

"You're here."

"The insurance didn't call me. I can't start working on it until the adjuster comes. Makes the estimate. Authorizes the work."

"So when are you gonna start?" Leo asked.

Gus shook his head, his mouth twisted in a half-grin, like Leo was an idiot.

Leo's face grew hot. The accident wasn't his fault. "So? When?"

"Monday at the earliest. Probably more like Tuesday."

"Tuesday?"

"Or Wednesday. Depends on the insurance."

"How long will it take to fix it?"

"Three, four days. If I get the parts."

Jenny's body was about to blow up. "I can't wait that long."

The mechanic shrugged. "It's an old car. Might be a total loss."

Leo's heart took off in his chest, racing, beating frantically like it wanted to escape. He was sweating and freezing at the same time. The breeze was giving him goose bumps. Jenny's apartment. The envelope by her side. His milk and bread in her empty refrigerator. He closed his eyes. Tess had her arms around him. She smelled like beer and cigarettes and patchouli oil. She smelled like home. He would take her home. Back to Maryland. They would leave Los Angeles as soon as possible. In L.A., the sun shone every day, but it was so cold at night. Huddled in the back of his car under his only blanket, he knew he had been deceived by Disneyland, seduced by the Rose Bowl and the Academy Awards. It always looked like summer, but Los Angeles was cold and dismal.

He had Jenny's little gun in the front pocket of his blue jeans. He patted it. But it couldn't help him here.

"You can call," Gus was saying. "Did you call your insurance? Call 'em."

"The police took all my information."

"They're not gonna call for you."

"The woman who did it, she died or something. The ambulance took her."

Gus sighed. He ran a hand through his curly hair. It was a habitual move. Leo saw a smudge of grease imbedded in his forehead from the repeated contact with the dirty heel of his hand.

Gus took a piece of paper off a notepad and picked up a pencil. "Okay. Here's what you do."

Leo looked down at Gus's head bent over the paper. His few gray hairs were even curlier, like wires springing through the darker waves. His right hand clutched the pencil as a child would, in his fist. His other hand held the paper flat. It was black underneath his fingernails, permanently.

"First accident?" Gus asked.

"Yeah."

"Okay. I got it written down for you."

Leo took the list. The man's writing was hard to read. The letters slanted in all directions and the spelling was unusual.

"If you get ahold of 'em, tell 'em I'm here 'til four."

He gave Leo his card. The corner was bent. There was an oily stain on the lower right.

"Thanks," Leo said, but he didn't mean it. "Can I get some stuff out of it?"

"Sure."

Leo walked over to his car. He had to yank to open the door. It made a terrible crunching sound. He looked inside. There was nothing, really. He grabbed his duffel bag and pulled it from the backseat. He bumped his head hard on the door frame.

He was suddenly sick. Too much breakfast after so little for so long. His intestines rumbled. His bowels cursed the pancakes and especially the sausage. And the bacon. He ran back into the office.

"Use your bathroom?" he said to Gus.

He didn't wait for an answer. The bathroom was small and painted a grimy institutional aqua. Traces of Gus's last discharge lay in dark streaks at the bottom of the bowl. Leo felt it coming. He threw up. Coffee, pancakes, eggs, bacon and sausage. Again. And again.

He flushed. He washed his hands and face. He pressed a brown paper towel to his eyes. He wanted to cry. He would take his duffel bag and go back to the apartment. He had only until four o'clock. Then he would go back to the diner. The night hostess would remember Tess. Everything would change. He thought of Jenny's swollen, deformed hand and gagged again. There was nothing left in him, he heaved and strained without result. He leaned over the bowl, his shoulders shaking, his knees trembling. Tess had beautiful hands with long fingers and short nails. He loved the chips in her fingernail polish, the pink nail showing beneath the blue sparkly color she usually wore. She would sit beside him on the couch as they watched a movie, eating potato chips with one hand, jerking him off with the other while he leaned back and watched her hand go up and down, the fingernails catching the light from the television.

chapter thirty

Note #162 09/23/01

To everyone in the entire world:

Please publish this in every newspaper in the country and the world.

Everyone listen to me! I want to help you. I want you to know what I know. The world is a goner. There is no god. What we think of as god is really our own desperation.

The only thing up there is aliens. The aliens will come and take our brains. They already have. Some people's brains are gone. You know that. Read the front page of this newspaper. Many famous people have no brains.

I walk around every day and I'm amazed that more citizens aren't jumping off of buildings or running their cars into walls or walking into the ocean if you live near it. The end will be horrible.

Don't say I didn't tell you. I have tried to tell everyone. Please publish this in the newspaper. Please read it on the television. I want to save mankind. Follow my example. Jump.

Follow me. Only in death are we are safe.

Very truly yours,

Roger G. Griswald

This note was taped to the door of the stairway leading to the roof. It was typed on a sheet of white paper that had been handled a lot and folded again and again. There was a hole in the paper from a pushpin, but the door was metal. It wouldn't take the pin. I found it lying on the floor nearby. The point was bent. Griswald had tried hard to get that pin in there.

Then, according to Julio Garcia in the pharmacy downstairs, Mr. Griswald, married, father of two, came in and bought a little dispenser of Scotch tape. He also bought a chocolate bar, but he didn't eat it. We found it, sort of, in his shirt pocket—and a lot of other places, too. Why did he buy the candy? That bothers me. I wonder about it. He had so much time between trying to get the pushpin into the door and then returning to the roof with the tape. What during that fifteen minute trip might have made him change his mind? What if it had been Julio's funny wife, Sophia, at the store that night? What if she had told him one of her jokes? What if she had kidded him a little? What if he hadn't had the money? Because $2.95 is expensive for tape when you're only going to use an inch. What if he stopped outside the store, looked up at the night sky, and ate that chocolate bar? Is chocolate enough to keep a man alive? Maybe for some it is, maybe that's all it takes; the taste of something delicious, the night air on your face, the way the headlights of a car driving toward you turn into stars in your eyes. If Roger Griswald had taken one more moment, to eat the chocolate or to look up at the sky, the night watchman might have come along and put the padlock on the door to the roof. Some Type-A guy, still working, bleary-eyed with his tie undone and his shirt wrinkled, might have been coming down the hallway as Roger stepped off the elevator, might have said, "What are you doing here?" or "Can I help you, buddy?" If there had been just one more moment, one way or another, if just one connection had been made, maybe all of them would not have been broken.

chapter thirty-one

L et me show you something," Steve said.

They were lying in his bed with the covers pulled up. His arm was around her. Madelyn's head was on his chest. She laughed.

"You've shown me enough for one day."

"This is something else."

He turned away from her and she felt the shock of the rest of her life. Without his skin touching hers, the world burst back into the room. She looked at the clock. She should leave. The kids, her kids, would be home. She had to make lunch and wrap a birthday gift. There was still laundry in the dryer from yesterday. It would be so wrinkled. She should stop and get milk on the way home.

Steve leaned over the edge of the bed and brought up a large picture book. It had no cover; she couldn't see the title. There were papers sticking out of it. He sat up and put the book on his lap. She sat up next to him. Her legs, her fat legs that she hated, made two long, wide, burial mounds under the comforter. On his side, the comforter was smooth. She pulled her legs up, curved them one way, then the other, finally sat up very straight and crossed them, Indian style.

He opened the book.

"What is it?"

"A book of epitaphs. You know, the things people write on their tombstones."

Madelyn looked at Steve. His face was shining, happy, excited as he paged through the book looking for his favorites. She rubbed her cheek against his bare shoulder. His skin was cool and smooth. She didn't want to read other people's tombstones. It made her stomach hurt to think of dying now.

"May I read to you?"

"Well—"

"You read it, for yourself." He handed the book to her. She needed her glasses, but she was not getting out of bed, naked, and getting them out of her purse in front of her much younger lover. She handed the book back.

"I just meant—the time—I should go."

The light went from his face. He took the book from her and closed it.

"I'm sorry," she said. "I—"

"Of course."

She waited for him to turn to her, to say something more. He pushed the book off his lap. He turned away, lifting his body with his arms, putting his back to her. She leaned toward his back, but stopped.

"Steve," she said again.

"What?"

"Never mind."

She threw back the covers and stood up. She picked up her underpants and her bra. She sat down on the edge of the bed again to put on her underpants. When she spread her legs she got a warm, wet whiff of sex. She blushed and turned, but he was wrapping his stumps.

They sat back to back on opposite sides of the bed. Like old married people, she thought. As if their bodies held no allure, no fascination anymore. The same old, same old. After enough time, even Steve would be familiar. But not in a bad way. She slipped her silly summer dress over her head.

"Well," she said as she stood up.

He looked at her over his shoulder. He squinted at her. His eyes were electric blue in his porcelain face.

"Don't leave," he said.

"I don't want to, but I have to."

"No. Don't leave until you push my wheelchair back over here."

Steve nodded at his chair. She had kicked it when they lay back on the bed. It had rolled away, too far for him to reach.

"Oh my God," she said. "I'm so sorry."

He shrugged.

"Has that ever happened? I mean, what do you do?"

"I have a neighbor I can call. I can crawl if necessary."

She pushed the wheelchair over to him. She picked his jeans up from the floor and handed them to him. He stayed on the bed, holding his pants. She waited and then realized he didn't want her to watch.

"I'm going to use the bathroom," she said.

She splashed cold water on her face to keep from crying. She had crossed a line in her life. She had eaten the apple; the garden would not hold her. From now on, she should wiggle on her belly like a snake. Her hands shook as she dried them. The towel smelled like him. She missed him so much. There was a throbbing in her throat and her chest, and she hadn't even left yet.

"I'm going." She called to him from the hallway. She didn't know where he was. "Steve? Steve?"

He was in the kitchen at the sink. Her warm water had gone cold. The bubbles had disappeared. He let the stopper out and watched the water drain away. He wheeled back off the ramp and turned to her. He looked up at her, not smiling, his face hard.

"So?" he asked.

"So what?"

"Sex with an amputee—did you like it?"

Madelyn didn't know what to say.

Steve continued, "We call them Devotees. Amputee Devotees. There are people who fantasize about us. Sometimes one will follow me on the street. Or stare at me in the grocery store. Then she—or he—will go home and masturbate. It's the only fetish where what I'm missing is more important than what I have."

"Stop it."

"I've had sex with other women. You can pay women to have sex with you. Even if you have no legs. I tip them well. And you have to tell them when you place your order, you know, over the phone. I always say, "Be sure to tell her I have no legs.""

"Shut up!" Madelyn had to shout to get him to stop talking. "You idiot. I'm in love with you."

He was quiet. She sat down on a kitchen chair. She knew she was late; she had to go; she was too late to stop for milk. She knew she couldn't leave now.

He rolled over to her, put his hands on her cheeks, and lifted her face to him.

"Sex is not the same as love."

"Don't patronize me," she replied. "I'm not stupid. Sex with an amputee is pretty incredible, but even if you weren't missing both your legs, I'd love you."

She kissed him. He kissed her. She really had to go.

chapter thirty-two

Dorothy cranked the radio. She had the windows down. She liked Michael's car—only a year old, foreign, fast, with a rainbow-striped triangle on the back window signifying his sexual persuasion. Maybe she would meet a woman. Or was it only a gay-guy sign? Michael had driven down from San Francisco for the wedding. He had picked up Jane at the sanitarium in San Luis Obispo on the way. He hated Los Angeles, but he had managed to stay out all night his first night here. Her brother had the life; that was for sure.

It was early Saturday afternoon, but Dorothy came over the rise and the freeway slowed to sludge. Bumper to bumper, cars lined up in all four lanes for as far as she could see. Dorothy sighed. What else could she expect? She was stopped. Then she jerked forward. Then stopped again.

She fiddled with the tuner to find her favorite station. Saturday-afternoon jazz. She sang along. Her voice was getting stronger; she could hear it. The singing lessons were beginning to work. She hadn't been practicing as much as she should. Now she would have more time. Now she could sing all the time. Lewis used to ask her to stop; he would tell her to stop singing, he was trying to compose his own song. He was always writing songs he didn't want her to sing. Guy songs, he called them. She opened her throat and belted out the song, using her diaphragm and her stomach muscles, practicing.

The guy in the car next to her was waving. She glanced over, still singing, and saw him motioning for her to roll down her window. She hit the automatic-window button and turned off the radio.

"Hi!" the guy yelled.

He was cute. A barbecued-ribs-and beer kind of guy, in a pale blue golf shirt, with his hair parted carefully on the side and trimmed neatly over his ears.

"Hi!" he said again.

Dorothy waited, frowning. She had a flat tire. Her back door was open. She had done something wrong to her brother's car.

"You have a beautiful voice," the guy called to her.

Dorothy blushed. "Thank you."

"Here!" he said. "I want you to have this."

He held out a sheet of lined school paper. They were moving slowly, under ten miles per hour, but still they were moving.

"Watch out!" she shouted.

He put his foot on the brake and stopped just in time to avoid rear-ending the car in front of him. Her lane moved ahead. She pulled away from him.

"Wait! Wait!"

She heard him shouting behind her. His lane moved. The car in front of her moved, too, but she stayed where she was, letting a long space grow between her and the car ahead. She glanced in her rearview mirror. The woman driving the minivan behind her looked curious, but not annoyed. Not yet.

"Thank you," the guy said.

He put his car in park and climbed across the gearshift to the passenger side. He handed her the paper. He was close enough for her to see his brown eyes, the wrinkles on his forehead, the gray in his chest hair curling above the top button of his shirt.

"What is this?" Dorothy asked.

"It's my number."

The car behind him beeped, once.

"My name's Eric," the guy said. "I'm a songwriter. Please, please, call me."

The car behind him honked again, once, twice and then leaned on the horn only letting up when the driver yelled out his window, "Fuck her later!"

The minivan behind Dorothy was honking, too, and the car behind that. It was a sudden fusillade of car horns.

"Okay," Dorothy said, just to get rid of him. "Okay, Eric. I'll call you."

She put her foot on the gas and leaped forward. She looked back over her shoulder. The guy waved, oblivious to the angry drivers behind him. He would catch up with her again. She sighed. She put on her blinker and slithered aggressively across two lanes. The next exit was only half a mile away. She headed for it, driving up the shoulder. Just let some cop try and give her a ticket. Just let him try.

She exited on Gower. Turned right and immediately right onto Franklin. She hadn't been this way in a while. She never came over here, to the Hollywood Hills. There was a strip of new cafés. Trendy couples in leather jackets sat at sidewalk tables, drinking lattes in the smog. The women were beautiful. The clock on the dash said 1:30. She should be in her wedding dress.

The next light turned red. She stopped and looked at Eric's number, handwritten in blue ink.

"Please call me," he had scrawled along the bottom. "I'll write you a fantastic song."

Dorothy sighed. The desperation of the creative people in this town just made her tired. The waiters who were really directors. The girls walking down the street in tight pants and ridiculous shoes, always auditioning. The writers eavesdropping and scribbling at every coffee shop. Sometimes she listened to Lewis and the guys in the band talk about their plans and dreams, and she just wanted to curl up and go to sleep. Wake me when I'm old, she thought, when ambition is gone, when all the little frantic voices around me, wanting, wanting, wanting, have all given up.

Another red light. She stopped and leaned her head against the steering wheel. She closed her eyes. Under her eyelid, her right eye flashed pink. On. Off. On. Off. Brighter than before, it left a little glitter of pain behind.

She opened her eyes to drive. The pink sparks continued. She felt a wave of nausea. She needed toast and a cup of coffee. No, tea with lemon. She passed the convenience store where she had called the cab. Almost home.

Lewis's truck was in the driveway. Her left eye began to pulse with green spots. She turned off the car and sat for a moment with her eyes closed. She tried to visualize a desert, the sandy expanse dry and hot and still. She willed her stomach to be calm.

The front door wasn't locked. Her wedding dress, the new one, was thrown over the arm of the sofa. The wedding cake was on the dining-room table. Something about it wasn't right. She looked carefully between the sparks flashing in her eyes and saw the plastic bride and groom on top upside down, heads planted in the frosting. Someone— probably Lewis with his sweet tooth—had used a finger to scoop some cake from the bottom layer.

She dropped Michael's car keys on the table next to the cake with a surprisingly loud jingle. A man walked out of her bedroom. He looked terrible, like he had been crying or sick or wrestling with someone. Dorothy felt awful for this distressed man in her house. She wanted to help him somehow.

"Dorothy," he said.

"Oh, no," she said. It was Lewis. She had forgotten who he was once again. Only for a moment, but it could not be good to forget the man you were supposed to marry. It wasn't healthy to not rec-ognize the guy you had lived with for two years. He was her . . . her . . . Oh, whatever he was, Dorothy thought with annoyance. He was Lewis.

"Sorry to disappoint you by being here," he said, "but this is my house. I *do* own it. I lived here before you did."

"That's not what I meant," she said. "You look kind of horrible. Are you feeling okay?"

"I feel fantastic."

She could tell he didn't mean it.

"I have to take a shower," she said.

"Dorothy."

"What?"

"You can't just walk in here and take a shower."

She looked around. The wedding presents were piled on the floor in front of the television. They looked like they had been tossed there. Some were lying on their sides; a few had the corners badly dented. There was something she was supposed to say, something that Lewis was waiting for, but she felt so fuzzy. If she could just move that dress, lie down on the couch for half an hour.

"Whose car is that?" Lewis asked.

"Michael's."

Lewis nodded. Dorothy smiled. It was good to have the right answer, even if it was an easy question.

"You found him," Lewis said.

"He showed up at the hospital."

"Dorothy," Lewis said again.

"What?" He didn't answer. "What?"

"Never mind." He walked away.

"I do mind," she said. "Lewis. Talk to me."

He turned back to her, but stayed on his side of the room, the dining-room table between them.

"I don't know," he said.

"How's the cake?" she asked.

He frowned at the big white baked thing on the table as if he didn't recognize what it was. Then he nodded. "Good. Banana."

"Every layer is different," Dorothy told him. "Try the middle. It's chocolate."

He dug two fingers into the second layer, gobbled up a big bite of chocolate cake with a frosting flower.

"This is better," he mumbled through his full mouth.

"The top is spice. Your favorite."

"Marry me."

Dorothy looked at him, not sure she had understood.

"I'm sorry about your mother." He wiped crumbs from the corners of his mouth. "I just wanted to marry you so much. I didn't want anything to get in the way. I'm glad to see you." He came around the table toward her. "Marry me. Now. Later. But soon."

This really was Lewis, Dorothy thought. He looked so odd, she decided, because it was Seth she had been dreaming of when she was asleep in the hospital. It must have been Seth who was the man in her mind during her accident-induced slumber. She had been thinking of Seth when she woke up.

"I can't," she said. "Not today. Well. Definitely not today."

"Don't leave me," Lewis said. "I can't live without you." He stretched his arms to her.

Dorothy shook her head. She suddenly couldn't get her breath. He took a step toward her. She saw the chocolate under his fingernails. She backed away from him. Her heart was pounding. Her eyes flashed, pink and green and pink and green, in rhythm with her heart. She had to concentrate on taking the next breath and the next.

The phone rang.

She leaped for it. The sound of normal life. But as she picked it up, she thought, it will be his mother, Lani, my brother. Why did I answer the phone? She almost hung up again, but didn't.

"Hello?"

A woman's voice. "Dorothy Fairweather, please."

There was that familiar sinking feeling; no good could come from a call that started that way. Dorothy sighed. "This is she."

"Good afternoon. I'm calling from St. Francis Insurance. Did you have an accident last evening?"

"Yes, I did."

"Did you file a report?"

"I was unconscious."

"Oh."

Dorothy could hear the rustling of papers at the other end of the line. She looked at Lewis. He was digging into the top layer of the cake. He would have to watch his weight in another few years.

"Can you tell me something?" Dorothy said into the phone.

"Yes?" The paper shuffling stopped.

"The other two people, the cars I hit, are you sure they're okay?"

"Actually, we represent the Mercedes. I'm not at liberty to say how the driver is feeling today." Shuffle, shuffle. "The third car was totaled."

"Wow. Really?"

"Yes, I'm afraid so. Now, let's see. Can you tell me what happened?"

"What about the person driving?"

"What person?"

"In the car that was totaled. What about that person?"

"I have no report of an injury. That doesn't mean there wasn't one."

Lewis had sat down at the table to eat. He was shoveling it in with his fingers. Bite and lick. Bite and lick. Dorothy had to look away.

"I'm not feeling well," she said into the phone. "How about we talk tomorrow?"

"I don't work on Sunday."

"Then call me Monday." Dorothy hung up before the woman could complain.

The phone rang again. Dorothy ignored it.

"I have to go," she said to Lewis.

"Back to the hospital? Want me to come?"

"I'm not going to the hospital," Dorothy said. And suddenly she knew she wasn't. "I'm going to see Seth."

"No."

She picked up Michael's car keys and her purse from the floor behind the front door where she had left it that morning.

Lewis stood up. The frosting ringed his mouth, clumped in the corners. There was a brown smear of spice cake, or maybe chocolate, on his cheek.

"Don't do that."

"I have to see him."

"Dorothy, please."

Lewis took a step toward her. She stepped away. He fell on his knees. She had never seen him on his knees before.

"Don't go." There were tears in his eyes. "Don't go to him. I love you. I can't live without you. If you leave me, I'll die."

"No, you won't." She wanted to wipe his face. "What is the matter with you, Lewis? Why are you acting this way?" He was the one in charge. He was the one who was definite and never sentimental. He carried his emotions tucked away in his wallet. She had never seen him cry.

He sobbed. She was sorry for him, but she didn't think she really had anything to do with it.

"What is it that you want?" he cried. "Tell me what you want."

She looked at him, on his knees, on the floor, with tears on the face she couldn't seem to recognize.

"I love you!" he begged. "What more do you need?"

She backed toward the door.

"I have to go. I have to."

"To Seth?"

"I have to."

"If you do that, don't come back."

That was the Lewis she knew. She smiled at him.

"Do you hear me? Don't come back!"

Let him eat cake, Dorothy thought as she closed the front door behind her.

chapter thirty-three

eo was asleep on the small blue sofa in Jenny's apartment. The Bible had fallen from his hands onto the floor. He had dozed off reading the words of Isaac to his son, "Bring me savory food, such as I love, that I might eat and bless you before I die." Isaac, whose father had wanted to kill him, had lived to be an old man, a father himself, asking his sons for favors.

His stomach gurgled and bumped. Still asleep, Leo turned on his side, pulled his knees up. The upholstery was rough under his cheek. In his dreams he could smell a woman's perfume, buried in the couch fibers.

A knock woke him.

Knock. Knock.

He sat up. The blank white apartment wall scared him. A hospital, a prison. Where was he?

Knock again. A woman's voice, "Jenny?"

The raincoat in Los Angeles, the tacky plastic shoes. The neighbor had arrived, just as Leo had known she would.

"Hold your horses," he called.

He put his T-shirt on. He walked over to the door and undid the locks, hoping his breath smelled as bad as it tasted. Hoping he looked terrible enough to scare her away.

She held a paper plate covered in aluminum foil in her hands.

"Hello," she said, looking around him, trying to see down the hall into the rest of the apartment. "Remember me?"

"Of course."

Leo exhaled in her direction. She winced but stepped closer to him. "May I come in?"

"Jenny's sleeping," he said. "She's not feeling well."

"Oh, my." The woman's mouth pouted in concern, but her eyes were blinking, darting here and there, furtively inquisitive. She expected the worst and couldn't wait to get it.

"Sorry I can't ask you in," Leo said. "Jenny needs her sleep."

"Maybe she could tell me what to get her? I could run out to the pharmacy."

Leo smelled the woman's musty spinster smell. A cat on her lap. A dirty litter box. No one knew if she changed her underwear.

"Do you live alone?"

"Why?" Her eyes narrowed. Her mouth flattened into a hard lip-less line.

"These are such small apartments." Leo said. "I mean, for two people."

"I have Freddy," she said.

Leo frowned.

"My cat."

He nodded, pleased with himself.

She tried to step around him. He blocked her path. "Here, now," she said. "Just let me in."

"I said, no."

"I'll just put the cookies down and leave."

"No."

"I'd like to see Jenny."

"She's not here."

"I thought you said she was sleeping."

"Right. I did. I meant, she's here, but she's not here. She's in dreamland."

"Jenny?" the old woman called. "Jenny?"

"Shut up." He didn't want the other neighbors to hear her.

"Jenny? It's me, Marion." She was yelling now. "Jenny!"

"Shut the fuck up."

"Don't you talk to me that way."

He grabbed her arm. The flesh was soft, without muscle. He pulled her into the apartment, closed the door behind her with his foot.

"Let go of me!" she screeched.

He slammed her up against the wall. Her head shook, her feeble neck wobbled.

"Shut up," he said. "You have to be quiet."

She looked at him. He let her go. She opened her mouth and screamed, high-pitched, earsplitting. She rocked her head back and forth against the wall and shrieked.

Leo grabbed her and threw her against the door. She bounced back into his hands. He threw her again, harder, pushing her head into the metal door with the three "Security King" locks. Guaranteed to keep you safe. Her head hit lock number one, scraped against lock number two as she slid to the floor. There was blood in a streak on the door.

"Be quiet," he said.

Finally. She lay without a sound. He took a step toward her and crunched something beneath his sneaker. One of her cookies. Chocolate chip. His favorite. Homemade. Ruined, scattered in the hallway because she wouldn't shut up.

He nudged her with his foot. "Go home. Get up and go home."

The woman did not move.

Leo went to the kitchen. He filled the only glass with water. He took it back to her.

"Here. I brought you some water."

He knelt beside her. "Hey," he said. "Listen. I'm sorry, but—"

Gingerly, he cupped one hand under her chin and lifted her head. Her eyes stared straight at him, not angry, not suspicious, only empty. He let go. Her head fell. He heard a bone crack. He stood up quickly, spilling the water on her. She was dead. She was really dead.

Stupid woman. Idiot. He had only pushed her. He had not hit her hard at all.

There were cookies to sweep up and blood on the door and another body that would swell and distort and start to stink. He put his hands under her arms and tried to lift her. She was heavier than she looked. Her pouchy stretched stomach, her sagging thighs. He couldn't think of it. He dragged her down the hall and across the living room. He held her propped against his leg as he let go with one hand to open the bedroom door. The buzzing of flies. He imagined flies and maggots, but it was quiet in the bedroom. He didn't look at Jenny as he pulled the old woman up next to her. He had to step on the mattress. He had to walk backwards across the blanket, dragging the old woman. He felt Jenny's body roll toward his leg. He flung the old woman back and jumped from the bed. He ran from the room, slamming the bedroom door behind him.

chapter thirty-four

It was a regular shift. Slow. Hayden and I helped a guy change a tire, gave directions to a tourist, stopped a gardener in a pickup truck with a broken taillight. Beverly Hills was beautiful. And ridiculous. Every enormous house had a front lawn of lush, well-watered grass trimmed to perfection. Never mind that Beverly Hills is naturally a desert. To hell with what's natural. A tour bus went by. I saw the guide pointing out the houses of the stars. I saw the tourists with their cameras clicking. I'd seen it a hundred times, a million times. I turned my back on them. They were all so excited to be here. I looked at my watch. I figured Dorothy was married. She was dancing with her new husband. She wasn't drinking anything, not even champagne, because her head still hurt. She was looking at him, Lewis Lapinsky, and the rest of her life didn't scare her. Not now. Not anymore.

It was last Thanksgiving and I was sitting in the airport. I was on my way to visit my mom for the holiday. I hadn't seen her or my sister for more than two years. I grew up with my dad in San Diego until he died, and then I lived with my uncle in Los Angeles. My mom and sister live in Denver. Linda wasn't coming with me. She said she wanted to go to a spa in Phoenix with her sister. Of course, now I know why. I know why whenever I called the hotel, she was "having a treatment."

That day in the airport, I had a magazine open in my lap, but I was really just looking out the window, looking around, watching the other passengers. I'm a nervous flier. Every time I get on a plane, I wonder, are these the people I'm going to die with?

So I was sitting there, uncomfortable as hell in those plastic chairs, and the woman next to me picked up her cell phone. I couldn't help but overhear her. She spoke loudly into her cell phone, as if she was home or in her office, not some public place. She called a colleague to tell her she wouldn't be at some meeting. She was going to Denver for a funeral. Her niece had killed herself. Class valedictorian, partial scholarship to Yale, but she dropped out and flew home the first of November. Her mom was completely surprised. She had taken the girl to a psychiatrist who prescribed an antidepressant, but the mom didn't know if she had been taking it or not. The day after her nineteenth birthday, she slit her wrists and bled to death in her bed. Her little brother found her.

She must have known how to do it. It's not easy to slit your wrists and actually die. The woman in the airport talking on her cell phone was angry with her sister-in-law. Why didn't she do more? she kept saying. Why didn't she stop her? I had to get up and walk away to keep from yelling at her. It's not her fault, I wanted to shout. Sometimes you do everything you can and it's not enough. Sometimes you can be right there, just downstairs, just pouring yourself a glass of milk, and you can't stop them. Maybe your presence only eggs them on. Maybe they need to accomplish something, despite you. Or maybe looking at you just makes them feel so goddamn bad.

In Denver, I did some asking. I got a copy of the note. It must've killed that mom to read it.

Note #206 11/18/02

To Whom It May Concern:
  Give my clothes to Goodwill.
  Give my books to the library.
  Give my shoes to the dog.

                              Belinda Wainwright

This is what happened to me. I was downstairs, having a glass of milk. I was sixteen years old. My homework was finished. I was thinking about turning on the television. I heard a thumping from upstairs, from my dad's room. I heard the bed slide across the floor and the dresser fall over and the glass break when the lamp went down. I ran up there. His door was locked, but I heard him moaning inside. I was strong even then. I broke the door down. He was on the floor. He was convulsing. The pain must have been something. His body was contorted. The furniture was overturned. He couldn't help it. He had flailed, writhed, desperate to alleviate some of the agony. There was vomit and shit and his skin had turned a terrible color.

"Dad?" I screamed. "Dad!"

I ran back downstairs and called 9-1-1. I know now that the amount of poison he ingested was remarkable. He was an amazing man to keep swallowing it, even after vomiting the first time. I know now there was nothing I could have done. Nothing more than what I did. He wanted to die so badly. He was such a tough guy. And of course he didn't leave a note, no message at all, not one word left behind.

Hayden put on the siren and we sped after a guy who had run a red light. I thought about my dad and Dorothy and what I would say to her if I wrote the note to her. I decided I had nothing to say except "Good luck."

chapter thirty-five

Madelyn was standing at her kitchen sink when Mitch and the kids came home. She had walked in the door five minutes before they did, without milk. She had not wrapped the birthday present or made lunch. She stood exactly where she had been standing when they left in the morning. She stared out the window at the same pile of dog poop under the same rusty swing set on the same dead grass. There were the same breakfast dishes in the sink.

"We won!" Morgan crowed.

"How about you, Mason?"

Her son trudged through the kitchen and out the back door without saying anything. She could see the tracks of sweat in the dirt on his face.

"They lost," Mitch said. "Guess you could tell."

She felt guilty, a dry taste in the back of her throat, a clench in her chest. Even though it wasn't rational, his loss felt like her fault. If she had been there at his game instead of where she was, instead of naked with Steve, the Brentwood Pumas might have won.

"We came home between games," Mitch said. "I saw your note. I called the chiropractor; they said you never came in."

Her heart raced. "It was crowded," she said, thinking hard,

thinking fast. "Honestly, to sit on those waiting room chairs for an hour—it'd be worse for your back than not going at all." She tried to laugh. "Maybe that's the idea. Maybe they plan it that way."

"So where'd you go?"

"I went to a bookstore. You know the one over there. I browsed. I saw that book on photography that I want. But I didn't get it. I came home and napped."

Mitch had stopped listening after she mentioned the bookstore. "I have to shower," he said as he walked out of the room.

Once you started lying, she realized, it was hard to stop. You told the first lie, and others had to follow. She wanted to tell Mitch the truth. She wanted to confide in him, lie on the bed while he dressed and tell him all about it. She had an epiphany today, a whole sensual, sexual world had opened to her, now, in her forties, when she was sure it was too late. Mitch should be happy for her. But he hadn't been her friend for a long time. Since Mason had been born, and then Morgan, since he had made so much money and become such an important person, they were husband and wife, a family, but nothing more.

She stood at the kitchen sink and remembered Steve's hands on her face as she said good-bye. His blue eyes brilliant with tears. I love you, she said. Don't think I'm saying that just because we had sex. I really do.

The clock above the stove told her she had left him less than an hour ago. It felt like they had been apart for years. It felt like the morning had never happened.

Driving home in her bruised black car, she had slipped two fingers inside her underpants and brought the smell of him to her nose. Earthy and pungent, the garden he grew flowed from him. She had reveled in her dampness. She knew, finally she knew what everybody was talking about.

"Mom," Morgan said, stretching the one-syllable word into three.

"What? What?"

"You haven't been listening to a word I've said."

"Sorry."

She walked to the kitchen table. She sat down in one of the four antique chairs she had bought for her furniture-restoration class. She had refinished one and gotten bored and dropped out and hired her teacher to do the other three. She leaned her chin on her hands.

"You don't feel well." Morgan put her arm around her mother's shoulders. "Don't move. I'll do everything."

Madelyn did not want to move. She was lost somewhere inside her own head, not really home with her husband and her children; obviously, painfully, not with Steve. She went over the morning and over it again. She thought of his hand on the table and on her skin. She sat watching Morgan, but not seeing; listening, but not hearing. She was transparent, a Madelyn ghost haunting her own life.

Morgan was opening cabinets and banging pots and pans, fussing with measuring cups and two large mixing bowls. She dropped a ceramic bowl. It clunked against the hardwood floor but didn't break. Madelyn looked at her daughter.

"What are you doing?"

"I said, I'd do it." Morgan stood with one hip out, the teenager she would become in her exasperated expression.

"Do what?"

"I'm making crepes for lunch. I told you."

What a mess. But Madelyn was in no position to complain, to deny her daughter anything she wanted. I love you, she said. But was it just the sex? She remembered her orgasm, his fingers, his hand, and the way he looked into her eyes as she exploded. She shuddered and squeezed her legs together. She should go out and talk to Mason. He was unhappy. She could hear him shooting hoops in the backyard, the drumming of the basketball as he dribbled, the crash and rattle against the backboard when he took a shot. She heard his groan and the admonishment he gave himself, "You suck." Her heart broke for him, but she didn't move. It was her fault. All of it.

Her life had been like a science-class frog, post-dissection, splayed open, pinned back on the board, even her organs no longer her own. Everything in her was removed, examined, then discarded or put back wrong. She had been alive when it started, but she had died on that board, her heartbeat slowing as Mitch and then the children had watched. Exposed, she had been left to rot, the end of her life closer than the beginning. She had had her time. She had her marriage, her kids, her house and the house in the country, too. What more was there to wait for? Her daughter's wedding? Her son's acceptance to medical school? The end.

Her mother and father died together four years ago. They were driving home from a Christmas party back in Ohio, where she was from. The roads were icy. It was cold and windy. Her dad had just been diagnosed with colon cancer. They slipped, slid, and sailed off the bridge. They landed in the water. The river was frozen, but not strong enough to catch them. The rescue team found them holding hands. Their fingers had to be broken to get them apart, to put them in separate caskets.

Four years ago. Just lately Madelyn would realize she had forgotten something: if her dad liked sugar in his coffee, if her mother—or was it Mitch's mother—beat eggs with a fork, never a wire whisk. Small things, ridiculous things, but she hated to not remember. Each time it happened, she felt them leave her a little more, take two steps farther away. And if they were farther from her, it meant she was closer to her own departure. After the funeral, she had cleaned out the closets and drawers in her parents' house, the house she grew up in. Mitch stayed in California with the kids. She had not cried. She had sorted and bagged without sentiment. If these items were all it came down to, what was the point of any of it? She had not kept anything that was her mother's. She had let it all go. In these last four years, Mitch had wanted a new dining room table and chairs, an enormous television. He had hired a contractor to enlarge their bathroom, put in a hot tub. She never said no, but it made Mitch angry that she wasn't excited.

Madelyn got up from the kitchen table and went to the bathroom to pee. She let out a soft fart as she sat down, a new trait, her body expelling an old person's odor. She looked at her hand reaching for the toilet paper and saw her mother's hand, the prominent veins, the skin between her thumb and forefinger loose and cross-stitched with tiny wrinkles. She had lain naked next to Steve, blanketed only in sunlight, while he traced her breasts, her hips, her outline. Memorizing, he said. She flushed the toilet and shuddered. She washed her hands and avoided her reflection in the mirror above the sink.

In the backyard, Mason slumped against the wall of the house. She walked up to him and he let the basketball fall from his fingers. It rolled off the cement pad, into the dead grass and under the swing set. Into the dog poop, Madelyn thought, but she didn't say anything. She put her arm around her son and was surprised, as always, at his height. He grew and grew. He never stopped. Sometimes she looked at his long legs and changing face and was exhausted by the churning and stretching of his bones and muscles. Six months ago, she could put her chin on the top of his head. Now he bumped her nose with his forehead. And it was all a progression in one direction, to death. You spent so much effort growing up and then the grass grew over you.

"Our team sucks," Mason said.

"I'm sorry."

Maybe she should have argued, denied it, reminded him about the game they won last week. Instead she pulled him to her, hugged him hard, smelled in his sweaty hair a lingering spoor of the baby he had been. He turned to her and laid his head on her shoulder. He was too old to cry, but she knew he wanted to.

"Dad was so mad," Mason said. "He kept yelling at me."

In all the family movies, the ones every studio and even her husband had produced, the mother was always dead. The children in the film lived with distracted and ineffective and occasionally grieving dads who gave them too little supervision. The kids could get into scrapes, discover the bad guys, save the day, because no one was there to make them go to bed on time or give them a healthy dinner or pick them up after school. At the end of the movie, the father and his children—always a boy and a girl—came to an understanding. They hugged each other and usually the dad's new girlfriend, too. In the movies, kids without a mother were free.

Madelyn would be crazy to leave Mitch. She would hate it if Morgan and Mason's weekends were spent with Dad. She knew plenty of divorced families. She saw the ex-husband and wife circle each other at the soccer games, avoid contact except to talk about schedules and responsibilities. She had seen the way the women put on weight and the men pierced their ears or started wearing odd European shoes. She thought of how much Mitch's mother would hate her. What a relief that would be. It would be so honest to be hated, to not pretend love anymore, to acknowledge that you never got along, you never really even liked each other. Mitch's mom came to visit and Madelyn felt her toes curl inside her shoes. She accepted silently the role of serving girl, chauffeur, kitchen slave, and screamed at Mitch the moment his mother left.

Steve. His name was on her tongue, the first word she wanted to say, wanted to keep saying.

"Tell Dad, will you?" Mason was pleading into her shoulder. "Please, Mom?"

"Of course."

She didn't have to listen to know what her son had said. She'd had the same conversation with Mitch a dozen times. Don't yell at him. That's not the way to reach him.

"Mom!" Morgan was screaming in the kitchen.

Madelyn ran inside. The frying pan was lying on the kitchen floor, smoking. The crepe inside was burned black and crispy. The burner on the stove was turned up as high as it could go, the flames tall and dancing. Morgan was still screaming.

Madelyn turned off the stove. "You had the temperature too high, that's all," she said calmly.

"I asked you to help me!" Morgan squawked at her mother.

"You did not."

Mitch shouted from upstairs, "What the hell is going on down there?"

"It's okay," Madelyn called back to him.

But she heard the hard soles of his shoes clatter down the stairs. He came into the kitchen, hair wet from the shower, dressed as if for work.

"Has everybody gone crazy?" he said to Madelyn.

"We didn't have far to go, did we, Dad?" Mason said from the back door.

Madelyn laughed. Morgan and Mitch stood next to each other, hands on their hips, glaring at her. They were father-and-daughter dolls, the same face, the same superior expression. If she could just take Mason and go. Get out of here. Get the hell out of here.

She would drive her smashed car to some small town where Steve could write a book and she could walk to the library. Very first thing, she would legally change Mason's name to Jack. He'd like that. He would become Jack. Jack was a strong, solid name. Not like Mason. Or Montana. Or Scout, or Byrne, or Windlass. Yes, Windlass, some northeastern nautical term. Mason and his friends were doomed by their names from the start. How well could any child do when he was named Windlass Horowitz? She and Mitch were just as bad. It had seemed such a fun idea at the time, the "M" thing. Then why hadn't she named them Mark and Mary?

"I have to go," Mitch said.

Madelyn nodded. That was usually what he said. He turned on his heel. He walked out of the room. He closed the door. He left. He was always leaving. Early to work. Out to a dinner meeting. Late for a golf game, the health club, the office office office.

And she was always standing in the kitchen, looking at the mess and her children.

"When will you be back?" She followed him into the living room, watched as he checked his hair in the antique hall tree with the carved swirls and Victorian curlicues she used to love.

"I'll meet you at the restaurant for dinner."

"You can't come home first?"

"Madelyn, I don't know." He was annoyed.

She watched him put his cellular phone in his shirt pocket, hook the earpiece to his ear, clip the microphone next to the first button on his shirt.

He softened. "I'll call you later." He put his hand on her shoulder and kissed her cheek. "I'm glad you're feeling better."

She hadn't said that she was.

Then he looked her up and down. "Why are you wearing that dress?" he asked.

She shrugged.

"Don't wear it to dinner, okay?"

He was out the door before she could speak. He was gone and the door closed behind him before she could tell him she loved this dress, tell him how easy it had been to remove, tell him to go fuck himself.

"I'm hungry," Mason said.

Something crashed in the kitchen.

Madelyn didn't think they'd be having crepes for lunch. There was tuna fish, she thought, or maybe turkey if it hadn't gone bad. She had to wrap that birthday present. The laundry was still wrinkling in the dryer. She had to pack overnight bags and deposit her kids at their respective parties. She had to shower and do her hair. She had to be at Celadon, the restaurant, by herself, by 7:30.

Oh. And she had to change her dress.

"One phone call," she said to Mason. "Then I'll make lunch."

She took the stairs two at a time. She went into her calm blue bedroom and picked up the phone. She dialed Steve. Her heart beat faster and faster, imagining the worst. He was bothered by her, unhappy she had called, he didn't know who she was, there were women with him.

"Hello?" he said and she gasped.

He sounded like him. His voice made her body answer.

"Hi." She almost whispered.

Silence. Then he said, "How are you?"

"I'm fine." But she wasn't. "I was wondering, I mean, well, how are you?"

"Everything all right? You got home in time?"

She loved that he didn't answer her. That he was more concerned about her than telling her how he felt.

"Everything's fine."

Another silence.

"My house smells like you," he said.

"I'm sorry."

"I'm not. Not at all. What are you doing tonight?"

"Going out to dinner with some of Mitch's partners from work."

"Where?"

"Celadon."

"Good. I've been there."

"Why?"

"I just want to know where you are. I want to imagine you eating, drinking, laughing. I'm jealous."

"Don't be." She wanted to laugh. She was the only first wife in the group. The two other women were definite trophies; Mitch's partners wore them proudly like wreaths of laurel. No one noticed her.

"What will you wear?" Steve asked.

What she always wore. "Black pants. Black shoes. Black sweater."

"Are you in mourning?"

"For you," she said. "Because you're not with me."

"I'm here."

"I wish I was."

"Mom!" Morgan was screaming again. "Mom! I need your help. Right now!"

"I have to go," Madelyn said. "Good-bye."

"Wait—"

"I can't."

And she hung up. She hurried down the stairs to her children waiting at the bottom, two baby birds with their mouths open, needing, needing, needing only her.

chapter thirty-six

Leo stood at the pay phone inside the diner where he'd had breakfast. Just in case Tess happened in, he wanted to be here. Problem was, the phone was down a little hall by the bathrooms. He couldn't see the front. If she came in and picked up an order to go, he could miss her.

He would have to ask the insurance person to hold on, he decided, while he stepped out of the hall to check the front counter.

He was pissed off with himself. He should have just spent the day here. He didn't need to go check on his car. He didn't need to go home and see that stupid neighbor. Stupid dead neighbor.

What a goddamn idiot he was. He patted his pocket. The little gun pressed against his thigh. He couldn't just leave it at Jenny's.

"Midway Insurance," a man answered. "This is Wallace. How may I help you?"

Leo had followed Gus's instructions and called the 800 number on his insurance card. The phone spit back his thirty-five cents. That was good.

"Hi," Leo said. "Uh, I was in an accident last night? And I can't drive my car anymore." He waited, but the man didn't say anything. "It wasn't my fault," Leo added quickly.

"Your name please."

"Leo Martinez."

"Spell the last name for me."

"M-a-r-t-i-n-e-z."

"Is your address 1408 Perry Circle, Gaithersburg, Maryland?"

"I'm in L.A., visiting. I mean, that's where the accident was. Is that a problem?"

"Mr. Martinez, your policy has expired."

"What?"

"It expired February sixteenth."

"But I had no idea."

"We sent you more than one notice."

"I was in L.A. I didn't get any notice."

"The grace period has expired."

"I didn't know."

"I'm sorry, sir."

"Can I pay you now?" Leo couldn't remember how much his insurance payments were, but he probably had enough.

"We can reinstate you, yes."

"Then you'll fix my car."

"Well. No. The accident you had last night is still not covered. That was an uninsured accident. You didn't have insurance when you had the accident."

"I didn't have an accident. I mean, it was her fault."

"That'll be $124.69 to reinstate your insurance. I'll just need some new information. You can mail the check, or money order, to Midway Insurance, 2300 Rockville Pike—"

"Wait!"

"Yes, sir? Was I speaking too fast?"

"What about my car?"

"You'll have to take that up with the guilty party's insurance company."

"I don't know the guilty party."

"I'm sorry, sir. Check with the police."

Leo thought of Jenny, and the old lady, waiting, swelling, back at the apartment.

"Mr. Martinez? Would you like to reinstate that policy now?"

"No!" Leo shouted. "I don't have a goddamn car anymore!"

Leo slammed the receiver down. A busboy, Latino, hair restrained in a thick black net, peeked around the corner and down the hall.

"What are you looking at?" Leo said.

Shit. How was he supposed to get his car fixed now? And he'd been on the phone for almost twenty minutes without checking the front once. Tess could have come and gone. Leo picked up the receiver and banged it into the wall a couple of times, and a couple more, just to make himself feel better. He was surprised to see the mouthpiece-sized dent in the plaster. The phone was harder than he thought.

The busboy again appeared around the corner. Another guy, a cook maybe in white pants and a dirty apron, a bigger guy, came and stood behind him. Leo tried to hide the crumbling wallboard with his shoulder. The first busboy crossed his arms, looked Leo up and down. Leo walked toward them, nonchalant, trying to stay between them and the hole in the wall.

"You eeet?" the little guy asked.

"What?" Leo hated the way these stupid Mexicans talked.

"You gonna eeet?" He mimed a fork going to his mouth.

"Oh. Just a cup of coffee."

"No."

"What?"

"You go."

The bigger guy said something in Spanish. He blabbered at Leo as if he should understand.

"Speak English," Leo said, "You're in America. Speak the goddamn language."

"Bye-bye," the big guy said.

He took Leo by the shoulder. Leo shrugged away. The little one grabbed Leo's other arm. Leo wiggled free and came back swinging.

His first punch caught the short guy in the cheek and sent him back on his butt. His second punch hit the big guy in the shoulder. The big guy grunted but didn't fall. He lunged for Leo. Leo danced away. They had to let him stay. He had to wait for Tess. He couldn't go back to that apartment. Star charts and maggots. The smaller guy stood up and seized Leo around the waist. The big guy wound up to let him have it. Not fair, Leo thought, two against one, as the fist came toward him. He turned his head and it caught him in the ear.

"Okay, okay!" he shouted. "You win."

He pretended to surrender. He stopped struggling and let his face fall as if he was sorry, or afraid.

The boys backed off, nodding at each other.

Leo jumped forward and hit each of them again, on target this time, as hard as he could. One. Two. He sucker-punched them, just as they deserved. The little one went down. The big one rolled away, holding his eye, and ran down the hall shouting something in Spanish. Reinforcements, Leo thought, the police.

Leo looked around. There had to be a back door.

There wasn't. Maybe he could run out the front while the guy was screaming.

Leo darted down the hall, out and across to the front door and smack into two policemen just entering.

"Get him!" The little busboy was up.

Leo tried to dodge the cops and get out, but they were fast and grabbed him. He couldn't hit a cop. Even in his rage, he knew it was not good to hit a cop. He let himself go limp. The policeman hit him anyway, in the stomach. As he doubled over, his eyes going blurry, he saw the hostess, the same unwashed woman from this morning, taking an order over the phone. She smiled and nodded into the phone, ignoring him collapsing to the floor, the busboy shouting, the cops voices deep and serious. The hostess said something into the phone, something that looked like "Thanks, Tess."

Leo watched her hang up the phone. Wait, he wanted to say, but he couldn't get his breath. He stretched out a hand, tried to crawl to the hostess station.

"Stand back," one of the cops said to the busboy.

"He coulda' busted my nose!" The busboy's face was red, the tendons on his neck distorted. "I'm an actor, man. My face is my livelihood."

Leo laughed. The larger cook snuck in around the cops and kicked him hard in the head. The pain exploded. The constellation Leo burst in front of him, and then the sky was black.

chapter thirty-seven

Dorothy felt the old excited flutter in her stomach. Her hands tapped the steering wheel in anticipation. Her foot stepped harder on the gas. Faster, faster. Saturday afternoon. Please let him be home. As long as she had been with Seth, going to see him, calling him on the phone, even thinking about him had produced this queasy bumpy feeling. She never had this feeling with Lewis. The excitement, the panic, was always missing.

Sick to her stomach. Eyes not working very well. Unwashed with dirty hair. She realized there was a new power in her. And if she had this ability suddenly, if men were attracted to her right now as never before, she knew how to use it. Seth would come back to her. Seth would love her again and more than ever. He would need her desperately, as she had loved him. She would never bathe again if that's what it took. She would bang her head and let her eyes go blind; she would have a million car accidents if it would keep him interested.

Seth, she thought, Seth. She let herself remember him, all of him, let him bubble to her surface. She had kept him under the lid for so long. She felt his steam rising from her knees, through her stomach, up into her throat. The car could not go fast enough.

His house was hidden behind a tall wooden fence. It ran along a ridge, overlooking the dip into Hollywood. On the north there was a huge Spanish-style house with a pool. To the south, a Cape Cod, incongruous among the bougainvillea and bird-of-paradise. Dorothy pulled in behind Seth's old Volvo wagon. Her head hurt. Her hands felt weak. She had barely the strength to take the key out of the ignition. She decided to leave it in the car. It was Michael's car, anyway.

She didn't ring the bell. She knew where the key was hidden in the dying cactus by the door. It had been dying two years ago when she last saw it. It was not dead yet.

She opened the gate to the oasis inside, a verdant jungle of plants. Lavish, growing. His studio sat down a little hill to the right, behind a cluster of bamboo. The house, small and delicate like a dollhouse, but falling apart, was beyond a path and a murky pond. She could smell the earth and the stagnant water, the moldy odor of decomposing leaves.

She did not call out. She crept, not sneaking, but not wanting to be seen, along the path. She crouched behind an enormous rhododendron bush. The front door was open. She could see in. She could see Seth reading. He was sprawled on the sofa, facing the door with his stocking feet on the coffee table and a beer sweating next to him. He looked terrible. He was pale. He had one of his eye infections. She could see the eye dripping. She watched him dab at it with his knuckle. He had put on weight. His hair was more gray than she remembered and he needed a haircut. He looked better than he ever had.

Her foot hit a rock and it clunked beneath her. Seth did not look up. He was absorbed. She had imagined him in the kitchen. She had imagined him sleeping. She had imagined him knowing somehow that she was coming. She had not thought of him reading.

Seth had always been a big reader. In bed, at night, he would read for hours. She would be waiting, but when he finally rolled in her direction it was to talk.

"Listen to this," he said with the book in his hand.

The pleasure on his face, the excitement the words created, made her want to curl away onto her side, put her back to him. She knew it was ridiculous of her to be jealous of the book he was reading, but she was. She was jealous that he thought of his book during the day and looked forward to returning to it at night. He held it like a lover, opening it with anticipation, one hand on the spine, the other stroking the page, tracing the words with his fingertips as his eyes caressed them, then gently lifting and turning to the next page. She resented the way he pursued a book, layer by layer, until all that had been offered was exposed. And if he went to sleep while reading, if the book fell open on his chest, she hated it even more. His sparse, wiry chest hairs against the paper, the submissive book waiting as long as it took for him to wake and continue. She could never be so patient. But if she moved the book, he woke up and went back to reading.

"Isn't that remarkable?" he would ask. "What beautiful language."

"Yes," she always replied. "Beautiful."

Remarkable. Whatever he said. She read what he told her to read. She sat quietly in his house on Sunday afternoons with a book dutifully open in her lap when really she wanted his head in that spot between her thighs, her hands in his hair, her skin and smell and taste translated into words he never said.

Dorothy stepped out from behind the bush. She walked toward the open door.

Seth looked up over his book. He did not smile or seem particularly surprised. He just looked at her. He looked into her eyes. She looked back.

Finally he gave a small smile and said, "Dottie."

Why was he the only one to call her that? Why did it make her cry? "Seth."

She stopped in the doorway, half in, half out of his house. Some new canvases leaned against one wall. There was a new stain on his blue rug. Everything else was the same and Dorothy took a deep breath, inhaling the smell of paint and turpentine, of coffee and cinnamon. The way his house always smelled. The way she smelled when she left.

Seth marked his place with a scrap of paper and closed his book. He put it on the couch next to him, took his feet off the coffee table, and stood up. Still looking at her. Dorothy's eyes sparked, the green and pink flashes like daggers of light. Her head throbbed more painfully, more insistently. She had to close her eyes for a moment. She tried to think of Lewis, but it was as if he had never existed. He was just a dream she had, a fantasy of making Seth jealous. I'll meet someone else. He'll want me to marry him. I'll buy a white dress. But then I'll run a red light and I'll wake up. The clock on Seth's old piano said it was past wedding time. She would be married now, if she hadn't had a car accident, if her mother hadn't flipped out, if she had remembered the word for what Lewis was to her.

"You look like shit," Seth said.

Dorothy laughed.

"You look wonderful," he said. "Your hair is great."

He came to her and put his arms around her.

"You're shaking," he said.

She was. She vibrated. She tried to pull out of his embrace.

"Stop," he said. "It's okay."

His hand went up the back of her shirt, against her bare skin, over her braless back. Her trembling grew more violent.

"Shhh," he whispered. "Dot Dot Polka-dot."

Say it again, she thought. That's who I am. She quivered now because she was warm and melting, pudding left in the sun. He kissed her. He kissed her perfectly. Their mouths open, tongues touching, he tasted just the same as always.

It's working, she thought. Whatever odd appeal she seemed to have, since the accident, since not showering and not getting married, was affecting Seth, too. He kissed her face, her eyes, her neck. He couldn't stop kissing her.

"I'm so glad you're here," he breathed against her skin.

She put her hands on either side of his face as they kissed. She slid one finger into their joined mouths. He pulled her toward the couch. They had made love many times on this couch. The leather creaked and sighed as they fell on it. He loved this couch. It was like a cowboy's favorite saddle, getting softer with age, bearing the marks and scratches of so many rides.

He pulled her T-shirt off over her head as she knelt beside him. He moved his book to the coffee table as he stared at her breasts. She pulled his face to her chest and kissed his hair.

She moved, she responded, but her mind went away. She hoped she could stay with Seth tonight, but she had to get the car back to Michael. Would her father come to the hospital? She wanted to be there when he came.

"Seth," she said and extricated herself. He reached for her when she got off the couch and stepped back.

She tilted her head and looked at him. His T-shirt was still on, his jeans unzipped and open to his underwear, and his socks—those brightly clean socks—were glowing at her from the end of the couch.

"I want to go to India," she said. "I want to learn how to dread-lock my hair. I want to learn about astronomy and take a class to build my own telescope. I want to keep singing and sing more and go to lots of auditions. But first, I want to go to India."

Her father didn't want to see her. Her mother wanted only him. Michael would survive without his car. He could rent one. He would be furious with her until the police called and told him they'd found his car by the side of the road, no note, no signs of foul play. She would be far away, in India.

"Okay," Seth said. "Sounds great. Do we have to go right now?"

Dorothy smiled. "You mean it?"

"I've always wanted to go there."

Dorothy laughed. Her eyes did their glittery thing. It looked like fireworks going off around Seth's head. When she got married, there were supposed to be fireworks.

Seth reached out and took her hand. She was naked in front of him. So much quicker to remove her clothes. She shivered again, this time from the chill.

"I'll call the airlines," Seth said.

He looked warm and familiar, but not too familiar. "Don't call right now," she said.

"No?"

"Ten minutes." She stretched out next to him.

"Fifteen."

"Twenty."

chapter thirty-eight

L eo sat in the back of the police Chevy Tahoe. There was metal mesh between him and the officers up front. The doors had no handles. His face felt funny, all tight and stiff, as if he'd been crying for a long time and the tears had dried and made a mask.

"Uh-huh," he said to the officers, agreeing with them, but not listening.

They had established that he wasn't Hispanic, that he didn't speak Spanish, that he was new to L.A. from Maryland. Leo even told them he was looking for his girlfriend. As soon as he got a chance, he would show them the picture. They ate here at this diner; maybe they'd seen her. If she had come in, they would have noticed her right away.

The two cops were nice now, but they were hungry, and hunger could make people crabby. He had to watch his step with them. Tess got nicer and nicer the hungrier she was, giggly, soft somehow. She was a bitch after a big hamburger and fries, said she hated feeling full and fat. He had interrupted these officers on their way to lunch, kept them from their coffee and relaxation, from watching the waitress's legs and her orthopedic shoes.

"Where do you live?" the younger, bigger cop asked him.

"Huh?" Leo's heart began to gallop. This was the question he did not want.

"Where do you live?"

"Uh . . . I'm staying with my cousin, my friend, distant cousin, really distant, in . . . uh . . . Hollywood."

"Close to here?"

They couldn't go back there with him. He didn't want them to drive him home.

"Not really," Leo said.

The officers looked at each other and sighed. Leo was sorry they sighed. He knew they didn't want complications. They wanted a simple guy who got annoyed with the phone and took it out on the busboys. No one had said anything about the big dent in the wall.

"Where exactly?" the other officer asked. He was sitting in the passenger seat, turned sideways to look at Leo. He put a hand up against the wire screen. His fingernails were too long. There was a look in his watery eye that reminded Leo of his dad.

Leo looked at the Hollywood hills rising in the distance through the windshield.

"Up there," Leo said. "In the hills." He shrugged, rolled his eyes at himself. "I can get there, but I don't remember the address. Beachwood. That's the name of the street."

He thought of that street because he had camped there in his car a couple of nights, under the Hollywood sign, until he realized the neighborhood was too upscale. These people didn't want a guy sleeping in his car on their street. He knew the type; rich farts who gave big donations to homeless organizations, mostly so the organization would gather up the street people and keep them out of sight.

"Listen," Leo said, "I've got a picture here. Have you seen my girlfriend?"

He reached in his pocket to pull out the wrinkled picture of Tess. He reached into his back pocket, but suddenly remembered the little pistol in the front. He lay the picture facedown over the bulge on his thigh. Jesus Christ, he was an idiot.

"Wait a minute," the young cop said. "I know you. You were in that accident last night, weren't you?"

"Yeah," Leo mumbled. "Yeah."

"How are you feeling?"

"I'm okay. I'm fine."

"Whose car you driving?"

"My cousin's." His only chance was to distract them. He held the picture up against the screen. "Have you seen my girlfriend?"

The older officer shrugged. "You gotta go in and file a missing persons."

The younger guy was back on track, "Now if the guy in there wants to press charges, assault and battery, it could be a real drag for you."

"He hit me first." Leo knew that wasn't true, but it seemed the right thing to say.

"That's not what he says."

"There were two of them," Leo whined. "And you saw that guy kick me when I was down. I was on the floor and he kicked me. For what? I didn't hit him that hard."

"Okay, okay. Calm down. I don't think there's going to be any more trouble. But let's just say this place is off-limits for you."

"But I gotta wait for Tess. For my girlfriend. I told you, she sent me a postcard from here. From this restaurant." He heard his voice go up a couple of octaves. He couldn't stop the words from coming faster and faster. "I don't know where else to go. I went to every movie studio, paid to take the tour, hung out outside, showed her picture to those fat guys in the guard booths. I've been to the beach. I've looked everywhere."

"I could just take you in," the older cop said. "Then it'd be really hard to find her."

Leo shut up. It'd be okay if they would stop asking questions and let him out. He knew Jenny wasn't his fault, but it might be hard to explain. That old lady wasn't his fault, either. He had only pushed her. It wasn't his fault she bumped her head on the lock the way she did. He didn't mean to hurt her.

He put his head down, stared at the picture of Tess. She grinned back at him. The flashbulb in her face made her eyes look hard and glittery like glass. He noticed for the first time how pointy her chin was and the way her nostrils went wide and flat at the end of her nose. This was all her fucking fault. Why the hell was he looking for her? He stared at her picture. He didn't even love her anymore. She was a complete and total bitch. But he'd keep looking. And when he found her—when he found her. Leo smiled a little thinking of the things he would do to her when he found her.

He folded the picture in half, cutting her face in two, and put it in his T-shirt pocket.

"Yes, sir," he said. "I'm sorry. Guess I've been a little upset about my girlfriend."

The older officer nodded.

The younger officer gave a big exhale of relief. "Okay, then." He got out of the Tahoe and opened the back door for Leo.

"Thank you," Leo said.

The other officer got out, too, and came around to stand by his partner. They wore bulletproof vests under their navy blue shirts. They looked uncomfortably massive around the middle. The dark-haired one, the blond one. Like Beverly Hills Police Department salt and pepper shakers.

"You'll find her." The pepper shaker nodded at him.

"Yes, sir. I will."

They watched him go to his car, take the keys out of his pocket, and get in. They waited until he had left the parking lot, heading north or east, whatever it was, up into the hills.

chapter thirty-nine

I t was lunchtime and I just wanted to sit down and eat. I wanted a cheeseburger, medium rare, and some well-done french fries. I wanted rice pudding for dessert. I'd been thinking about it. I'd been listening to Hayden's weather report go on and on and thinking about what I wanted to eat. I love a big pink hamburger on a fresh toasted bun with cheddar cheese melted over the edges. I picked the place. We got there and my mouth was watering, just smelling the hot grease. I couldn't wait to sit down and order, but instead we walked into a goddamn fistfight. And in the middle of it, there he was. Leo. How weird was that, running into him again. I'd kept thinking that morning about Dorothy and her accident and her wedding. I'd been wondering why the hell I was still thinking about her. Then here was the guy who had hit her. Right in front of me.

Beverly Hills has only sixty patrol officers, so we all do everything. Traffic. Robbery. Drugs. Whatever. And I do end up seeing the same people sometimes. Like Leo. I didn't like him. Something about him wasn't right. I'd thought it the night before at the accident. He worried me. I didn't like the way he picked at the cuticle on his thumb. He was thinking too hard when he answered our questions. Maybe he had killed that girlfriend of his. Maybe he had come out here and killed her and was just waiting to get caught. A lot of perpetrators actually want to be caught. They make a stupid mistake; they leave one piece of evidence behind that links them to the crime. I'm not a detective, but I see it all the time. Some guy robs a jewelry store and instead of walking away and blending in with the foot traffic, he runs. It's like he's screaming, "Look at me. Look what I did." People want to be seen. They need to be known. It's life and death to them.

Seven miracles a day. When my father was happy, he counted miracles. There were seven miracles in every day if you just knew where to look. A parking place in front? One miracle. A pretty leaf on the sidewalk? Miracle number two. If he dropped a bottle of beer and it didn't break, that was miracle number three. On and on. He had a bell on his key chain, and he would ring it every time he experienced another miracle. Some days the bell didn't stop ringing. And on those days I was the biggest miracle in his life. When he was up, he'd stare at me and tears would be in his eyes.

"Where did you come from?" he'd ask. "You can't be my kid. You're a goddamn miracle."

But the other side of seven miracles was a hole the size of hell. He wouldn't get out of bed. He drank and drank. He cried. And he'd look at me and shake his fist and hate me for being born and then hate me even more for making him feel guilty about hating me.

My mom finally kicked him out. She'd had it. I knew it was coming. I was ready. I followed him. I begged him to let me stay with him and he did. Mom said it was okay with her. She had my little sister, who was easier. And in six months she had a new boyfriend and soon after that another baby. I think she thought it'd be good for him to have me around. I know she hoped that I would take care of him. I tried. My mother loved my father. She just couldn't live with him.

I watched Leo drive away. Maybe he really was looking for his girlfriend. If so, he loved her a hell of a lot to drive all the way to L.A. to find her.

I thought about driving to Phoenix on my day off instead of the plan I had in mind. I thought about showing up at her new front door and demanding something. What, however, I didn't know.

I could remember when I met Linda, but not what she was wearing. I knew we'd gone miniature golfing on our first date. I couldn't remember our second date, or our third. Whole hours of our wedding were lost to me. I looked at the pictures once and didn't recognize the place or the band or the food. When had we moved into the apartment? When had we bought that couch? It was all muddy in my mind. I could hardly remember our life together, but I wanted to die because I didn't have it anymore.

"I'm going to eat," I said to Hayden.

We got out of the truck and went back into the restaurant. All of a sudden, the cheeseburger didn't sound so great. Or the french fries. Or even the rice pudding. I shook my head. I couldn't eat enough food to fill me up.

I sat down in the booth across from Hayden. I took out a little pad I'd bought and a pen. I opened it up as if I had something to write down. It was just to keep Hayden from talking. He got up and went to the men's room. I ran my hands over the Formica table and felt how smooth and cool it was. I touched the electrician's tape on the vinyl seat. I moved my shoes back and forth across the crusty floor. I pushed a crumpled napkin out into the aisle with my toe. I watched the pastry case rotating, displaying coconut cake, apple pie, and my rice pudding in a tall parfait glass, one after the other, around and around.

I looked down at the pad of paper. The lines were pale blue, as always. Who decided to make the lines on paper blue? I hadn't had any thoughts about my note, the note I was going to write. I just kept thinking about some of my favorites and the people who wrote them.

Note #147 05/13/01

Dear Lucy,

Don't think this is your fault. My life and my death are not your problem.

You tried to help me. When you told me to grow up and get a life you were right. You tried and I thank you for that.

You've been the best friend you could be.

You are the only thing I will miss from this world. Even when you snubbed me, or said mean things, I still liked you. Tell the other girls I liked them too. But not as much as you.

As I said before, this is not your fault.

I chose your room to die in because I know you will understand.

May you always have flowers and sunshine,

Beth

chapter forty

Madelyn made tuna-fish sandwiches. Morgan liked hers with pickles. Mason without. She shook the last broken potato chips out of the bag into a bowl. The night before last, the night before her accident, the night before she called Steve and everything changed, she had sat on the couch watching television and eating chips one after the other until the whole bag was almost gone. Mitch had been working late again. The kids were asleep. And she had nothing to do. Steve had not been real then. She had not thought to call him. He called her, but he was just a voice on the phone, the light in her mornings, not something she could touch.

She cut up an apple, arranged the slices on the two plates like fans. Years ago she had shown her children the star inside an apple, the five-pointed shape the seeds made when you cut an apple crosswise. There was a story about the star, a folktale or a myth, that she didn't know anymore.

"Remember the apple star?" Madelyn said to Morgan as she set the plate in front of her.

"You say that every time."

Madelyn cleaned up the kitchen. Her children sat at the dining-room table and ate and bickered, their voices the dissonant sound track to her life. She wiped up crepe batter and washed bowls. She swept the burnt crumbs into the dustpan. She went to the basement and emptied the wrinkled clothes from the dryer into a laundry basket. Her head had stopped hurting. Her back, too. At Steve's house it had all gone away, stopped hurting, felt fine. She filled the washing machine with a white load and turned it on. The washing sound was so comforting, churning and working, the hot sudsy water cleaning and cleaning. She leaned her head on her arms on the top of the vibrating machine. The enameled metal was cool against her flushed face.

If Mitch died, she would be free, without divorce, without the lawyers and the papers and the hate. Mitch drove too fast. He drank at lunch. Anything could happen. The day would come when there would be no more of his laundry to wash. Not another sock, not a wadded-up handkerchief under the bed. He would all be washed and put away. She had thought so often about her own death, about suicide being her release. There were other ways, ways to stay alive.

"Mo-o-om." Morgan again. Morgan as always. Morgan called down the stairs, "We have to go. I'm gonna be late."

The present wasn't wrapped. Mason was still in his soccer uniform. The lunch dishes were on the table, apple slices hardly touched, crusts of bread discarded beside Mason's plate, all the potato chips gone.

"Mason, change your clothes, get your stuff," Madelyn said and turned to her daughter, "Did you pack your sleeping bag? Toothbrush?"

"I thought you were gonna do that."

"Go do it. Right now."

Morgan scowled at Madelyn and tossed her long hair over her shoulder. Then she turned and flounced out of the room, huffing through her nose. Madelyn watched her dark curly hair bounce away, the long spider legs, the curveless hips. So much beauty she would grow into, that she had only an inkling of as yet. The glorious Jewish hair, the ivory skin and pale Episcopalian blue eyes. Morgan knew how to put her head on the side, toss her hair back, pout after licking her full bottom lip. One day soon she would not waste her knowledge on her mother.

Once upon a time Madelyn had known these things. She had used her blond hair and her round breasts to her own advantage. She had known how to laugh low in her throat and lean toward a guy. She had known, but she had forgotten. She turned to the mess her children had left on the table. Then she smiled. Her eyes closed and she felt the fabric of her dress move against her skin. She had forgotten, but today she had been reminded. More than that. She had been given what she'd always been missing. Steve, she thought, and went to the phone to call him.

"Me again," she said.

"Hi."

"Are you busy?"

"No."

"I have to take my kids to . . . oh, never mind, here and there, I'll be near your house; can I stop by?"

"Today?"

Madelyn grimaced. "Yes. No. That's okay. I'm sorry."

"You want to stop by? Again?"

"I just thought—" Her mind worked, she looked around her kitchen, thought of him at home, in his bedroom. "I have a book I want to give you."

"Great. Sure, come by."

"Really? I mean, I can give it to you next week."

"Next week?"

"Well, if we see each other again."

"If we see each other again?" She heard him sigh. "Just come by, okay? As soon as you can."

Madelyn ran upstairs. She hollered at the kids to hurry. She washed her face, brushed her teeth, put on fresh makeup. She decided to change, but into what? She might never see him again.

She stepped out of her dress and threw it on the bed. She pulled on the black pants she would wear tonight. She got out her favorite sweater. Blue was good on her. She always got compliments. It was a little too heavy for the warm weather, but it was her favorite.

"What did you change for?" Morgan was standing in the doorway. She frowned at her mom.

"I was freezing," Madelyn said.

"Now you're sweating."

Madelyn put on perfume. She found her stylish black shoes, the ones even Morgan liked.

"Come on!" she called to her kids as she clumped down the stairs.

Mason, in shorts and an enormous T-shirt, stood at the top of the stairs. "I'm not sure," he said.

"What?" Madelyn looked up at him. His hair needed washing. He should have taken a shower.

"I don't think I want to spend the night at Montana's."

"Everybody's spending the night. It's a slumber party."

Other kids went anywhere, sleep-away camp, friends' houses, trips to Catalina and Idlewild. Mason refused to sleep anywhere but his own bed.

"You won't do any sleeping anyway." Madelyn smiled at him. "You know you'll be up all night."

"But—"

Of course when both kids were away for the night, which didn't happen very often, Mitch always wanted to light candles and drink scotch together, make wild and passionate love. He asked her to scream, to wake the neighbors. She shuddered. Not tonight.

"Call my cell phone," she said. "We'll pick you up after dinner. It'll be late."

"What time?"

"Eleven."

"Maybe I'll stay."

"You can call me either way."

The sweater clung to her back and between her breasts. It was the wrong choice. She didn't have time to change. She hustled the kids to the car with all their gear. She turned the Mercedes' air conditioning on high. She was almost to Morgan's sleep-over when she remembered the book. She had no book to give him.

chapter forty-one

I t was just like Seth not to ask her what was going on, why she was there, how she had ended up back on her back on his couch.

Dorothy put her clothes on. He was in the kitchen. She heard him rummaging. She walked into the kitchen and he tossed her a bottle of water.

"Take this," he said. "Grab your purse."

"Where are we going?"

"India."

"Now?"

"Trust me," he said. "You never trust me."

"Sure I do."

He grinned. She smiled.

Her lips were sore from his kisses. Her wrists were sore from his grip. The insides of her thighs were rubbed raw. She was weak from transcendent pleasures and forgetfulness.

"Where are we going?" she asked again.

"India," he said. "I told you that."

He lit a joint, took a deep drag, passed it to her. She shook her head. He offered again. She shook her head again. He pulled her to him, kissed her openmouthed and exhaled his long toke into her lungs. All decisions abdicated. None of it was her doing.

One evening after work, a year and nine months after Seth had left her, the phone rang and she picked it up. She was half-dressed for meeting Lewis at the bar, half out of her hairdresser clothes: she wore her comfortable shoes and her black push-up bra, she had a stretchy short skirt in her hand.

"Hello?"

No response, then faintly she heard a gasp and a sharp exhale. Then many staccato breaths, huh-huh—huh, exploding into tears. A baritone, a man, was crying into her phone.

"Hello?" she said again. "Who is this?"

The sobs subsided.

"Can I help you?"

The man wailed and wept harder.

"Please," Dorothy said, "please let me help you."

The crying turned into snuffling.

"Where are you? Are you hurt? Do you need an ambulance? Who is this? Michael?" Even as she said it, Dorothy knew it wasn't her brother. "Seth? Seth, are you all right?"

The man was grunting, hiccuping, weeping uncontrollably and suddenly he laughed. He whooped with laughter and hung up.

Dorothy had stared at the phone. She was living with Lewis. She was getting married in three months. Her hands had been trembling as she put on her skirt and kicked off the shoes. She was pulling on her thigh high stockings when the phone rang again. She wanted to let it ring. She wanted to ignore it.

"Hello?" she said. "Hello?"

"Hey, babe," Lewis said. "I'm at the bar, waiting for you."

She had felt both relief and regret.

She looked at Seth as he stood at the open refrigerator, eating blueberries. She watched his familiar, fat-fingered hands put the dark berries one by one into his red mouth. His cheeks shone in the cold refrigerator light. The hand holding the green plastic basket also held the joint, between two fingers like a cigarette. He let it burn. So much abundance, conservation did not occur to him. He put the fruit away without offering her any. She hadn't eaten in a long time. His cock had been the last thing in her mouth. And before that Lewis's. She put her hand on his back, felt his warmth through his button-down shirt.

"Are you dealing?" she asked. "Are we just driving to some big score?"

"We're going to India," he said. "I'm going. If you don't want to—" He shrugged.

She let herself relax. Her headache winked at her from the distance, reminding her of its existence. One false step and she would run right into it, head-on. She took the joint from his fingers. He nodded approvingly as she took a lengthy, surrendering toke.

"Let's take your car." He kissed her hair. He breathed into her ear.

She could not remember where they were going. She had waited so long to be right here.

"What are you driving?" he asked.

"It's Michael's car."

"Perfect."

chapter forty-two

Madelyn dropped Mason off last. She walked with him up to the front door of his friend Montana's house. It was a tall, skinny, ultra modern house with huge windows. Montana's dad had designed it. Montana's mom, Phoebe, was a potter. She had a studio in the back and every year at Christmas Montana gave his teachers lumpy, arrogantly handcrafted mugs or bowls.

"Come in," Phoebe said to Madelyn. "Have a cup of chai tea."

Mason went inside and immediately disappeared up a flight of stairs, all blond wood and open risers.

"'Bye Mason!" Madelyn called. He had been so tentative about going. Now he was gone.

"I just love that sweater," Phoebe continued. "I didn't realize the temperature had dropped that much."

Phoebe wore tight capri pants and a fitted sleeveless blouse. There was an appropriate smudge of clay on one slim hip. Her hair was artfully, purposefully disarrayed.

"I can't stay," Madelyn said. "Mitch and I are going out."

She could tell that Phoebe wanted to chat, but she didn't have time. She had to get south on the 101 and it was Saturday afternoon, traffic could be bad, and then home to change and then back to the restaurant. She thought of Steve, waiting for her. Her mouth opened. Her breath came faster.

"I have six boys here," Phoebe was saying, "and I guess I'll just order a couple of pizzas. I made a salad. And a big bowl of fruit. They can't stay up that late. I rented a movie, but not too scary. PG-13. Although I find that rating deceptive. You just never know. You know Montana has blood-sugar problems; he really needs his sleep. I give him that herbal sleeping remedy. Does Mason like cucumbers?"

Madelyn was already opening the passenger door of her car and crawling across the gearshift to the driver's seat.

"Sure!" she hollered back to Phoebe.

Madelyn put the keys in the ignition, started the motor.

"What happened to your car?" Phoebe was coming down the steps.

"Car accident!" Madelyn called. She waved gaily, amiably—she hoped—and leapt away from the curb. Away.

My God, Madelyn thought, was she that boring? Were they all that deadly dull? Discussions of pizza and movie ratings. Cucumbers. But what else did they have to talk about?

Madelyn imagined another conversation, "Hi, Phoebe. No, I can't have a cup of ridiculously expensive herbal tea in one of your lop-sided, desperate attempts to have some kind of life through pottery. I need to have one more orgasm with my new lover—did I tell you he's a double amputee?—before I go to dinner with my husband and his business partners."

She had to turn around. She had missed the freeway entrance. She still had time, if she didn't screw up again. She liked to drive. She got on the freeway. Traffic was moving. She checked her face in the rearview mirror. Her eyes looked very blue. She was on her way to meet her lover, her boyfriend, her secret affair. She was having an affair. Even if it was only for this one day, she could say she was one of those women who'd had an affair.

One night at the Suicide Prevention Hot Line, she had a call from a woman who was about her age. The woman had announced it proudly, "I'm forty-one," when Madelyn answered the phone, wanting Madelyn to know she wasn't a depressed teenager, that her problems were serious. But the woman didn't sound like she had problems. Her voice had an open, airy quality. She wasn't suicidal, at least not anymore, but she had been and she wanted to tell Madelyn about it.

"I was going to kill myself," the woman said. "I was. It all seemed overwhelming. I quit eating. I was sleeping all the time. The kids were going to school in dirty clothes and with just a bag of Fritos for lunch. My husband and I were barely speaking. And I thought they all would be so much better off without me."

"How do you feel right now?" Madelyn asked.

"Fine. Now, I'm fine. But back then, I went to my doctor and asked him for some sleeping pills. He could tell I was depressed, but he wrote me a prescription anyway. I just changed the number. I wrote in an extra zero on his little slip so I'd get a lot more. The pharmacist didn't even blink an eye. I had the kids with me. I'm a mom. I bought the pills and I went right home. I put a video in for the kids, and I went upstairs to my bedroom.

"I sat down on my bed and I had this lovely moment when I first held the pills in my hand. I took them out of the pharmacy bag and I looked at the little blue plastic vial and laughed out loud. Suddenly, my death was completely my own. I could die at any time. I was free. Life could not be a prison when there was an open door waiting in my palm. Like the Bushido warriors, who consider themselves already dead, I held death inside me. So I decided not to use the pills. Not right then. I wanted to hold on to this feeling of controlling death a little longer.

"The next two weeks of life were wonderful. Nothing bothered me. I didn't care about traffic or the kids whining. I saw the beauty in everything because I recognized the world's temporal nature and I accepted it without fear. I was temporary, too."

"But what happened?" Madelyn asked.

"What do you mean?"

"After those two weeks, what happened? When was this? Why are you calling me?"

"My son got the stomach flu and I was up all night. The next morning the car broke down, and we didn't have the money to fix it. I had to get a job. I got busy and I forgot to die."

"You still could," Madelyn said, then winced. That was not what she was supposed to say.

"I'm having too much fun," the woman replied. "I like my new job. I'm having an affair."

"Oh." At that moment, it seemed to Madelyn that everyone was having an affair. Except her. Since the kids were born, she never even considered it a possibility. She never flirted with anyone or even smiled at the guy in the car next to her. She didn't think of it. How did women—married women—have affairs? Who did they meet? She knew only the fathers of her kids' friends, the rabbi, Mason's overweight soccer coach.

"Will you leave your husband?" Madelyn asked.

The woman laughed. "This is just for kicks. But it's amazing how everything improves after a good fuck."

"What are you going to do with the pills?" Madelyn asked.

"I still like having them."

"It might be dangerous for you to have them around. What about next time you get depressed?"

"Maybe. Maybe you're right. But I think that's what they're for— to keep me from getting that desperate again. I'm telling you, the freedom, the power I felt just holding them in my hand. I wanted to tell you guys to suggest it to people who call. People who are suicidal. Tell them to hold on to the pills, or the gun, or the rope for a while. Feel that. Maybe that's all it will take."

"That's an interesting theory," Madelyn said.

"It worked for me. I just wanted you to know."

There was a sound in the background, a child's voice, a boy, calling, then laughing.

"I have to go," the woman said. "Thanks."

"No," Madelyn replied, "thank you. Please call us anytime."

The next day, Madelyn called her doctor to make an appointment. She told the receptionist she hadn't been sleeping. But then she canceled. She was too embarrassed. She pulled up in front of Steve's house. She had butterflies in her stomach, but vampire bats in her mind. This could go nowhere. He didn't care for her. She was crazy to jeopardize what she had. She had to go in. She needed his hands on her body. Did he think she would live with him in this tiny house in this bad neighborhood? She could just imagine the look on Mason's face as she moved out. She could see Morgan's smug disgust with her trampy mother. Mitch would give her nothing. Steve would get tired of her. She would be on the street, a homeless crazy woman, lurking outside her children's private school, desperate for a glimpse of them.

He opened the door before she got to it. She saw him and her black thoughts flew away. She hurried up the steps to him. Then she stood there in front of him, looking down. The chrome on his wheelchair shone in the afternoon sun. It was awkward that they couldn't really hug. She bent and put an arm around his neck, kissed his cheek.

He held her face so he could kiss her lips. With his other hand he wheeled backwards into the house. She followed bent over, lips on his. She giggled.

"I'm so glad you came back," he said.

"I don't have long," she said.

"Dinner with the partners."

"I just wanted to make sure you really exist."

"Without you, I'm an ephemera. I materialize only for you."

"You're an angel."

"I'm in heaven."

They didn't make it to the bed, but stopped at his couch. It was wonderful. Again. Amazing that it worked so well a third time. She'd been given more orgasms in a day than she had in the last twelve years combined. He didn't completely unwrap his stumps. She never took off her sweater. He stayed sitting up on the couch. She straddled his lap and looked out the window at the empty street, the children gone, no cars going by, no one in the world but them.

chapter forty-three

Leo had read an article by a doctor, which said the body was a vessel to hold your past. He believed it. He believed that the sorrows and the joys were buried deep in muscle and tissue. He believed you remembered them viscerally through release or, more often, pain. Leo sat in Jenny's car and his legs trembled. He had pulled over, almost there, just around the corner from her apartment. He couldn't drive. He couldn't go forward. He turned the car off. His back recalled his father's belt. His skin shuddered like a horse's flank, rippling away from the memory. He felt chastised, punished, stupid, eight years old. He sat in the car. He was afraid to go home. At the apartment, there were two women rotting as they lay in wait for him. Like his mother waiting. His right arm ached, remembering her grip on him. His nose wrinkled recalling his mother's old-person smell, her dirty hair, her feet slopping damply toward him, the thick yellow toenails curling toward the floor. And grabbing him, always holding him, keeping him. He cringed. Sitting in Jenny's car, he tried to shake himself free. His head hurt. His heart skittered, taking his breath away. He couldn't stop his body from remembering.

In the apartment—her apartment—were cold beers. He had bought a whole six-pack. With her money. Bought them with her money. Death money. Money for the funeral. Stop it. Think about the beers, he told himself. Two would help, three could give him peace. He started the car. He would go in. He would grab the beers. He would leave. He would sit in the car to drink them. He would park across from the restaurant, but behind that palm tree so that fucking busboy couldn't see him. He would wait for Tess.

His gut did not respond when he thought of Tess. His head throbbed and his hands clenched, but his stomach didn't hurt. For once, for the first time maybe, he didn't feel his penis tingle. She was retreating. His body was moving her. He nodded. She was sliding to another part of him, someplace tougher. His fingers twitched. He knew his hands would not betray him. Wouldn't she be surprised. Her face would light up; she would smile sweet and sexy at him, but not for long.

He turned the corner onto Jenny's street. He pulled up and parked right in front. He didn't use the parking lot behind the building. He was just going to run in.

An old man stood on the sidewalk, wearing pants too big for him, his head tilted, watching the front door. He turned, shifting his cane, and looked through the windshield at Leo in the car. The man frowned. Leo froze. The man squinted. His lip came up in a sneer. Leo's teeth began to chatter. He noticed the old man's brown sweater was buttoned wrong. The ends lay unevenly against the sagging crotch of his pants. It bothered Leo how the dark triangles hung so terribly askew. How could the guy not know his sweater was cock-eyed. Leo wanted to fix it. And while he was at it, he wanted to straighten the old man, yank his shoulders back, up and out of that question-mark curve.

The old guy was still staring at him. Leo was tired of old people. He was tired suddenly, exhausted, by everything. He got out of the car.

The old man shuffled toward him. "Do you live here?"

If the guy didn't know, then Leo assumed it was safe to lie. "Yes."

"I live next door." The old man made a small stiff gesture with his head, tipping it toward his house, offering Leo the hairs sprouting from his ear and the wrinkled wart on his temple.

Leo looked over at the little clapboard house squeezed in between this apartment building and the next. There were bars on the windows and bars on the front door and a six-foot chain-link fence all the way around. It needed paint. The yard was only dirt. Leo had assumed the house was empty, being prepped for demolition.

"There's a cat inside."

"In your house?" Leo asked.

"No. In your building. It's been crying for over an hour. It's making me crazy."

"Oh," Leo said. He knew which cat.

"I'm a screenwriter."

The old man coughed and spat on the sidewalk at Leo's feet. Leo stepped back from the yellow gelatinous blob.

"I can't concentrate. I'm under deadline." The old man squinted at Leo. "I have very important contacts."

"Maybe you know my girlfriend," Leo said. It was just something to say. He asked everyone who talked about working in the movies.

"Yeah? Who's your girlfriend? Julia Roberts? I know Julia Roberts." The old man tapped his cane with one long arthritic finger. "We worked together. One of her early pictures."

"My girlfriend's not Julia Roberts." Leo laughed. If she was, he wouldn't be planning to kill her. He laughed again, a high-pitched hoot. "Yeah, right."

"She's a doll. Like a beautiful doll. I'm writing something for her now."

"Tess Connor. That's my girlfriend. Tess Connor."

"She a big star?" the old guy asked.

"No."

"Nah. I don't know her." The old guy shook his head. "You must be an actor. Those eyes. That physique. The Hollywood execs really go for you Mexican boys."

Yeah, Leo thought, to park their cars. "I'm not Mexican," he said.

"You speak really good English."

"Fuck you," Leo said.

The old man took a faltering step back. "I don't care," he said, "I don't care what you are."

"I'm not Mexican. And fuck you."

Leo raised to the balls of his feet. He bent over the crooked, cowering man. The old guy's eyes were cloudy with fear. He gripped his cane. Leo wanted to invite him in. Introduce him to the two dead women on the bed. Take your pick. Have fun.

Instead he turned his back on the guy. He went up the three steps to the building's front door. Behind him, he could hear the old guy shuffling home. If that disgusting, deformed creature knew Julia Roberts, then he was the King of England.

At the foot of the stairs, Leo paused. He heard a low whine. Or a baby's cry. It was that fucking cat. He would have liked to leave it crying, just to drive the old guy completely wacko, but someone else in the building would complain. Animal services would come. Officials. The old lady would be missing. Leo tried her door. It was locked. Stupid paranoid bitch. She took a plate of cookies to the upstairs neighbor and locked her door. He wiggled the knob, tried to force it open.

He took a deep breath. Her keys must be upstairs. In her pocket, probably. On her body. Next to Jenny. On the bed. In her pocket. He would have to get the keys. The cat had shut up while he tried the door. As he walked away, it started up again, louder. Don't leave me. Come back. Pleading. Insistent. Leo felt his legs go weak, his arm ache. He wouldn't let the memories come. Instead he stamped his feet on the stairs, pounded the banister with his fist. Didn't anybody or anything—besides him—have the courage it took to be alone?

chapter forty-four

Madelyn straddled Steve and tried to curl her larger body against his slight chest. His arms were still around her. She pressed herself against him. She wanted to be fused to him, absorbed by him. He sighed and she inhaled his breath, tasted the essence of him. He shifted his hips a little. She was afraid she was squishing him.

She slid off his lap and sat beside him, facing him on the couch. She started to put her head on his shoulder, but he bent forward, reaching for his pants, and his arm collided with her face.

"Sorry," he said.

"Sorry," she said.

He struggled to pick up his pants. She retrieved them easily and handed them to him. He snatched them from her. He wiggled into them. She tried not to watch his stumps twitch. He was angry. She had done something wrong."Don't you have dinner plans?" he asked.

"I don't care," she said.

"Mitch cares."

"What?" His name was a shock. He didn't belong here. She didn't want Steve to even say his name.

"Your husband," Steve said belligerently. "Remember him? Isn't that his name? Mitch?"

Again it was like an assault. Madelyn closed her eyes and prayed. Mitch could be dead already. He drove away this afternoon, talking on the phone before he reached the end of the driveway. He never paid attention. He was always having near misses and close calls. She imagined the scene: she walked into her house and the phone was ringing. No, she went to the restaurant and Rusty and Scott were waiting for her, their eyes soft and sad.

"What?" she would say, "What is it?"

"It's Mitch. He's gone."

Would Steve be the first call she would make? Before Mitch's parents? What would she say? My husband's dead. Can you come over? But her house was a terrible house for Steve. There were stairs to the front porch and stairs going upstairs and even one step up into the family room off the kitchen. She imagined installing a long ramp down her curving staircase. Mason could ride his skateboard. He and Steve could have races.

"Here," Steve said. He handed her underpants to her. They were black and nylon. They felt like lead in her hand.

"Where are you going again?" he asked.

"Celadon."

"Do you know what celadon means?"

"No," she said. "I'm sorry." She didn't give the restaurant its name. She was only going there.

"Literally it means green, but originally it meant a new and tender lover. An innocent. Someone new at love."

"Like me?"

He laughed. "Not exactly."

Madelyn looked into his blue eyes. His long dark hair framed his lovely alabaster face. His skin was flawless. The sex and now his anger had put a flush of perfect rose in his cheeks. She knew she looked coarse, older, red, and used. A breeze blew through the open window and chilled the sweat on her neck. She shivered.

"Steve," she said.

He looked at her. He looked at her and she was afraid he was angry enough to say good-bye, to tell her never to return. She would do anything to keep him.

"Kiss me," she begged.

He opened his arms for her to come to him. He let her kiss him and then he kissed her back. His arms wrapped around her. He pulled her tight, crushed her face against his until she could feel his teeth against her lips, his tongue deep in her throat. It hurt. She would never get enough.

He let her go. She fell away from him.

"You don't understand," she said. "I've never felt this before. I told you that. On the phone. I told you, I didn't like it. Sex. I never enjoyed it. I told you that."

He didn't believe her. She had to convince him.

"This is the first time for me." She wouldn't look at him now. "I've been married for fourteen years. All those years, all that time, I never cared about it, except to procreate. I wanted my kids, wanted them enough to do it a lot, whatever it took. But that's all it was to me."

Steve frowned. He pulled a strand of hair from her damp temple, stretched it straight and let go.

"Even before I was married, I never saw the point. I could take it or leave it. No one ever did it for me. No one. Really. I told you that a month ago. It's true. I never felt anything much. Until today, last night. Today. Until you."

The anger, the little bit of color, fled from his face. All at once he looked ill. She had said too much. She had scared him.

"You're going to be late," he said.

She nodded and stood up. He sat on the couch with his pants unbuttoned. He gripped the arm of his wheelchair. The veins on the back of his hand were blue and pronounced, like a topographical map of his life flowing through him. She could almost see the blood move. What he was missing made what he had so much more remarkable.

She got dressed. She went to his bathroom and fixed her hair, wiped the mascara from under her eyes. She couldn't cry. She'd be a mess when she got to the restaurant.

He was still sitting on the couch when she returned.

"You look a little"—he paused—"windswept?"

"No one will notice." That was for sure.

"Have fun," he said.

"Oh, please! If you knew what agony these dinners are for me."

She saw the challenge in his face. Then don't go, he wanted to say. You're a grown woman. Make yourself happy. She had. She was.

"What do you want?" he said to her.

She wanted to be everything to him. She wanted to be enough for him. She was just an aging, married woman with stretch marks and ten extra pounds. She did not need to die to be invisible. She wanted Steve to see her.

"You," she said.

He grabbed a handful of her sweater and pulled her to him. She almost fell over him on the couch. He buried his face in her side. She kissed the top of his head. She kissed his forehead, his face. They were kissing again. She couldn't stop kissing him. Mitch lay in his silk-lined coffin. Morgan looked tragic and adorable in black velvet for the funeral. Today was the first day of spring. By December, she could have a Christmas tree.

chapter forty-five

Seth took an odd exit off the freeway. They bounced in Michael's BMW over broken pavement into an industrial park, now out of business, the metal accordion doors on the warehouses permanently locked. The only color was a big splash of triumphant graffiti, words that Dorothy couldn't read.

"What are we doing?" she asked.

Seth pulled the car around to the back of the farthest building. There were train tracks behind them through a chain-link fence and up a gravel hill. Dorothy looked at Seth. He lit another joint and passed it to her.

"It's a long trip to India," he said.

He exhaled smoke through his nostrils like a cartoon bull spouting twin jets of angry steam. Dorothy had not seen Seth for a long time. He looked like himself, but she stared at the dark red spatters on his faded jeans. Paint. Blood.

"You've changed," he said to her. His voice was low.

His eyes were glassy, stoned. "I can't stop looking at you. I've never wanted you so much."

Dorothy took a deep breath. She had dreamed of this. But not sitting here, in her brother's car, framed in train tracks, garbage, and failed attempts.

"Is this India?" She tried to laugh.

"Would you just relax? Let me touch you."

His hand went to her breast. His mouth skidded down her neck. She leaned back against the seat. She still wore her seat belt.

"Let's get in back," he said.

Dorothy didn't want to. She felt something that seemed like fear. But it was Seth. His lips moved to hers and she forgot to be frightened. He transported her with his mouth. Kissing him was meditation, release from self, a melting into the supreme universe. Maybe this was India.

He undid her seat belt. He leaned across her and opened her door for her. She got out. Got in the back. He jumped in beside her. He must have seen the look on her face because he kissed her again, right away. He didn't let her stop; he didn't let her speak. The back door of the car was open and her jeans were on the littered ground. A train went by as he thrust into her, and she thought of the travelers on the train, where they were going, and the story she was giving them to tell when they got there. She wrapped her legs around him. She put her hands up in his hair. She saw the hazy Los Angeles sky through the back windshield. A twist of black bird. What was the word for what Lewis was to her? History. An ancient memory of childhood. Seth dug into her and her back scraped against the rolled edge of the leather upholstery. The pain sent her away, down the tracks, running after the departing train.

chapter forty-six

The key wasn't in the first pocket Leo checked. The key wasn't in the second pocket. The two front pockets of the old woman's ugly beige raincoat were empty except for a silver gum wrapper so soft and wrinkled it must have been there for a hundred years.

Leo stood back and tried to focus on just her clothing. He tried to keep his eyes looking for pockets. He did not want to look at her face. But then he did. Rigor mortis. Already. It had pulled her lips back; her teeth gleamed crooked and exposed. Her face was the color of a mushroom, but stretched so tight it shone. It reminded him of his public-school urinal, never dry, never white. Her hands grabbed the air, the tips of her fingers swollen and red. Blood made a maroon cloud on the sheet beneath her head. He could smell her. Jenny had not been so horrible.

He leaned over the old, dead neighbor lady and unbuttoned the coat, trying to keep his fingers light, to touch her as little as possible. He pulled the coat open. She wore a housedress underneath, like a nightgown, faded and pathetic pink. There was a pocket down low on one side below her hip. It was the kind of pocket that held old, snotty tissues. Crumpled. Moist. He could see it bulging with the Kleenex. But also possibly the key. His fingers tingled, retreated into fists. He went over his options. Leave the cat. Eventually it would get so weak from hunger it would stop crying. It would starve to death. Then the whole apartment building would begin to reek of rotting flesh. And before that happened the guy next door, that ancient screenwriter, Julia Roberts's best friend, would call a cop to complain.

Leo held his breath and tiptoed two fingers into the pocket. He leaned over the disgusting corpse with his shins against the mattress and his feet on the floor. He shuffled his feet to get a better angle. His toe caught a corner of the bedspread and he slipped. Without thinking, he put his hand down to catch himself. He put his hand right on her chest, half a fucking flattened breast under his palm. Her body was hard beneath him but mushy, too, like a balloon covered in wet foam rubber. He screamed and pushed off her. The housedress stuck momentarily to the sweaty palm of his hand. It came up, revealing an old lady's terrible thigh and, worse, her underwear. He could see her pubic hair, a lumpy shadow underneath the awful nylon panties, a couple of hairs springing through the weave. Dark hairs, he couldn't help but notice, not gray.

He took the hem of her housedress and flicked it down toward her knees, covering her again. He kneeled on the bed and put his hand in her pocket. He felt the putrid tissue and nothing else. Then he saw it. A string around her neck, a flattened pink shoelace with the words "key kaddy" written over and over in white. It was long and the key itself was hidden under her housedress, but that had to be it.

The tendons of her neck bulged. He gritted his teeth and pulled the string up from under her housedress. Her breast wiggled. He didn't know how long he could stand this. He had to get out of this apartment. He had to get out of here. He wanted his car fixed. He wanted to find Tess and go home to Maryland. People were so god-damn weird here. It was all her fault, Tess, the bitch. He yanked so hard on the string that the old lady's head snapped forward and made a cracking sound. He yanked again, pulling it from around her neck. It tangled in her hair. He tugged hard. It came free. He had the key in his hand.

And he was exhausted. And sore. His ear hurt where the dumb Mexican had kicked him. His hands hurt from fighting back. He needed a couple of aspirins. He went to the bathroom and washed his hands with soap and hot water before taking a good long piss. And afterwards he washed his face and his hands again, for a long time, with the water as hot as he could stand and lots of Jenny's flowery soap. He looked at himself in the mirror. Jesus, he was handsome. Even he could see it. But everyone got ugly when they died. First old. Then ugly. Then dead. And then uglier.

He took the key off the string and put it in his pocket. He tossed the string on the bed. He saw Jenny's manila envelope, half-crushed under the old lady's arm. He pulled it free. He would take it with him. He looked at Jenny's swollen body under the blanket. He wished he had someplace else to put the old lady. Shit. Suddenly, his eyes were watering. His nose was hot and full. It was the smell. The stink. The work was getting to him. How could Jenny's mother hate her so much? Jenny's star was in his name. Jenny's light twinkled in his constellation. Jenny wasn't trying to be a star, she already was a star. Leo nodded at her blanketed form.

"Don't worry," he said out loud. "I'll take care of it."

He would find Tess; then he would leave Los Angeles and track down Jenny's mother. She needed to hear a couple of things.

It was good to have a plan. Leo felt better. He got a beer from the refrigerator. He sat down for a moment on the couch. The breeze blew in from the open kitchen window. It was a nice apartment. Jenny had chosen well. It was a good, solid couch. Quality. Her car was nice, too. Leo put his face in his hands and sobbed.

chapter forty-seven

After lunch, I was working alone. I was driving an "L-Car" which means without a partner. I thought I couldn't wait to get rid of Hayden, but when I was actually driving, I missed him. I missed somebody or I guess I missed everybody. It was getting late. My final afternoon was fading. Beverly Hills was quiet. There was nothing to think about except how sad I felt.

Finally a call came in. A 3-4-8. Suspicious activity. In Beverly Hills, we always respond. The L.A.P.D. has to pick and choose; we absolutely always respond.

It was a routine call, if there is such a thing. Routine for Beverly Hills, anyway. There are a lot of old people here and a lot of them have time on their hands. They should be woodworking, or knitting, or playing bridge, but instead they spend their time spying on their neighbors. We get a lot of calls about something suspicious going on next door. Most of the time—99 percent of the time—it's nothing. Sometimes I think the older folks are just looking for company. Even a cop. They always offer us coffee and a piece of bundt cake or something.

I pulled up in front of a single-family home below Wilshire Boulevard. It's the less expensive, but not inexpensive area of Beverly Hills. The house was a sixties ranch, wide and a little run-down. Someone had gardened once. Now the yard was overgrown. There were clumps of weeds and an old newspaper on the walk. It had a two-car garage with the door closed.

The neighbor lady stood on the lawn of her house next door, the one on the garage side.

"He's had that car running in the garage for an hour," she said. "It's making the windows rattle. I called, but no one answered."

A car with a full tank of gas will idle for a long time. I looked in the garage door windows. I saw what I expected to see. The garage-door wasn't locked. It opened right up. I held my shirt over my face to turn the car off. A Caucasian male, seventy-five to eighty, was in the driver's seat. He sat back with his eyes closed and almost a smile on his face. He had his hands in his lap.

His wife, Caucasian, his age or a little younger, had changed her mind. She had been sitting in the passenger seat, and suddenly something made her want to live. Maybe her head hurt from the carbon monoxide. Maybe she was coughing. Maybe she hadn't thought that dying would be so damn uncomfortable. She opened her car door. She fell, or tried to crawl, out of the car, before she succumbed. That's how I found her, half in, half out of the car, one hand reaching toward the clean air.

I staggered out of the garage. I looked up to keep the tears behind my eyes. The sky was getting dark. The color seemed washed out of everything, even the grass and the flowers by the front door were faded as if they had been left in the sun too long.

The old lady from next door screamed, or tried to. Her vocal cords weren't what they used to be. Then her eyes watered when she told me what good neighbors they had been. I thought I saw envy on her wrinkled face.

In the kitchen, propped up against the toaster, I found the note:

Dear Kids:

You're right, we're getting too old to take care of ourselves. We don't want to end up in a nursing home or (Heaven forbid!) living with one of you. And neither of us wants to be alone if the other dies first. Don't worry. Don't be sad. We didn't suffer. Be happy for us.

All our love forever,

Mom and Dad

If only I had gotten there sooner. If the neighbor had called earlier, when she first noticed the car running and running. It wasn't what they wanted. Definitely not what she wanted. She wanted to live. Even without him, she was willing to live.

After my dad died, I moved in with my uncle. My mom didn't want me back. She didn't want a teenager, especially one who had the potential for being really screwed up. My uncle is a conscientious guy. He sent me to college. I gave it a good try, but it was hard for me to sit so still. I decided to be a cop. I haven't regretted it. But it hasn't been exactly what I thought it would be. By the time the police get there, so much has already happened. It's like going to a resort when the season is over. The stores are closed. The ice cream parlor is boarded up. The sign on the souvenir shop is faded and hanging by one hook. Why didn't I come sooner? I missed it. I hate that feeling. I hate to be too late.

chapter forty-eight

D orothy."

"Dorothy."

The voices were there, just out of reach, just through that next door, around that next corner. She almost had them.

Dorothy woke up. Seth was still driving. The freeway went on and on. They rolled past an enormous warehouse of office supplies, a store for baby furniture, a car dealership a mile long.

"Sorry," Dorothy said.

"You were tired."

"Yes."

"So how is it?" Seth asked.

"What?"

"Married life. How is being married? Obviously something's not all there for you." He laughed.

"I'm not married." She couldn't believe he thought she was.

"What do you mean?" Seth took his eyes off the road. He looked at her, frowning. "I ran into Junior. He said you were getting married."

"I was."

"That was a hell of a long time ago."

"It takes a long time to get married!" she shouted.

She took a deep breath. There was no reason to be so defensive. There was no reason for him to look so annoyed.

"So, are you getting married? Is this—you know—a sort of last-gasp, wild-oats kind of thing?"

Dorothy tried to decipher if that was what he wanted it to be. "Why?" she said.

"Don't you think I might like to know?"

Dorothy looked out the window. The car dealership had given way to a junkyard, piled with the rusted carrion of family cars, work cars, cars that had taken people where they wanted to go. New cars, old cars, and she and Seth rode somewhere between. Traveling, traveling, never able to stop the trip.

"We broke up," Dorothy said. "I was supposed to get married today. Today. But my mother flipped out—"

"Again?" Seth interrupted.

"That's what Lewis said. I went to the hospital. Instead of the wedding. That was that."

Seth laughed. Dorothy had to snicker with him.

"I had a car accident yesterday," she said. "I hit my head."

"And you wanted to see me," he said.

That's right, she thought. "I never thought I'd see you again."

"You always were a girl of absolutes. Never. Forever. Nothing is that permanent."

"I woke up in the hospital, after the accident, and I couldn't remember who Lewis was at first. Then I knew who he was, but I couldn't remember what he was to me. What's that word?"

"What word?"

"For Lewis."

"Who's Lewis?"

Dorothy couldn't answer him.

"I'm just glad you're here," Seth said. "I didn't realize how much I missed you until I saw you standing in my doorway."

"I want to be in New Delhi. Or Bombay. Or Calcutta."

"We are moments away."

"Where are we going?"

"Los Angeles is a remarkable place," Seth said as if she hadn't lived there for twelve years. "It has many pockets of ethnic diversity. Chinatown. Little Tokyo. Little Armenia. And, last but not least, Little India."

"Artesia, you mean."

"Known as Little India. Ever been there?"

"No."

"Me neither. Today is Saturday," he said. "Saturday afternoon. The place should be hopping."

They exited the freeway onto Artesia Boulevard. They turned right at the light, drove two long suburban blocks past the fried-chicken place and the Chinese food express. They kept driving until they saw a sign for the Bombay Palace and then one for the Delhi Hut. India was paved and sterile. The street was empty. Dorothy had expected saffron and curry. She had anticipated umbrellas on the sidewalks, dark-skinned men squatting over bright madras cloth, women wearing bangles and bright saris carrying full plastic European-style shopping bags. She expected life.

Seth parked. In the store windows, behind the glare from the sun, Dorothy saw products from India. An inlaid wooden box. An elephant. Small gold statues of deities. She didn't come to buy. She didn't know why she was here. What she wanted was not found behind the counter.

"Well," Seth said.

He looked at her expectantly. He took her hand. A tuft of his wavy reddish hair stood up over his ear. This was the man she wanted, had always wanted. Forever. She pulled her hand from his sticky grasp.

She got out of the car. The sun was bright, but not warm. She shivered. And at once her head swelled with pain. And expanded. It threatened to kill her. Her legs felt weak. Her palms opened. She looked at Seth, but he was looking down the empty street. She was a supplicant begging him for scraps. The little bits of mica in the cement glittered around his feet.

"Maybe if we walk left or right," he said. "Maybe if we get off the main drag."

She bowed her head and followed him to the next intersection. She hunched her shoulders against the sunlight. He looked right. He looked left. In both directions, as far as they could see, were square stucco houses with slanted shingle roofs and dead lawns. A postwar middleclass neighborhood become immigrant barracks without any flavor from home.

Dorothy sighed.

"I've heard such great things about this area," Seth said. "Come on. Let's explore."

Her head would burst if she didn't get out of the sun.

"Why are we here?" she said to him.

"I can't take you to India," Seth said. He put his hands on either side of her face. "Not today. But I will. I promise."

It was good to be promised to. It suggested a future.

"In here," she said at the very first door.

Inside it was dim and refrigerator-cold. Dorothy felt the capillaries in her head contract and her headache recede. There was a clean smell of sandalwood soap. She took a deep breath. She looked around. It was a clothing shop, a tablecloth shop, an everything shop. Linens, shirts, socks for children, silk scarves and cotton sweaters. A case along one wall displayed jewelry. A shelf along the back held cooking pots and frying pans and a rice steamer and a cookie jar in the shape of a giant red apple. The store had everything the modern Indian woman would need.

Dorothy put her hand on a folded pile of tie-dyed cloth. It was not as soft as it looked.

"Do you have Mehendi supplies?" Seth asked the woman behind the counter.

The woman smiled at Seth. Women always smiled at Seth. Dorothy had not seen him for a long time. She knew her back was scraped. He had slapped her thigh when he was done and grinned.

"That's my girl," he had said. He stood in the trash-strewn parking lot with his pants around his ankles and she saw love on his face. She had fantasized that moment, this day, so many times. He would turn to her; he would tell her he wanted her, he could not live without her. She put a hand on Seth's shoulder, felt his indisputable warmth through his button-down shirt. She leaned her cheek against his arm, breathed in his familiar scent of deodorant soap, marijuana, and turpentine. She closed her eyes. Time fell away. She had never met Lewis, never bought a wedding dress; she was still waiting to be asked. She was sore between her legs. She had the evidence she needed.

The Indian woman shopkeeper pulled out a box full of little yellow packages and plastic bags of paintbrushes. She was dressed like any other older American woman, in polyester pants and a big sweatshirt appliquéd with patchwork flowers. But her hair was black and long and piled on her head, and her fingers were articulate and brown. Her hair looked dry and the color was flat. She probably dyed it herself. Seth was right. Dorothy felt very far from home.

"Do you have it in larger quantities?" Seth was asking. "I'm an artist. I'd like to use it for my work."

"No," the woman said. "But I can give you a deal on this whole box. I am the biggest supplier anywhere in Artesia."

"I need more than this."

They haggled. The woman was shrewd. The genes that had gotten her to America, helped her open a store, and turned her into a successful civic leader, were strong. Seth bought the box.

"How about a cup of coffee?" Dorothy asked when they were back on the street.

"I thought we'd have an Indian dinner a little later. Let's shop some first."

"I don't want to shop."

"We can talk to some people. Indians."

"Is this about drugs? Are we here on some kind of deal?"

He pulled his lips in. His eyes went flat. "This is about you," he said. "We're here for you."

She had not remembered that his arms were so freckled, his nose so small, that his Irish blood was so pronounced. She realized she had become accustomed to a different body type. Seth seemed fleshy and distorted. But right, she thought, exactly right. At home, nine thousand miles away in Los Angeles, Lewis was sitting at the dining-room table using two fingers to destroy their wedding cake. Jane was lying in her hospital bed. Michael paced in the hallway, waiting for his father and his car. She stood on the sidewalk with the man of her dreams, but wide-awake.

"Seth." She looked up at the sun. "I should have been married by now. At this exact moment, I should be dancing at my stupid reception, but I'm on a corner in Artesia with the one man who smashed my heart into a million pieces, and he wants to shop."

"Don't cry," Seth said.

She hadn't realized that she was. "Why shouldn't I?"

"I'm sorry," he said. "I'm sorry. I didn't know I hurt you. A million pieces? I had no idea."

Suddenly Dorothy was furious. The rage bubbled in her throat, exploded from her mouth. "You asshole! How could you not know? I loved you. Remember? I tiptoed while you painted. I made you food. I bagged kilos for you. I tried to be everything you wanted me to be. You threw me out. What did you think? I wouldn't care? I almost died!"

But instead of feeling sorry, she watched him swell with pride, expand with the realization of his own irresistible masculinity.

"Really?" he said.

Dorothy shook her head.

"Oh, Dorothy," he said. "No wonder I've missed you."

She felt the familiar flutter of hope in her heart. He had missed her? His eyes were green. The red hair on his arms sparkled in the sun. There was blue paint under his fingernails. Her heart yearned to curl up again in his variegated world.

"No one has ever loved me as much as you."

"Except you!" Dorothy shouted. "You love yourself more than anyone else ever could!"

"What's wrong with that?"

"Give me the car keys." She had no answer for him. She had no answers at all. "Give me."

"Why?"

"I need to get back. I have things to do."

"I don't want to go."

"I'm not asking you to go."

"You can't leave me here."

"You should have taken your own car."

"I'm here for you."

Too angry to speak, she stamped her foot. Her head detonated, and Seth burst into more than the million pieces of her heart. Shards of Seth, bright and sharp like glass, flew into the air. In each tiny piece she saw his whole reflected. It was raining Seth. She opened her arms to collect him. She felt the sticky ooze of sex in her underwear. She collapsed to the shiny sidewalk. She closed her eyes and hid from what she had done.

"Dottie."

"Dottie."

Seth crouched beside her. "Dottie," he said again.

She sat up and put her arms around him. She sobbed into his shoulder. All day long men had fallen in love with her, wanted to take care of her, offered her coffee and dinner and themselves. Seth sat down on the sidewalk with her, he held her, but he was not giving anything. He was incapable of it. If she spent the rest of her life with him—the rest of her life—this was as much of him as she would ever have. Behind her tears, her eyes had resumed their concussion-induced sparks of color. She opened them to calm them down. Her right eye flared with neon green spots. Her left eye flickered electric pink diamonds. Seth looked deep into her flashing eyes. Could he see the damage he had done?

chapter forty-nine

Leo began to feel ridiculous. He was crying. He was a grown man. He never cried. He didn't cry when he was a kid. He snorted in and swallowed his snot. He wiped his eyes with the back of one hand. The other hand held the manila envelope. He looked at it. The number waved at him. Jenny's insistent "CALL!"

"Okay, okay," he said out loud. "Okay."

He picked up the old lady's key and headed downstairs to take care of the cat. Cats gave him the creeps. They squirmed in your hands and their flesh felt separate from the fur. He hated the way their tails switched, the way they hid their claws between their toes. They weren't good for anything. They didn't protect you or do tricks. They lay around licking themselves. Girls liked cats. They could relate to useless beauty.

Tess loved all animals. One night out by Dickerson Quarry, they had parked at the end of a pseudo-country road. Actually, there was a housing division just over the rise in every direction. Leo had his hands on her breasts when Tess said, "What was that?"

They listened. Ax murderers were not unheard of. Then "meow." A tiny sound.

"It's a kitten," Tess said.

"Yeah." He had resumed his touching.

"It's lost."

"There are houses right there," Leo had said. "How can it be lost?"

Tess had opened the door and gotten out of the car, leaving Leo hard and without support. He followed her. Didn't want her walking around alone. Ax murderers.

She found the kitten. It was tiny. It was scrawny. It looked blind, the eyes crusted shut, the nose oozing pus.

"It's half-dead," Leo said. "Leave it."

"Take me to the vet."

"What vet?"

"There's a vet on the Pike. Below the college."

"Come on, Tess."

She looked at him. He wasn't getting any. He drove to one vet. It was closed, but a sign on the door gave the address of the emergency pet clinic. He drove there. Tess kept the kitten. It was only blind in one eye. She named it Cyclops. She had that cat until she left for L.A. It was the only thing she said she was going to miss.

Leo was glad he didn't meet anybody in the hall. He could hear people in the apartment next door to the old lady. Spanish voices, a woman and a man. The cat was quiet, but when he put the key in the lock he heard it cry once. He opened the door. The place stank of cat. Cat food. Cat litter. That sweet dirty smell. Tess's bathroom had smelled that way. He wouldn't go in there if he could help it. He hated the way the spilled litter would crunch under his feet. The old lady's cat ran to him, then ran away. It was gray and white. Fat. And over the cat smell, something else. Something warmer. The cookies. She had baked those cookies.

"Here, kitty," he called.

The cat ran back down the hall into the apartment. He followed. It was a mirror image of Jenny's apartment, the same hall and little living room, same kitchen through the archway, but it was as full as Jenny's was empty. Photos in cheap frames crowded every wall up to the ceiling. Massive furniture that had once belonged to a much larger house was crowded together like a secondhand store. There were throw rugs on top of larger rugs on top of the apartment carpeting. Between the furniture and the cat stink, Leo couldn't catch his breath.

It was obvious where the old lady spent her time. A Naugahyde recliner, with a faded towel over the back and a flat cushion in the seat, sat in front of a mismatched footstool. The television was drawn up, almost in the center of the room, facing the chair. That was her spot. He could see her in it. He could smell her. Long greasy hairs stuck to the towel.

The cat ran into the kitchen. Leo tripped over a throw rug, stumbled after it. "Shit," he muttered, "I hate cats." The cat had hopped onto the counter. It sat among the cookies that had been put out to cool on brown paper bags. Everywhere Leo saw hair. The cat's hair. Her hair. In the empty bowl of cookie batter that lay soaking in the sink. Stuck to the cabinet door, beside the dark smudge of fingerprints around the handle. Even in the oven. The door was open, the rack slimy with old food, and Leo saw a long white hair.

He reached for the cat. It hissed at him and arched its back, highstepping through the cookies away from him. He tried to grab it and it attacked, scratching him on the backs of both hands. He needed something. A pair of gloves, a towel. And then what? Think, he told himself. Do this sensibly. He was smarter than a goddamn cat.

He went through the bedroom, into the bathroom. Just like in Jenny's apartment, there was a small linen closet built into the bathroom wall. He opened it. It was crammed full of sheets and towels and napkins and even candlesticks and a china figurine of a shepherdess and sheep. He was looking for a pillowcase. The figurine teetered, almost fell, but he caught it just in time. He set it on the back of the toilet. That was good. His reflexes were quick. His hands were bleeding—two long scratches on one, a shorter but deeper scratch on the other. Feline leukemia, AIDS, rabies flashed through his mind. The cat looked healthy. The old lady probably took great care of it. He found a pillowcase after dumping most of the linens on the bathroom floor.

He went back to the kitchen. The cat sat on the counter, nonchalantly licking one paw. Its yellow eyes slid sideways to look at him. It looked away, pretending not to care. At that moment, he grabbed the dish towel and threw it over the cat. He picked it up with one arm and held it wiggling, claws flailing, against his chest. It took only two tries to dump it into the pillowcase. It thrashed, the claws came through the faded fabric, but it couldn't get out. He had only one new scratch. On his stomach, right through his T-shirt. The shirt wasn't even torn.

He carried the cat out of the apartment. He locked the door but kept the key.

As Leo left the building, an older Mexican man was coming in. He looked at the bag, then at Leo. The cat had grown still.

"Sick," Leo said. "Sick cat."

"Bueno," the man replied. He nodded at Leo as if he was doing a good deed.

Leo put the cat on the passenger seat in the car and held the top of the pillowcase closed with one hand. The cat got to its feet and crouched, alert. It gave one short meow.

"Shut up," Leo said. He thumped it on the top of its head. It crouched lower. He heard it growl deep in its throat.

He drove up into the hills where he had told the policeman he lived. The Hollywood sign perched above him. He couldn't remember why he had been so impressed when he first arrived. Hollywood. In enormous letters. A beacon to people from all over the world, but to what? A racist, cold, expensive, ugly city.

The higher he went in the canyon, the nicer the houses. Bigger. Set back from the road. One of these rich assholes would take a cat, Leo thought. They'd see the poor fat thing and take it in. Their maids could clean up the shit.

At the very top of Beachwood, the road curved around to the left.

The hills gave way and opened into a view of Hollywood and even, very distantly, the ocean. There was a scrubby sage-filled slope down to a park, well-maintained green grass nestled in a hollow in the hills. Leo saw children with blond hair playing on the swings. A man threw a ball to his yellow Labrador retriever. The sun was setting, the park luminescent in the yellow glow of the good life.

Leo dumped the cat into the brush. It sat still and looked up at him. He stamped his feet and waved the bag. The cat ran away, down the hill. The mother of the blond children looked up at him. She shaded her eyes to see him better. Ever watchful. She was like an animal, too. She looked at him, then glanced at her children. She took a step in front of them, toward him. Don't come near them. Her legs wide in the playground sand. One hand on her hip. The other on her forehead. He got in the car—Jenny's car—and left.

chapter fifty

Dorothy stared out the window as Seth drove them home. Outside, this day was turning to evening. Even the car dealership and the outlet mall looked pretty in the waning sunlight. Seth drove with both hands on the wheel, eyes straight ahead. She was worn out from her anger and tears. She didn't speak. He had picked her up off the sidewalk, put her in the car, sighed as he walked around to the driver's door. She was ashamed of herself. She was shrinking from embarrassment. By the time they reached Los Angeles, she would be a doll in the seat, too small to even open the door.

She put her hands to her nose. She could smell Seth on her fingers. She closed her eyes, took a deep breath. His smell made her happy. His odor was more real to her than he was. It was what she remembered, what she dreamed of at night. The smell was what she wanted. And how that smell had made her feel. Desirable. Wanted.

"How are you feeling?" he asked.

"I have a concussion," she said. "Just like in the cartoons, I see stars."

He pushed her dirty hair off her forehead. She smiled at him. Maybe he had changed.

"What will you do now?"

She shrugged. "I guess I need an apartment."

She waited for him to say the right thing. He drove silently. She had wanted Seth to show up at her wedding. Now she could admit it. In her secret heart of hearts, she had expected him to appear at the back of the church shouting, "Don't do it!" But he hadn't even realized she was getting married today. He hadn't seen the announcement in the newspaper. He thought she had become a wife long ago.

They were home. At Seth's house. Back in the Hollywood Hills. The sky glowed like a sapphire, the last blue before night. India, both Indias, even that California version of India, seemed like a dream. She had wanted that. She had wanted Seth. She had wanted to love him that much again. The weight of that love settled in her thighs. It had fallen from her heart and immobilized her. She couldn't get out of the car. Seth opened his door and looked at her. She glanced at him, tried to smile.

"What a day," Seth said. He shook his head as if he had been the one in the car accident, almost married, whose mother had stopped traffic in her bathrobe. "What a day."

He reached for her. His hand stopped just above her shoulder. He didn't touch her. She had wanted him to love her.

"Dot Dot Polka-dot," he said.

She waited.

"I want you back. I want you in my life. I've missed you. I didn't know how much until today. There you were. In my doorway. You appeared like from a magic act. Like the woman who vanished in the locked trunk and reappeared magically in the birdcage."

"Can I take a shower?" she asked.

"Sure, of course. Sure. Sure. *Mi casa es su casa.*"

She opened her door. She stood up. She felt the last cup of her love for him slip down her legs and puddle around her ankles. She stepped away.

"Where're you going?"

"Changed my mind. I better get to the hospital."

"You can call."

"I have to give Michael back his car."

"He's figured it out by now."

He stood with the full light of the setting sun in his face. In their two years apart, he had aged. His cheeks drooped, there were deeper lines on either side of his nose, his neck was soft. She found him even more attractive. But the eyes that looked at her were the same, a child's eyes, self-centered, demanding, and completely terrified.

"'Bye," she said. "Thanks for taking me to India."

"When will I see you again?"

"I'll call you."

She took the keys from him and got into the car. The seat was warm. She was done crying.

"Hey," he said.

"What?"

"Don't get married."

"Why?"

"Until you talk to me. Don't do anything until you talk to me."

Her heart broke again, not because of what she felt, but finally because of what she didn't.

She closed her door and started the car. He stood in the driveway watching her back out. He raised his hand in farewell. She kept both hands on the wheel.

Her mother, her brother, and possibly her father waited at the hospital for her. She stepped on the gas. She needed to get there.

She came around a curve to the ridge on Mulholland Drive with a beautiful view. It overlooked a small park and the skyline of Hollywood, golden in the sun's very last light and sparkling like her eyes. She pulled over. She and Seth had walked here many times to smoke a joint and watch the sun set. In the park below her, a mother was walking her two kids to her minivan. A cat, long-haired, gray and white and plump, ran out from under a clump of sagebrush. It paused right in the middle of the street with its back legs bent. Its tail twitched; its ears perked forward. Dorothy heard the minivan start and begin chugging up the hill.

"Go," Dorothy whispered. "Go!"

The cat leapt away.

chapter fifty-one

The later it got, the more hypersensitive I felt. I drove my regular beat through residential Beverly Hills. I watched my pale hands move on the steering wheel. I saw every hair on each knuckle, every freckle. I was aware of the moistness in my nose and the way my tongue fit against the back of my teeth. I listened to my heart beating. I pulled over to look up at a tree branch against the darkening sky. Just as I turned off the squad car, the streetlight above me flickered on. I heard the fluorescent buzz and felt my pupils shrink in the brighter light. I got out of the truck. My body was a good machine. I wished the machine was enough. I crouched on the sidewalk. I saw the shiny meandering track of a snail. And one last time, I thought of Dorothy P. Fairweather. By now, she was leaving the reception, kissing her mother good-bye, gathering her long white skirt to get into the car with him. I stood up. I took my wedding ring off and put it in my breast pocket. I buttoned the flap.

I began to run, in my hard police shoes with my equipment clanking. Faster and faster, my legs pumping, my arms working. I couldn't remember the last time I had run as fast as I could. My hat blew off. I leapt through the amber pools of street light. Dogs barked. My body worked and I ran, but I was a ghost flying down the street, already mostly gone to that better place or that different place. If anyone had looked out their window, they would have thought they imagined this spectral me. I ran until I collapsed in a yard of green grass.

I gulped in great mouthfuls of air. I cupped my hands over my mouth and nose to smell my own exhale. The grass pricked the back of my neck and my scalp through my hair. My legs were trembling. For a moment I felt good. Then I smelled something cooking. Garlic and tomatoes, roasted meat. The odor of home wafted over me. I sat up. I was in the front yard of a stately stone house. There were nice cars in the driveway, lights on upstairs and down. I saw movement in the far right window, the kitchen window. I imagined the family coming together for dinner. The husband walked in from work and kissed his wife hello. He let his hand linger on her waist. Their son interrupted. He wanted to tell his dad about the tennis game he won while his sister danced as she set the table. Everyone was so glad to be home.

The sun was gone. Suddenly the sprinklers started. I heard the click. I smelled the water coming and then it came, right where I was sitting. It was cold. I jumped up. I laughed. It was the rain I had wished for. I closed my eyes and let it fall on my face. I bent my head so it would shower on my neck and shoulders. Then I shook like a dog. I walked back up the street. I picked up my hat. I was almost ready for this day to be over.

I drove over to the coffee place. I wanted to say good-bye to Bridget, but she wasn't there. Instead, a pimply guy with long hair took my order. The place was empty except for a fat girl reading a book and Hayden. Of all people. I wished I'd seen his cruiser before I went in. I would have gone someplace else.

"Hey, Suicide Man," Hayden called to me. "Aren't you lucky?"

Everyone had heard about the old couple. Of course. News travels around the department pretty fast.

Hayden kept talking, "Glad you were there, and not me. Was there a note?"

I got my coffee and walked over to his table.

"Lemme see," he said.

"What?"

"The note."

"It's evidence," I said. "I bagged it. Turned it in."

He just snickered.

"That's two in two days," he said. "That must be some kind of record."

"Could be." I started to leave.

"Maybe it's you." His voice was loud. The girl looked up from her book. I turned back. I wanted him to keep his voice down. I moved closer to the table.

"Maybe you make them do it," he said, his voice just as loud. "Maybe you give off the suicide vibe; you make people think of it. Maybe people are just 'dying' to see you." He laughed.

"Shut up, Hayden," I said. "Shut up."

"It's a funny thought, isn't it, Suicide Man?"

"Go to hell."

"Remember. Three's the charm! One more. Maybe tonight! You can do it, Suicide Man!"

I had nothing to lose. I grabbed Hayden by the collar and pulled him up out of his chair. The fat girl gasped. The pimply guy at the counter stared at us with his mouth open. Hayden's meaner than I am, but I'm twice his size.

"What did you say?" I asked.

"Fuck you, Cork."

I threw him back in his chair. He started going over backwards, but caught himself with his hands. He pushed off and jumped to his feet.

"You wanna take this outside?"

I could see the cords in his neck. A vein full of blood pulsed in his temple. There was dandruff along his hairline. I didn't hate him anymore. I turned away.

He shouted after me, "You haven't heard the last of me!"

Yes, I wanted to tell him, I have.

Back in the Tahoe, I leaned my head against the leather headrest. I could smell aftershave or hair stuff left over from the officer on the earlier shift. Why the hell hadn't I chosen a better job, something where people were happy at least sometimes? Too late now. My choice had been made. I started the truck. I was sorry Bridget hadn't been there. Ronnie would talk to her next week. She'd ask him where I was. Why the hell did people buy four-dollar cups of coffee, anyway? I drove out of the parking lot. I had only four hours and seventeen minutes until my shift was over and it would be time for me to go home.

chapter fifty-two

Madelyn was late. The sun had set. What if Mitch had come home? Where could she tell him she had been? She didn't know. Tea with Phoebe. Another aimless trip to a bookstore. She didn't care. It was all worth it. Horribly, wonderfully worth it. She was a woman with a secret. She would never see Steve again. No one deserved to be as happy as he made her. She would give him up. Maybe one more time, then she would never see him again. She would say something to Mitch. She could say anything to him. One more time; then she would never lie again.

Anyway, she thought, Mitch won't even be home.

And he wasn't. She ran into the house, put on more makeup, found her fancy earrings. She didn't change her clothes. She could smell Steve on her sweater and her hands.

She took the vodka from the freezer and had one quick snort, right out of the bottle. She imagined her neighbor looking through the kitchen window and watching the housewife next door swigging straight alcohol. The liquid flared in her throat, singed her nose.

In the car she felt the warm rush of the drink in her bones, in her brain. She hadn't eaten since his omelet. She hadn't had a drink in months. She looked at the clock on the dashboard. She still had time. She didn't want to be the first one to get to the restaurant.

She drove slowly. She used side streets instead of the freeway. She rolled the windows down. She rolled them up again. Her hair was frizzy enough from sweating with Steve. She let go of the steering wheel. She missed him already. She wanted him beside her. She would move to New York City, San Francisco, the isle of Crete. He would come to visit. He would never leave.

She swerved out of her lane. The car behind her honked. The guy went around, yelled, "Crazy mother!" In her case, he was right.

chapter fifty-three

L eo had read about a cat—he thought it was a cat—who ate its own dead owner. Or a dog. Definitely a pet of some kind, not some animal off the street. Probably a cat. Well-loved and cared for. Then the master dies. Old person in their apartment alone. No one coming by for days. Not even Meals on Wheels. The cat gets hungry and starts sniffing around the master's tough old body. Feed me. Feed me. One way or the other. They were animals, after all. When he was old, he wouldn't have a pet. He hated animals anyway.

He'd also read somebody famous who said you always die alone. But that was bullshit. Most people died in hospitals with at least a nurse standing by. His dad, the asshole, died with a third of the family—and that was a lot of them—sitting all around him. Christmas eve. Heart attack in the Naugahyde recliner watching *Rudolph the Red-Nosed Reindeer* on TV with the grandkids. Suddenly he made this funny growling noise and flapped one arm like he was trying to fly out of the chair. The kids had all giggled. One of them— Ryan? Brian?—had imitated him, thinking Grandpa was doing something funny. But Grandpa never did anything funny. Leo'd been coming in from the kitchen with a beer in his hand and he knew it wasn't right. He could hear the way his dad couldn't breathe. He could see his back arching and that right arm flapping.

Leo walked up to the chair and looked down at his dad. Looked him right in the eye. The kids were quiet now. They could see Grandpa turning blue. The hand on the end of the flapping arm grabbed the bottom of Leo's flannel shirt. Leo remembered the tug, how strong his dad was, even dying. Maybe it was dying that made him that way. Terrified. Knowing what was waiting. He gave a mighty yank and pulled Leo over, almost into his lap. Still he didn't speak. If he had asked for help, spoken his name, Leo would have done something. Instead they just stared at each other. His dad needed a shave and his beard was coming in white as snow. His big brown eyes were watering, the tears spilling over the wrinkled pouches and down his lined cheeks. His nose had little veins on it. He was a handsome man made ugly by a nasty spirit and too many mean secrets. Leo's sister Nadine came running into the room then and screamed and ran around, and his sister Mary Beth and his brother Tom came in and they pulled Leo out of his grasp. Tom said for them to open his shirt. But nobody did. Mary Beth ran and got a glass of water. But then she just stood there with it. Everybody just stood there. Dad closed his eyes and died with his wife and four of his kids and two of the husbands and nine of his grandkids all watching.

Leo had saved that old lady from getting eaten by her cat. He didn't want to go back to the apartment now. Even for a beer. He would get a burger at a fast-food place and then drive over and watch the diner. It was late for dinner, but if Tess had worked all day—and she was such a worker, she always had a regular job—then coming in for dinner at seven o'clock wouldn't be so weird.

He had that phone call to make. On the floor in front of the passenger seat was Jenny's manila envelope. He had carried it with him. Kept it the whole time. CALL! it said. CALL! He would. He drove down out of the hills under the Hollywood sign. There was a restaurant at the first stop sign and a little grocery store and two pay phones. He parked and went in the grocery store.

"Change for a dollar?" he asked the girl behind the register.

She was Mexican or something. Her hair was black and gushed down her back like dark water. Two inky rivulets framed her face. Her shirt, under the store's apron, was too tight. Her bare arms reminded him of one of his sisters or his mom, a hairless cardboard-colored arm reaching across him to cut his chicken into little pieces.

The cashier smiled at him as she gave him his change. "Calling your girlfriend?" Whatever the hell that meant. She was flirting. She thought he was the same as her.

"I'm Italian," he said.

"Yeah. And I'm Irish," she replied in perfect English.

She laughed and he saw her teeth were crooked. Every other person in the store was white. The only brown people he ever saw in L.A. were doing the shit work.

"You here alone?" he asked.

She looked around and frowned, confused.

"I mean, you work alone?"

"Why?"

There were customers now behind him. He jingled the coins in his hand.

"You shouldn't be here alone," he said.

"Come on, kid. Make time on your own time," the guy behind him growled.

He was an older white guy, with a big potbelly and a gray beard. He wore sandals and black socks. Leo was glad he didn't have to look at his bare feet.

"Come around over here," the girl said. She gestured beside her, behind the counter. Then she whispered something to him in Spanish. She looked down the line of customers and back at him and giggled.

Leo flushed red. He shrugged, looked at the fat white guy and shook his head. He didn't know what she was talking about. He rolled his eyes. Shrugging, shaking, rolling. The guy probably thought he was a retard.

"Thanks for the change." He hurried out.

The sun had set. The night was beginning. Another night in Los Angeles. He would have to sleep on that couch. He would have to spend as long as he could in the car across from the diner. He had nowhere to go. There was a light over the pay phones. They were clean and free of graffiti. The rich people up here, Leo thought, have a whole fucking team of brown bodies that wash the phones, pick up the trash, change the lightbulbs.

What had that stupid Spic girl said to him? Why him?

There was a bulletin board under the building's overhang conveniently located next to the phones. It was neatly covered in advertisements and notices. There was a flyer for a dog-walking service and two for psychic advisors. There was a car for sale and a lost dog and a basement apartment for rent. "Mediterranean charm," read the ad. "Hwd floors. Exp. beams. Eleven hundred dollars." More than a thousand for a one-bedroom apartment with six-foot ceilings, no windows, and the moldy smell of damp dirt. This town sucked.

Leo dialed. The phone rang and rang.

A woman answered. She sounded breathless, hopeful.

"Yes?" she said. "Hello?"

"Who is this?" Leo asked.

"Who is this?"

"My name is Leo. My girlfriend gave me this number." It was easy to lie, always easier.

"Who's your girlfriend?"

"Jenny." He had forgotten her last name.

He heard a sigh, then the woman's voice, more quietly. "I'm driving," she said. "Let me pull over so we can talk."

"I'm sorry," Leo said.

"No. Wait. Hold on."

He waited.

"Are you still there?"

"Yes."

"How is Jenny? Is she all right?"

"Who are you?" Leo asked. "How do you know her?"

"How did you get my number?"

"I found it," Leo whispered, "in Jenny's house. She wrote it in red. She circled your number. It seemed important."

"I'm a counselor," the woman said, "with the Suicide Prevention Hot line." The woman spoke slowly. Leo could hear her understanding, her resignation. "I gave Jenny my private number for emergencies. Where is Jenny? Is she with you?"

"No," Leo said.

There was a pause. The woman took a deep breath. "Are you worried about her? Where is she?"

"At home."

"Does she seem depressed?"

"No." Not anymore.

"Why are you calling?" the woman said. Then she continued without waiting for him to answer. "I've been talking with Jenny since I started at the hot line. I didn't even know she had a boyfriend. I'm glad."

"I shouldn't have called."

"It's fine. I'm glad Jenny is okay."

Leo was quiet. He wasn't going to be the one to tell her. Her voice was soft. It sounded like she really cared.

"You know," the woman continued, "we can talk a little about her. There are things you should watch for. There are ways to know how she's feeling, without asking her all the time. You know how annoying that can be."

The woman laughed a little into the phone.

"Who are you?" Leo asked. "I mean, what's your name?"

"Madelyn," she said. "My name's Madelyn."

He knew from her voice that she was overweight, her breasts like pillows. He wanted her arms around him. He wanted to put his head in her lap.

"Can I meet you?" he asked. "Can you meet me now, anywhere?"

There was a pause.

"I can't," she said. "It's not allowed."

He heard the harder edge in her voice suddenly.

"Let me give you the regular hot line number. I'm there on Mondays. I'm happy to talk with you, over the phone, then. But there's someone there, right now. You can talk to anyone who answers. We have some counselors who specialize in family and friends. I'm sure you'd find them more helpful."

Now she sounded like a therapist. Leo hung up.

Then he dialed again.

"Hello?" Her voice was wary.

"Me again," he said.

"Yes?"

"The thing about Jenny—"

What was the thing about Jenny. There were no things about her anymore. She was a lump of decomposing flesh. All her things, the things that made her Jenny, were gone.

"Sometimes suicide seems like the right answer," Leo said.

The woman, Madelyn, did not reply.

"Are you there?" he asked. "Did you hear me?"

"Are you feeling suicidal?"

"Homicidal," Leo answered.

He heard her staccato intake of breath. It warmed him. "To kill someone who's suicidal—that's not really murder, is it?"

"Of course it is." She sounded frightened. "Where are you?" she continued. "May I speak to Jenny?"

"Jenny can't come to the phone right now." Leo laughed. "But if you'd like to leave a message, she'll get back to you as soon as she can." He beeped, high and loud.

"Leo," the woman said. "What's going on?"

When did he tell her his name? That was stupid.

"I have to go," he said. "I'm sorry I called."

"No, no, no. I'm glad you called back."

Leo dug the toe of his sneaker into the dry dust around the base of the phone booth. He rocked his forehead back and forth against the phone case, felt the cool smooth metal.

"Leo?"

"What?"

"Would you ask Jenny to call me?"

"How old are you?"

"Forty-two."

He knew that. He knew that and he knew lots of other things about her, too. She had dark hair and big brown eyes and skinny long legs, but there was fat around her middle.

"I wish I could meet you," he said.

"Maybe I could meet you and Jenny together," she said.

She was hedging. She was afraid of him. He didn't want to hurt her. He wanted to squeeze her a little, that was all, push against her, feel her arms around him. Maybe her legs weren't so skinny. Maybe there were not too many wrinkles on her face.

"Leo?" she said again. He didn't want her to keep saying his name. "Where are you?" she asked. "Right now?"

"Never mind," he said.

"Are you at Jenny's house? Where does she live? Leo? Answer me."

"Never mind," he said again. "Shut up."

"Leo."

"Stop it."

"I'm sorry," she said softly. Then. "Leo?"

He hung up. He pushed off from the phone. His legs trembled. His palms were sweating. He needed to eat something. He felt sick to his stomach. He needed to do something. He should have met her. She should have met him. A girl went past, in skintight exercise pants and sneakers, a baseball cap on her head. A pretty girl with a bag of groceries. She glanced at him.

"What are you looking at?"

She hurried away without a smile. Usually he could get a smile from a girl like that. In Maryland she would have smiled at him. He

266

loped after her. He patted the gun in his pocket. He had forgotten about it. He was glad to have it. His belly felt tight. His jeans hung on his hips. His hair was too long. She didn't look back, but she knew he was there. Her legs were muscular in those stretchy pants. He watched the cloth wrinkle behind her knees.

He saw her shoulders hunch forward. She dug in the pocket of her sweatshirt and took out her car keys. He saw her hold them through her fingers, keys out and pointing. As if she thought they'd be some kind of weapon, some protection. As if she thought the scrape of the sharp end of a key would deter a man with a purpose. The sun was gone. This day was finally coming to a close. Another fifteen minutes, maybe, and it would be really dark. This girl would be much more frightened in the dark. Her hair hung down her back in a dyed-blond ponytail. That L.A. hair. It all looked the same. She pointed her car-alarm control at her small black Japanese import. She was too far away for it to work. He picked up his pace.

If he reached her before the alarm worked.

If she turned and looked back at him.

Her car alarm wasn't responding. He saw her thumb frantic on the control, pushing, pushing, pushing. He was one car-length behind her. She was opening the car door the old-fashioned way.

If her ponytail fell over her shoulder as she tried to get her key in the lock.

If she dropped her groceries.

If she looked at him.

She yanked the door open and the car alarm went off. The siren whooped and pulsed. She got in, grocery bag on her lap, closed the door. The car screamed.

He walked by, right next to her window. He heard the automatic door locks click into place. She left the alarm blaring. He turned and grinned at her through the windshield. She stared back at him, her mouth in a soft "O," her eyes two scared circles in her face. Locked in her car, the alarm going, the keys in her hand, she was still terrified of him. He wanted her to know, the alarm wouldn't help. No one would come. He stood there. She started her car. Still she didn't drive away. Then he saw her bend over, reach for something. She sat up. It was a cell phone.

He shook his head. He'd been hoping for a gun. He couldn't wait to pull out his own little gun. Jenny's revolver. He was looking forward to a showdown and then the windshield exploding, the glass covering him, the moment before she died when she realized she had been stupid.

He walked away.

There were other ponytails in Los Angeles. The city was filled with them. Filled with white female hands clenched on steering wheels, reaching for cell phones, hitting the button for the automatic locks.

Tess had white hands. She had the palest skin he'd ever seen. Her ancestors had lived in the dark and the cold. But her hands were the whitest. It was not her belly, not the soft inner flesh of her thighs, it was her fingers and the veinless knuckles of her hands that glowed in the television's light.

He shuddered now to think of them. They swelled in his memory until the woman he had loved had hands like Mickey Mouse, three-fingered bright white cartoon gloves at the ends of her stick arms. He wondered how she had brushed her hair or held a fork.

And all at once, he knew he would never find her in Los Angeles. Never. He had come all this way for nothing. She was hiding from him. She knew he was here. She had seen him that first day six weeks ago, his long, slow cruise under the palm trees of Beverly Hills, the wide streets, the million-dollar homes crammed together for the right zip code. She had recognized his dirty car with Maryland plates; she had ducked behind the white drapes in that large stone house, waited until he had driven away to reveal herself.

His seven-year-old nephew had said as much. Brendan, skinny and dark, had a special gift for knowing things. Brendan had said, Uncle Leo, don't go. You'll never find her. Don't go. Brendan always knew when someone in the family was going to get sick. Brendan knew what was in the Christmas packages. He showed up for dinner right on time, never had to be called from outside. Want to know the future? Ask Brendan, his mother said.

Uncle Leo, don't go. You'll never find her.

Forget her. That's what he should have done, but her marshmallow hands had been too sticky. He couldn't get free. He had wrecked his car. He had put a cat in a pillowcase. He had let Jenny die.

If he could turn back the clock. The permanence of all these events sat on his chest. He was having a hard time breathing. He could not find the cat. He could not go back, take a different route, an earlier left turn, miss that intersection entirely. Too late to call 9-1-1. His arms were weak and weighted. He heard his heart thumping in his chest. He listened and listened, afraid he would hear it stop. He shook his head, cleared his throat, afraid listening would make it stop.

Brendan could tell him about Jenny. Brendan would know if Jenny was at peace.

Leo went back to the pay phone. He took the phone card from his wallet that his mother had given him for emergencies. He dialed the many numbers and then his sister's house.

"Hello?"

"Sherry?"

"Well, well, well. Leo. Where the fuck are you?"

"Lemme speak to Brendan."

"What are you, nuts? He's asleep."

"Lemme talk to him."

"It's ten o'clock."

"Wake him up."

"I will not. You know, you coulda' called Mom. She's been worried sick about you."

"Yeah, yeah."

He spoke to Maryland. To home. To the brown plaid couch and the big tree outside the bay window in her split-level.

"How're you?" his sister asked. "What's goin' on? Seen any movie stars?"

"Is it spring there?"

"Raining. Cold as shit. You got sunshine?"

"All the time."

"That hot southern California sunshine."

"Yeah. Yeah."

"Call in the morning. Mom's coming over to watch the kids. I'm going to yo-ga with Mary Beth. Doesn't that sound like I'm in La-La Land? I'm going to yo-ga. You can talk to Brendan."

"No school?"

"Tomorrow's Sunday. Stupid."

He hung up. Felt the chill from the last winter rain in Maryland.

Where had he been going? Last night. It was only last night, twenty-four hours ago, that the accident had wrecked his car, that he ate a doughnut, went to the bar, met Jenny. Twenty-four hours ago, Jenny was still alive. Why had he hit that car? Why had that woman run the red light? Was she dead, too?

If he could find her, maybe he could start it over. If he could go back there. That's what he would do. Go back there. He would drive to that intersection. He couldn't remember where he had been going, but he remembered where he had been. Yesterday seemed so long ago.

chapter fifty-four

Madelyn shook her head. Her mouth was dry. She stared at her cell phone. Maybe he would call again. She should have said something. She could have done more. She was a lousy counselor. An awful mom. A terrible, deceitful wife. Wasn't there something they said, something in the handbook about dealing with angry boyfriends? Of course, she couldn't remember. Her head was so filled with Steve, with his scent and his breath fogging her judgment. Stupid selfish woman. She could have helped him. That guy. Leo. She could have helped Jenny. But it was too late. Leo was gone. Jenny was only a first name, one of a thousand Jennys in Hollywood. Steve would have known what to do. She tried to let the thought of Steve make her feel better. She was loved. She had made him feel good, which made her feel good.

Of course, other women had affairs with men who had legs. Her affair was the best she could do. It was with Steve, a depressed, suicidal double-amputee. She was thinking of leaving her husband for a man who could be dead in five years. Then where would she be? Almost fifty years old with angry children, an ex-husband with a new trophy wife, and astronomical psychotherapy bills for all of them. Of course, she would have to pay those bills, she caused her family's trauma, and she didn't even have a job. How would Steve go to soccer games? Would she push him across the lumpy grass? The other mothers would turn to each other and whisper, "She left Mitch for *him?*" But if they only knew, she reminded herself. If they had felt his fingers on her, his lips, how well what was there worked.

Madelyn stopped at a mini-mart for a soda or some water. She pulled into the parking lot, but then she sat in her car. She just wasn't very good at counseling. She wasn't a good cook. She didn't bake. She wasn't firm enough with her children. They were spoiled. They were self-centered. She often recommended that her callers speak to a different counselor. She would wave at someone across the room, hold up her fingers to tell the person what line she was on. "Wait a minute," she would say, "I know someone who understands exactly what you're talking about." The other counselor would pick up, and she'd run to the bathroom or outside for a smoke. She listened to them, but she had so little to say in return. Leo sounded bad. She didn't like his mention of homicide. She recognized his frustration. She watched the Indian man inside the mini-mart. She could see him with his turban and full dark beard. He was picking his nose and inspecting what he found on his finger. She decided against the soda. She just drove on to the restaurant.

She was the last to arrive. The partners, Rusty and Scott, looked up at her and away. Their wives—what the hell were their names? Model Number One and Two took in her outfit, her messy hair, didn't care. Mitch was sitting there, annoyed.

"She finally shows up," he said.

"I need a drink," she replied.

Scott laughed. "Get this girl a cocktail."

Rusty raised his eyebrows. She liked Rusty. She liked Scott, too, truth be told. They were honest about their women. Made no bones about the fact that these two models were the girls they couldn't get in high school. She wondered why Mitch kept her around. Maybe it was his way of being unusual. He was the only "Father Knows Best" character in the partnership, probably in the entire studio. Rusty and

Scott had kids with their first wives. Kids they never saw. It was Mitch who went to soccer games and birthday parties.

"You let your hair curl," Rusty said. "Looks good."

"Thanks." Her first compliment from one of them, ever.

"Is that natural?" Model Number One asked.

"Yes. Are those?" Madelyn returned, glancing down at her impossibly perfect breasts.

Model Number Two snickered. Madelyn looked at her. She didn't have a curl in her body. Straight eyebrows, straight nose, legs like sticks. Even her pubic hair was probably straight.

"What are you drinking, honey?" Madelyn asked Mitch.

Mitch frowned. She was not her usual quiet self. "Vodka," she said to the waiter. "On the rocks."

"Make it a double," Rusty said.

"Yeah," Mitch said. "Right."

"Yes, please." Madelyn smiled at the waiter. "A double."

The waiter wrote the order on his pad. A tattoo on his wrist peeked from beneath the cuff of his white dress shirt.

"What's that?" Madelyn asked. "What's that tattoo?"

"He's working," Mitch said.

"Does it say 'mom?' Madelyn put a hand out to stop him.

The waiter laughed. He unbuttoned his cuff, revealed his soft young wrist to her. She watched his fingers fold back the fabric. Slowly. The tattoo was dark blue and fluid, a swirl across his veins.

"That's beautiful." Madelyn sighed. "What's it supposed to be?"

"It's a special design just for me. A Maori man in Atwater does it. He's a master. He meditates on your energy force and then draws his vision. Every one is different."

Madelyn wondered what it would be like to have the waiter's hand on her body. She wondered if her lips would be able to tell the difference between his pure skin and his tattoo.

"Does it hurt?"

"Hurt like hell when he did it."

He was proud and faintly superior. Madelyn wished she had a tattoo to show him. Complicated. Inspiring. On her shoulder. She could open the neck of her sweater, expose her white skin to him.

"Andrea has a tattoo," Rusty said. "Show him."

Model Number One stuck her tongue out at Rusty. Rusty laughed.

Mitch laughed harder.

"Come on, baby." Rusty was grabbing for the waistband on Model Number One Andrea's pants. "Stand up. Show him your tattoo."

"It was a long time ago," Andrea said. "I was young."

How young? Madelyn thought. Six? It was a tattoo of Barney the singing dinosaur.

Rusty grabbed. The waiter waited.

"Stop it!" Andrea's voice was sharp.

She stood up and stepped away from Rusty. She bent to get her purse from the floor. Her shirt came up and everyone saw the naked tan skin on her back. The fine hairs. A single freckle.

Mitch was still snickering behind his hand, like a boy waiting his turn to look at the girlie magazine. "Now, your tattoo I'd like to see," he said to Andrea.

"I'm going to the ladies' room," she replied. Her eyes narrowed as she looked at Rusty and then Mitch. She walked off with surprising dignity, her white denim-covered hips sashaying, glowing through the dim restaurant light.

"I'll get that drink." The waiter retreated.

There was an uncomfortable silence at the table. Model Number Two looked up at the ceiling, fascinated by the lighting fixtures. Scott played with his fork. Rusty shrugged, telling himself something. Madelyn realized that Mitch was growing angry with her.

The waiter returned with the drink. Madelyn took it silently.

"I'll be back in a moment to take your order," he said.

No one even looked at him.

Madelyn took a big gulp of her vodka and shuddered.

"When did you start drinking?" Scott asked her.

Alcohol and sex, she wanted to say. They go together, don't they? I had the best sex of my life today. Tonight I felt like a drink.

She wanted Steve. She wanted him here. She wanted to know what it was like to sit across from him, to look into his eyes through the candlelight, to flirt with the waiter in front of him.

She blushed. She was ridiculous. Old enough to be the waiter's mother. She heard her own voice too high, her absurd giggle betraying her. She saw her sagging flesh next to his perfect form. There was no place on her body for a tattoo. No skin worth revealing. No wonder Steve turned his back to her. I love you, he said. It was the sex talking. Funny how loud sex could be, how much it chattered, had those convincing conversations in your brain. It said love, love, love, but it meant fuck, fuck, fuck. Madelyn's nose got hot; her eyes watered. She missed him and then missed him even more. She put one hand to her nose, smelled him faintly on her fingers. She put her other hand on Mitch's thigh. He was a good guy. He knew her long ago when there was something to know. He could remember her brief moment of midwestern prettiness before the kids, before life. He was still around.

Mitch put his hand on hers. "Are you okay?" he asked.

"The accident," she said. "I think it made me crazy."

Andrea came back from the bathroom. They ordered dinner. Madelyn splurged and asked for risotto, red meat, a mozzarella and tomato salad, fattening foods even though she wasn't particularly hungry. She wanted the insulation, padding against the future that looked so much like the present.

She grew quiet. She finished her drink and listened to the men talk around her, business, those goddamn writers. The models talked to each other. Madelyn smiled at them, her way of telling them she didn't mind being left out.

She heard a familiar squeaking sound. She turned. The room swayed. The temperature rose ten degrees. Steve was rolling in. Steve.

It was really him. He had a beautiful young Latina woman with him. He wore a blue shirt the color of his eyes, and his hair was long and clean. He looked at her as he entered. He was looking at her. She watched him go by.

"Do you know him?" Scott asked.

"What?" Madelyn turned. "Oh. No." She had been staring. "Well. Maybe. Doesn't he look familiar?"

"I think I'd remember. Poor guy."

Rusty leaned in. "I don't know. Look at the chick with him."

They laughed, uncomfortably. Madelyn realized everyone was embarrassed by Steve. They squirmed in their chairs, unconsciously checking to make sure their legs were still working.

Steve and his friend took a table behind them. Who was that woman with him? Madelyn couldn't see him without turning around, but she could feel him. She could feel him watching her. She wanted to think he had his eyes on her. She sat up straighter. She tried to pay attention to the conversation, but it was less intelligible than before. She watched each person speaking. Their mouths moved and sounds fell out, but not words, not words that she could understand.

There was sweat on her temples and her upper lip. Why was he here? What was he doing? Didn't he know how hard this was? He was her torturer as surely as if he held the red-hot poker to her skin. She turned to see him. He was smiling, laughing at something his companion had said. It bothered Madelyn how much he was enjoying this.

The waiter came by. He put another drink down in front of her.

"I didn't order this," Madelyn said. She looked at Mitch. "I didn't."

"The guy behind you, in the wheelchair, he sent it. With this." The waiter handed her a folded cocktail napkin. She opened it and read:

"My Epitaph:

Goodbye does not mean forever.
Eternity will not end his love.

Even death cannot it sever.

He lies here for what he could not have above."

Madelyn gasped. Mitch grabbed the note out of her hand without asking.

"Hey," Madelyn said.

It was her private note. She didn't want Mitch's hand on the napkin, his big thumb covering Steve's architectural print. The vodka bubbled in her stomach.

"That's mine," she said.

Mitch snorted. He read it aloud.

"Jesus Christ!" Rusty said.

"What does it mean?" Model Number Two asked, not surprisingly.

"Is this guy gonna kill himself for you?" Andrea and her tattoo spoke.

Madelyn saw on her face a voyeuristic envy. For her. For the overweight mother of two in the out-of-season blue sweater and the same pair of black pants as always.

Mitch crushed the napkin and tossed it on the table. "He's a sick fuck." He pushed his chair back. "I'm gonna go talk to him."

"No," Madelyn said. She stopped her husband from speaking to her lover. "No. It's just the hot line. I know him from the hot line."

"What hot line?" Scott asked.

"Suicide Prevention. I work there one night a week. I, I—" She thought hard, lying, always lying suddenly. "I didn't recognize him at first. He comes on after my shift. It's a joke. The quote. The whole epitaph thing. You're all taking it much too seriously."

There was a collective exhale of relief.

Rusty grabbed the waiter as he went by. "Send our wheelchair friend a bottle of champagne, and tell him this'll help a man forget his troubles."

Everyone laughed. Everyone nodded, admiring Rusty's quick wit and generosity. Only Mitch was quiet.

Madelyn turned in her seat. Steve was watching her. She smiled. Politely. Raised her drink to him in thanks. He did not smile back. It was not the response he wanted. She could not give him anything else.

She picked up the crumpled napkin, smoothed it, folded it, and put it in her lap. She fingered it through dinner, the many courses she could not eat. She drank the second vodka. She wanted him to see her drink it. She was drunk.

They were still sitting with coffee and brandy when Steve rolled by on his way out the door.

"Thanks for the champagne." He looked at Mitch.

Again Madelyn saw how uncomfortable Steve made her husband. Not the threat, but the suggestion of what could be.

"Sure."

Madelyn was too drunk to speak. She didn't trust her voice. Steve looked at her. Her eyes filled with tears. And her nose. She sneezed. And blushed.

Then Steve smiled.

"See you when I see you," he said to her.

"Good night," Rusty said.

"Good night."

She listened to his squeaky wheel until the front door closed and she couldn't hear him anymore.

chapter fifty-five

Dorothy stood in the hallway outside her mother's hospital room. She heard a man's voice inside. She heard her mother answer. They spoke softly and in order, like a song she knew but had forgotten, punctuated in laughter. She didn't want to go in. She wanted to listen to the voices. She closed her eyes. She leaned her head against the wall next to the door. Her headache hurt less. Her eyes were quiet for the moment. She listened. The man's voice. The woman's.

Footsteps. She opened her eyes. The little Indian, Dr. Swarup, was walking down the hall. He was looking at her. A smile started below his nose. She ducked into the hospital room. Her mother looked up from her bed. Her father, Jim, stood beside her. He was larger than she remembered, but his form and features were more muted, as if he'd been drawn in pencil a long time ago. The paper had yellowed. The lead was fading away. He looked up, too, but reluctantly. Her mother frowned.

"Dorothy," her mother said.

"Dorothy," her father said.

Dorothy backed away. She backed out of the room. She didn't

want to hear it. Not like this. Those were her voices. They were the voices from her dreams. But she had always thought they were calling her. Instead, they were rebuking her, disappointed in her arrival, saying her name but telling her "not now." Not ever. She had found them. They wanted to be lost.

Dorothy backed right into Dr. Swarup. He was lurking outside the door, waiting to snare her. She looked at him and shook her head. Not tonight, she thought.

"I waited for you all day."

"Have you seen my brother?"

"He left, some hours ago. With a friend."

"I have to go," she said.

"We are having dinner. I have been here since three o'clock when my shift ended. I have been waiting for you."

"Another time." She wanted to tell him how bad she was feeling, but perhaps that would not be a deterrent for a doctor. She could mention that another man's semen was still crusty in her underpants, but that might only heighten his resolve. Men were so weird. She had no idea anymore what turned them on or off.

"I thought you were going home to clean up," the doctor said as he looked her up and down.

"I am. I was. I went to India," she said. "Oh. Never mind."

She skittered down the hall into the stairway. He called after her.

"Miss Fairweather. Dorothy. Wait."

She only waved above her head, telling him to fly, to go bye-bye. But who was she to be ungrateful? He was probably a very nice man. She was the awful one.

She opened the door to Michael's car and got a giant whiff of Seth. She could smell paint and pot and body odor. She rolled down the window. She couldn't wait to be home. Her mother's face. Her father frowning at her. Dorothy. Dorothy. Her father had seen her. Now he knew where she was. He could come and find her. Michael knew. Her mother knew. Her father could call and invite her out to lunch. He probably had. Jim and Jane were probably calling the house from the hospital room right now. Lewis would be there. He'd answer the phone. Her mother would tell him they'd seen her. Jim would get on the phone and introduce himself. When she got home, Lewis would be waiting. Take a shower, he'd say. Let's have dinner with your dad. Let's get married and your dad can give you away.

chapter fifty-six

The intersection was empty. There was no traffic in either direction. Saturday night. No one going anywhere. It gave Leo the creeps. He parked Jenny's car against the curb and watched the lights change. Yellow, red, green. Yellow. Red. Green. The traffic lights seemed obvious. How could she have missed them?

He got out of the car. He ran catty-corner across the intersection and looked at the flower bed where she had ended upside down. It seemed untouched. The flowers quivered full and white in the night air. There was a black skid mark against the curb and one on the metal railing, but they could have been there for a long time. Her car had been blue, he remembered, but he saw no blue paint on the white railing.

It might never have happened. Except it had. A car stopped at the red light. The driver, a man in his forties in a golf shirt and short dark hair, alone, looked over at Leo. Leo put his hand over the gun in his pocket. He didn't want the outline to be seen. He shivered. The night was growing chilly. His jacket was back at Jenny's apartment. He regretted leaving anything there.

The light changed. The man drove on. Leo crouched in the flowers, looking for evidence. Nothing. Not a bloom out of place. One by one, systematically, Leo broke the flowers off their stems. He plucked and yanked and tossed the blossoms into the street. He pulled up the grass and threw clods of dirt at the backside of the railing. He did not stop until every flower was destroyed, until the bed was mutilated and the surrounding lawn mangled and deformed. For Jenny, he thought. He stood up. The white petals looked virginal, a bride's first bower, strewn across the black asphalt. He picked up a single intact bud. He would take it back to Jenny.

Headlights caught his knees. A car came toward him. Again he put his hand over the weapon in his pocket. It did not take a gun to kill anyone. The car drove over the broken flowers. Leo grimaced. He squatted and looked into the car.

Two old ladies, bridge club friends, movie friends, rich and satisfied. He saw the red nails gleaming, the skinny overexercised arms. Too old for arms that narrow, that chiseled, that bony.

The passenger looked at him. She almost smiled at the flower in his hand. Then she looked past him at the mangled lawn behind him. She turned to her friend in alarm. Her hand waved at her friend to go, to go. The light was red. Go, waved the hand.

Leo grinned. Their fear emanated through the rolled up window. It was palpable in the tires vibrating on the road. They had crushed Jenny's flowers.

The driver saw him, too. Her hair, frozen solid with hair spray, didn't shift as she turned to face him, then quickly turned away. She stepped on the gas and inched into the intersection even though the light was red.

He dreamed of hitting them. He dreamed of driving the giant truck that would barrel through the crossroads and flatten them. He dreamed of how much he hated them. The gun meant nothing. It was annihilation he was after. The little gun would not send their automobile with them.

They went away. He went back to his car. He went in search of something, someplace, someone to take this feeling away.

chapter fifty-seven

You certainly made the evening fun. First you practically had an orgasm all over the waiter and his ridiculous tattoo. Then that handicapped guy sends you a drink. Which you needed like another hole in your head."

The tassels on Mitch's loafers were twitching. He spat out the word "handicapped" as if it were an addiction, or worse, something tasteless you might choose to do like wearing spandex to a funeral. Madelyn stood once again with her head bowed in the front hallway of her lovely house. The house was dark, illuminated only from the streetlights outside. She had left without turning on a light, without leaving the porch light on to welcome them home. Fighting was better than sex, she thought. She would scream if she had to have sex with him tonight.

She lifted her head.

"So?" Mitch asked.

"What?" She moved into the kitchen.

He followed her, flipped on the harsh overhead fluorescent. She turned away. Her freezer door gleamed, reminding her of the friendly vodka it cradled within. Her dinner cocktails had worn off; she wanted another drink, oblivion. Wouldn't that be nice. "What do you want me to say?"

"You made a fool of yourself with that waiter."

"I asked to see his tattoo."

"You're ridiculous."

"Why do you even want me to go out to dinner with you?"

Mitch sighed and shook his head at her inability to understand him. He got out his vitamins, bottle after bottle, the twenty-four-capsule twice-a-day regimen to keep his hair curly, his skin firm, his memory and his dick straight. She was three years younger than he, but after the first child she had caught up; after the second, she had passed him. He still had the legs of a teenager, slimly muscular, with soft, dark hair. She had the varicose veins and cellulite of his grandmother.

She got out the vodka and a juice glass.

"Oh. That's great," he said.

"I almost never drink."

"You're making up for it tonight."

"What do you care?"

"You're gonna feel like shit tomorrow."

"I repeat," she said and took a long swallow, "what do you care? I'm sure you have to work tomorrow."

"Who was that guy?"

"Don't you have to work tomorrow? Sunday?"

"Yes."

"How come when I asked Scott what you were doing at the office today, he said you hadn't come in?"

"I don't know. He wasn't there. I work harder than either of them."

"Uh-huh."

"Who was that guy?"

She knew exactly who he was talking about. "I told you. I met him at the hot line."

"What happened to him?"

"He was walking across the street to buy his girlfriend some ice cream and got hit by a truck."

Mitch laughed.

"Stop that." Madelyn put her drink down hard enough to clatter on the tile counter. Vodka sloshed over onto her fingers. "Don't you dare laugh at him."

"What is he to you?"

She saw his hand on the brown plastic bottle of vitamins. She saw the whiteness of his fingertips, saw how all of his blood burned in his furious face. He knew, he knew, he knew. He knew. This was not the time to remember Steve's breath on her neck, the cool smoothness of his skin, his fingers moving against her. She closed her eyes and gripped the countertop.

"I asked you a fucking question."

"Don't speak to me that way."

"I saw the way he looked at you. The way you—" He broke off, wanting her to stop him, wanting her to interrupt.

She picked up her drink and walked into the living room. He had to say it. She would not give him anything. But, yes, she wanted to scream at him, yes. He's the one. The one. The only one.

"It's like the plot of some movie," Mitch muttered. "The noble cripple."

"One of *your* movies," she called back to him.

"That's it. That's *it!* You hate what I do. It's not intellectual enough for you."

This was the argument she knew. She breathed a sigh of relief. The familiar litany of rage and disappointment. My job pays for this house, your photography lessons, your power-yoga classes. My job keeps our kids in private school. She was supposed to apologize and pay homage, do penance for denigrating the almighty studio.

"I can't do this anymore," he said suddenly.

"What?" she called to him.

He stood silhouetted in the kitchen door. He had his special water bottle in one hand, the bottle he bought from the health-food store with the copper and hemp casing and the special plastic that did not leach impurities even when microwaved. As if anyone would want to microwave a water bottle.

She worried about that guy, Leo, who had called her. And Jenny. She should check her cell phone for messages.

But Mitch was speaking. She sipped her vodka, tried to focus on his dark face. She didn't know what he was saying anymore. It had been so long since he had really spoken.

The phone rang. She jumped.

"Who the fuck could that be?"

"I'll get it," she said, trying not to sound desperate.

"I'm standing right here."

He walked back into the kitchen. She heard him. "Hello?"

Then his deep sigh. "Oh, brother."

Steve. It was Steve. He had asked for her.

But then she heard Mitch continue, "Jesus Christ. You're thirteen years old!"

It was Mason. Calling from the slumber party. Wanting to come home.

"I'll go," she called. She picked up her keys from the table by the front door.

"Is anybody else going home?" Mitch was shouting into the phone. "They're asleep? Then go to sleep. Why can't you? Jesus, Mason. When are you going to grow up?"

"He's only thirteen," Madelyn said.

"We're not coming," Mitch said into the phone.

"I'm going."

"No. Tough it out. You'll be fine. If you stay up all night, so the fuck what!" Mitch slammed the phone down.

"You're mad at me," Madelyn said. "Why take it out on him?"

The keys were heavy in her hand. She turned to go.

"Don't you dare go get him."

"He wants to come home."

"You've babied him his entire life. You've ruined him."

Madelyn stepped into her spotless formal dining room and dropped the keys onto the table. She sat down at the dark Mission-style table. It had cost them a fortune, this table and the matching chairs. She lay her head down on her arms. Why had she bought this table? They never used it. They never had the big dinner parties, Thanksgiving feasts, birthday celebrations she had imagined. The first winter after her mother's death, she had tried to make Christmas dinner. She had unpacked and washed her mother's special holiday china, bought red and green napkins, decorated this room with pine and reindeer. Mitch had been furious. We're Jewish, he reminded her. Other Jews have Christmas, the Santa Claus and snowflake kind. Then she apologized. She had not been very sensitive to his feelings. Her mother and father were dead. What did they care? She had put it all away. They ate the roast beef that night in the breakfast room, like always. This dining room would be better used as storage. Well. She supposed that's what it was. Attractive storage.

She heard the door to Mitch's office slam shut. Maybe Mitch was right. Maybe if they were tough this time Mason would get over it. One night wouldn't hurt him. One night spent curled in his sleeping bag, sobbing into his pillow. It was just one night. It wouldn't hurt. She would pick him up early tomorrow morning. He had Hebrew school anyway. They were celebrating his bar mitzvah in only two months. There was so much to do.

She had forgotten her drink. Maybe she had had enough. The vodka burned in the back of her throat, festered in her full stomach.

"Mitch?" Madelyn called. "Mitch?"

He didn't know. No one would know. No one could ever suspect that she had slept with another man. Not with her sloppy stomach and saddlebag thighs. Steve was probably home right now laughing at her. He and his young, beautiful Latina dinner companion were chuckling over the desperate housewife. Together. In bed.

Madelyn knew she would not sleep tonight. She missed her children. Lately, even when they were home, she missed them. She missed the children they had been, longed for their little bodies in her lap, the way they collapsed against her chest. When they were small and she fought with Mitch, she would go into their room—in their first tiny house where the children shared a room—and lie down on the floor next to their bunk beds. She would inhale their young breath as they exhaled, draw their love for her into her lungs. They kept her young. They aged her beyond recognition. She would stroke their flushed cheeks as they slept and study their hands curled on the blanket, under their chins, against the pillow. They were born in such perfection. When did the imperfections begin?

Mitch came out of his office.

"I'm going out," he said.

"Where?"

"I can't do this.

"You said that before."

"I'm going for a drive."

"Want company?"

He looked at her. She saw that she was what he wanted to escape. He put his cell phone in his pocket. He picked up his keys.

Madelyn followed him into the living room. She picked up her drink and stared into the glass. She focused on the ice, the patterns made by cool liquid against frozen. Where did the shadows come from?

The front door closed.

"'Bye," Madelyn said.

chapter fifty-eight

pulled into a mini-market with a phone booth. One of the parking-lot lights was flickering on and off. A soda can lying on the asphalt glittered and then went dark. I went to the phone booth with a handful of change. It's easy for cops to get some things. I made my first call. I got the phone numbers I wanted. I dialed the first number.

"Hello?" It was him.

"I . . . " My voice sounded funny even to me. "May I speak to Linda?"

"Who is this?"

He knew, but I told him anyway. "Her husband."

"She doesn't want to talk to you."

"Ask her."

"She's not interested."

"I want to talk to her."

"She's not coming to the phone."

"She needs to talk to me."

"I'm sorry."

"Come on." I hated to beg.

"I'm sorry. She's made her choice."

"Are you aware that I'm a police officer?"

"Yes."

"Well?"

"Since when is love illegal?"

He hung up.

I watched the can shining in the alien-green light. Abruptly the lamp went out. There was no rhythm to the light and dark. I waited, but it stayed off. Linda would go on with her life. There was no reason for me to ever see her again. Divorce can happen in the mail.

I looked at my pad. I dialed the next number. I was surprised when a man answered. I had expected an answering machine.

"Hello?" he said. "What? Who is this?"

The man was crying, obviously upset. Something was not right, and I admit my depression took a tiny shift from black to navy blue.

"Is Dorothy there?" I asked.

"Who is this?"

I paused.

"Is this Seth?" he asked. "I have something to say to you, asshole."

"This is Officer Cork with the Beverly Hills P.D."

"So what do you want?"

"May I speak to her please?"

"She's not here."

"Where is she?" They had gotten married that afternoon, I thought. Had she run out for milk? Shouldn't they be in a hotel somewhere, or at least in bed together?

"I don't know where she is. I don't care. I don't care."

"I thought you were getting married."

"I thought so, too."

He snorted. I heard him take a drink of something.

"Is this about the accident?" he asked.

"No. Yes. Just a follow-up call. You have no idea where she might be?"

"Her mom is at St. John's. I guess she's there."

"And the wedding?"

"Fuck the wedding. Fuck her. Do me a favor, okay?"

"What?" The navy blue turned aquamarine.

"If you see her, tell her to go fuck herself. Tell her I hate her." I heard him sob.

"Well. Thanks very much."

We hung up. I turned from the phone booth. The light overhead zapped on again. I picked up the soda can and put it in the trash. I heard the police radio crackle, calling me. I hurried to answer. As soon as that call was dealt with, I was going to the hospital.

chapter fifty-nine

Dorothy pulled up in front of the house she shared with Lewis. Something white fluttered on the front lawn. For some reason, she was always finding plastic bags in the yard. Because the house was on a corner, or possibly due to the prevailing wind, the bags got caught in the low jade plants and rustled and flapped. She peeled one from the shrubbery every day, or at least every other day. Usually they were white, sometimes khaki-colored, printed with the names of cheap clothing outlets, supermarkets, drugstores. One, white with purple lettering, had come all the way from an adult video store in Las Vegas, Nevada.

The house was dark. The porch light was not on. Dorothy got out of her brother's car. She shivered. The first day of spring had turned into a Los Angeles winter night, dry and briskly chilled. Sweater weather. She had packed new brown pants and a tight sleeveless T-shirt for tonight at the hotel after the ceremony and the reception. She and Lewis had planned to sit on the balcony of the bridal suite and drink champagne and talk and laugh before going inside to make love. She would have been freezing.

"Lewis?" she called pointlessly.

His car was gone. The house was darker than she imagined it could ever be. She stood on the front walk. There were many white plastic bags in the bushes and on the ground. They were quiet. They swelled in the breeze, but didn't crackle and crunch like plastic. She walked over to the closest one, in the tallest bush. It wasn't a bag. It was a piece of white silk with a subtle floral design. Her wedding dress had been shredded. Her new wedding dress. The one she really liked, that Mr. Lee had given her. There were scraps all over the yard, tatters of fabric snagged on bare branches. The largest fragments looked trampled, stamped into the dirt by angry feet.

The chill crawled up her spine. She took a step away. She backed toward her brother's car. She wrapped her arms across her chest. Headlights turned the corner, a car, no, a truck like Lewis' coming toward her. She ducked behind the bushes. It slowed. It passed. She got up and ran to Michael's car. She could not run fast enough. She drove down her street to the dead end at Sunset Boulevard, and then she sat there in the car, doors locked, windows rolled up. Right. Left. There were no other options. One hundred and fifty people had planned to be at her wedding today. Eighty of them were Lewis's friends and family. But she had loved ones, too. Her great-aunt and uncle were at the Holiday Inn in Glendale. Cousin Stan and his wife, what's-her-name, were at the Roosevelt in Hollywood. Susie from elementary school and her husband and baby were staying at the Magic Castle. Her mother and father were together at the hospital. Right. Left. Left to Lani, her best friend, who liked Lewis so much and had been so excited about the wedding. Her maid of honor, if they were doing that kind of hoopla. She would go to Lani even though just the thought of it made Dorothy tired, made her head so heavy she didn't think she could hold it up for the ten-minute drive over there. Left. Left. Her left eye flashed its annoying sparkles in sympathy.

Lani's kooky Silver Lake house was lit up for a party. It was always a party at Lani's house. Multicolored lights twinkled over her front porch. The Tibetan lanterns in her garden swayed and sparkled. A battery-operated plastic lamp, a replica of a life-sized goose, glowed by the door.

Dorothy stepped over the blue glass bottles, each containing a burning candle, that crossed the front walk in regular intervals. The pattern was Lani's complicated and ridiculous design to catch evil spirits.

Missed me, Dorothy thought as she got to the front door. Missed me again.

There was music inside, the blues, and voices. She heard Lani's braying laugh. The door was ajar. She pushed it open and went into the living room. It was empty, but there were drink glasses on the coffee table and incense burning. Lani had made her living room look like the inside of a wealthy bedouin's tent. The pillows were scattered on the floor.

"Lani?"

"Darling!" Lani ran in from the kitchen, still in her outfit for the wedding, lustrous red Chinese pajamas. How great those would have been with the new dress, Dorothy thought; how beautiful she would be standing next to me wearing Mr. Lee's favorite dress.

Lani put her arms around Dorothy. She held her tight. Dorothy could smell the marijuana and the sweet orange liqueur that Lani favored for cool evenings.

"You really fucked things up, didn't you?"

Her arms were warm, but her voice was cold.

"What?"

Lewis entered from the other room. And two of his band members. They stood in the arched doorway. An absurd orange tassel hanging from the ceiling tangled in the hair on the top of Lewis's head.

Lani stepped back into line with Lewis and his buddies. They crossed their arms, spread their legs, frowned. They looked like a poster for a bad '70's cover band, Lani in red, the boys in black, the Indian bedspread covering the wall behind them.

Dorothy laughed.

Lewis hung his head.

"No," Dorothy said, "I didn't mean—"

"You better go," Lani said.

Where? Why didn't Lewis go? Wasn't Lani her friend? "Where?" she said out loud.

"I'm helping Lewis right now," Lani said. "You've hurt him very, very badly."

"I didn't mean to laugh."

"I wasn't talking about that."

"Where am I supposed to go?"

"What about Seth?" Lewis spoke. His voice was thick and nasal, as if he was coming down with a cold. "That's where you want to be."

Dorothy thought of Seth's leather couch. Of his cold studio and the bottles of expensive beer in his refrigerator.

"What did you do to my dress?" she asked. She turned to Lani. "Did you see what he did to my dress?"

Lani only shrugged. Lewis sobbed once, a guttural hiccup filled with snot and liquid, and ran out of the room. Lani ran after him.

Dorothy stumbled out the door. She wasn't crying, but she couldn't see either. The edges of her sight were fuzzy, as if the aperture were closing.

She heard the tinkle of broken blue glass as she kicked a bottle down the walk in front of her. And another. She couldn't see the bottles.

She heard Lani's door close behind her.

Her head hurt. She got into her brother's car and closed her eyes. They pulsed and sparked under her lids. She needed aspirin or something stronger. She had always wanted someone to take care of her. When she was young, she wanted a mother—a real mother, not a crazy one. In high school, she had Lani to tell her what to wear and what kind of music to listen to. And then, when she grew up, she wanted a man—Seth, Lewis, whoever—to have all the answers. Not anymore, she thought. From now on, she would take care of herself. She started the car. It was all she had and it wasn't even hers. In Los Angeles, there was always someplace to go. She'd drive until she figured out where that was.

chapter sixty

Leo traversed the streets of Beverly Hills. He drove up and down, back and forth, left and right, drifting but not without purpose. He was simply waiting for the choice to be made for him. He wanted the decision out of his hands. He had let women lead him his entire life. He would not stop now.

He lifted his ass, still driving, and wriggled the gun from his pocket. It had dug into his hipbone, prevented the seat belt from lying straight. He set it on the seat beside him. He kept his hand on it. He kept the other hand on the wheel. The streets were quiet, the windows dark in every mansion that he passed. Only the palm trees moved, swayed against the night sky and clapped their hard, spiny leaves together as he passed by. Thank you, he thought. Thank you very much. He turned down Rodeo, the famous shopping street. A police car idled at the curb. Leo looked over as he passed. The officers glanced back over greasy lips and working jaws. There was nothing open, no doughnut shops. Only window after window of tiny clothes strung on emaciated plastic models, nothing to eat and all of it designed to make you want more and more, more food, more money, more sex. The policemen must have brought their late-night dinners from home.

Leo turned the corner away from the cops. He made a mental note not to go down Rodeo Drive again. They could already be running his license plate, realizing he's not Jennifer Dunlop. They could be dropping their sandwiches and chicken legs into their hard cooler lunch boxes, putting the patrol car in gear and coming after him. He did not speed up. He did not hide the gun. He did not turn another corner. He went straight, heading for Wilshire Boulevard and the possibility of traffic, activity, choices.

No cops behind him. Who cared if a handsome Hispanic guy drove an old two-door rice burner. He was just coming home from work, the catering job, the cleaning service, dishwasher, busboy, nobody. The traffic on Wilshire was all heading in one direction, home. He thought again of the officers' sack lunches. Last night's leftovers packed for today. Drumsticks and ham on white. An apple. Peanut-butter cookies. Leo had to get something to eat. He was dying of hunger. He was dying. He had to eat something. He was sick of burgers and fast food. He wanted broccoli. He wanted roast chicken and broccoli and a twice-baked potato. He wanted it served in a white china bowl. His stomach complained. His navel was rubbing up against his backbone. His belly was concave, scooped out with a dirty serving spoon. He wanted a table in front of him and someone passing him the butter. The rolls. His head hurt. His eyes closed. The car swerved.

Honk. The horn opened his eyes. He had crossed lanes, cut off the car behind him. He looked in the rearview mirror. A young woman, in thick gothic makeup and white-blond hair, flipped him the bird. She had a dozen bracelets on her arm. It was Saturday night. He just remembered. She was out. She was alone. He pulled over and let her go ahead. Then he pulled in behind her. He caught her looking at him in her rearview mirror. She shook her head and her bleached hair didn't move.

Did you hear about the suicide blond? She dyed by her own hand.

He saw her mouth say, "Asshole." The choice was made. He was not responsible. She had given him the instructions, and all he could do was obey.

She ran a yellow light and he followed. She zipped onto the 405 freeway northbound. He zipped right behind. She drove a miniature truck, a half-pint sport utility vehicle with a bumper sticker that read "Bad Girl." It wasn't his idea. He said it again to himself. He said it out loud. Bad Girl. This was your idea. He could see the blond hair, even at night, even on the freeway. He wondered how white her skin would be on the inside of her arms, under her shirt, above her hipbone. The bad girls were usually best.

She was aware of him. He saw her glance again into her rearview mirror. And again. She was worried now. His hand closed over the gun. He could wave it at her, show her he meant business. She might get too scared, call someone, drive off the road. He pretended to look elsewhere, at the watch he didn't wear. At the radio that wasn't turned on. He was only following her. Something he did well. When he got back to Maryland, maybe he'd get a job as a private investigator. He could drive along behind. He could take pictures of men with other women, women with men who weren't their husbands. He would pull the black-and-white photos slowly from the manila envelope and reveal them one by one to unhappy husbands. The husbands would gasp, exhale, cry, or rage. He would commiserate and then counsel the cuckolds to leave 'em flat, fuck 'em, they're not worth it. Maybe the guys would slip him an extra couple of hundred dollars to give their wives a final unforgettable memory.

She exited on Sunset. Leo sighed. He didn't want to be here again. Sunset Boulevard. Back and forth. But she came off the exit and turned left, west into Brentwood. A direction he had not gone before. He let a car come between them. Her truck sat high enough that he could see it over the BMW in front. She knew he was back there. She knew that road rage was about to change her life. But it wasn't road rage. She was wrong.

She made a sharp right into a driveway leading to the parking garage under a small apartment building. He pulled over to the curb behind her, at the start of the driveway. He revved his motor once. She was fumbling in her purse. Again he thought of a gun, a woman with a gun. Again he imagined the glass shattering, but it was his blood this time that sprayed like a fountain in front of City Hall. He saw his hand palm up and twitching on his lap before growing still.

He picked up Jenny's pistol from the seat. What was the stupid bitch doing? She leaned from her window. She had something in her hand. It was the key card to open the garage; she was trying to get it into the little slot. He could see her hand shaking. He could hear the ugly row of bracelets clinking together. He watched. He could slide behind her into the parking garage. Two cars could go through. The gates moved so slowly.

He waited. She dropped her key card. He saw it fall. He knew her moment of decision. Should she get out of the car? Should she try to get her card? Should she back out of the driveway and go somewhere else? Would he pick up her card and use it, wait for her? She opened her door. She slid one hand out, but her ridiculous mini-truck sat too high for her to reach the ground. She would have to get out. The door opened a little wider. She didn't have much room between her car and the machine. She squeezed out of her car. She was plump. That surprised him. She wore a flowered skirt that rode up her sub-stantial thighs as she bent to pick up the card. He had expected long, skinny legs and big black boots. Her calves were freckled and thick, her ankles hidden by white socks in funny red shoes. The backs of her knees were dimpled as she climbed back into her car.

He didn't have it anymore. His stomach hurt. And he just felt so sad. Used-up, the way his mom would say whenever one of the kids fought with her or said something mean or spilled their milk at dinner. I can't do it anymore, she'd say, I'm just all used-up.

He drove away. The girl buried her face in her hands. She was crying. He was leaving. There was no reason to cry.

The only home he had was with Jenny. She had wanted him to stay. She had offered to love him forever. If he had said yes, would she have lived? Or had she already taken the pills? Now he couldn't remember. It seemed she had killed herself because he didn't love her. He didn't know her then. Not like now. She could have given him some time. He loved her now. He did.

He pulled into the parking lot of a big, beautiful supermarket. He would buy vegetables and one of those chickens already cooked. He would go back to the apartment and eat dinner with Jenny.

chapter sixty-one

Madelyn was dreaming of a garden. The plants grew wild and bloomed in profusion before her eyes. Even in her dream, she laughed. Flashback, she said. Her lips moved against the sofa cushion. She had fallen asleep on her living-room couch. She was alone in her house. Her children gone. Her husband gone. The phone sat on the coffee table beside her. She had wanted to speak to Steve, but she had been afraid. She had curled up on her couch. She had closed her eyes, just for a moment. In her dream she was beautiful. In her dream her friends surrounded her. Her mother and father were not dead; her sister and brother and their families were just behind the next stand of trees. In her dream it had begun to snow, but it was warm, like snow in a commercial on television. No one felt the cold; no one had a red nose or watery eyes. Everyone was delighted with her.

Before Madelyn awoke, she reached for something. Her hand went out, her fingers clawed at the air, but she found nothing. She opened her eyes and sat up. She picked up the phone.

She dialed her husband's cell phone. It rang once before the answering service clicked in. It meant he was on the phone. Who was he talking to this late at night? Rusty? Scott? Complaining about her. She hung up. She dialed Steve. His phone rang once. Twice. Four times. If he's not there, she thought, I'll kill myself. An expression they frowned on at the Suicide Prevention Hot Line.

"Hello." Steve sounded sleepy, almost annoyed.

"It's Madelyn."

"Come over," he said. "Come over here. Right now."

"I can't."

"Why not?"

"What would I tell Mitch?"

"Tell him you're grocery shopping. Tell him it's the best time to grocery shop. No crowds. No whining children."

"But I won't have any groceries when I come home."

"I'll give you a bag. A roll of toilet paper. A box of crackers. I think I have a loaf of bread. Please?"

"I can't."

"A cup of tea. That's all. I promise."

She would not think about his penis. How it felt hard but coated in silk in her hand, how deeply it entered her. "Why did you come to the restaurant?" she said.

"Are you angry?"

"Of course."

"Come over."

"Do you know how hard that was for me?"

"I'll make it up to you. Right now."

"No."

She could see the new pattern of her life. She would sneak the moments to talk to him. Her heart would beat in her chest as she dialed his number. The thrill would be in doing it. They would talk and flirt and once a week, if possible—maybe less, maybe more—she would get away to unwrap his stumps, to climb aboard his wheelchair for an hour, or two at most. It would never be enough. It was better than nothing.

"Don't be angry," he said. "I wanted to see you. I missed you. I knew you were there and I had to come. I had to."

"You made me miserable."

"I know. I'm sorry. Was that your husband sitting next to you?"

She didn't want to talk about Mitch. She didn't want to think about him. She wanted Steve to ask her to come over again, to demand it.

"Steve?"

"Yes?"

"Never mind."

He sighed.

"I'm not going to last long," he said.

Her stomach gurgled. Not death. Not now. "What do you mean?"

"I can't keep this up. I don't want a part-time, guilty, occasional screw. It was fun today. It was great. But I want more."

"Better than nothing?"

"Yes. For now. But I don't know for how long."

Out of the frying pan. Her mother's mind put her kids and her in his little house. Weekends with dad, homework with her, the awkward moments at sporting events and holiday pageants. Who would go to the parent-teacher conferences? What about the dog?

"I love you," she said to him. "I'm sorry. I love you."

"It's okay," he said. "You can't scare me."

"Good night."

"Sleep well."

Madelyn hung up and began to cry. Her hip was still sore from the accident. She deserved that. She should be hurt worse, wounded. She should have her face destroyed, become a horror to her children.

But Steve wouldn't care. He didn't seem to care about any of it. She should follow Mitch, show up at his office. Next weekend she would surprise him with a room at a hotel on the beach. They would stay up late, take a bath together. She could make it happen. She could give up photography and the hot line. Of course she would give up her Monday nights at the hot line. She would concentrate on the kids, spend more time helping them, encouraging them. And when they were a little older, she could go back to school for social work. She could be one of those women who does good. She would make it up to Mitch. She would.

chapter sixty-two

Mitch was in his enormous new Sport Utility Vehicle, a truck that wasn't really a truck. It was made to stay clean and carry only briefcases and the dry cleaning. It was just two months old; it still had that tart new car smell. He dialed his cell phone.

"Did I wake you?" He whispered into the phone, even though there was no one who might overhear, no reason to whisper. "Are you awake? I'm coming over. I love you. I can't live without you. I'm telling her. Tomorrow. Tomorrow."

He didn't feel guilty. He had waited for Madelyn to get her life together. He had waited for ten years for her to get off her fat ass and do something. She had so much promise before the kids, before the house, before his success. She had turned into her mother.

"What are you wearing?" he said into the tiny cell phone. As if that was original.

And he laughed under his breath and he could already feel his dick getting hard and that, to him, was love.

chapter sixty-three

<u>Note #151 07/17/01</u>

Without some reason to go forward, I can't think of why not to die. I'd rather meet the inevitable head-on, face front, best foot forward. The futility of life depresses me. If there were just one flower that only I could grow, it would be enough.

James

I hurried down the second-floor hallway of St. John's Memorial Hospital to Room 262. A plump nurse huffed along beside me. She had nodded wisely when I asked for the room, when I said I was looking for Dorothy P. Fairweather. She panted to me as we trotted together that Dorothy had behaved so oddly, that she had run out of the hospital earlier after being terribly rude to Dr. Swarup.

We went in. Dorothy's mother was sleeping. Dorothy's father dozed beside her in a hard chair. The nurse woke her. Dorothy's mother was not happy to see me.

"I'm trying to find Dorothy," I said.

She waved a hand.

"It's important."

"We have no idea where she went," her father grumbled. "She has her brother's car."

"What kind of car?" I asked.

"'99 BMW 528. Black. California plates. His name is Michael Fairweather." The dad knew just what I needed.

"Thanks."

"Is she in trouble?" he asked.

"No," I said. They frowned at me, puzzled. I realized how odd I must seem to them. "I was at the accident yesterday." I didn't know what else to say. "I just need to talk to her."

Dorothy's mother, Jane, sat up and looked me in the eye.

"You find her," she said. "Go get her."

As I ran back out of the hospital to the "emergency parking only" where I'd left the squad car, I felt a little guilty. I was still on shift. But I was working. I would work if something came up. I had answered that last call. It was nothing. The alarm had gone off in a warehouse off Veteran. I went before going to the hospital. I went inside, talked to the security guard. We found no one and no sign of entry. It must have been a tremor or something. Happens a lot.

I got in the cruiser and started it up. I hoped another call wouldn't come in. I used the computer. I spoke to dispatch, asked them to put out an APB on a '99 528 black BMW. I gave them the license plate number.

I drove back to Beverly Hills. It was 11:26. I had only half an hour left on this shift. My last shift, but I wasn't thinking about that. I was thinking about Dorothy P. Fairweather, about what had happened to her and how sad she must be. I didn't know what I'd do when I found her, but seeing her seemed the best last thing I could do. I kept my eyes open as I drove. There are at least one million black BMWs in Los Angeles.

chapter sixty-four

Dorothy sat before the welcoming glow of the twenty-four-hour supermarket. This was exactly what she needed. Aspirin. Soup. It was all here as advertised. She had found a parking space in the first row. She took it as a good omen. The store was huge. It was more than just a grocery store, it was Food Nirvana. She sat in her car and watched the checkers and the baggers and the customers working, bending, gliding, performing through the glass picture windows in a suburban ballet.

A tear ran down one cheek. It was less a tear than a leak. She released it and her shoulders relaxed. She was glad to be here, even if she had nowhere else to go. She was so happy not to be driving. She was having trouble with her eyes. She could see only what was right in front of her, right at the end of her nose. Anything peripheral was missing. The edges fell away into darkness.

She got out of the car. The big glass doors slid open automatically. Welcome. Welcome. We've been waiting for you. She entered. A checker looked up and smiled at her. The artificial light caressed her. She admired the yellow tint it gave her hands as she took a cart and started down an aisle. The wheels made a rhythmic hum on the shiny linoleum floor, keeping time with the ambient synthesized music that had no words or emotion. Everything anyone could ever want was right here, twenty-four hours a day, seven days a week, in every weather, no matter what happened. It was good to have one thing you could depend on.

She stood back and let her spyglass eyesight survey the stacks of food. Right away something caught her damaged eyes. A lovely box of powdered doughnut holes. She put it in her cart. The box had pink and yellow bunnies hopping across the front. New, it said, for Spring. Pink and yellow and lavender doughnut holes. She licked her lips. The coolness of the sugar, the crunch of the fried dough, the way the lard and sweetness would coat her tongue.

A lot of the food in the store was decorated for spring. She had never noticed before how the food changed with the seasons. Not the actual food—doughnut holes were doughnut holes, after all, but the decorations changed, the toppings went from white to pink. The canned spaghetti advertised flower-shaped pasta. The cereal boxes displayed spring pictures of young animals and children with kites. And over her head there were bright crepe-paper streamers of pink and green and yellow, cardboard baby chicks hanging down, and plush stuffed rabbits on top of every shelf unit. Many many rabbits as if they'd believed their own cliché and procreated with abandon. It was a spring festival in the grocery store.

Another tear. Her head throbbed, but just a little. The cleanliness, the bright lights, the abundance were soothing to her.

She wandered back by the deli counter. A shadow moved in the edge of her right eye. She turned to look. A young guy, a little too skinny, Italian maybe or something, stood at the hot-food case. He stared at the whole roasted chickens as if he were waiting for one to get up and leap into his basket. He ran a hand through his long black hair. Dorothy walked a little closer. Chicken might be good. With the doughnut holes.

He glanced up at her. His eyes were yellow, dark, like melted butter about to burn. She stared. She couldn't help it. He stared back.

And he looked so familiar. But not in a good way. He was not someone she was happy to see again. A flash of neon green flared in her left eye. She groaned. She did not want the sparkling in her eyes to begin again. She needed to get away from him. She backed up, but the grocery cart wheels were turned the wrong way. She couldn't make it go. She pushed forward. She pulled back. It wouldn't behave.

He kept staring and his yellow eyes were not friendly, not warm, not springlike. They were the amber of desert and hot sun, the ochre-colored eyes in an Egyptian sarcophagus.

He took a step toward her.

She could not get her cart to move.

Another tear slithered from her eye. She knew her nose was getting red.

"Are you okay?" he said.

"I bumped my head," she said. "My eyes are acting weird."

He took another step toward her. "Where are you from?" he asked. "Where do you live?"

She wasn't going to tell him. She picked up her box of doughnut holes. She would leave the cart right there. His hand patted the front pocket of his jeans.

She turned and tripped over something she couldn't see at her feet.

She stumbled and he grabbed her arm as if to help her, but then he didn't let go.

"You're skinny," he said.

His voice sounded very far away. Aneurysm. Hemorrhage. The words kept flashing in her brain.

She wiggled her arm. She looked down. She could see his fingers closed around her sleeve. She saw that he bit his nails. She could see the scratches on the back of his hand. From some other woman's fingernails, she wondered, a woman whose arm he had held earlier today? She had no nails.

"Let go," she said. "Please."

"Why?"

"Stop it."

"Why?"

"I need to go. My boyfriend's waiting in the car."

"No, he's not. I saw you sitting in your car. I saw you come in."

"What do you want?"

Where did he begin? I want a home-cooked meal. I want a bed with sheets. I want to be in Maryland. I want to wring your neck. I want you to love me forever. He felt her slipping from his grasp. He tightened his hold on her thin arm.

"Am I scaring you?"

"No. Yes."

She wanted to tell him what he wanted to hear.

"I'm going to scream," she said.

"That's a terrible idea."

He pulled her down a quiet, empty aisle, away from the front of the store, away from the deli case and the hot roasted meats.

"Why do you make me feel this way?" he asked.

And she did. He looked at her and he wanted to protect her. He wanted to feed her warm soup and cut the crusts off her toast. He wanted to save her. He wanted to kill her.

"Please," she said. "I'm sorry."

She apologized. To him. She apologized and immediately he knew that if he could make her feel better, it would all be okay. Everything would be fine.

Her beautiful market had become cavernous and forbidding. She clutched her doughnut holes as he yanked her farther down the aisle. She looked for weapons, but she was surrounded with cellophane packages of chips and popcorn, nothing more lethal than a bag of pretzel rods. She kept thinking she saw faces in the corners of her hurting eyes. She turned but it was just the bunnies on the top shelf leering down at her. The little yellow chicks grinning at her fear.

"Okay, okay," she said. "Let's talk about this."

They were heading toward the gray double doors leading to the stockroom. It was dark through the glass. She let the doughnuts fall.

She reached for something, anything, and grabbed a tube of ready-to-bake biscuits from the refrigerator case.

"Okay," she said. "Just a minute."

He stopped.

"What?" he said. "Whatever you want. Let me help you. The dark. It's too bright in here."

He could see that she was frightened. But he wanted to get her away. He wanted her alone with him.

"Don't," he said. "Don't be scared. We'll get out of here. You'll feel better."

"Let go. You're hurting me."

Stop it, he almost shouted. Can't you see I love you?

"You think I'm a fucking moron, don't you?" he said.

"No. No. No."

That wasn't what he meant to say.

"I'm not," he told her. He wanted desperately to tell her the right thing. She was sliding out from under him.

He gave her arm a yank up, pulled her onto her toes. He stared into her eyes, willing her to see him.

She looked him in his weird yellow eyes. She had seen him before. Someplace. On a wanted poster. On the wall at the post office. Oh God, someplace. She felt horrible. She was going to throw up. Her legs would not hold her. She dropped the biscuits and found his waist, held on to him to keep from falling down.

"Let go of me." She had no expectations.

"Hold on," he said.

Her eyes closed. Her knees buckled. She let herself slump.

Leo held both of her arms. He held her up. She was as light as a song. She made him feel enormous.

"Don't worry," he said.

"Please," she said again. "I'm sorry for whatever I did."

"You didn't do anything. You didn't do anything. You did nothing at all. Nothing."

She heard the biscuits rolling, rolling, rolling. She leaned her head against his chest. She couldn't help it. She felt the furious rhythm of his heart against her cheek. His arms went around her. He sighed. He held her tight.

"Yes," he said, "I'm here. I am."

She wasn't beautiful. She wasn't even pretty. She was too skinny and she looked dirty; he could see her hair needed washing and there was stuff on her shirt and her jeans. But she was helpless and her neck was long and white and he wasn't sure he could live without her. She was exactly what he had been waiting for. Her head hurt. She was crying. There was snot in her nose. He could fix it. All of it.

"Stop right there." Another voice. A man's voice. Deep and authoritative.

"I think she fainted."

"Stay where you are."

chapter sixty-five

D ispatch called. They had found the car. It was parked in front of the huge gourmet grocery store on Wilshire Boulevard. I shopped at that store sometimes. It was expensive, but it had strawberries in the spring before anyone else and Linda's favorite clementines at Christmas. I knew just where it was.

I pulled in and parked next to the BMW. My hands were sweating. My stomach was jumpy. I checked my hair in the rearview mirror. I was afraid I was crazy. Tomorrow hovered in the corner of my mind; what I planned to do, what I would do, what would happen then. My hand rested on my gun. This was it, then. This was my last chore.

I nodded at the checker as I went in. I think she recognized me. The store looked empty. I headed for the frozen foods. I wasn't hungry, but I could pretend I was shopping. Pretend I just ran into her. I couldn't wait to see her. I didn't know what I was doing there.

I came around down an aisle toward the freezer and I recognized him right away. Leo. That dumb kid from the fracas at the diner and the car accident. The one with the sad story about looking for his girlfriend. There was a girl with him. Didn't look like he was looking anymore.

But then I saw the shiny blue tube of biscuits rolling away from her. She turned her head down the aisle toward me. Her eyes were closed and her face was all puckered and scared. It was her. Dorothy

P. Fairweather. I held my breath. My first thought was how glad I was to see her. Then I was confused. This was not the guy she was supposed to marry. This was the guy whose car had hit her. And she did not look happy.

I thought about how weird the world is, you know, that they knew each other. That the kid with the yellow eyes was the same kid I'd been seeing for two days. At the car accident where she got hurt. At the diner. Now here. With her. I knew she didn't live in Beverly Hills, and he had told me twice he lived in Hollywood. But here they were again, in my neighborhood.

Then I saw his eyes slide over to me and his face go a kind of sick, bruised color. He recognized me, too. Me, the police officer.

"Please," I heard her say. "I'm sorry for whatever I did."

He whispered to her, but she squeezed her eyes shut. She was trying to sit down. Her head fell back. He was holding her up. His hands on her arms were not the hands of a friend. He was squeezing too hard.

"Yes," he said louder. "I'm here. I am."

He started dragging her, heading toward the stockroom.

"Stop right there," I said.

"I think she fainted."

"Stay where you are."

I walked toward them. I knew her. I knew him. But I was confused. Did they know each other? Did the kid know she was the one who ran the red light and caused the accident?

"Leo," I said because I remembered his name and it always helps if you know their name. "Leo, what are you doing? Is she all right?"

"She fainted," he said again. Then he shook her. "Wake up."

He was holding her too tight. She was a dead weight in his hands. Her legs collapsed. Still, he didn't help her down. Her arms were above her head. Her feet were backwards on the floor. I could see a strip of her belly from her shirt being pulled up. I could tell by the color of her throat she was not feeling well. She should be home lying on the couch in front of the TV, I thought. She should have her legs on a pillow, a little above her heart. Not good to move around too much with a concussion.

"Let me help you," I said.

I reached for her and he turned away from me.

"No," he said.

"I'll help you."

"No!" Now he was shouting. "She's mine!"

I didn't like that. I could tell by the look on his face, it was not a good "mine." It was not a good thing at all.

"Leo." I used my most authoritative voice. "Do not move."

"Don't you see?" he said. He looked down into her face. He was crying and then I thought maybe he did know her because he was crying over her. "Wake up," he said to her. "Please wake up."

He gave her a shake.

She groaned a little.

"Don't do that!" I shouted. "She's hurt!" You should never shake a head injury.

He looked at me. The tears ran down his face like rain, like a spring rain. I'd seen those tears before, once, a hundred times, a thousand. He'd gotten himself someplace, but he couldn't get out. He looked down at her.

"Please wake up."

Then he screamed at her. "Wake up!"

Her eyes opened. She was terrified. "No," she said. She had it in her to struggle a little. "No."

"I want you to put her down. Gently," I said.

Leo just slid her under one arm. She was such a little thing. He wrapped one arm around her waist, leaving her sort of bent over. With his free hand, he reached in the pocket of his blue jeans and I knew it before I saw it, I knew it was coming, he pulled out a gun. Damn it. I knew it was there. I should have seen it in his face.

It wasn't much of a gun, it was what they call a lady's derringer, but I knew the damage it could do. I turned away from him, unsnapped the holster guard, and unlocked the safety on my gun.

316

"Get back," he said.

I stepped back.

Dorothy squirmed a little. "I want to sit down."

"Tell me you love me," Leo said to her. "I love you. I came all this way to find you. I've looked everywhere. All the places I thought you might go. I waited outside of that acting school you told me about. If I saw a movie truck, I'd stop and show them your picture. I had almost given up, and then I found you."

And I knew Leo had gone completely nuts. His tears kept coming and he recited his speech for the other girl, that girl from Maryland he was looking for.

"I've looked everywhere for you. Why did you leave me?" I could see him sweating.

"Leo," I said. "Let her sit down."

For the first time, she heard me. She turned her face to me and her eyes widened when she recognized me. She knew who I was. I saw her relax a little. I could see her faith in me.

"Tell me you love me." I heard desperation in his plea. He was angry, but he was begging her.

I nodded at Dorothy. I smiled a little. "It's okay," I whispered.

She turned her face up to Leo.

"I love you," she said. She stared into his eyes. She almost made me believe her. "I love you. I love you."

"Okay, Leo," I said. "You can let her go now."

But he just kept staring at her.

"Leo?" I wanted him to look at me. I didn't want him to realize, even for a moment, that Dorothy was not the girl of his dreams. I saw his hand fingering the gun. He brought it up to his face. He pressed Dorothy to him. She was against his chest as tight as a Siamese twin. I didn't know where the gun was headed.

"You found her, Leo," I said. "Let's go buy a bottle of champagne. Let's celebrate. You found her. Jesus, Leo. That's terrific."

"Don't leave me," he whispered to her.

"I love you," she replied.

317

She brought her hands up as if to caress his chest. Instead, she pushed him. She pushed hard and when he wouldn't let go, she slapped him. Still he held on. She tried to get away. He grabbed both wrists and brought the gun up to her face.

"You bitch," he said.

"No!" I shouted.

Leo swung around and fired at me. I was close. He wasn't far off. The bullet grazed my ear and ricocheted in the shelves of popcorn and cake mixes.

I heard Dorothy scream and then I wanted to live. I absolutely did not want to die. I rolled back from him and came up with my gun aimed.

And he dropped her. Just like that.

He dropped her—no—he kind of threw her from him, like he didn't want to touch her anymore. Then he ran and I yelled "Wait!" or "Stop!" but he didn't and she fell and bumped her head hard on that industrial floor. It was bad. I heard the crack. I felt it.

But I had to go after him.

I took off, shouting, "Stop! Police!" which is what I'm supposed to say, but it never stops them anyway. Once they're running, it doesn't matter what I say. And he knew I was a cop. He headed for the door and I got on the wrong stupid side of the cheese thing, that refrigerated case like an open casket in the middle of the floor.

"Stop!" I yelled again. But I had to run around the cheese and he was already out the door.

"Dial 9-1-1," I called to the checker as I ran by. "There's a girl in the back. Get an ambulance."

One of the other checkers, younger, pregnant maybe, was standing there like a statue. Her mouth was hanging open. I could see her pierced tongue. But I saw the other checker dialing the phone before I was even out the door.

Leo was in his car. He was backing out of the parking lot. And there was this moment when I had to decide what to do. Should I follow him in the truck? Shoot at him? Cops can only shoot out the tires in a movie. I'm a good shot, and I would have missed. So I memorized his license-plate number. He was going fast. He was backing all the way out of the lot. I could see his face through the windshield. He was sobbing now. His face looked like a kid, a little kid. A fucking crazy little kid with a big adult problem.

He was going way too fast. There was a screech of brakes and a fancy-ass SUV swerved to avoid him, slid to the left and flipped over the decorative brick wall in the median strip and landed upside down in the opposite lane. A sedan going the other way rammed right into it. Couldn't help it.

I was sick to my stomach. And I was really glad that the ambulance was on its way. The guy driving the SUV was hurt. Seriously. I knew it.

Traffic stopped in all directions. Except for Leo. Leo gunned it and took off. He kept driving, dodging around the stopped cars until I couldn't see him anymore.

I could have gone after him, but I was worried about the driver of the SUV and Dorothy. I had Leo's plate number. I knew eventually we'd find him. She was lying on the supermarket floor, Dorothy P. Fairweather. Jesus, I love that name.

I jogged across the road, hopped over the rubble that had been the brick wall. I hurried to the driver's side of the SUV and crouched down. It was a man and he was definitely dead. No one could live with their neck in that position. Blood trickled from his mouth and maybe his ear, I couldn't tell exactly. A woman came running up from her car and she screamed. Then a guy came over and another, and another woman. 12:32 A.M., Sunday morning, and this guy's mangled death was attracting a crowd. I stood up.

"Step back," I said to them.

And they did. I looked at the body in the car. His eyes were open, but he wasn't seeing anything. And suddenly, I was filled with sadness and horror for this man's death. He had a life, all that we know of life he had, and now it was over. I didn't feel like he was better off. I didn't feel that at all. I thought of Dorothy and I so fiercely wanted her to be alive and okay. I looked at the crowd and I saw each person standing there living. I was filled with awe watching them, the miracle of them thinking and wanting and alive. One woman was crying and her tears sparkled on her cheek in the streetlight.

There was something on the side of the road and it was singing, making noise. I looked over. It was a cell phone. Ringing. Playing "Take Me Out to the Ballgame." The guy must have been holding that cell phone when the accident happened. I picked it up, pushed the little green button.

"Hello?"

"Mitch?" It was a woman's voice. "I'm sorry. Come home. I'm really sorry."

It seemed like everybody was apologizing. And I had to apologize to her, the woman on the phone. I had to give her instructions. I had to listen to her be completely quiet on the other end of the phone. I know that silence too well. I'd rather they scream and cry.

Uniformed officers and the ambulance showed up really quickly. I gave the officers Leo's information, license plate, etc. Then I ran back inside to Dorothy with the paramedics, two guys I know, Kenny and Rick. I was afraid there would be blood, a minimal concussion turned fatal. Aneurysm, I thought. Hemorrhage. If she's dead, I don't know what I'll do. We hurried. She was lying on the floor with the checker kneeling next to her.

Her eyes were closed and she was an odd color.

"What's her name?" Kenny asked me.

"Dorothy," I said.

"Dorothy?" Rick called to her. His voice was gentle. He rubbed her cheek. "Do you hear me?"

She didn't respond. Rick frowned. I couldn't stand that frown on his face. I'd seen it before.

"Dorothy," I said. "Dorothy!"

She groaned. Her eyes opened for a second. "I'm sick," she said.

Kenny was quick. He rolled her onto her side, but she only dry-heaved. A little spit came out—that was all. They rolled her back. There wasn't any blood on the floor under her head.

"Better?" I said.

She looked at me and smiled. I thought I knew that smile. People are happy to see policemen—when they need them. It's the smile they give a priest after the exorcism. Now go away. I want to pretend this never happened.

But she kept smiling.

"Hi," she said. "What are you doing here?"

She started to get up, but Rick put a hand on her shoulder to keep her flat. He kneeled over her. Took her blood pressure and her pulse.

Kenny shined his penlight in her eyes.

"What's your name?" he asked.

"Dorothy Fairweather."

"What's your address?"

"One sixty-five Juniper," she said. "No. Wait. That's where I grew up. I . . . I'm sort of between places right now."

She blinked a few times. Then she smiled again. A big smile this time.

"My eyes," she said. "They're fine. I can see just fine."

We all grinned at her. We were happy for her. We couldn't help it.

"Can I sit up?" she asked.

"Slowly."

I had already explained to the guys that Dorothy had a slight concussion, that she had been in a car accident only yesterday. I looked at my watch. 1:11 A.M. Her accident had been the day before yesterday. For some reason, I felt relieved. It was Sunday. The first day of spring was over.

The paramedics told her to see her doctor on Monday, but there was no reason she couldn't go home.

She laughed when they said that.

They helped her to her feet. She wobbled a little, but she walked all on her own over to where Farley, one of my colleagues, was waiting. He had to ask her some questions. I wanted to know why she was there, how she knew Leo. I wanted to listen to her answers, but another officer, Smitty, had to talk to me. She was done first. I watched her leave the grocery store.

"That's it," I said to Smitty. "That's all I know."

I ran out to the parking lot.

Dorothy was leaning against her car, her brother's car. She didn't look unhappy or even worried.

"Still here?" That was a clever line on my part.

"I'm trying to decide what to do next," she said.

"There's a good hotel just over on Brandywine."

"I was thinking of the bigger picture."

"Why don't you come home with me?" I said. I couldn't believe I said it. I'm not like that.

"Are you in love with me?" she asked. "Do you want to take care of me forever?"

"No," I said. And that was the truth.

"Thank God," she said.

She followed me back to the station, where I checked out. I didn't do any paperwork. I didn't want to keep her waiting.

We went back to my apartment. I told her to park in Linda's space. She had the longest shower I've ever known a woman to take. But I didn't mind. I gave her a clean shirt—couldn't do much about the pants.

When she came out, she looked shiny, as if she had been scrubbed with a brush. She smelled great. Even though I knew it was my shampoo, it smelled completely different on her.

"You need some different shampoo," she said. "I'll get you some."

"You will?"

"And a haircut," she said, "Later I'll give you a haircut."

"Okay." That was the last thing I expected from her. "How do you feel?"

"Tired."

She slept on my couch for four and a half hours. I read and then I took a shower myself. Linda's hair in the shower stall had been washed away. I knew my heart was broken, but I also thought it would mend. However long it took, I figured I could make it.

I went out in the living room and sat in our one good chair and waited for her to wake up. 4:43. My least-favorite time of day, somehow not so bad.

The sky was just beginning to lighten when I looked over and saw her eyes were open. They were pretty eyes. Gray on her driver's license, but green in the sun.

"Hungry?" I asked.

"Starving."

I emptied the cupboards and made her canned soup and noodles and sliced an apple. I gave her everything there was. It wasn't much, but she ate it all.

"How did Leo know you?" I asked her.

"Who?"

"The guy in the grocery store."

"What guy in the grocery store?"

"Don't you remember?"

She shook her head. "I was going to buy some doughnuts. Then I remember this lovely warm feeling. I felt like someone was holding me, cradling me in their arms, rocking me gently. And then I woke up when you said my name. I was in a car accident," she said apologetically. "I have a concussion. But you know that."

There wasn't any point in me setting her straight. I figured she would remember whatever she wanted to when she wanted to.

"What about your fiancé?" I asked. "Where is he?"

"Oh, my God!" she shouted. She jumped up from my little card table and hopped around the room. "That's the word I've been looking for. Fiancé! Fiancé! You are a genius."

The first rays of sun peeked between my blinds. It was the worst time of day turned the best. I grinned. It was good to be a genius. I had the rest of the day off. No place to be but here and nothing else to do.

chapter sixty-six

The sun rises again over Los Angeles. Six million people wake up on the second day of spring, go to the bathroom, think about breakfast. Not all of them get to eat. Not all of them even have a bathroom, but they are all pretty much the same anyway.

Leo Martinez can't wake up because he didn't go to sleep. At a rest stop outside of Las Vegas, he stole a car while the owner was taking a leak. He thinks he's safe driving home to Maryland. He never wants to leave again. He takes the picture of Tess from his pocket and lets her fly out the window.

At Jenny Dunlop's apartment building, the landlord is walking up the front steps. The guy in 1A called to complain. He has a water stain on his ceiling. The landlord uses his key to let himself in the building. He has keys to all the apartments. The girl in 2A doesn't have a phone. He sighs. If she's not home, he'll have to go in and check.

In Jenny's living room, Leo's mother's Bible lies facedown on the floor by the couch. It is open to the page in Genesis where the bad son, Jacob, tricks his blind father into believing he is the good son, Esau. "See, the smell of my son is as the smell of a field which the Lord has blessed."

The Bible has Leo's home address in the front. It even has his mother's telephone number.

And in the bedroom, Jenny and her neighbor lie in the bed. They are beyond worrying about a stain on the ceiling or the blessings of their fathers or whether this spring their lives will really be different. Soon the landlord will be knocking on the door. With the window closed and the door closed, Jenny's bedroom has gotten warm. There is a faint odor, sweet and acrid, creeping under the door.

Far away, Leo catches a whiff of that now-familiar smell. He swerves to miss the dead dog in the road. Suddenly he is overcome with exhaustion. He pulls over in the next rest stop, parks between two semis, and sleeps. Right away he dreams that he and Tess are driving very slowly down an endless highway. She has her hand on his penis. Her nail polish glitters in the sun. They pass the dead dog. They're driving so slowly they can hear the flies buzz. And then a cat. And another cat. And a raccoon. And a goat. The road is littered with maggots and fur and flattened animals.

Madelyn has called Mitch's family. She woke them in their suburban mansion in northern California. His mother screamed and screamed. They're taking the first plane this morning. She has made the decision to let the kids sleep at their respective slumber parties. She'll tell them in the morning, soon now, very soon. She has called Scott and Rusty. Rusty cried. Then he told her that he had a fight with his wife, Model Number One or Two.

"I just can't seem to make her happy," he said. "Nothing I do is good enough."

Madelyn has not cried. She has been silent and capable and driven in her damaged car to the morgue to identify Mitch's body. She is afraid she made this happen. She is afraid she wanted it too much. Her children will never forgive her. She has not called Steve. In her imagination he was the first call she would make. Instead she has forgotten he even exists, except as a weapon, except as the way she killed her husband.

Dorothy P. Fairweather is full and clean and well rested. Her head hurts, but her eyes are fine. She reads the Sunday paper sitting on the floor in Ray's apartment where she can feel the morning sun warming the back of her neck. She is circling possible apartments for rent. She likes this cop named Ray, but she has already called the airlines about her trip to India. And she has left a message for her mother in the hospital and her brother at his hotel. She has given them her current number. If they're interested, they can call her.

Ray is in the other room, making more coffee. His hands shake a little as he spoons coffee into the filter. He thinks about what he had planned for that day and his muscles clench, his breath comes faster. His gun is on the secret shelf under the bed. Where it belongs.

"Dorothy?" he calls.

"Dorothy?"

She looks up as he comes into the room with the toast. He is smiling. And she answers him.

"Here I am."

chapter sixty-seven

Note #3 03/26/99

Dear Mom and Dad:

I feel so happy and at peace. Spring has finally come. Relief. Rejoice. Rebirth.

Be glad for me.

all my love,

Peter

Actually, in suicide notes, people don't apologize as much as you would think. By the time they do it, they're done apologizing. They've spent their lives apologizing; sorry they were born, sorry they weren't happy, sorry they were so sorry. They have no questions anymore, no decisions left to make, just the business of dying to complete. They've achieved a calmness that I find admirable, even enviable.

But for me, I guess I'm too afraid I might miss something. I never read the last chapter of a book first. That means that Camus was wrong. If the unexpected makes my life worth living, then dying for it doesn't make sense. I need the discovery from page to page. Anything can happen. The next event could change my life forever.